IMMORTAL CITY

IMMORTAL CITY

BY SCOTT SPEER

razor
bill

An Imprint of Penguin Group (USA) Inc.

Immortal City

RAZORBILL

Published by the Penguin Group
Penguin Young Readers Group
345 Hudson Street, New York, New York 10014, U.S.A.
Penguin Group (USA) Inc., 375 Hudson Street, New York, New York 10014, U.S.A.
Penguin Group (Canada), 90 Eglinton Avenue East, Suite 700, Toronto, Ontario, Canada
M4P 2Y3 (a division of Pearson Penguin Canada Inc.)
Penguin Books Ltd, 80 Strand, London WC2R 0RL, England
Penguin Ireland, 25 St Stephen's Green, Dublin 2, Ireland (a division of Penguin Books Ltd)
Penguin Group (Australia), 250 Camberwell Road, Camberwell, Victoria 3124, Australia
(a division of Pearson Australia Group Pty Ltd)
Penguin Books India Pvt Ltd, 11 Community Centre, Panchsheel Park,
New Delhi – 110 017, India
Penguin Group (NZ), 67 Apollo Drive, Mairangi Bay, Auckland 1311, New Zealand
(a division of Pearson New Zealand Ltd)
Penguin Books (South Africa) (Pty) Ltd, 24 Sturdee Avenue, Rosebank, Johannesburg 2196,
South Africa

Penguin Books Ltd, Registered Offices: 80 Strand, London WC2R 0RL, England

10 9 8 7 6 5 4 3

ISBN 978-1-59514-506-2

Library of Congress Cataloging-in-Publication Data is available

Printed in the United States of America

To my parents, who taught me to believe.

CHAPTER ONE

At 3 a.m., the Pacific Coast Highway was nothing more than a gray ribbon winding through the ocean fog. Despite being more than a little buzzed, Brad downshifted, smashed the gas pedal, and sent his BMW M5 surging forward. His iPod had shuffled to "California Love," by 2Pac. He turned it up.

"California! Knows how to party!" Brad sang out. Except when he sang it, California came out *"Caaafna,"* and party sounded more like *"parry."* It didn't matter; in his head he was performing for a sellout crowd at the Staples Center, and they loved him. In the rearview mirror the lights of Santa Monica twinkled. The Pacific Wheel on the pier glowed like a neon disk reflecting on the black mirror of the sea. Up ahead, the rocky shores of Malibu lay dark and silent. The music roared and Brad depressed the gas pedal almost involuntarily. He couldn't help himself. Gladstone's and Sunset Boulevard streaked by as the world accelerated into a violent blur.

He took each turn a little faster than the last, pushing the limits of the machine. He felt a surge of adrenaline as the headlights suddenly illuminated the churning Pacific just beyond the rocks. He stomped hard on the brake and yanked the wheel over, pointing the BMW back toward the curve he had nearly missed. He let out an exhilarated breath. *This would make such a cool music video*, Brad thought. *Dangerous and exciting*. Up ahead he saw another sharp turn in the road. This time, he would be ready. He pumped the brake, threw the wheel over, and punched the gas pedal hard. The car growled in protest but managed to stay on four wheels. Brad let out his best rock star scream as he half-skidded, half-flew around the turn.

Right into the headlights of an oncoming car.

Brad tried to brake, but he had finally pushed the BMW too far. Antilock brakes grabbing and releasing, he was a missile rocketing toward the other vehicle, a pickup, at eighty miles an hour.

That's when it happened.

It occurred so fast Brad didn't even see it. But he certainly felt it.

It hurt like hell.

It was a hand. A hand grabbing him and pulling him out of the car. To the oncoming driver it must have looked like a magic trick. In one instant Brad was there, wide-eyed and terrified in the driver's seat, and in the next, gone.

Suddenly the pungent smell of sea air filled Brad's nose. Salt-spray flicked across his neck. He realized he was standing on the side of the road, watching a fantastic collision unfold. His BMW slid across the centerline and collided head-on with the pickup. The bed of the pickup leapt up over the cab and sent the truck toppling end-over-end, over the retaining rail and down the rocky slope. Safety glass sprayed across the rocks in glittering crumbs. Then the truck hit the water, upside down, with a sickening smack. Brad's BMW ricocheted off the cliff wall and spun across the road, breaking through the retaining wall on the opposite end and soaring into the air. It entered the water nose first, gracefully, like a diver. The spectacle was all so violent it was almost beautiful. Then, sputtering and steaming, both vehicles began their slow descent under the icy waves.

Brad shivered against the breeze. He was so staggered by what he had just seen that he didn't immediately notice the figure standing next to him. Turning, he at first saw only a pair of wings silhouetted against the full moon. Six feet in both directions and razor sharp, the broad appendages rose and fell with the heave of a great breath. The figure stepped forward, and Brad recognized his Guardian Angel.

"Oh my God, it's you," Brad said, trying his best to sound sober.

The Angel smiled but said nothing.

Brad became aware of something warm and wet dripping down his left arm, forming small, trickling droplets at the end of his fingertips. He lifted his fingers to his mouth and tasted. It was blood.

"I'm bleeding," he said.

The Angel's eyes twinkled in the moonlight. When he spoke, his tone was even and smooth. "I had to pull you out through the window," he said. "It was the only way."

Brad remembered it now, as if recalling a nightmare. He remembered the white-hot pain of traveling through the glass window, the tiny slivers lodging in his face, and the way the jagged edges had felt as they sliced through the living skin. He shuddered.

"The cuts on your arm and shoulder are superficial and will heal," the Angel continued. "But your hip is fractured. It's very common in this type of save. I've taken the liberty of calling an ambulance to take you to the hospital. It should be arriving momentarily."

Brad took a cautious step forward, then cried out as his right hip erupted in pain. He stepped back and quickly shifted his weight. He blew out a ragged sigh.

The Angel hadn't moved.

"Oh, right," Brad said, embarrassed. He fumbled for his wallet in his pants pocket. "Sorry, this is my first time, you know," he mumbled as he flipped the wallet open and struggled to pull a Platinum American Express card from its sleeve. His fingers were already numb from the cold.

"There's no need," the Angel said, dismissing the effort with a wave of his hand. "The funds have already been transferred out of your account."

"Oh," Brad said. He returned the billfold to his pants pocket. "How much . . . was this?"

"One hundred thousand dollars, in addition to your monthly rate."

Brad's gaze drifted to where the cars had landed in the water. His M5 was already submerged, but the back end of the pickup still protruded from the surf, bobbing in the swells like a corpse.

"What about him?" Brad asked.

"Him?" the Angel asked.

"Yeah," Brad said, and pointed to the tailgate as it slipped under the waves. "Him."

The Angel looked at the sinking pickup as if seeing it for the first time.

"He didn't have coverage," he said.

Brad nodded numbly.

The headlights of an approaching ambulance swept over the scene.

"Good night, Brad," the Angel said, and smiled.

"Good—" Brad began to reply, but trailed off as he realized the Guardian was already gone. Alone now, standing in the cold, Brad began to shake uncontrollably. The realization had only just hit him. The realization that he should be dead.

CHAPTER TWO

Maddy woke up to the drone of her alarm clock. It was early, the dawn dim and gray outside her window. She had been dreaming she was lounging on the shores of some faraway tropical beach, the ocean glittering, diamond-like, as it reached to the horizon. Maddy wanted to stay in the dream, still feel the warm sand under her feet, nothing to do but simply enjoy the sun on her face, no one to be but *herself*. But the sound of the alarm was unrelenting, and her eyes began to open, unwillingly.

Lifting her head, she looked out the window. There it was, like a ghost in the misty half-light—the Angel City sign. It loomed huge and silent on the hill, perfectly framed by Maddy's bedroom window. She sighed. The final remnants of the dream faded to nothing, replaced by the reality that she was still living in Los Angeles. Still stuck in the Immortal City.

She swung her legs out of bed and tried to shake the remainder of the sleep away. Kids at school complained about first period starting at 8 a.m., but for Maddy, the day started at five. Every day. She groped for a pair of jeans off the floor and pulled a striped long-sleeved tee from her closet and changed into them. Nothing fancy, and that's the way Maddy liked it—simple and comfortable. She didn't have the time—or the money, for that matter—for much else. She grabbed her favorite gray lightweight hoodie before leaving the room. Then she brushed her teeth and ran a comb through her hair before heading quickly down the stairs.

The light outside was fuller now, and she could tell by the way it illuminated the haze that her uncle, Kevin, would already be plating the first orders. This was their routine and had been since Maddy's freshman year. He would wake before Maddy and open the restaurant, taking the first orders so she could get a few more precious minutes of sleep. Then he would put on his apron and take up his position in the back as cook. It was Maddy's responsibility to bring the orders out and work the rest of the morning shift until she had to leave for school. Like most mornings, she would be the only waitress on duty. Maddy was used to it, though. And even though it could get annoying to spend most mornings working after late nights up doing schoolwork—especially in the winter, when it was totally dark through a lot of her shift—it still made her feel good to help Kevin, to be the one he really counted on. She knew he appreciated it.

Maddy grabbed her backpack off the living room couch, which was covered in laundry, and quickly scanned the room to see if she was forgetting anything. Knickknacks and pictures lined the walls, hanging over the worn furniture and haphazard laundry-folding job Kevin had apparently started the night before and then stopped halfway through. The home was modest and could've stood a remodel in 1987, but it was all she had ever known—and, to be honest, all she'd ever really needed. Satisfied she wasn't leaving anything behind, Maddy dashed out the door and down a narrow path that led from the front door through the sloping yard to the back door of Kevin's Diner.

When she was eleven, she had tried to get her uncle to change the restaurant's name to something more original, but Kevin was a bit of a traditionalist, and Kevin's Diner it remained. She went in through the back door, slipped into the tiny office, and changed into her waitress uniform, which she kept in the office so she could head straight to school at the end of the shift. The uniform couldn't be more traditional either: a simple pin-striped dress and white apron. The waitresses were *theoretically* supposed to wear pumps with the outfit, but most of the time Maddy managed to sneak her black Chucks past her uncle, who always seemed to look the other way.

Maddy could already smell the sharp aroma of fresh brewed coffee, sizzling bacon, and freshly poured pancakes as she emerged from the back and walked down the narrow hallway toward the kitchen. Just as she expected, Kevin was already hard at work behind the counter, plating the first three orders of the day. Maddy shoved a notepad and pen into the pocket of her dress and pulled her hair into a ponytail.

"Morning, Mads," Kevin said, slapping butter on some whole-grain toast. "These go out to four and seven." He indicated the plates. He was an average-looking man, if a little more weathered than most, but the lines of worry that crisscrossed his face were offset by a smile that always crackled with resilience and optimism.

"Cool," Maddy said, yawning and deftly stacking the plates up her outstretched arm—a seasoned pro at seventeen.

"And Mads?" Kevin added. "Get yourself some coffee. On the house." He winked. Maddy laughed sleepily, then, balancing the plates on her arms, swung out of the kitchen and into the dining room.

The dining room was like the rest of the restaurant—old and unremarkable, with fluorescent lights flickering over a scuffed black-and-white linoleum floor. The diner was laid out like an L on its side. The long part was bordered by a counter and stools on one side and cracked beige vinyl booths on the other. The booths ran along the windows that looked out to the street. The short part of the L faced back toward the house and the hill, giving those booths, like Maddy's room, a near-perfect view of the famous Angel City sign. Maddy dropped off the orders to tables four and seven, then turned to head back for the water pitcher and coffee carafe to refill drinks.

"Excuse me, miss?" an overweight woman in one of the booths asked as Maddy passed. "Can you fix the TV?"

Maddy looked up at the ancient Magnavox propped in the corner. On the screen was nothing but rolling static, which tended to happen a lot. The woman's cheeks were flushed, and her face wore the expectant expression of a child. "Didn't you hear? There was a *save* last night in Malibu." She emphasized the word *save* as if it was the most exciting, most important thing in the world.

"Oh, really?" Maddy murmured noncommittally. She placed one knee on the woman's table and reached up, banging on the side of the set. After a moment the signal came in, and the diner filled with the sound of ANN—the Angel News Network. If it were up to Maddy, she'd rather watch anything else, but the customers always insisted on hearing the latest news about the Angels, and so ANN it was.

"A terrible accident but a dramatic save in a two-car collision in Malibu last night—and the Guardian had one of the NAS's trial Angelcams!" announced the news anchor, her face obscured by smears of dust on the Magnavox. *"We'll have first-person, thrilling footage of the save and an exclusive interview with Archangel Mark Godspeed coming up within the hour, right here on ANN."*

At the word *Angelcams*, the woman in the booth sat up straight and watched the screen with wide, excited eyes as it previewed the tantalizing footage of a misty hairpin curve on the Pacific Coast Highway.

"Oh my gawd! Can you *imagine*?" she said, her eyes fixed on the screen. "Can you imagine having one of them Guardian Angels always watchin' over you, keeping you safe no matter what? And wakin' in in their big, strong arms, with everybody having seen it?" Her eyes remained on the TV. "One day *I'll* be saved."

But Maddy was already walking away. The truth was, she just didn't understand the big deal about Angels. Ever since they had revealed themselves to the world over one hundred years ago—the Awakening, as they called it—and turned their lifesaving abilities into a business, the Immortals seemed to be the only thing anyone cared about. Everyone, that was, except Maddy. It's true she lived in Los Angeles— the Angel capital of the world—but she had never been able to go along with the crowd around her and get caught up in the mystique of their fame, fortune, and lavish lifestyles. She didn't buy clothes from their clothing lines or sample their Angel-themed perfumes, and she certainly didn't read about them in *Angels Weekly*. When you can't afford any of that stuff, it's just easier not to be sucked in, she had long since concluded.

The morning rush passed quickly, Maddy expertly wielding her pen and notepad to scratch down orders, dealing plate after plate of eggs, French toast, and sausage to the steady breakfast crowd. Near the end of her shift, when Maddy went back to the kitchen, she found another steaming plate of food waiting for her on the counter. There was no ticket with it. She frowned and looked at her pad.

"Kevin? Who ordered this?" she asked, flipping through her tickets. Kevin looked at her over the counter and smiled, the skin crinkling like paper around his eyes.

"You did."

Maddy looked down at the plate again, her mouth flooding with water. Scrambled eggs with seared peppers and onions. It was her favorite dish at the diner.

They sat in one of the booths in the back, the customers having thinned enough that Kevin could hang up his apron for five minutes.

"Thanks again," Maddy said as she scooped another forkful of egg into her mouth. "You didn't have to cook for me."

Kevin shrugged as he glanced out the window. He took a sip of coffee. "Sometimes I still can't believe you're a senior, and that you'll be graduating in the spring. You've always been my little Mads, but you're not little anymore. My niece has grown up into a smart and beautiful young woman."

Maddy blushed and looked down, fiddling with her fork. She wondered why she could never stand to have anyone compliment her looks. She didn't think she was unattractive, but as a realist, she knew she was average. She had shoulder-length brown hair, brownish-green eyes, and a normal, if slender, body. The only makeup she had were some things that her best friend, Gwen, had given her for her birthday, and she almost never used the stuff. Gwen also launched an exasperating campaign every six months or so to get her to dress "cuter," which Maddy always evaded—she didn't care about all that. She had to work the morning shift, get good grades, and maybe, just maybe, get into college on a scholarship. No time for clothes and makeup—or boys.

But if she was honest, part of it was that if she even began to think about what would happen if she put on makeup and dressed "cuter"—about the attention she would get, or maybe worse, the attention she *wouldn't* get—her stomach flipped in anxiety. So she mostly just hid behind her gray hoodie and her iPod earbuds. It seemed easier that way.

"I want you to know I'm proud of you," Kevin went on, "and your parents would be proud of you too." Maddy paused, another bite of egg poised in front of her mouth. Kevin rarely mentioned her parents. They had both been killed in an accident when Maddy was a baby. Kevin was a kind man, and a good man, but if she was being honest with herself, she missed having parents. She missed their role in her life, and she missed *them*, even though she had no memories, no recollection to hold onto at all.

Kevin was still talking. "I know it hasn't always been easy in our little family. I know working at the diner isn't your favorite—"

"It's fine, Kevin," Maddy interrupted, feeling guilty.

"It's no dream job, I know. But I want you to know that I really appreciate your help." Maddy smiled at him over her cup. "And besides," he went on, brightening, "I think our luck is due to change this year. I really do. Just you watch, Maddy, this place is finally going to take off!"

Maddy's gaze drifted out the back window, out once again to the view of the famous sign on the hill. Giant white letters, fifty feet high, spelled out the iconic words ANGEL CITY. To everyone else the sign was a symbol of glamour, an icon of the Angels' wealth and power. Maddy just couldn't bring herself to care. Housing was actually pretty cheap up on this side of town, and all the sign really meant was that she had to endure those annoying Angel Tours tourist buses coughing blue exhaust on her walks to and from school. People all over the world would kill for a chance to live in the middle of the action—in the glorious Immortal City—but as far as Maddy Montgomery was concerned, she couldn't wait to get out.

Suddenly Maddy realized her uncle was staring at her.

"I'm sorry?" Maddy asked.

"Our luck, Maddy," Kevin said, "I feel like it's finally going to change."

"Right. Me too," Maddy said, and tried her best to believe him.

The door jingled as more customers came in. It was starting to get busy again.

"I better get back to it," Kevin said, "But have a great day at school, okay?" Maddy nodded, and Kevin rose and left. After he had gone, her eyes fell once again on the view out the window and the famous sign. Maybe her uncle was right. She was a senior now, and next year hopefully meant college. Maybe things *were* looking up for her.

Then, realizing she was about to be late for school, she ran to the back to change.

The walk to school took Maddy down Vine Street and through the heart of Angel City. She passed under the towering billboards of Angels selling jewelry, sunglasses, designer handbags, and luxury cars. Half-naked Immortal bodies were the alluring backdrop for labels like Gucci, Chanel, Louis Vuitton, and Christian Dior. Maddy only casually glanced up at them. She had never had fancy things, not that she was complaining. Most of her clothes were from Target or were secondhand, and she didn't own any jewelry, or even a proper handbag for that matter. She was also one of the only seniors without a car, and if you didn't drive in Angel City, you didn't exist.

Listening to her iPod shuffle, Maddy barely noticed as she turned onto Angel Boulevard and strode down the famous Walk of Angels. She unconsciously stepped over the names bronzed in the sidewalk, the names of the most famous Guardian Angels placed in stars to be forever celebrated. She passed the souvenir shops selling little plastic Angel statues, fake wings, and T-shirts with slogans like SAVE ME! on them. She wove her way through the wide-eyed tourists looking around excitedly, hoping to catch even a glimpse of a flawless Immortal. Eyeing them, Maddy wondered if there was something wrong with her. Why couldn't she bring herself to care about what the rest of the world seemed to be so obsessed with? What were they seeing that she seemed to be missing?

Suddenly Maddy had to stop herself from crashing into a throng of excited tourists blocking the sidewalk. They had gathered around a shiny new star with no name on it—the star of a soon-to-be Guardian Angel. A couple girls let out screams of delight as they posed for a picture next to it.

"What's going on?" Maddy asked.

"Don't you know?" a woman replied. "That's Jackson Godspeed's star! He's being Commissioned this week!"

This Angel, of course, Maddy had heard of—everyone had. He was the hottest, wealthiest, and most eligible young Angel in Angel City, or so she had been told. To Gwen and millions of other screaming fans, he wasn't just an Angel. He was a god. Tourists held their cell phones high, taking video of the star and chatting excitedly as Maddy squeezed through the crowd. *How can you get so worked up over a sidewalk?* she thought.

While waiting for the light to change at Highland Avenue, she didn't even glance up at the screens breathlessly reporting a "MIRACULOUS LATE-NIGHT SAVE IN TWO-CAR COLLISION IN MALIBU. WE'VE GOT AN EXCLUSIVE WITH THE PROTECTION— ANGEL CITY'S NEWEST CELEBRITY, BRAD LOFTIN!" After a moment she crossed the street, dodging a shiny new Mercedes that had no intention of slowing for her, and hurried the remaining three blocks to school.

Angel City High was not what you would think. It was not, as the name suggests, where the rich and famous Angels go to school. Years ago that might have been the case, but that was long before young Angels were pulled from the public school system and put in exclusive private schools. Despite the plaques on the wall recording the famous Angel alumni who had once been students there, the last Angel at Angel City High had graduated in 1969. Nowadays it was just another subpar public school.

After passing through the chain-link fences and metal detector, Maddy walked under the faded HOME OF THE ANGELS sign and entered the crowded hallway. Like a well-worn routine, no sooner had she arrived than she was joined by Gwen, who was reading her

BlackBerry. Gwen was wearing a jean miniskirt and revealing halter top she would probably be made to change out of by lunch.

"OMG," Gwen murmured as she scrolled through paparazzi photos, "Vivian Holycross looks so cute in those boots. And did you see the Malibu save? It's all anybody's talking about this morning."

"Of course," Maddy said ruefully, "Angels." Angels were pretty much the only thing that seemed to matter to Gwen at all. Every day she read the Angel blogs and tuned into Angel television to hear the latest and greatest about the Angels' perfect lives. The clothes they wore. The places they went. The fancy cars they drove and the amazing houses they lived in. Gwen had been known to obsess for weeks on a save if it had been one of her favorite Angels. She kept track of who was friends with who, who was Protecting who, and, most importantly, which young Angels were dating each other. Gwen was definitely what they called "Angel Crazy."

"And who is Vivian again?" Maddy asked as they headed to their lockers.

"Honestly, Maddy," Gwen said. "How can you live in this city and not know these things? Vivian is only the most beautiful Angel on the planet. We would so be best friends. If I can't marry Jackson Godspeed, I want her to."

Maddy leaned over her friend's shoulder and looked at her Berry. On the screen was a picture of a stunning brunette running with a handful of shopping bags, hiding behind a pair of Chanel sunglasses.

"Why do you read that stuff?" Maddy asked for the hundredth time. "That guy Johnny whatever who blogs about the Angels is such a jerk."

"I can't believe your uncle won't get you a BlackBerry," Gwen said, wrinkling her nose. "You're, like, missing out on life."

Maddy pulled an ancient-looking flip phone out of her backpack and did her best Uncle Kevin impersonation. "Only for homework and emergencies, Maddy, homework and emergencies," Maddy said, laughing and dropping the phone back in her bag.

"Your uncle is such a dinosaur," Gwen said. Maddy shrugged.

"I'm sure he would get me a new one if he could afford it."

Maddy and Gwen reached their lockers, side by side, middle row. This was how they had met in seventh grade. Even in a school of three thousand, *Montgomery* and *Moore* were somehow always right next to each other, and it had been that way since middle school. At the beginning Maddy was quiet, especially around someone as outgoing as Gwen, but after only a few weeks of seeing each other day in, day out at the lockers, Maddy had started to let down her guard. Soon they were real friends. Then later that year, Gwen's parents split up. A lot of her more popular friends didn't feel like dealing, but Maddy was there for her the whole time: she knew what it was like to feel abandoned. They'd been best friends ever since.

"I try not to read the blogs," Gwen said, setting up her mirror and makeup inside her locker, "but it's like an accident on the freeway. As much as I try not to, I just have to look."

"Or you're obsessed," Maddy said as she shoveled in books.

"I'm not *obsessed*," Gwen said defensively. "I just know I'll be Protected someday. I want to be *ready*."

Maddy stopped unloading her books. "Gwen, you bought one of those maps on Sunset Boulevard and tried to get me to go with you up to their houses. On your learner's permit." She turned back to her locker and smiled. "Obsessed."

"That was so forever ago," Gwen huffed.

"That was last summer," Maddy said.

Gwen nodded. "Exactly." She paused. "Besides, if I was *really* obsessed, I would have already shown you this footage of Jacks shirtless at the beach that leaked onto SaveTube last night."

A roar of laughter echoed down the hall behind Gwen and Maddy. They turned and saw a group of four boys heading toward them.

"Hey, Gwen, what's up?" one of the guys, Kyle, said. He was tall, with broad shoulders and lank brown hair. He and Gwen had dated for the first semester junior year but ultimately decided it was better to be just friends. Maddy secretly felt like her best friend might still have some feelings for him, even though Gwen swore up and down against it. He and Maddy had bonded slightly over how they didn't care about the Angels, not the way most people did.

"Hi, Kyle," Gwen said, pushing back her hair. They gave each other an awkward hug.

"Hey, Maddy, have a good Columbus Day weekend?" Kyle asked.

"Um, yeah," Maddy said, wishing she hadn't put her hood down when she'd gotten in the school. She felt . . . exposed. Sometimes when it came to guys, Maddy found herself a bit tongue-tied, even if it was just her best friend's ex. Like, why hadn't she asked him if he'd had a good weekend too?

"Are you guys coming?" the boy standing next to Kyle eagerly blurted out to Maddy and Gwen. He had long hair and glasses, and Maddy thought his name was Simon.

"Dude, of *course* they are." This came from Tyler, with whom Maddy had been in government class sophomore year. With every school year he seemed like he'd gotten a little "edgier": he was wearing black skinny jeans and a little too perfectly ripped-up Vans. "Hi, Maddy," he added as an afterthought, waving slightly even though he was only five feet away.

"What are you talking about?" Gwen asked.

"Ethan's having a party later this week," Kyle said, clapping his hand on the shoulder of the last of the boys, who hadn't spoken yet.

"Yeah, you should come. My mom's out of town," the guy said, stepping forward slightly.

Maddy realized she recognized him, but not from school. He sometimes came in to eat at the diner. They'd had a few brief conversations at the restaurant—he had recently moved to Angel City, to somewhere up the hill from the restaurant, and he'd come in and eat sometimes when his mom was traveling for business. Today he was wearing a navy T-shirt, cargo shorts, and sandals, and as her gaze reached his face, he smiled at her. But that wasn't what caught, and held, her attention. It was his eyes, which she hadn't really noticed before. Dark hazel and expressive, they pierced out from under sandy-colored, beach-boy hair. It was almost as if they were talking to her all by themselves.

"The party's going to be amazing," Simon said. In an almost reverent tone: "He got a keg."

"Er . . . hey," Gwen said to Ethan, flipping her blond hair the way she did around cute boys.

"This is Ethan. He's new to this beautiful institution," Kyle said, motioning to the cracked paint and dingy hall of Angel City High. "E, this is Gwen and—"

"It's Maddy, right?" Ethan interrupted, still smiling at her.

"Yeah, she's Maddy," Gwen answered for her. Maddy elbowed her friend.

"We know each other already," Maddy said, feeling a little shy. "So you're going to school here now?"

"Yeah," he said, "Just transferred a couple weeks ago."

"I'm sorry to hear that," she said, joking.

"I know, me too," Ethan said, and laughed.

"So are you guys coming on Friday?" Kyle asked. "I know Gwen will. But, Maddy, you should definitely come too. It'll be fun. I promise, no SaveTube and no ANN." Kyle looked at her and gave her a flirtatious smile. Confused, Maddy glanced down.

"*ANN,*" Tyler repeated with scorn, rolling his eyes. He was "alternative," and part of that was being against all the Angel glamour and glitz—although Maddy sometimes suspected that if someone offered one of the alterna-kids the chance to become a famous Protection, they'd still do it in a heartbeat.

"Yeah, come to the party," Ethan said.

"Oh, um, the weekend . . ." Maddy said, stalling. In truth, she had no idea what to say. Getting invited to parties was Gwen's thing. Whenever Maddy wasn't doing homework or working shifts at the diner, she usually just listened to music or curled up with a good book. Parties were pretty much unknown territory for her. She thought about the stack of college applications waiting for her back home. The weekend would be her only time to work on them.

"I'd like to," Maddy finally said. "But I have college apps, so . . ."

"So that means no, right?" Ethan said, sounding downcast.

It was Gwen's turn to elbow Maddy. She gave her a look and turned to Ethan.

"It just means she might have some other stuff too," Gwen said, improvising. "She's pretty popular, you know," she added. Maddy felt her cheeks beginning to flush.

"Well, if you want to come, I can give you directions," Ethan said.

"Maybe she should get your number?" Gwen offered. Simon and Tyler slightly snickered under their breaths. Now Maddy was sure she was bright red.

"Yeah, totally."

Maddy fumbled in her bag for her old phone as Ethan slipped his iPhone out of his pocket. The two exchanged information, Maddy awkwardly asking Ethan to spell his last name, McKinley, while the other boys stood there watching. Maddy couldn't believe how embarrassed she felt. "The party should be cool," Ethan said as he slid his phone back in his pocket.

"Um . . . okay," she said. "Thanks?"

"Keep it quiet, though, he doesn't want the whole school coming, you know?" Kyle added. Maddy could've sworn he winked at her. "See you guys later."

"See you Friday," Ethan said.

Simon and Tyler also said goodbye, and the group of senior guys strolled casually down the hallway. Ethan gave her a final smile over his shoulder.

"OMG," Gwen breathed.

"OMG?"

"OMF-ing G!" Gwen could hardly contain herself. "You *know* him?"

"Kind of," Maddy said, tossing another book in her locker and untucking her hair from behind her ears. "He comes in to eat at the diner."

"That's the new guy everyone is talking about. I guess he moved to Angel City with his mom and she wanted him to do his senior year in public school or something, but word on the street is he's totally loaded. He even did an around-the-world trip earlier this summer. And the big rumor is that he *knows* the Angels," Gwen continued excitedly. "He sometimes surfs with them off Malibu. He might be the only student at school who will get an actual *Guardian*; they just haven't announced the Protections yet, not till Friday. And, of course, he's gorgeous."

"Well, I don't know why you said I could go. Because you know I can't," Maddy said.

"What?" Gwen gasped. "We're going and I'm your wingman!"

"I still need to finish my apps, and you should see those financial aid packets. They're like books. Besides, Kevin would kill me. He always says parties are dangerous, you know, dumb kids and alcohol, that whole thing."

"Maddy," Gwen said sternly. "Don't you realize you guys just had the moment?"

"The *moment*?" Maddy asked.

"Of course," Gwen said, explaining: "That's when a boy sees you in the perfect outfit, and the light is falling on you just right, and you're laughing or smiling, and everything about the moment is so perfect that he falls in love with you. I mean, he's seen you at the diner, of course, but he hasn't *seen* you-seen you until right now!"

Maddy looked down at her jeans and hoodie. "Gwen, I barely said anything to him," she protested. Besides, what was up with Kyle giving her that wink? Gwen hadn't seemed to see it, thankfully.

"Trust me," Gwen said with a knowing smile. "You guys just had your *moment*."

Maddy looked down the hall in the direction Ethan had walked. He'd always been totally friendly when they'd interacted at the diner, but she couldn't remember having felt, like, sparks. Still, he was definitely nice-looking.

"Maddy," Gwen said, her tone suddenly pleading, "You've never had a boyfriend; you've never even been on a real date. Please, you can't let me down now."

Maddy looked into Gwen's eyes and sighed. This wasn't a battle she was going to win today.

"Okay," she said, "I'll think about it."

"Perf!" Gwen squealed.

Maddy turned back to her locker—and froze. She stood there, trying to figure out why her mood had suddenly flipped to a feeling of suffocating dread. She glanced down the hallway. Next to her, Gwen typed away on her phone, not seeming to notice that anything was wrong. But to Maddy the corridor seemed gaping and haunted. Distorted sounds echoed through it. Maddy had experienced this before—a bad feeling coming out of nowhere—but never this strong. Never this vivid. She forced herself to take a deep breath and closed her eyes. When she reopened them, the hallway was once again normal. The banks of lockers, the scuffed linoleum, the yellowed ceiling tiles—it was all as it should be. She shook the lingering feelings away.

The bell rang, a nasal monotone drone, and students scrambled into their classrooms. Gwen gave Maddy a hug, then skipped away down the hall. Maddy affectionately watched her go and wondered what it must feel like to be so bubbly and blissfully happy all the time. Then she grabbed her backpack and closed her locker with a metallic click.

CHAPTER THREE

Jackson Godspeed was still asleep when his maid, Lola, came into the room.

"Time to get up, Jackson," she said in her warm Latin accent. "Breakfast will be served in five minutes."

Half-unconscious under the sheets, Jacks reached a hand out and fumbled for the remote on the nightstand. His fingers found the thing and powered on a sixty-inch plasma television, which descended from the ceiling. The sounds of Angel Television, or A!, as it was simply known, came over the speakers. Tara Reeves, the morning anchor who always wore spaghetti-strap minidresses and too much makeup, was unusually energized as she announced the day's top story.

"Brace yourselves, ladies, this is the week you've all been waiting for! Angel superstar Jackson Godspeed will be Commissioned as a Guardian this Friday, making history as the youngest, and some say hottest, Guardian Angel ever! That's right, it's Commissioning Week in Angel City, and we will have your live, breaking coverage of all the Angels right here!"

Groggily, Jacks began to wake up. He'd had his final Guardian test the day before and afterward had gone out to celebrate with his best friend, Mitch. Lola went to the window and pulled back the curtains, revealing a panoramic view of Angel City, downtown Los Angeles, and the ocean beyond. She went to the closet and laid out Jackson's clothes for the day: a Calvin Klein suit, YSL shoes, and Ray-Ban sunglasses. Meanwhile, Tara continued excitedly on the plasma.

"Of course the questions on everyone's mind are, will Jacks be able to live up to the pressure at his age? Can he step into the shoes of the glamorous Godspeed Guardians? And maybe most important of all, who will be Jackson's first Protection? Guesses include presidential daughters, pop stars, and even Bill Gates's oldest daughter. Thousands of girls across the nation will undoubtedly be hoping—or maybe just wishing—that it will be them, and who can blame them? Who wouldn't want to wake up in Jackson Godspeed's arms as his first save?!"

Jacks sat up in bed, his broad chest and chiseled midsection framed in the shaft of light from the window. With flawless model-like features and pale blue eyes, Jacks was the image of perfection, Angel or otherwise. Reaching out his arms, he spread his wings in a sudden, dramatic motion, stretching after a night of deep sleep. Not the fluffy white wings of Renaissance paintings, Jackson's wings were sleek and muscular, with feathers sharp enough to cut. A warm blue glow lingered around them, a glow that grew astonishing at night. No other Angel had wings with this luminescence. Each Angel was born with his or her own signature wings, with special features and marks. But nothing like *this*. The wings were just as famous as his face. Many breathless commentators said they marked Jacks out for something even more special than just being the youngest Angel ever to reach Guardian status. The mania surrounding Jacks's Commissioning had all but drowned out the coverage of the other Angels unfortunate enough to have to share the spotlight this year with *the* Jackson Godspeed as they were commissioned too.

"So keep it locked to A! all week long as we bring you exclusive coverage of the parties and events, the glamorous red carpet, and the ceremony itself as Jackson Godspeed and nineteen other Immortals become Guardian Angels this Friday! And don't forget to follow all your favorite Angels online at Aonline .com or on Twitter at AngelcrazyA!"

Jacks yawned and retracted his wings. They disappeared into his bare back, leaving only two small marks below his shoulder blades. The marks were graceful spirals, almost like tattoos that glowed supernaturally. These were his Immortal Marks—the mark of every Angel—which indicated Jacks was not human.

As he brushed his teeth, Jacks tuned out the stock footage of girls camped out outside his house, screaming for him at events, and running after his custom red Ferrari in the street. This was the biggest week of his life, and he needed to focus. Lola was making his bed when he emerged from the bathroom, fully dressed. He picked up the Calvin Klein jacket, looked at it, and threw it over a chair back. Instead he opted for a vintage-looking—but obviously new—Led Zeppelin T-shirt, J Brand jeans, and Converse. He kept the glasses.

"Thanks, Lola," he said, giving her a kiss on the cheek, and headed out the door and into the hall.

The Godspeed mansion was breathtaking. A neoclassical, Italian palazzo–style villa, it contained vaulted ceilings, dramatic marble staircases, and a sleek, modern interior design. The house had been featured in numerous architecture and design magazines over the years, but to Jacks, it was just home. He headed down the stairs, pausing when he reached the bottom to look at the full wall of framed magazine covers that stood across from the landing. They were his covers and went all the way back to when he was little, the boy Angel wonder of the famous Godspeed line. He reread some of the captions, from "SUPER TOT!" and "ANGEL IN WAITING!" in his early years to "HOLY HOTTIE!" and "HALO HUNK!" as he got older. The most recent covers depicted Jackson as a heroic Angel with smoldering eyes and an increasingly unbuttoned shirt, his signature wings often spread just behind him. It suddenly occurred to Jacks that he had grown up on these covers, and the world had watched. Now they would be watching as he took the final step—the step he had been working toward for so long—and became a Guardian Angel.

Jackson's entrance into the kitchen went unnoticed by his stepfather, who was scanning a work report on his laptop. Jacks thought he glimpsed the letters HDF on the screen in the report as he passed by to kiss his mother, Kris, who brightened at the sight of her only son.

"Morning, honey," she said. Even in her bathrobe, Kris radiated the refined beauty for which she was famous. Before she had children, she'd been one of the most popular Guardians. Now she helped administer the largest Angel charity and was always running from one fund-raising event to another across Angel City. "Ready for your big week?"

"He better be." Mark folded his laptop screen down. "He's been waiting for this his whole life. Haven't you, son?"

"Absolutely, Mark," Jacks said, trying to sound confident.

"Ready to make that first save?" Mark asked.

It was a loaded question coming from his stepfather. Mark had been one of the most famous Guardian Angels of all time, and his first save had been brilliant. He had gone on to become one of the most famous and powerful Archangels, though he still handled a few select Protections—in fact, apparently, he'd come home late from one the night before, although Jacks hadn't seen any media coverage of it yet. Most of Mark's time, though, was taken up being the lead Archangel in charge of disciplinary issues, making the tough decision when a Guardian should have his wings removed after a failed save, which was a rare but painful ordeal for the Angel community. Gabriel and the entire Council of Twelve had nothing but faith in Jackson's stepfather, and his achievements were a lot to live up to.

Jacks's gaze drifted down to Mark's Divine Ring. It was the ring worn by every Guardian, a symbol of responsibility and power. It was all Jacks had ever wanted, ever since he could remember, and Mark had been an encouraging—and demanding—taskmaster on the path to getting it. Jacks watched it glint in the sunlight. Then he looked up at Mark.

"Well, I do feel unprepared," he admitted. "I wish I had a better idea who the Archangels were putting under my protection."

Mark gave his stepson a sly smile but said nothing, and returned to his laptop.

The side door to the kitchen swung open and the family chef, Juan, guided in a silver breakfast cart piled with pastries, fresh fruit, juice, and coffee. It had always been this way for the Godspeeds, every morning, as long as Jacks could remember. He would have been impressed, except he had never known anything else. Mark took a cup of coffee for himself and handed a glass of orange juice to Jacks.

"Jacks, you know I'm not going to say a word about your Commissioning," Mark said. "You're my son, and I love you, but that doesn't mean I'm going to treat you any different than any other young Guardian out there."

"I know that, Mark—"

"And I'm not going to take it easy on you this year, either," Mark went on, grabbing a plate and loading it with pastries. "You'll have to prove yourself to me like any other Angel."

"Mark—"

"And Jackson . . ."

Jacks looked up from his own plate and met his stepfather's gaze.

"I like it when you call me Dad."

"I won't let you down . . . Dad," Jacks said.

Mark nodded. "I know you won't."

Kris cleared her throat, flashing her husband a pointed glance. "Mark. Can we please have a nice breakfast as a family and put work talk aside for a minute?"

"Sure, honey. Of course," Mark said, but he held Jacks's gaze a moment longer before heading to the table. He meant what he said. Jacks leaned against the kitchen island and took a bite of pastry. He knew his stepfather was right. He thought about his training, in which he'd broken records and shocked his teachers with his prowess. He'd gotten early Angel endorsements, even as young as fourteen. And now he would be taking his place as the latest Godspeed Guardian. The eyes of the entire world would be on him this week, and on that first save. His time to perform had come.

Footsteps echoed down the stairs as Jacks's younger sister, Chloe, burst into the kitchen. The full-blooded child of Mark and Kris, Chloe had much more the look of her father: sharp, almost severe features, a kind of beauty so intense it was almost cold. As usual, she had her head buried in her BlackBerry.

"Oh my God, did you see these pictures from yesterday?" she announced. "They actually came *in* to the store with me and were, like, hiding behind stuff, trying to see what I was buying." She wrinkled her nose. "I hate the paparazzi; they are *so* annoying. That shirt looks really cute on me, though," she said, showing her BlackBerry to Kris.

"You look great, sweetheart," Kris said lovingly.

"I know, right? Dad, can't we sue them or something?"

"Well, it depends," Mark said, chuckling. His cell phone rang and he rose to take the call, walking over by the window to talk in an undertone.

Chloe's fingers flew over the keypad as she went to different blog sites, looking at the different pictures the paparazzi had gotten of her and reading the comments. She walked over to the breakfast cart and, with her free hand, poured a glass of orange juice.

"Hey, Jacks, ready for this week?" she said without looking up.

Jacks smiled at his baby sister. "I didn't know A! paid you all to interview me over breakfast."

Chloe rolled her eyes. "You better be ready. Don't let the family name down." She took a swig from her juice and made a face. "Ew. Juan!" she yelled, letting her voice carry through the kitchen as she continued to surf her Berry. Juan's sweating face appeared in the doorway. "This juice tastes funny. I think something's wrong with it."

"My apologies, Ms. Chloe," Juan said. "I squeezed it fresh this morning."

"Well, it tastes funny to me," Chloe said. "Make it again, okay?" Looking confused, Juan obediently took the jug of juice away.

". . . destructive addiction that must be dealt with!" Mark snapped, startling his family. "I want to meet with you at ten to discuss this." He ended the call and returned to the table. "Not to worry," he said calmly, sitting back down and pouring more coffee.

"If you say so, honey," Kris replied, looking concerned. He leaned over to whisper in her ear.

Chloe grabbed the remote on the island and powered the downstairs TVs. Two flat screens in the breakfast room and one in the living room blinked to life, all set to A! The same breathless anchor, Tara Reeves, had moved on from headlines to photos.

"Hot photos! Vivian Holycross was spotted as she stepped out to do some shopping yesterday on Rodeo Drive. The Angel beauty picked up accessories from Fendi and Valentino while trying to avoid those pesky paps."

The flat screen showed the image of Vivian running with shopping bags while trying to hide behind a pair of Chanel sunglasses.

"Her boots are *so* cute," Chloe breathed, then glanced over at Jacks. "She is so hot, Jacks. You should have never broken up with her." As if in agreement, Tara continued on-screen.

"But while she looks amazing as always, the question we really want to know is, are they or aren't they? Is Vivian secretly back together with drool-worthy Jackson Godspeed?"

As she spoke, the footage cut to a photo of Vivian from an ad for her own fashion line. Her wings extended out behind her, displaying finely spun gold spirals that spread out in delicate patterns, glittering. They were considered by some to be the sexiest wings of all time. *"Vivian's publicist would neither confirm nor deny, but the rumors are swirling. Together or not, they remain, easily, the hottest Angel couple on the planet!"*

The kitchen had gone quiet. Kris raised her eyebrows knowingly. Mark turned toward Jacks with a pregnant expression. Jacks sighed.

"We're just friends," he announced to the room. "We are *not* getting back together."

"Well, we like her very much, son," Mark said. "You know that."

"Yes, that has been made abundantly clear to me," Jacks said with a laugh.

"Jacks, we would *so* get along," Chloe said pleadingly, coming around the kitchen island to pull on her half brother's arm. "Now that I'm older, I can totally see her and me being best friends."

"Let's give the young Angel a break for now," Mark said, winking at Jacks. "He'll be seeing her this week."

Feeling suddenly tired, Jacks put his glass in the sink. He went out to the foyer.

Keys hung on a rack under the security camera monitor: Jacks's Ferrari, Mark's M7, Kris's hybrid Lexus, and Chloe's Porsche—which, Jacks thought, was a little ostentatious for such a young Angel. He grabbed his keys and returned to the kitchen, where he kissed his mother and snatched a final piece of toast off the cart before heading toward the door.

"Jackson?" Mark called after him.

Jacks turned in the doorway.

"Good luck this week," Mark said.

"There's no need for luck when there are Angels in the world," Jacks replied.

"Who taught you that?"

Jacks smiled. "You did."

With that and an approving nod from his stepfather, Jacks disappeared out the door and into the blinding southern California sunshine.

Jacks cruised down Sunset Boulevard in his cherry-red Ferrari, passing the famous boutiques, restaurants, and rock clubs of the Halo Strip. It was going to be a busy day, as usual. In an hour he was scheduled to make an appearance at the *Angels Weekly* style lounge, where he would share his thoughts about his Commissioning in an exclusive interview and then pose for pictures with lucky fans. He wasn't a fan of the magazine—*AW* was one of the most notorious Angel gossip rags—but Darcy, his publicist, had more or less forced him to do it. *Keep them happy*, she had told him, *keep them off your back*.

From there he would make a quick stop at the Lexus Angel's Flight VIP room, where he would do another interview and would most likely have to decline an offer for a free Lexus LF-A. Again. He had already told them—and it was the truth—that there just wasn't any more room in the garage, but he knew that wouldn't stop them from offering again. Maybe he could donate it to charity, he thought, and made a mental note to do so. Then he would rush over to the EA Saved! 2 video game launch party. The new version gave players the option of being Guardian

Jackson Godspeed, and experts were predicting it would easily become the best-selling game of the year. As part of the endorsement deal, he would be giving ten awestruck contest winners the chance to play against him during his agreed-upon one-hour appearance. Finally, he would try and make it to his own *Halo Magazine* Pre-Commissioning party.

Taking the turn onto Melrose, Jacks passed the Pacific Design Center and flipped a quick U-turn into the valet for Urth Caffé, an Angel City landmark and hot spot for Immortals. Girls screamed, people shouted, and paparazzi reached their cameras over the car's hood as Jacks eased the Ferrari into the sudden human swarm.

"JACKS! JACKS! JACKS! OVER HERE, JACKS!" A barrage of camera flashes erupted as Jacks stepped out of his car. *"WHO'S GOING TO BE YOUR FIRST SAVE, JACKSON?"* one of the photographers shouted. *"ARE YOU BACK TOGETHER WITH VIVIAN?"* another yelled. *"SAVE ME, JACKS!"*

A few security personnel managed the paparazzi and fans. These guards were also useful for the occasional weirdo stalker like the one who'd followed Jacks's every move last year, who was now in jail, or for the wacko anti-Angel activists who arrived at the café every few months or so and started making a ruckus. Jackson waved the photographers and fans off with a friendly smile as he ran up the steps to the patio, where Angels sat at tables sipping lattes and socializing. All eyes turned to the brightest star in the Immortal City as he made his way through the tables.

He found Mitch sitting at a table drinking a green tea latte and eyeing the female Angels at the next table.

"There he is!" Mitch said, getting out of his chair. "Ready for your big week?"

"Not you, too," Jacks said, groaning, and the two friends embraced. Mitch was short for an Angel but stocky, like an athlete. He had rich brown eyes and a dimpled smile for which he was famous. They sat and Jacks ordered coffee from a gawking waitress, who brought it promptly.

"Check it out," Mitch said, nodding toward a female Angel with long black hair who had just sat down at a nearby table. She was stealing glimpses at Jacks as she chatted with her friends.

"That's Elena. She just did the new Versace campaign."

"Mm-hmm," Jacks said absently, enjoying his coffee.

"And check out by the steps." Mitch said.

Jacks glanced over and saw a tall, striking platinum-blond Angel looking in his direction.

"I'm just saying, look at those Marks. I mean, perfect, man." Mitch whistled. The Angel turned and Jacks could see she was wearing a backless shirt that revealed her Immortal Marks. They were feminine and ornate, with curlicues and shimmering, delicate lines that reached all the way down to the small of her back. She looked over her shoulder to see if Jacks had noticed, but he was back to drinking his coffee. "You should go talk to her," Mitch encouraged. "She's incredibly hot."

"I forget her name," Jacks said, uninterested. Mitch sighed.

"Kelsie Godchild? The face of Burberry? She's on the entire side of that building at La Cienega."

"I'll take your word for it."

Mitch just shook his head. "So how excited are you for this week, man? This is going to be like a weeklong party. Last night was just a taste. Here, let me read you your schedule." He grabbed Jacks's iPhone from the table and pretended to scroll through it. "Party. Party. Party. Get drunk. Get drunk. Get drunk. *Then* get Commissioned. And then get drunk again." He leaned back in his chair as if visualizing it. "I don't know about you, dude, but I can't wait."

Jacks put his hands behind his head and looked at his best friend.

Mitch loved the Angel way of life, and it loved him right back. He always seemed to be turning up on the pages of *Immortal* and *Angels Weekly* at various events and parties, always with a new Angel beauty on his arm. But the truth was, he was a genuinely nice guy, and a bit of a class clown. They had become close friends their first year of training, ever since Mitch had started making fun of Jacks's wings, and had stayed that way ever since. Though the public knew very little about Angel training, the NAS released tidbits about Jackson and Mitch's progress over the years, playing up their friendship. One photo in particular of them was famous: two cocky thirteen-year-olds with their arms crossed across their chests, Jacks with his luminescent wings behind him, Mitch's wings showing intricate mazelike patterns. Together the two had gone through the mind-numbing math of Basic Aerodynamics, all the way up to courses such as Multiple Frequencing and Advanced Flying 406, until a few months ago, in a shock, the NAS announced that Jacks would be jumping a year in his class to become the youngest Guardian ever Commissioned. Mitch had been a good sport about the whole thing, but sometimes Jacks wondered if he still hadn't been hurt by it.

"I don't know, man," Jacks said, taking his iPhone back. "I'll go to some events, sure, but I don't want to get too crazy."

Mitch looked stunned. "Are you *insane*? Everyone knows the whole point of becoming a Guardian Angel is the *parties*. The *females*. And this is pretty much a once-in-an-eternity thing here, your early Commissioning. This is supposed to be the best week of our life, and you're going to miss it?"

Jacks ran a hand through his hair and took a swig of coffee. "I just . . . I've got to focus, Mitch."

"Oh," Mitch groaned. "Here we go again. Why does everything always have to be perfect with you?"

"It's not that it has to be *perfect*—"

Mitch set down his cup. "Highest grades in school. Top of the class in simulation training. First to fly in Basic Flying—"

"Okay, I get it," Jacks said, mildly embarrassed. "But that first save does have to be perfect. You know what they say—you never forget your first save. It's someone's life. It's a big responsibility. I just want to make sure I get it right."

Mitch leaned forward. "As your best friend, let me tell you something you already know. You're talented. Like ridiculous. Way more talented than me—"

"That's not true—"

"That is true. And I can tell you, whoever your Protections are going to be, they'll be in great hands. So please. Do me a favor and at least *try* and enjoy yourself this week."

Jacks held up his hands in surrender. "I promise. I'll enjoy myself."

A Mercedes G550 pulled up to the valet at the curb. As much as the attendant was clearly trying not to stare, he couldn't take his eyes off the driver—and neither could anyone else. Emerald-green eyes, flawless features, and glossy, dark brown hair: Vivian Holycross was without a doubt the hottest female Angel on the planet. Compared to her, the human supermodels at the next table looked downright plain.

Being only seventeen, Vivian wouldn't be Commissioned for another two years, but she was already everywhere in the media. She came from one of the older, more powerful Angel families, and her life up to that point had been nothing short of charmed and effortless.

Fans and paparazzi swarmed as security guided her up the sidewalk and onto the patio. She wore a pair of leopard-print Miu Miu shoes and a red jersey tank dress that revealed her bra and Immortal Marks. Her outfit was perfectly accessorized with a Louis Vuitton bag and Bulgari sunglasses.

"Don't look now, man," Mitch said as he watched the chaos of Vivian's arrival, "but we have an unexpected visitor. Vivian's here."

Jacks stiffened. "Great. Any chance she won't see me?"

"I don't think so," Mitch said. "She's coming this way."

At that moment Vivian noticed Jacks and Mitch—or pretended to—and sauntered over. She made sure to put a hand on Jacks's shoulder as she arrived.

"Oh hey, boys, didn't expect to run into you," she said in a seductive, soft voice. She turned her face toward Jackson. "Hey, Jacks."

"Hey, Viv," Jacks said casually. There was no bad blood between them, but run-ins with Vivian could get tricky. He didn't have anything against her; he had just had gotten tired of playing the role of the "It" Angel couple—the events together, the ravenous photographers, the magazines covering every supposed change in their relationship. It was exhausting, and even though Vivian would seem outraged every time a piece of gossip about their private life surfaced, Jacks sensed it was mock outrage and that she was secretly into it. It had caused his feelings for her to gradually fade, and they'd broken up that past summer. But since news had broken about Jacks's early Commissioning, Vivian had resurfaced with a vengeance.

"What time are you guys going tonight?" she asked.

"You know, I hadn't decided if I'm going," Jacks said. Vivian blinked at him.

"It's *your* cover and you haven't decided if you're going?"

"You know how those things go." Jacks shrugged. "They're all the same."

Vivian smiled mischievously. "Well, if it would make you feel better, I'll go with you and keep you company." She looked deep into Jacks's eyes.

"That's okay, Viv," Jacks said, backpedaling. "But if I end up making it, I'll see you there, right?"

"You absolutely will," she said, her green eyes twinkling. Vivian bent over and gave Jacks a kiss on the cheek. As she did, what sounded like thousands of shutters clicked from behind the hedges. Jacks knew she had done that on purpose—she had maybe even called the paparazzi and set the whole thing up. Vivian was a nice girl, but Jacks felt like she somehow tried too hard. After going out with her for five months, Jacks had started to feel more and more like she was with him just because he was *Jacks* and what that meant to the outside world. It was hard for him to explain even to himself, but sometimes when she was holding onto his arm, it felt like *he* wasn't actually there. That he could have swapped in a Jacks look-alike and Vivian wouldn't even notice.

He also knew how much Mark wanted to see them together, and though he was usually anxious to please his stepfather, in this case, conversely, it made him even more hesitant.

Jacks let out a long breath and glanced at Mitch, who gave him an encouraging look. Vivian tucked her hair behind her ear.

"So then," she said, "I'll see you tonight?"

CHAPTER FOUR

"There have always been Angels among us."
New History of Angels, McGraw-Hill, 2nd ed., p. 1

Maddy sat curled up in her desk with her history textbook open in front of her, trying to keep from dozing off while taking notes on Mr. Rankin's History of Angels in America lecture. The early-morning shift at the diner was starting to catch up with her, and she shifted in her seat, willing her eyelids to stay open.

"I hope you all did the assigned reading over the long weekend," Mr. Rankin said as he paced down the rows of desks. "And no, having read *Angels Weekly* does not count."

A laugh rippled through the class. Mr. Rankin was a small man of about forty with a trim beard and balding hair. He held their AP U.S. History textbook aloft as he spoke. "To those of you who didn't do the reading, staying silent will not help you. The less you participate, the more likely I am to call on you." The class let out a collective groan.

Maddy might not follow the Angels, but she *had* done the required reading. However, she was always quiet in class. As Mr. Rankin got started, her eyelids grew impossibly heavy.

"So, who can tell me about the history of Angels before the National Angel Services formed?" A hand shot up in the front. Mr. Rankin pointed.

"Well, in the beginning, miracles were performed anonymously," a boy said. Mr. Rankin nodded.

"And how were Angels on Earth governed?"

"There was a royal class?"

"Legend has it, yes," Mr. Rankin said. He paced down Maddy's row. "As with much about the Angels, they will not confirm or deny many things about their existence here on Earth, including much about their early history. Some historians speculate there was even a battle long ago between the Angels and Dark Angels, or demons, for supremacy on the planet, a battle won by these royal classes." Maddy sat up in her chair again, trying to look as awake as possible as he passed. "So the Angels were anonymous. Then what happened?"

"The Civil War," someone in the back called out. Maddy felt her eyelids closing.

"The American Civil War, correct." Mr. Rankin went to the board and wrote *Civil War*. "After the awful bloodshed of that conflict, brother killing brother, Angels decided there was no longer any point to staying hidden and serving man out of kindness." He paused. "To put it bluntly, we didn't deserve it. So the original Angels, the True Immortals—twelve Archangels, mostly male, but we'll talk more about that when we discuss the suffragette movement—came forward and presented their case to the U.S. government. They were led by Gabriel and came to be known as the Council of Twelve. With the help of President Grant, Angels made their power into a service and entered American capitalism."

Mr. Rankin wrote *American capitalism* under *Civil War* and circled it. He began slowly pacing in front of the room again. "The Angels organized themselves into classes, formed families, and started having children. These Born Immortals matured to adulthood at a human rate, but then their aging almost came to a halt. Born Immortals do appear to slightly age over a very long span of time, although the Council officially claims they are immortal. They, in turn, had more children. As their numbers grew, the National Angel Services was formed. Now, who can tell me about the NAS?"

No takers. Mr. Rankin's eyes scanned the room and fell on Maddy curled up in her chair, her head nodding.

"Maddy?"

Maddy looked up, surprised. "Yes?"

"We're waiting."

"I'm sorry, could you repeat the question?"

Mr. Rankin gave a tight smile and walked toward her. "Repeating the question won't do any good if you haven't done the reading."

Maddy sat up and cleared her throat. She felt confidence flare in her quiet gaze, and the small history teacher stopped walking and stood where he was.

"The National Angel Services opened in 1910 in Angel City, and a group of Born Immortal Archangels was created to oversee it. The original Council of Twelve male True Immortals granted the NAS powers to regulate the employment of Guardian Angels all over the world, and the system was called protection-for-pay. The governing body of Archangels spread Angels across the globe, but everything stayed headquartered in Angel City."

Mr. Rankin's eyebrows rose. He opened his mouth to speak, but Maddy continued: "Still, no one knew where the Angels came from. Every religion and culture has their own stories of supernatural protectors and messengers, guides. According to the Council, and then the NAS, this was who the Angels were. Beyond that, where they came from depends on what church you attend—if you attend church at all. The Council left the debate to the scholars and preachers, keeping most of their secrets from the public. Most people just accepted the Angels, like you accept the sun coming up in the morning."

"That's right, Maddy, very good—"

"The Angels charged a lot of money for what turned out to be a priceless service, and as they got richer, they charged even more." Then she stopped and added, "Not that I care, but it seems like a pretty lousy thing to do."

The classroom went dead silent. Mr. Rankin opened his mouth to reply but was cut off by a sound coming from the hallway, a sound that made Maddy's blood run cold.

It was a scream. Raw and terrified.

Frantic footsteps echoed down the hall, followed by more horror-filled shrieks. A blond junior, Samantha Cellato, burst into the classroom, sobbing. Her shirt and hands were covered with dark crimson stains.

Blood.

Mr. Rankin blinked, then rushed to the girl. Maddy just stared, trying to make sense of what she was seeing.

"It exploded. It just exploded," Samantha mumbled over and over. "I think she's dead."

More muffled screams rang out down the hall. Maddy looked through the door to see kids running for the front of the school as smoke began to fill the corridor. Somewhere in the building a fire alarm wailed.

Reacting more than thinking, Maddy leapt up and ran out of the classroom. She wasn't even sure where her feet were taking her, but she could see smoke pouring from the biology lab at the far end of the hall and headed in that direction. She burst through the doorway to the lab and nearly gagged at the grisly scene in front of her.

The remains of an exploded propane tank lay on the ground. Mrs. Neilson, the bio teacher, was lying on the floor next to several other kids. Dark pools of blood were spreading out underneath them, reflecting yellow licking flames. Both of Mrs. Neilson's hands were gone.

"Maddy?"

Maddy's eyes popped open. She was panting, as if out of breath, and she could feel dampness on the nape of her neck. She looked up at Mr. Rankin, who seemed to be patiently awaiting a response. That tight smile back on his face. Maddy remembered what she was going to say.

"The National Angel Services was formed, and . . ." Maddy trailed off. A shaky, clammy sweat had broken out all over her body. She trembled.

"And?" Mr. Rankin looked confused.

All at once Maddy leapt to her feet and dashed down the row of desks. In a flash she was past Mr. Rankin and out the door. She knew she would have no more than a few seconds. She could only hope she wasn't too late.

Running as fast as her legs would carry her, Maddy sped toward the biology lab at the far end of the hall. She burst through the door.

"Excuse me, young lady!" Mrs. Neilson shrieked, standing over her Bunsen burner. Maddy had already focused her eyes on the gray metallic lighter in Mrs. Neilson's hand.

"Don't!" she screamed.

Mrs. Neilson raised the lighter as she opened her mouth to respond, and in one fluid movement, Maddy lunged at her. She tackled Mrs. Neilson, linebacker style, and sent them both tumbling to the floor. Mrs. Neilson's head hit the tile with a vicious crack, but she seemed to be okay because she began punching and kicking Maddy in an uncoordinated frenzy.

"Oh my God, help! Help! I'm being assaulted!" she screamed. Several of the students stood up, but no one made a move toward the front of the class. They all just stared at the bizarre sight of a teacher and a student wrestling on the ground. Maddy batted away Mrs. Neilson's slaps and punches as she wrestled the lighter out of her hand, trying desperately to avoid creating any sparks. Mr. Rankin came running into the classroom.

"What the hell is going on in here?!" he demanded.

Gasping for breath, all Maddy could choke out was, "Check the propane tank." Mrs. Neilson stopped struggling and gave an inquisitive look to the large, spherical tank just a foot away from her. Then she scrambled on her hands and knees away from Maddy and sat in the corner, wiping her nose between sobs. Mr. Rankin walked over to the tank and examined it. He put his ear to the valve, and his eyes grew wide.

"It's leaking," he said with alarm. "We have to evacuate this classroom. Now."

Maddy spent the next period in the nurse's office, which smelled of Band-Aids and alcohol, before being called before the principal's desk. Mrs. Neilson agreed not to press charges, and in exchange, Maddy was given lunch detention the following day. Conversely, she was also thanked for helping detect the gas leak, although no one could quite figure out how she had known. Maddy, who didn't want to open the can of worms that telling them the truth could cause, said she had smelled something walking past the lab. She was sent back to class and tried to finish out the rest of the day ignoring the whispers of her classmates.

The day had gone in her mind from hopeful to disastrous. She felt like a freak, like someone entirely different and out of step with the world. But that, she told herself, was nothing new.

After the final bell buzzed, Maddy pulled her hood over her hair and walked quickly home. She didn't bother going inside but hurried across the yard and down the small hill to the office door of Kevin's Diner, where she changed into her waitress's uniform. Since Tracy had scheduled the night off, Maddy would be spending the rest of her day working the evening shift.

"How was school, Maddy?" Kevin called from the kitchen as Maddy threw her backpack in the office, pinned on her name tag, and pulled her hair into a ponytail.

"You know, uneventful," she replied, trying to sound as convincing as she could.

"Really? Classes were okay?"

"Yup," she said, coming into the kitchen and smiling vaguely. She hated to lie, especially to Kevin, but she couldn't see any way around it. She wasn't going to tell him about what happened. Being a freak at school she was willing to accept, but she didn't want to be one at home too. She grabbed her notepad and pen and swung into the dining room before Kevin could ask anything else.

After about an hour, Gwen, Gwen's friend Jessica, and Samantha Cellato came in. Jessica and Samantha were both juniors, and Sam had been in the biology lab for Maddy's little performance with Mrs. Neilson. Maddy put them in a booth in the rear, and they all ordered the hamburger dinner. They had, undoubtedly, come in to talk over the incident at school.

"You made the Lunch Special," Gwen said as Maddy arrived with their Diet Cokes. Of course, Gwen wasn't talking about food. The Lunch Special was the gossip blog of Angel City High, where a junior named Blake Chambers dished on the goings-on of the school. Gwen held out the Berry for Maddy to read.

The screen featured a blowup of Maddy's hideous junior-year

picture and the headline "MADDY MONTGOMERY ATTEMPTS TO TORCH BIO LAB." She read Blake's words aloud.

"'Dear Maddy, thank you, on behalf of the student body, for trying to set fire to the school. It would be an improvement, no doubt. Next time, though, please wait until the fire starts before beating up Mrs. Neilson for giving you an A–.'" Maddy winced. Jessica giggled.

"Did you get in trouble?" Sam asked, her eyes wide.

"Lunch detention tomorrow," Maddy said. "I don't really care. It will give me time to work on my applications."

"Well, I mean, but how did you *know*?" Jessica asked as she plopped a straw in her Diet Coke and took a deep pull. Gwen looked at Maddy, her face sincere.

"Did . . . it . . . have to do with what happens?" she asked quietly.

"Happens?" Samantha asked avidly.

"Nothing," Maddy snapped, glaring at Gwen. "It's nothing. I'll be right back with those hamburger dinners." Maddy left the table, annoyed and a little embarrassed. Gwen lowered her voice.

"Maddy has this thing. She . . . sees things sometimes."

"What!?" Jessica gasped, her eyes lighting up.

"Shut up, Jessica!" Gwen hissed, but not before Uncle Kevin peered inquisitively out from around the fryer. Gwen gave him a wave. Kevin waved back.

"Not all the time," Gwen whispered, "just sometimes, she'll start to see things that don't really make sense. But they're usually bad—"

"Three hamburger dinners," Maddy interrupted as she returned from the kitchen with a tray of food. Samantha and Jessica just stared at her. Maddy stared back.

"What?"

"You, like, *see* things? Like what?" Samantha asked. Maddy shot daggers at her best friend, who shrank down in the booth.

"Not really," Maddy said, shrugging, "I guess I'm just a little weird. That's not exactly news." She set down the plates and a bottle of ketchup. "It's just one of those things, like being double-jointed or something."

"Like being double-jointed?!" Jessica blurted incredulously. "You're like Wonder Woman or something!" A few other customers turned to look. Maddy felt her face going red. Uncle Kevin came around from behind the counter and approached the table.

"How's everything going over here?" he asked with a friendly smile.

"Really good, Uncle Kevin," Gwen offered. "Just having girl talk." Gwen had taken to calling him Uncle Kevin, just like Maddy, something Kevin liked.

"Oh, okay, sorry to interrupt," Kevin said, hovering awkwardly. "Dessert is on the house. You girls come by anytime."

"Thank you!" the girls chorused.

"Would you shut it, Jessica!" Gwen scolded after Kevin walked away. "God, you're hopeless." Maddy waited till her uncle was well out of earshot, then crouched down by her friends.

"Listen, if you guys don't mind, please don't say anything about it? Kevin doesn't know what happened and I'd rather it stay that way. Please?"

The three girls nodded. "Sure," Gwen said, seeming to feel bad about the whole thing. "It's our secret."

Relieved, Maddy stood up as the crackling Magnavox filled the silence that had overtaken the table.

"*Stay tuned as our life and style correspondent Jamie Campbell will be at the* Halo Magazine *party later tonight for an exclusive interview with the one and only Jackson Godspeed. She'll continue reporting on his every move as he prepares for his upcoming Commissioning! Plus more on the absence of bad-boy Angel Theodore Godson from a special gala charity event today. Has his latest divorce already caused ripples in the social world of the Angels?*"

"OMG!" Gwen squeaked, turning her attention to the TV. "Jackson Godspeed's Commissioning!"

"His what?" Maddy asked, craning her neck around to see. Was that what the girl on Angel Boulevard had been talking about?

"Commissioning, duh," Jessica said, shoveling a fistful of fries in her mouth. Maddy gave her a blank look. "Youngest Guardian ever? First Protections? First save? What city have you been living in?"

"See, everybody but you knows this week is his Commissioning," Gwen explained, "which means a bunch of parties and events, and then all the Angels dress up and get together and there's a ceremony where they announce his Protections. And it could be me!"

"If your parents had a crapload of money, which they don't," Jessica said snidely through a mouthful of fries.

"They don't need a bunch of money," Gwen huffed. "I have the NAS Protection Lottery." Every month Gwen put most of her allowance into the lottery in the hopes of winning a Guardian for life. On top of their regular protection-for-pay services, it was a big moneymaker for the NAS although five percent of the proceeds went to fund development in Africa and Asia, where only a few disgustingly wealthy political leaders had Guardians.

"You and everybody else!"

"And don't forget about the NAS charity," Gwen countered, undeterred. "They raffle off one free Guardian each year."

"What are odds of winning that?" Samantha asked.

"About one in six billion," Jessica said.

"Or I could go on . . ." Gwen said. As if on cue, from the TV in the corner blared a promo for the season finale of *American Protection*, a show in which contestants competed against each other in seemingly arbitrary contests, with the viewers voting who stayed and who went. The ultimate prize was winning the services of a Guardian for ten years and a cash prize of a million dollars.

"Last season sixty-two million of you tuned in to see who YOU chose to be America's next Protection. You made Sarah the world's new Protection sweetheart!"

Maddy turned to look. She'd been studying for her AP finals in the spring and had never gone over to Gwen's to watch with her. On-screen flashed footage of a girl and a boy standing next to each other on a huge stage before an audience. A host opened an envelope and read the name Sarah. The runner-up grimly hugged Sarah as she jumped up and down in celebration. Seemingly from nowhere, a Guardian Angel, Owen Holymead, descended onto the stage, his wings flapping slowly as he landed. He gallantly stepped forward and took Sarah's hand. The host handed her an oversized check.

"Who will it be this year?"

"Lindsay!" Sam exclaimed at the Magnavox. Gwen rolled her eyes.

"It's totally going to be Addison, she had a way better performance last week, Lindsay's so lame."

Maddy knew the odds for winning the lottery or *American Protection* or getting a charity Angel were infinitely small, but Gwen and millions across the world still believed every month, every day, that they would be the newest Protection, instantly catapulted into the world of Angel glamour and fame, with their own Guardian. To be saved. Maddy kept her mouth shut.

Gwen took a french fry off Jessica's plate. "You'll be sorry when I'm Jackson Godspeed's Protection and I'm at all the parties with the Angels and everyone wants to be my friend, and you guys are still worrying about second-period algebra." Gwen turned to Maddy. "You're coming over and watching Jacks's Commissioning with us. I even got a little red carpet. We're totally dressing up. Then after we'll go to Ethan's party!"

Ethan's party. In all the excitement of the bio lab incident Maddy had almost forgotten.

"Gwen, I have three quizzes now on Monday. Two of which, I know for a fact, you do too. Plus my college applications are just sitting there. Look, I know I promised you I would think about it, and I have. The truth is, I really can't go." She flipped open her pad and began adding up their bill in her head.

"Come on, Maddy, *everyone's* going," Samantha said, as if that was reason enough.

"Maddy, how long have we been friends?" Gwen asked.

"Oh, don't be so dramatic," Maddy said, exasperated.

"When else are you going to have fun except this year? Kyle says Ethan's house is *amazing*, and what if he actually has a Guardian, and he makes a special appearance? He says you totally have to come, I bet that means Ethan is really into you. If you never do anything else for me ever again, please do this." Gwen folded her arms over her chest defiantly. It was one of those moments in life, Maddy thought, one of those moments where you had to choose between what you knew was right and your friend.

"Okay, relax," Maddy said. She put the check down. "I just have to make sure I can get my shift off and that Kevin doesn't find out." Gwen jumped to her feet and gave Maddy a hug over the table.

"This weekend is going to be the best ev-er!" she said, transforming the last word into two distinct syllables.

After the girls paid and left, Kevin came around from behind the fryer, holding a spatula in one hand.

"Did your friends have a good time?" he asked.

"Yeah," Maddy said, loading Gwen's dirty dish on her tray.

"What was all that yelling about earlier?"

"Oh, just some Angel Gwen is in love with."

"No, before that," Kevin pressed. "You girls were talking about an incident at school or something?"

Maddy paused, hoping her expression hadn't betrayed her. "Just girl stuff," she said innocently, not meeting Kevin's gaze. She piled Jessica's plate onto Samantha's and took them both on her arm. After a moment Kevin wiped his hands on his apron.

"Oh. Okay. Well, make sure to tell them to stop by again," he said, and disappeared back into the kitchen. Maddy didn't realize until he was gone that she had been holding her breath. Slowly and silently, she let it out.

It was the only secret Maddy had ever kept from him. Her visions.

Over the past several years, these strange images would come on her out of nowhere. Bad things, like what she had "seen" today. Except the difference was that this time, she actually recognized someone. That had never happened before. Normally the pictures in her head didn't make any sense.

Growing up, most of the time she had explained the visions away if Kevin happened to be around. The first time it had happened, they'd been at an amusement park for her ninth birthday, and she'd had flashes of horrible things happening on the rides—bloody, disturbing images. She became hysterical and Kevin was so worried he took her to the medical facility at the park. After a while she was able to calm down. And she'd lied, saying the roller coaster had upset her. Even from that very young age, Maddy never wanted him to know about the strange things she saw. And she certainly didn't want him to know that lately, it had gotten worse. She already felt like enough of a freak with the way she never felt fully simpatico around her peers. She didn't need her uncle thinking so too. She loved Kevin dearly, but the fact of the matter was, he wasn't her parent. Some things were just private.

Gwen often gave her a hard time about not dating, and Maddy usually used schoolwork and work at the diner as an excuse. And she *was* really busy with that stuff, but Maddy also knew that if she got close to someone, there was a chance one of those unsettling images would come in, and *then* what was she supposed to say? How could she explain her *thing*? Freshman year she'd been on a date with Adam Rosen, and halfway through, when they were holding hands, she'd literally run out of the frozen yogurt place they were in after a terrifying image of a car crash hit her from out of nowhere. Adam caught up to her, but she was still upset, and she had Kevin come get her and take her home. Just thinking about it still filled Maddy with shame.

But all of those earlier visions had been just random, like strange mental static of bad images. She thought she was just . . . okay, fine. Mentally sick. Today she actually *recognized* the people. And a lot of good it had done her: she'd finally made the Lunch Special.

Maddy looked up at the big plastic clock that hung over the dining room. 8:45. Still early. She sighed as she walked her friends' dishes to the kitchen. It was going to be a long night.

CHAPTER FIVE

Angel Boulevard lay dark and quiet. The palm trees stood motionless. By day it was the city's biggest tourist attraction, with people from all over the world flocking to the Walk of Angels. At night, though, with its neon signs off and the shops shuttered, this end of Angel Boulevard looked more like an eerie ghost town.

An old man stumbled over the gleaming stars, the streetlights casting looping streaks in his vision. Pockets of people were outside clubs farther down the boulevard, but most everything else shut down at dark, the crowds moving west to the Halo Strip. The man steadied himself against a trash can, then peered in. It was the usual. Angel maps and tourist brochures and fast-food wrappers. If you want to know the character of a people, he always said, look at their trash. He dug his hand down through the garbage until his fingers closed around the smooth, curving surface of a beer can. He pulled it out and leaned back, letting the remains of its contents dribble into his mouth and over his chin. Then he tossed the can back at the trash. He missed and the can rolled across the sidewalk and into the gutter.

He didn't bother picking it up. If the Angels wanted their boulevard to be clean, he told himself, they could come and do it themselves. They'd be cleaning a long time to get the dirt off this city.

He walked over and sat heavily in the doorway he had picked out for the night. It smelled vaguely of urine, but that didn't bother him. It was out of the wind, and out of the way of the shop owners and the straggling tourists who would still be walking by. With any luck, he wouldn't be kicked out tonight. He leaned drunkenly against the doorway and watched the glittering lights of the Immortal City spin around him. He smiled. If you had to be homeless, you might as well be homeless in the glorious City of Angels.

His eyes closed, and before he was even aware of his exhaustion, he fell asleep.

When he woke again, he wasn't sure how long he'd been out, but the boulevard had gone eerily silent. Even at night he could usually still hear the birds in the trees or the occasional stray dog looking for scraps. Tonight, nothing was making a sound. Nothing seemed even to move, apart from the palm trees trembling in the breeze. He sat up and blinked.

Something was wrong.

He was still drunk, that was for sure, but less so now. He could tell he was coming out of it because he could feel the first twinge of what would be his usual headache. This wasn't an alcohol-induced paranoia, he was pretty sure; something just seemed . . . off. He tried his best to focus his bleary eyes and looked around.

He saw only darkness. Nothing. But something was definitely wrong. He didn't know it consciously so much as instinctively. As his eyes searched the dark he was suddenly reminded of something he hadn't thought about in years. Even decades. He remembered being a kid and being afraid of the dark. That's what it was. It was a *feeling*. A feeling coming from the dark itself. The night around him seemed to be full of a feral, primitive presence, a gnawing, sweating animal instinct, like fear itself.

Then he heard the breathing and realized he wasn't alone.

"Hello?" he said nervously.

Someone was out there. In the dark.

"Is someone there?"

There was no response, but the breathing continued. A deep, rattling respiration. His eyes looked around wildly.

Then he saw it.

Even at his drunkest, he could never have imagined something so horrific. He opened his mouth, and the boulevard filled with the echoes of his screams.

CHAPTER SIX

Maseratis, Lamborghinis, and limousine car services jammed Sunset Boulevard, stacking up in a long line in front of the Chateau Marmont Hotel, bringing traffic on the glittering Halo Strip to a standstill. Dozens of personnel scrambled to control the scene, directing traffic, holding back the crowds, and coordinating the arrivals. Ranks of spotlights illuminated a red-carpet arrival area and a large white wall with the *Halo Magazine* logo repeated over and over on it. Nearby was an oversized blowup of the *Halo Magazine* cover featuring Jackson Godspeed crouching on a rooftop, wings out, the wind in his hair, under a caption that read "HOT HERO: *Jackson Godspeed prepares to make the leap into Guardianship.*"

Directly across from the wall and the display, an army of photographers, reporters, and journalists waited. Jamie Campbell, the life and style correspondent for ANN, set the glamorous scene as she stood breathlessly in front of her camera.

"We're here, live at the Halo Magazine *Commissioning Week release*

party, one of the hottest events in the Immortal City this week, so much so that word is Angels are stuck up and down Sunset Boulevard just waiting to get in. Jackson Godspeed and his famous wings are on the cover this month, and the rumor is he'll be arriving anytime now!"

Like a procession of supernatural perfection, the Angels began to arrive on the carpet—Guardians in sharp suits with their Divine Rings glinting in the lights and lady Angels in backless dresses that showed off their Immortal Marks. Fans swelled against the barricades and screamed their throats raw. Pedestrians passing by stopped and stared, either incredulous at the glamour before them or transfixed by it. Security was thick: last year during Commissioning Week an operative from the fringe radical anti-Angel group, the so-called Humanity Defense Front, or HDF, had actually made it onto the carpet. Dressed up as a Guardian, he'd covered himself in fake blood and made a run for the cameras, holding a sign that said THEY'RE NO ANGELS. He'd quickly been carted off, but the incident had left its mark. The European branch of HDF had made an armed attempt to kidnap an Angel in Munich five months earlier, a plot foiled when the Angel overpowered his attackers. The HDF had never gotten violent in Angel City, but they were always making some kind of threat, and the Angels were taking no chances.

Love the Angels or hate them, you couldn't help but feel the excitement in the air, like a kind of electricity, as if their very Immortal presence could be felt.

The world seemed to explode as Jackson Godspeed stepped out of his car and into the lights. The sound hit his ears like a drawn-out thunderclap. He wore a gray Gucci suit, white shirt, and slim black tie. The paparazzi swarmed, and Jacks took a deep breath and smiled his practiced smile as the cameras devoured him. From behind the barricades hysterical fans screamed things like "Save me, Jackson!" and "I want to be your first Protection!" Jacks turned and made sure to wave at them. A tightly wound middle-aged woman in an all-black pantsuit hustled over to him. Jacks grinned in relief at the approach of Darcy, his publicist ever since he could remember.

"*You* look incredible," Darcy said, giving him the once-over. "I couldn't be happier if you'd shown up naked."

Jacks cracked up. His stepfather liked Darcy because she had, hands down, the most elite client list in the business. Jacks liked Darcy because she was crass, honest, and unrelenting. Sometimes her antics were the only thing that got him through these events.

"It's the usual press, Access Angels, *Angels Weekly*, Angel News Network, oh, and A!" Darcy punched something in on her BlackBerry as she talked. "Vivian's already here, so remember"—she stopped typing and pointed her Berry at him like a weapon—"do *not* answer questions about your status. Be vague."

Jacks shrugged unhappily. "Is it really that big a deal?"

"*Buzz* is the really big deal, Jackson. Talk. Tweets. Gossip." She smoothed the lapel of his jacket. "If it creates buzz, then it's a big deal, and it does, so it is. For both you and Vivian. You want this cover to sell well? Just keep them guessing, okay?"

Jacks searched the carpet up ahead until he found Vivian. There she was in a one-shoulder dress that was probably from her fashion line. As much as he might try, Jacks couldn't deny it. Vivian looked incredible. He would have to remind himself to keep his distance. They weren't getting back together, he had decided. No matter how happy it would make Mark.

"You okay?" Darcy asked, snapping Jacks out of his reverie.

"Sure," Jacks said, and shook the image of Vivian out of his mind.

"Great, let's go." Jacks fixed another charming smile on his face, and they started down the long press line.

"Here he is, Jackson Godspeed and his famous wings, the Angel everyone is talking about." It was Jamie Campbell for ANN. "You're only a few days away from becoming the youngest Guardian Angel of all time. Can you describe what you're feeling right now?"

"I've wanted this for as long as I can remember," Jacks said, having to yell to be heard over the screams of his fans. "I used to go to bed dreaming about that Divine Ring."

"Any idea about your first Protections? We have a lot of girls watching tonight who are hoping it's going to be them!"

Jacks had answered this question in almost every interview now, and the answer was always the same. But somehow that didn't stop anyone from asking.

"Well, as you know, it's really out of my hands. The Archangels will assign my Protections, and it's my job to safeguard their lives."

"And, as you likely know, William Beaubourg, leader of the Humanity Defense Front, was just released from prison two days ago. He's already started making threats against Angels on amateur videos on the Internet, and you've been singled out in one of them. What do you think about that?"

Jacks felt annoyed for a split second. He put on another smile, fake this time. "Honestly, if we worried about every crackpot with a video camera, an Internet connection, and an opinion, there wouldn't be much time for anything else, now would there?" He realized he was basically repeating what Mark had told him to say when encountering this question. Now his annoyance was directed at himself.

"I see." Jamie glanced at her notes. "So let's be honest, Jacks, can we? What is the best part of being an Angel? Is it the lifestyle? Is it the parties? The fame? What's your favorite part?"

"Just having this chance," he said after considering.

"And what chance is that?" Jamie asked.

Jacks's blue eyes twinkled. "The chance to be a hero."

Darcy gave a "time's up" signal to Jamie, who thanked Jacks

enthusiastically and turned back to the camera as he stepped away. He moved down the red carpet, stopping to answer questions here and there but using only half his attention. Watching the event unfold, he felt that strange sensation of disconnect overtake him once again. It was as though he wasn't really present, as though all of this fuss, all of this grandeur, just needed a Jackson doll at its center and not him at all. He'd thought it was just his relationship with Vivian that made him think that way. But now it seemed this feeling had more widespread roots.

Jacks walked past a human being interviewed—a guy on crutches with a hip cast and a bandaged face—and guessed that he was the Protection from Mark's save last night, soaking up the limelight that came with the territory. Up ahead, Vivian modeled her dress for the Access Angels camera. The reporter, a girl with a fake tan who wore a sequined minidress, nearly fell out of her heels as she fawned over it. "Vivian, this dress is absolutely gorgeous! Tell us about it!"

"Well, Courtney," Vivian said, and spread the fabric of the skirt gracefully to give the camera a better look, "I thought this would be a great occasion to debut my new dress line. This is one of my favorites, so I'm wearing it tonight."

"So the line is dresses?"

"Not just dresses," Vivian corrected. "My line is the total package. I know that girls out there want to look like me not only for special occasions, but for everyday wear too. Even if they're, say, just going down to get a cup of coffee at Starbucks."

"Wouldn't we all like to look like you when we go to Starbucks!" Courtney gushed. Vivian smiled appreciatively.

"I'm also working with an amazing designer on my handbag line, which will be out in the spring." Courtney gasped.

"Well, Vivian Holycross, have a great time tonight; you look incredible!"

"Thank you," Vivian said, then added in a mock whisper, "I hope Jacks thinks so too."

An all-new eruption of shouts drew the attention to an arrival at the curb and Jacks saw his sister step onto the carpet. Photographers shouted as they leaned in for the perfect angle. Chloe posed and smiled, then shifted her weight, posed and smiled again. Then she gave them an over-the-shoulder and revealed she was wearing a backless dress with her Immortal Marks showing, looking almost childlike in the flashing lights. Angels gasped. Fans screamed. Jacks ground his teeth. He couldn't believe his mother had let Chloe wear that. One of Darcy's assistants led Chloe quickly over to the press line.

"Chloe Godspeed, how are you?" It was ANN again. "Are you here to support your big brother tonight?"

"Yes, of course," Chloe chirped.

"And congratulations are due to you as well on the success of your reality show, *Sixteen and Immortal*. The number-one-rated reality show on cable and already picked up for a second season, isn't that right?"

"Yeah!" Chloe beamed. "You can see it on Monday and Wednesday afternoons at 4 p.m. on A!"

Near the end of the carpet, Darcy pulled on Jacks's arm; he had been watching his sister. "Talk to A! Then we're done, okay?" she said as she led him over to Tara Reeves and her camera crew. They were broadcasting live from the event.

"And here he is, the Angel himself, Jackson Godspeed," Tara Reeves squealed. She looked beside herself with anticipation. "Well, it's no secret. You're a hit with the ladies. I'm just going to come right out and say it. You're *gorgeous*!" She blushed deep crimson and corralled a strand of hair behind her ear.

Jacks felt exquisitely uncomfortable. He shrugged self-deprecatingly. "Oh, come on—"

"—no really, how does it feel to know every lady Angel and woman on the carpet is worshipping you?"

"If you say so, Tara," Jacks said.

"So, the question on everybody's mind, and the speculation of girls and their moms across the nation, is, are you single? The big buzz this week is that you and a certain Angel are back together."

"Well, I'm not in a relationship, if that's what you mean."

Tara took a quick breath. "Can you characterize your *relationship* with Vivian Holycross, then?"

"She's a great Angel. I think she'll make a wonderful Guardian."

"But will she be wearing your Divine Ring one day?"

Jacks glanced at Darcy. She was glaring at him, stern and expectant. Tara's eyes narrowed.

"Well, I have to get it first. Then we'll see," he said finally.

"So it's still a mystery!" Tara shrieked into the camera. "Jackson and Vivian, are they secretly back together?!"

Jacks looked back at Darcy again. Her expression had transformed into relieved approval. She gave Jacks a thumbs-up. He felt that pang again, just for a moment. As though he wasn't even here.

Darcy led Jacks toward the throng of Angels sipping drinks, talking, and laughing in the lobby. He recognized a few of the other Angels who were going to be commissioned this week, like Milo Trinity and the Churchson twins. They'd been a class ahead of him until this year, so he didn't know them all that well, but it seemed they had shown up at his party despite the fact that the attention around Jacks had basically taken over their own Commissionings. Jackson had just pulled out his phone to text Mitch when he saw Vivian eagerly waving to him across the room.

"Good job," Darcy said while pounding the keys on her phone. "I'll leave you here. Go have fun, okay?"

"I will," he lied.

Jacks sighed as he watched Vivian walk toward him.

They entered the lobby together and Vivian took hold of Jacks's arm. Despite his attempts to disengage, she made herself inseparable from him, and they worked the party together. They chatted with the Archangels. They posed for pictures. It looked like they had never broken up. Finally they walked out to the patio to get some air.

"I just wanted to tell you I'm glad we took this break," Vivian said as she led him to a quiet corner.

"Great, Viv," Jacks said. "Me too." Maybe he had worried unnecessarily. Maybe she was starting to move on after all. Had she started to understand how he felt about the whole thing?

"You're young still," he said encouragingly. "You should, you know, see what else is out there."

Vivian stepped in front of him and put a hand on his chest, stopping him. Her flawless brow knitted together.

"I know what's going on, Jacks."

Jacks paused. "What do you mean?"

"I know this whole breakup thing is just for the press, a little publicity stunt before Commissioning, right? I get it."

Jacks blinked. He could feel the shock on his face.

"Vivian, I told you I needed time to focus before my Commissioning, and that's the truth," he said.

"Jacks, I *get it*." She smiled coyly. "I'll play along, even though, seriously, like you need any more publicity! With your wings and early Commissioning, you're going to be the biggest Guardian ever. I just want to hear you say we're getting back together after you get your Divine Ring."

He said nothing, too startled to be diplomatic. Vivian took a step forward and moved her body against his. "We'll surprise everyone. They'll discover our secret romance on some beach somewhere. Do you have any idea how much *press* that will get? The media will eat it up. And it will totally help sales for my fashion line."

"Vivian," Jacks began, but she put a finger against his lips. Her emerald eyes had becoming piercing and seductive. "You're Jackson Godspeed. I'm Vivian Holycross," she said. "It's just . . . *right*. Right?"

Jacks's gaze drifted desperately to a restroom sign with an arrow hanging on the wall. "Viv?" Jacks said. "Will you excuse me? I'm just going to use the restroom."

"Okay," she said, her eyes dancing, "But don't be too long."

He turned quickly and left. Her coy smile was still in place, but she watched him go, dissatisfied.

Jacks made his way down the narrow hallway that led to the bathroom. But he passed the door labeled Gentlemen and went instead through a back door leading to the parking lot. One of the valets was standing by the Dumpsters, smoking.

"Hey man," Jacks whispered. The valet's eyes grew wide when he saw Jacks. "Would you mind pulling my car around?" He held out his valet ticket and a hundred-dollar bill. "And would you mind being discreet about it?"

CHAPTER SEVEN

The sanctuary of the Blessed Sacrament Catholic Church on Sunset Boulevard was nearly empty. Detective David Sylvester, who, at forty, looked ancient already, sat alone in a sea of empty pews. He wore unremarkable clothes, wire-framed glasses, and a near-constant scowl. He sat hunched, as if the weight of the world were on his shoulders. His hands were clasped, fingers laced together as if he were immersed in prayer, but the detective's eyes remained open. They drifted up past the stained-glass windows of the sanctuary, to the vaulted ceiling, and beyond. They were intent, the eyes of a man more in conversation than prayer.

The classic cathedral glowed with beauty, lit only by soft candlelight from the altar. In the grotto, votive candles danced and flickered, illuminating the gentle and ever-smiling face of the Virgin Mary. It all suited Sylvester fine. He preferred an old, imposing church where you could feel the presence of God Himself whispering to you through the walls. He believed in the things of yesterday. He still listened to records, and his home phone still had a cord. Sylvester believed in the

Angel City of yesterday, and, if truth be told, he believed in the Angels of yesterday too.

The silence was interrupted by the chime of the detective's cell phone, an unfortunate necessity for police work. His fished the thing out of his pocket and looked at the number.

"This is Sylvester," he said into the phone tersely.

"Sorry to disturb, Detective," an officer from headquarters said. "But we need you on a scene. Right now." Sylvester frowned. He hadn't been on a real case in years. He looked around the empty church.

"I'm a little busy," he said, "Are you sure you need me?" The officer seemed to grunt.

"Jones or Chu would be more qualified, if you ask me, but the captain wants you on this one. Said something about your special background." Sylvester considered this.

"What's going on?" he said after a moment.

"You better just go down there and take a look."

Sylvester took down the address and pocketed the phone. He lingered for a moment, looking at the altar and its shimmering candlelight. Why was he being called? And why now? He wondered what could be going on. Then he stood without crossing himself and walked unceremoniously out of the church.

Sylvester's unmarked cruiser made its way toward Angel Boulevard, passing closed stores and shuttered cafés. Dark palms above shuddered in the night breeze. The city seemed naked, raw, without the neon, double-decker buses, and throngs of visitors. A pocket of drunken tourists staggered down the sidewalk on a side street. They had all bought matching SAVE ME! T-shirts and were taking pictures of each other. The detective shook his head. The Angels could only protect a few, but every year millions still dreamed it was somehow going to be them, that they were going to be on ANN with the Angels and other Protections, that they would be saved, and *everyone* would see it. They believed the lottery would come through. Or they'd make their millions and then have their own Guardian in no time, taking their rightful place among the Immortal City's beautiful and glamorous elite. The detective knew better. He had spent too many years observing the dirty truth about Angel City to get taken in by what he considered a fairy tale. Through it all, though, the Angels still seemed to keep clean. They'd moved up to their houses in the hills years ago to keep from getting splashed with the mud from down below. Sylvester turned right on Angel Boulevard, leaving the group of tourists laughing in the night.

The crime scene was alive with activity. Floodlights illuminated a section of the Walk of Angels cordoned off with yellow police tape. An Angel City Police Department chopper droned overhead, its searchlight slicing through the night. Sylvester pulled up in his cruiser and waited for a moment in the car, observing the busy scene through his windshield. It was the first time in a long while he had been at an active crime scene. He had almost forgotten the chaos. The adrenaline. The rush. He opened the car door and made his way out into the cold and noise.

"Hey, you can't come in here," a uniformed officer said as he approached the tape. Sylvester fumbled out his badge. "Oh. Sorry, sir," the officer said, and held up the tape.

Sylvester ducked under and took in the scene. On the sidewalk he saw a white sheet covering a lump directly over one of the famous Angel Stars. There were gangs in Angel City, and the occasional homicide was not uncommon. And it was certainly nothing that he was normally trusted with.

The one thing that caught his attention was that the bulge under the sheet looked small. Too small, he thought, to be a body. As he looked around for the sergeant, he thought he heard one of the officers mumble something as he passed. *Burnout*, he thought the man had said. Sylvester stiffened, plunging his hands into the pockets of his overcoat, and tried his best to put the man—and the past—out of his mind.

When Sylvester finally found him, Sergeant Bill Garcia looked especially upset.

"Hey Bill, what's going on?" said Sylvester. Garcia seemed surprised to see him.

"They put you on this?" Garcia said, worry edging his voice.

Sylvester nodded.

"Guess so. What's this all about?"

When the veteran sergeant looked at him again, Sylvester was startled to see fear glimmering in his eyes.

"Come on, sir," Garcia said. They walked together toward the sheet on the sidewalk. "Everyone keeps asking me if it's ever happened before. I tell them I don't know. I mean"—he paused—"not like *this*. I don't know these things, Detective, I just do my job."

"Settle down, Bill. What's going on?"

"I mean, we're running gang interdictions tonight, usual procedures, but this doesn't even seem like our jurisdiction anymore—" Sylvester stopped and held up his hand. The sheet was at their feet.

"Bill, stop. What's the big deal?"

Garcia pursed his lips.

"The big deal? Come take a look, Detective. I'll show you the big deal."

The sergeant knelt down and Sylvester followed. Out of the corner of his eye, Sylvester realized the other officers on the scene were staring in their direction. Either watching him or curious as to what was under the sheet. Or both. Garcia took the edge of the sheet in his hand and raised it.

The gory mess on the sidewalk was perfectly reflected in Sylvester's glasses. Two severed Angel Wings had been neatly placed over the Angel Star, crossed one on top of the other. Their ragged stumps glistened with thick, glittering Angel blood. Steam rose faintly from the wings in the cold night air. Whatever had happened, it had been very recent.

A jolt ran through the detective's body. He ran the back of his hand over his mouth.

"Is this for real?" Sylvester asked.

"Yes, sir," Garcia said, "This is for real. And read the name on the star."

Sylvester pulled a pen out of his shirt pocket and used it to lift one of the wings, just enough to look under. The gold lettering, though spattered in blood, was still readable.

"Theodore Godson," he read aloud.

Garcia nodded. "Theodore Godson was reported missing earlier today."

He pulled the sheet over the wings again, and the two men stood up. Sylvester looked down the length of the deserted boulevard. All of a sudden he seemed to have a terrible headache. He pulled his glasses off his face and began to polish them with the end of his shirt.

"What do you think, Detective?" Garcia asked.

"If someone cut off his wings, then he was probably mortalized."

"*Mortalized?*" Garcia said.

"Yes," Sylvester said. "He was made mortal." Sylvester was surprised to realize he was out of breath. A cold sweat had broken out on his forehead.

"Excuse me, sir, aren't Angels *immortal*?"

"Yes, well . . ." He paused again and had to lean against a wall. The ground had begun to move under him. Garcia looked at him, concerned.

"Hey, are you okay?"

"Just give me a second," said Sylvester, clutching the wall. A sudden wave of nausea had risen in his stomach.

"Sir, are you . . ." The sergeant trailed off, peering back toward the other police.

Sylvester steadied himself and after a few moments turned back to Garcia. The sergeant was looking at him with concern. So were the other officers, the forensics team, everyone. He gazed back into their disbelieving eyes. *No one thinks I can do this*, he thought. The spotlight of the chopper cut through the scene again, pointing at the severed wings on the sidewalk like a white finger in the night. Sylvester peered down the street. A few straggling tourists had seen the light and were coming over to investigate what was going on. Sylvester straightened and put his glasses back on.

"Get that chopper out of the sky," he suddenly barked. Then he turned to Garcia. "We're going to keep a low profile starting right now. Absolutely no press. You keep your men buttoned up, okay?" Garcia nodded. "Who else knows about this?"

"Just a few of the responding officers," Garcia said, surprised by the sudden confidence in the detective's voice.

"Okay, let's keep it that way," Sylvester said. "Document the crime scene and then clean everything up like it never happened at all. Have those wings taken to forensics and find out who they belong to."

Garcia had begun taking notes.

"Contact the Angels and get them involved. I want someone I can interface with on this, preferably someone close to the Council. Got all that?"

"Yes, sir."

Sylvester looked back at the other officers. They had all gone back to their work.

"So, what am I writing in the report then? Homicide?"

"Maybe," Sylvester said as he walked briskly back to his car. "We won't know for sure until we can find Theodore Godson. But if those really are his wings . . . it's not good."

"We've been getting reports of HDF activity in the run-up to the Commissioning. Do you think . . . ?" Garcia kept trailing Sylvester. "I mean, um, when was the last time something"—Garcia stumbled on his words—"well, something like this happened? In this way."

"Something on your mind, Garcia?" Detective Sylvester paused. The sergeant shook his head and dropped his head. Sylvester looked off into the distance as he continued, his expression hard: "It's been . . . a while."

Garcia crossed himself.

"I didn't even know it could."

"Walk with me," Sylvester said gruffly. They rounded the corner, and Sylvester stopped in front of a darkened souvenir shop. It was Sylvester's turn to question the sergeant.

"Garcia, are you going to be able to handle this?" Garcia considered, then nodded weakly.

"Okay, then I'm only going to explain this once. There are two kinds of Angels in the world. True Immortals and Born Immortals. True Immortals are, as the name suggests, truly immortal. Born Immortals can become mortal if their wings are removed and their supernatural powers are stripped. This is normally done for disciplinary purposes, by the Archangels, at the order of the Council." Sylvester looked into Garcia's eyes. "But last time I heard, Theodore Godson hadn't missed a save. He's not even in the Guardian ranks anymore; he stepped down from that a couple years after he was promoted to Archangel. Although judging by his recent behavior with women and drinking, he's been a bit of an embarrassment to the Archangels. Anyway, it wouldn't be like this." He motioned toward the boulevard. "Not this brutal. The Council is much more . . . civilized. This would be impossible to do, except for the most powerful Angels."

"Another Angel?"

"Only an Angel can kill another Angel," Sylvester said. "We're looking for an exceptionally strong, exceptionally powerful Immortal. Get on the horn with the Archangels and start taking statements from their people. Try to find out if Godson has any enemies among the bigwigs."

"There's an ex-wife. It's all over the gossip shows," Garcia said.

"Bring her in. Find out if she has a new man," Sylvester said. "And we need immediate saturation patrols for Angels in the area tonight. We need to talk to everybody."

"They won't like that," Garcia scoffed. "I know you haven't been on the front lines in a while, so let me just tell you, the Angels pretty much pretend we don't exist. I mean, they think they're above the law."

"Well, tonight they're not," Sylvester said flatly.

Garcia nodded and walked back to his cruiser to radio in the request. Sylvester stepped back to the darkened Walk of Angels and looked down the long, empty boulevard.

The whole thing felt unreal. Garcia was right to be afraid. Sylvester struggled to remember the last time an Angel had been mortalized. It had been a long, long time ago. And if it was happening again . . .

Garcia walked back over, his radio crackling. It echoed in the night air.

"Detective, lucky for you they're all in one place tonight. There's a big party down the street."

"Party?" said Sylvester. "What for?"

Garcia grinned. "You don't have a daughter, do you, sir? It's a Pre-Commissioning party for Jackson Godspeed." At the name, a moment of recognition flickered across Sylvester's face.

Garcia's radio squawked again, and he held the speaker close to his ear. "Okay. Everyone's accounted for. Actually, wait, everyone except one. He was spotted leaving in a hurry without talking to anyone. No one knows where he went."

Sylvester's eyebrow raised. "Okay, let's find him, and let's begin questioning those other Angels at the party. And start knocking on Angel doors up in the Hills, too," Sylvester said. "As for the one who left the party in a hurry, consider him a person—well, Angel—of particular interest. And before we hear otherwise, let's consider him potentially dangerous."

Garcia paused and looked at Sylvester. "You're not going to believe who it is," he said. Sylvester looked at the sergeant.

"Who?"

CHAPTER EIGHT

Jacks's Ferrari spun through the crisp Los Angeles night, the city twinkling all around him. He headed east on Sunset, just driving. He felt himself becoming more real, more free, with every mile he put between himself and the party. Was this disconnected sensation going to chase him all his life? He needed to get over it. He was Jackson Godspeed. It wasn't like he could just move somewhere and be anonymous. And, he reminded himself, he didn't want to. He'd been looking forward to saving people since he was a little boy.

After ten minutes his phone rang over the car's Bluetooth. Jacks checked the caller ID. It was Mark.

"That didn't take long," he murmured before picking up. "Hey Mark, I'll be home in a bit. I wasn't feeling well, so I decided to—"

"Never mind that now," Mark said, cutting him off. "Where are you?" His tone was urgent.

"Somewhere in Angel City. Why?"

"Get off the road."

Jacks sat up in his seat, alarmed. "What?"

"Something has happened. I'll explain later, but right now I need you to get off the road, go somewhere out of the way, and just blend in." His voice sounded almost panicked. "Make sure no one knows you're an Angel. And don't talk to any police. Do exactly as I say, all right?"

"Is Mom okay? Is Chloe? What's—"

"Don't ask any more questions," Mark snapped. "They're fine, but this is serious, young man. Do as I say. When you're somewhere safe, give me a call and I'll come meet you." With that he hung up.

Jacks's pulse quickened. He had never heard Mark so upset. What was going on? He took a hard left and zigzagged up side streets, through an Angel City he rarely saw, with modest homes and small, neglected lawns. Making a hard right, Jacks slowed and looked around, trying to get his bearings.

He had never been in this part of town before. He saw only one sign lit up, up on the left, a diner called Kevin's. His heart racing, he drove forward and pulled into the tiny lot. He parked, took off his suit jacket, and threw on a dark hoodie from the backseat. Then he looked at the diner again through the windshield. The place looked deserted. He wondered if this could all be about Vivian. No, he decided, it had sounded more serious than that. He should do exactly as Mark had said. He got out and pulled his hood up, locked the door, and walked toward the diner's front door.

Maddy was running a mop over the floor when the door jingled open and someone she had never seen before stepped into the diner. It was past closing and she realized, with regret, that she had forgotten to click off the neon Open sign in the window. Standing in the doorway was a boy Maddy thought looked to be about eighteen or nineteen. He was oddly dressed in tailored formal pants and a hoodie, and he had the hood pulled up over his head. Stabs of straight brown hair cut across his eyes. Maddy picked the mop up and set it back in its bucket. He looked out of breath and confused, unsure of himself even, and after a moment of what Maddy guessed was contemplation, he turned to leave.

"Hey," Maddy called after him. He turned around. "Can I help you?"

"Um, yeah," he said. "A table for one, please? If it's not too late?"

Maddy looked around at the nearly empty diner. Just a couple of regulars finishing up, one paying the check. By his tone she knew she could tell him they were closed, and he would accept that and leave. Still, it was her fault for not shutting off the sign. "No, of course not. Right this way."

She pulled a menu from behind the counter and led him to a booth by the window. As they walked to the table, Maddy realized that even dressed as he was and hiding under a hood, he was absolutely, strikingly beautiful. It was strange how it seemed to radiate off him. She could almost *feel* it, could almost taste it on her tongue. Maddy's head swam. Where was this coming from? She was around her share of what everyone would consider "cute boys": at school, at the diner, even just around Angel City. And sure, maybe they were attractive, but she had never felt herself gushing *he's beautiful*. That was Gwen's job. Maddy was supposed to be the levelheaded one.

She took a breath and tried to collect herself. He was a customer like any other, Maddy thought, and he would be treated as such.

"Here you are," she said, setting the menu down on the table. "I'll be right back to take your order."

Jacks slid into the booth and glanced at Maddy as she walked away. She was really pretty, he thought, even if she was just an ordinary girl. As she disappeared into the kitchen, he was surprised to realize he was still watching her. He pulled out his cell phone and texted Mark his location.

Kevin was hanging up his apron when Maddy appeared. "One more customer," she told him.

"Really?" Kevin asked wearily. "You didn't just tell him we were closed?"

Maddy looked down at the floor, thinking about her reaction to the cute stranger. "Uh, he seems a little shaken up. I didn't want to send him away."

Kevin gave Maddy a look. "All right, go get his order," he said, putting his apron back on. "The sooner he gets his food, the sooner we can go home."

Maddy poured a glass of ice water and placed it on her tray. She headed over. "Long night?" she asked as she set the water in front of Jacks and pulled out her notepad.

Mark's text came in. Jacks glanced at it: STAY THERE, COMING TO YOU. Jacks flipped the phone over on the table and looked up at Maddy.

"Something like that. I just needed to get off the road for a second."

"Well, you came to the right place. What can I get you?"

"Ah," he started, then stopped. Maddy waited. His gaze had drifted outside. Maddy looked up. Two ACPD cruisers had just pulled into the parking lot.

Jacks picked up the menu. "What do you recommend?"

As Maddy ran through the specials, Jacks's eyes darted outside again. The cruisers had parked in the lot, and two policemen stepped out.

"Any of that sound good?" Maddy asked, and waited for a response. Jacks watched as the officers examined his Ferrari with flashlights. At once they turned and looked in the direction of the diner. Jacks instinctively sank down in the booth, his mind racing. "The meat loaf's good too," Maddy continued, trying to spur a decision, starting to feel guilty that she was keeping Kevin.

"Actually . . ." Jacks said, trailing off. And then he noticed it. There was a sign in the window. Even facing away from him, he could still read the red lettering: HELP WANTED, and below that, scrawled in black Sharpie, *Part-time position available*. Jacks looked at Maddy. "I'd like to apply for a job."

Maddy blinked. "Okay, I'll bring back an application with your food."

"I was actually hoping I could apply right now," Jacks said, a little urgently.

"All right," Maddy said, a little surprised, "I'll bring you the application." Maddy turned to go in the back, oblivious to the officers approaching just outside the window.

"Miss?" Jacks called. Maddy turned. "Isn't there someplace we could go in the back? So you could interview me? I'd like to get that part out of the way." His eyes flickered to the door, where the police were just entering, their hands were on their holsters. He looked back at Maddy.

"Please."

There was something different about him, Maddy thought. Something beyond the obvious good looks. It was in the way his eyes caught the light. The way he looked at her. They way he held her gaze. The funniest thing was, it made her want to trust him.

She was surprised to find herself speaking.

"Okay, follow me."

Jacks jumped to his feet and followed Maddy around the counter and into the back. He couldn't believe she didn't recognize him, but at this point he didn't care. He wasn't concerned with anything except getting out of the dining room.

Maddy's uncle was cleaning the griddle as they passed. Before Kevin could look up, Maddy had taken Jacks into their tiny office and closed the door.

The room was dingy and cramped. A battered metal desk was covered in piles of receipts and bills, an old picture of Maddy and Uncle Kevin in a frame poking up out of the mess. Maddy's backpack, exploding with textbooks and college brochures, sat on the floor. She smoothed her uniform and found an application among a stack of forms. Jacks took a seat in the creaky chair opposite the desk and pulled his hood back.

"Thanks," he said.

"Sure."

Closed in the small room with him, the fact struck Maddy that this boy's beauty was nearly overwhelming. Who was this guy? It didn't even seem real. His pale blue eyes were piercing under strong, dark eyebrows, and his model good looks sat on a sturdy face, giving him a slightly rugged quality.

"Okay," she said, assembling her thoughts and grabbing a pen out of a nearby coffee mug. "I didn't get your name."

"It's Ja . . . Jason." Jacks looked over to a newspaper sitting on the desk and read the headline: STOCKS SLIDE AGAIN. "Jason Stockton."

"Okay, Mr. Stockton," Maddy said, "do you have any prior experience in serving?"

"No," Jacks said. Maddy looked up at him.

"Any experience in the restaurant industry at all?"

"No."

Maddy sat back in her chair. "You know, Jason, to get a restaurant job in Angel City it's pretty much required to have some experience serving."

Jacks's lips pulled up into a half-grin. "Well, how are you supposed to get experience if you can't land a job to begin with?"

Maddy folded her arms and leaned over the table. She was trying not to flirt, but she almost couldn't help herself.

"Okay, then, why should I hire you?"

Jacks looked for something, anything, that would keep him safely in the back room. His eyes drifted down to Maddy's backpack and a college brochure sticking out between two textbooks.

"To save money for college," he said, improvising. Maddy paused, her expression softening. Jacks looked at the image of the leafy campus on the brochure's cover. "Somewhere back east, actually. Away from Angel City."

"Really?" Maddy said, her interest piqued.

"Yeah . . ." Jacks said unsteadily. He took a deep breath and lied. "It's always been my dream. Problem is my family, well, we don't have a ton of money right now."

Maddy shook her head in empathy. "I know how that is. Did your dad lose his job or something?"

"Actually, he . . ." Jacks trailed off, searching Maddy's eyes. He was surprised she had unwittingly brought him back to the truth. "He died."

Maddy flushed. "Oh my God, I'm so sorry."

Jacks shrugged. "It's okay, I was young. I never really knew him at all."

"Yeah, but that doesn't make it any easier," Maddy said, her defenses collapsing with startling quickness. "I mean, I know just how it is. Both my parents died when I was just a baby. I never knew them either."

"Wow, I'm sorry. I thought *I* had it rough."

"It's okay," Maddy said, looking away. Jacks watched her. He felt a sudden urge to share something with her that he'd never told anyone.

"You know what? This might sound crazy, but I have no memories of him, right?" Jacks said. "So one day I just started making them up. Making up things we did together, places we went." He laughed in embarrassment, shaking his head. "Pretty stupid, right?"

Maddy was quiet for a long moment, but her eyes had returned to Jacks and studied him.

"At the park," she said finally.

"What?"

"My mother, father, and me at the park. Perfect day, you know, a carousel, swans floating on the pond, like one of those old postcards. That's my favorite. My favorite pretend memory."

Jacks smiled softly. "That's a nice pretend memory. The park. I hadn't thought of that one."

"All this time I thought I was the only one," she said. "I mean, you know the memories aren't real, you tell yourself that, but somehow, in some crazy way—"

"They help."

They said it together. Jacks and Maddy stared at each other as the seconds drew out, and she only now was aware that she had leaned closer to him. She couldn't be sure, but she thought he had come closer too. Now they were only inches apart. She leaned in, willing the moment to sweep them into a kiss, the most delicious kiss of her life . . .

Jacks spoke.

"I don't even know your name."

"Maddy," she said, holding out her hand. Jacks reached for it and, ever so gently, took it. His hand was hot to the touch, and Maddy thought she could feel a crackle of electricity, as if a current of energy was passing through Jacks and into her. From the look on Jacks's face, he had felt something too.

A loud knock boomed at the door.

"Maddy? What are you doing in there?" It was Kevin.

"That's my uncle," Maddy whispered to Jacks. "He owns the place." Jacks's eyes focused, brought back to the present.

"Listen, Maddy, I need to get out of here. Is there a back door?"

"Yes, in the kitchen. What's going on?"

"I'm not sure yet," Jacks said in a low whisper. "But I need your help. Will you help me?"

"Okay," she said, a little cautiously. "Stay here." She went to the door and opened it just a crack.

"Hey Kevin, I was just interviewing someone for the part-time position."

Kevin eyed her. "I do the interviews."

"I know, I just thought I would help out."

"Okay, well, I need you both to come out. There are two police officers here asking to see everyone."

"Okay, be right out," Maddy said a little too brightly. Kevin walked back to the dining room and said something to one of the officers.

"This way," Maddy whispered as she led Jacks out of the office and toward the back door. They were halfway across the kitchen when a voice shouted from the dining room.

"There he goes right there!" one of the officers yelled in alarm, drawing his gun. "Jackson, stop!"

"Stop right there, Jacks!" the other echoed as he lunged forward, sending a table and dishes crashing to the floor. Jacks stepped in front of Maddy, knocking her back with such force it took her wind away.

"Back up toward the rear door," he whispered. "Do it now."

Maddy did as she was told, her lungs gasping for air. One of the officers shouted again.

"Leave the young lady! Freeze right there or I will shoot you!"

Jacks stopped. He reached a hand back and touched Maddy's side, right on the curve of her hip. She could feel the heat of his fingers through her uniform.

"No," Jacks replied calmly, "you won't." Then he took another step back, still touching Maddy.

The officer's trembling finger squeezed the trigger.

BANG. The discharge of the gun was the last thing Maddy heard before a bright, white light filled the diner, as though the sun itself had risen in the restaurant. As her eyes adjusted, Maddy saw the most amazing sight of her life up to that point.

The entire dining room was frozen.

The two policemen were like statues, their faces masks of fear and surprise. One of them had knocked the coffeepot off the warmer, and it now hovered, mid-shatter, over the floor. Uncle Kevin was frozen too. He had dropped his spatula, and it was rendered motionless just beyond the tips of his fingers. Perhaps the most spectacular thing of all, the bullet that had been fired now hung in the air, absolutely still, like a model airplane on fishing line. Maddy looked up at the boy. His hand stretched out in front of him, as if telling the entire room to *stop*. He turned and looked at her with his perfect features and his piercing blue eyes. There was no other explanation. He was an Angel.

The front door burst open, and an impeccably dressed older man rushed into the restaurant, the rest of the diner remaining stock-still. He looked around at the frozen scene and then at Jacks.

"Jacks," he said sternly, "let's go."

Jacks held Maddy's gaze for another breathless second and then, without saying anything, turned to leave. Nonchalantly he grabbed the bullet out of the air and put it in his pocket. Only then did he let go of Maddy.

Time seemed to return to normal. *SMASH* went the coffeepot all over the floor, and glass and brown liquid rushed over the linoleum. Uncle Kevin's spatula clanged to the ground. Jackson and the older Angel vanished out the front door. The two officers peered at each other, confused. Maddy just stood there, immovable. It wasn't just what she had *seen*; it was what she had *felt*. As she stood there still breathing his strange, wonderful smell, a conversation came back to her, a conversation with Gwen and Jessica and Samantha from earlier in the evening. A name rose to the surface of her mind.

"Jacks . . . Jackson . . . Jackson Godspeed." Her face turned white with disbelief, then blushed pink with embarrassment. Finally, it turned deep crimson. With rage.

Outside, Jacks and Mark walked quickly to their cars. Mark turned to his stepson. "Are you okay?"

"Yes. What is going on?"

"We'll discuss it at home. I'll follow, and don't ever let me lose sight of you." Jacks got into his Ferrari and started the throaty engine. Mark went to his M7. He unlocked the door, but before he could get in, a hand seized him by the arm. Hard. With supernatural speed Mark spun around, ready to defend himself and Jacks.

It was Kevin. His stare was cold. Mark relaxed his hand, which was already around Kevin's throat.

"Hello, Kevin," Mark said calmly.

"You know the agreement," Kevin said, cutting him off. "I don't ever want to see you, or your boy, around here again."

"I'm sorry, Kevin, it was an emergency."

Kevin leaned into Mark's face.

"Stay the hell away from Maddy."

CHAPTER NINE

Kris was waiting as Mark and Jacks came in from the garage. Her eyes were puffy from crying, her face creased with concern. She rushed to Jacks and hugged him. On the flat screen in the background, A! was replaying footage of Jacks's arrival at the party.

"I'm fine, Mom," Jacks said in answer to her questions. "Is Chloe okay? Where is she?"

"Upstairs, in bed," Kris said. Jacks turned to his stepfather.

"Mark, what's going on?"

Mark picked up the remote off the kitchen island and turned the TV off.

"We don't have long. A detective from the ACPD will be here soon. Just let me do the talking."

Jacks looked between them.

"Would someone please just tell me—"

A buzz echoed in from the foyer. Mark stepped over to the security cameras and looked at the image of the police officer waiting in his unmarked car at the gate. Mark studied the face. It was different now, he thought. The years had dulled the edges of David's features. His eyes, though, still burned with that same righteous fury, and in that way, he was undeniably the same.

Mark activated the gate and watched on-screen as the vehicle pulled up the drive. Jacks gave Mark an expectant look when he returned. Mark looked at his stepson evenly.

"There's been an incident on Angel Boulevard. There's reason to believe an Angel was attacked. And mortalized. Perhaps even murdered."

It was several seconds before Jacks could fully absorb what his stepfather was telling him. Of course he knew Angels could be made mortal—he and every other Angel were warned relentlessly in Guardian training about the consequences for certain actions—but killing them wasn't something that happened. Not in modern times. Not in Angel City.

"What . . . how . . ."

The doorbell echoed.

"Remember," Mark said, placing a hand on Jackson's shoulder, "let me do the talking."

Mark walked to the door and opened it.

"Mark," Sylvester said.

Mark nodded. "David."

"It's been a long time."

"Yes, it has," Mark said. "Come in." The Archangel stepped out of the way and Sylvester entered with another policeman. "I thought you had retired," Mark said. Sylvester took a quick glance around the expansive house before returning his gaze to Mark.

"This is Sergeant Garcia," he said.

The two shook hands. Mark gestured toward the living room.

Sylvester took a seat on one of the leather sofas across from Jacks and Kris. Garcia stood near the back.

"I'd like to know what you thought you were doing trying to arrest my stepson," Mark said as he came in and sat with them.

"I could bring Jacks downtown right now, Mark," Sylvester said. "I could detain him up to forty-eight hours. I'm here out of courtesy. And respect."

"How could you suspect him of *anything* in this matter?" Mark barked. "It's an outrage."

"Jackson left the party in a hurry at the probable time the crime was committed, he was in the immediate area, and no one had seen him. Simple. We needed to bring him in for questioning. He resisted, attempted to abduct a young lady, and one of our officers was compelled to discharge his weapon."

Jacks stood up in protest, but Kris pulled him back down on the sofa. Mark dismissed Sylvester's words with a wave of his hand.

Juan, eyes bleary with sleep, pushed a tray in from the kitchen. Hot coffee, peanut butter sandwiches, cookies, and milk.

"Thank you, Juan," Kris said, and set out the late-night snacks. Sylvester pulled out his notepad.

"This will only take a moment. Jackson, please, can you just tell me why you left the party and where you went afterward?"

Jacks looked at Mark, who nodded.

"I just left to get some air. I was driving on Sunset, and then I stopped at the diner. Two officers came in, and you know the rest."

"They reported you were in the back, with a waitress."

Mark looked at Jacks curiously.

"Yes, we were just talking," Jacks said.

"Is that it? And you didn't do, hear, or see anything else?" Sylvester asked.

"Yes, that's it." Sylvester eyed him warily. Jacks cleared his throat.

"Will someone please tell me what's going on?"

Mark and Kris exchanged a look.

"They found . . ." Mark paused. "They found severed wings."

Very slowly, Jacks looked up at his stepfather.

"Whose?" he asked quietly.

"We don't know yet," Sylvester said, "But the wings were left on Theodore Godson's star."

"An Archangel," Jacks murmured, the enormity settling in. Mark and Sylvester exchanged a look.

"And you knew nothing about this?" Sylvester asked.

"Of course he didn't!" Mark exclaimed.

"I'm asking Jackson, not you," Sylvester said calmly.

Jacks shook his head honestly. "I'm telling the truth. I left the party, went to the diner, came here."

Jackson's stepfather turned to the detective. "We're doing this as a courtesy because even the faintest notion that Jackson could be involved with something like this is so absurd, I thought it best to get it over with. But if you want to continue this ridiculous questioning, I'm afraid there will have to be a lawyer present."

Sylvester narrowed his eyes. "Fine. We'll see. For your sake, I hope it all checks out. Otherwise we'll be coming back and won't be as polite." Sylvester stood up. "And Jacks? Next time an officer of the Angel City Police Department asks to speak to you, please listen." He turned to Mark. "Thanks for your time."

"Let me see you out," Kris said. Sylvester got up from the couch and walked to the door. Sergeant Garcia lingered in the living room, smiling sheepishly at Jacks.

"Excuse me, Jackson, um, do you think I could get an autograph for my daughter?" he said.

"Garcia," Sylvester said stiffly, "let's go." Garcia hurried outside without his autograph. Mark shut the door, then turned to Jacks.

"I don't want you to worry about this, Jacks. I'm going to address the issue with the rest of the Archangels tomorrow, and we'll more than likely be putting our own team on the investigation. You can't expect too much from the police."

Jacks nodded. He pushed his hand through his hair. Severed wings. It was horrific to think about.

"You've got a big week coming up," Mark continued. "What's important is that you don't lose focus. Now why don't you go upstairs and get some sleep."

"Okay," Jacks said, feeling himself sliding helplessly into the same pattern he'd followed his whole life—following Mark's suggestions, which were actually not suggestions at all. He turned to walk up the stairs, then stopped. "That man at the diner. What did he want after we left?"

Mark paused, then looked at Jacks evenly. "Oh. Him? He was just angry at the damage to the restaurant. I told him we would cover it."

"Why'd he mention Maddy to you? I heard him say her name. What's she got to do with anything?"

"Maddy? Who's that?" Mark asked.

"The girl. The waitress."

Mark shrugged. "I have no idea. Like I said, don't worry about this. Leave the police, this alleged incident, that restaurant, all of it to me."

Jacks looked at him, dissatisfied. Wordlessly, he headed up the stairs.

Lola had turned his bed down already, but Jacks wasn't tired. He pulled off his shirt but stopped undressing as his gaze drifted out the window. He walked to the glass door for his private deck, unlocked it, and stepped out into the cold night.

Angel City unrolled beneath him like a carpet of twinkling stars. For the first time ever he squinted and forced his eyes to search among the tiny, individual lights of the city. He spent almost a minute examining the lights below until he found it. A tiny, blinking sign tucked into the bottom of the hill.

The sign for Kevin's Diner.

For reasons he couldn't explain, his mind kept returning there, to the back room, and to the girl. That flash in her eyes when their hands touched. And what had he felt? He watched the sign. It blinked and blinked. Then went dark. Jackson let his eyes defocus, and the city returned to an unbroken, glimmering whole.

CHAPTER TEN

Maddy woke before her alarm went off. She had tossed and turned all night. In her half-conscious mind, the strange images of the frozen diner played over and over like some kind of surreal nightmare. And *he* was there as well, in the back room with her. She saw his pale blue eyes, his cruelly perfect features. Again and again, she relived him manipulating her. He was probably dying with laughter inside while he made up the whole story. He was making fun of her, and she fell for it. She must have looked so foolish to him. Yet under it all was a tiny voice, a lone note of discord in the chorus of her thoughts: it was the hope that what had happened between them in the back room—and what she had felt—was real. When she couldn't lie in bed any longer, she pulled a shirt from a stack of laundry, dressed, and went downstairs.

Outside, the morning was soft and gray, the Angel City sign barely visible on the misty hillside. Uncle Kevin sat at the kitchen table in his robe, reading the *AC Times*. When he looked up at her, his eyes were tired. His face, Maddy thought, had changed. It was lined with worry and looked somehow older.

"Morning," she said quietly.

"Morning. Why are you up so early?"

"I couldn't sleep," Maddy said, sitting on a step at the base of the stairs.

Kevin nodded. "Me neither."

He stood and took down a mug from the cupboard. He poured her coffee, then took two slices of bread from a bag on the counter.

"Toast?"

"Sure. Thanks."

Kevin placed butter and strawberry jam on the table. Maddy shuffled over the faded linoleum of the kitchen and sat down. She drew her legs up to her chest and rested her chin on her knees. He poured her a glass of OJ—they always had the generic store brand from concentrate, but Maddy thought it tasted pretty good. She picked at the toast Kevin set in front of her.

"I'm really sorry about last night," she said at last.

"It wasn't your fault, Maddy," Kevin said, his voice gruffer than usual.

"Well, I'm sorry I let things get as far as I did. Even though he asked for an application—" she said, then stopped herself. It was so embarrassing to think about in their little kitchen in the daylight. Interviewing the world's most famous Angel for a part-time position at Kevin's Diner. And the way he had . . . bewitched her. The way he had made her believe there was something between them. Stupid, stupid girl. "I just should have been more careful," she muttered, and took a vicious bite of her toast. "Are you sure you don't need help with the cleanup?"

Kevin shook his head. "No, it's really not that bad," he said. "Just some broken plates and glasses; we'll be open for lunch."

"Okay," she said, not quite meeting his eyes. She let the guilt wash over her.

She walked to school with her head down and her hood up, as usual. She waded through the usual crowds, not looking up until she got to school. When she did, she was surprised to see a curious pair of eyes staring back at her. A girl from calc, Maddy thought her name was Lucy, had been watching her. Maddy quickly looked away, hiding herself behind a curtain of hair until the girl had passed. It was odd. Maddy turned and saw a pair of guys, sophomores, looking at her too. Their gaze was curious, intent. Something was different.

As she approached her locker, she could already see Gwen there, waiting impatiently for her. Her eyes looked like they were about to bug out of their sockets.

"Hey," Maddy said as she approached.

"You little bitch!" Gwen exclaimed, holding her phone out. On the screen, to Maddy's shock, was a picture taken in Kevin's Diner. A picture from last night. There was Maddy standing just behind Jackson Godspeed, looking terrified, in her waitress uniform. Ew. The headline under the photo read in all caps:

"JACKSON GODSPEED TRASHES DINER"

Maddy could feel the hot blood rushing into her cheeks as she read the blog's embellished detailing of the previous night.

"You're on every Angel blog," Gwen said excitedly. "Now, I want details and they better be juicy!"

Maddy hazarded a glance down the hall. More intrusive eyes stared back. Assessing. Prying. Even the cheerleaders were looking at her. Everybody knew. She opened her locker and tried to use the door as a shield for her face.

"Nothing really happened," she said as she pulled her books out.

"What?!" Gwen shrieked. "Why don't you want to talk about it? This is my chance to, like, live vicariously through you!"

Maddy squirmed. "He came in, sat at a booth—"

"Which booth?!"

"I don't know. He ordered—"

"What did he order?!"

"I can't remember. Then some people came in, and he left. That's it."

"Okay, tell me *exactly* what he said to you."

Maddy thought about the lies. "Nothing. He didn't say anything."

"He must have said *something*."

"I think he said, 'Can I get the check?'"

"Can I get the check?!" Gwen exclaimed in astonishment. Maddy watched her melt as she pictured it. "'Hey, it's Jackson Godspeed,'" she said in her lowest male voice, "'Can I . . . get the check?' *Maddy!*" she screamed. A few people nearby turned to look.

"So you really didn't know it was him?" Gwen asked incredulously.

"No, like I told you. I don't follow that stuff."

"Okay, but you must have known he was an *Angel*," she pressed. "I mean, wasn't he impossibly, amazingly fine?"

Maddy's mind flickered to back to Jackson's divine features and the electricity that seemed to pass between them when they touched.

"I promise," she said, making her tone apathetic, "he was nothing special."

The bell buzzed. Gwen looked unfulfilled. "Okay, you can tell me the rest at lunch!"

"I have lunch detention," Maddy reminded her. Gwen frowned.

"Want me to try and bring you something from the cafeteria?"

Maddy smiled, grateful. "Sure."

A ping went off and Gwen was looking at a blog alert on her BlackBerry again. She crinkled her nose. "Ew," she said. Maddy looked over her shoulder and saw a picture of a man with a wild, dark beard and short hair. His eyes were black and intense, almost—the thought occurred to her unbidden—infernal. The blog headline read: *HDF leader William Beaubourg releases new video, threatens Angels.*

"Those guys are such losers," Gwen said. "Why do the Angel blogs ever even mention them?"

Maddy's classes crawled by. In AP History she sat in the last row, hoping it would make it harder for her classmates to stare at her. Somehow, they managed. At least Mr. Rankin didn't call on her again. He had learned his lesson. In English she asked questions about *Hamlet* to which she already knew the answers to pad her participation grade. In Spanish she listened to the whir of the overhead projector fan. Finally, the lunch bell rang.

She reported to the administration office and was taken by the assistant principal, Mr. Leihew, to an empty classroom.

"No visitors," he said, sounding sort of apologetic about the whole situation. "But you're free to study, of course. I'll check back in on you in a few minutes." Maddy thanked him and he left. She fished a stack of college applications out of her bag and paged through to an essay prompt.

Please describe what you consider to be the most difficult moment of your life. Maddy groaned. She heard the click of the door opening. Mr. Leihew must really not trust her, she thought. When she looked up, her heart nearly stopped in her chest. It wasn't Mr. Leihew.

It was Jackson Godspeed.

He stood there in an untucked white collared shirt rolled up at the sleeves, designer jeans, and tie. Even dressed casually, he looked like he had just stepped off the cover of a magazine. Maddy was a statue of a girl in a desk. She couldn't make sense of him in this place. Jackson

Godspeed and Angel City High—they were like puzzle pieces that wouldn't fit together in her mind.

"Hi," Jacks said, closing the door quietly behind him.

"*You*," Maddy hissed in disbelief. It came out harsher than she expected. It was almost hateful. "What are you doing here?!"

"I wanted to talk to you," he said, smiling. He came into the room, and it was as if the dusty, cramped classroom could hardly contain him. He took a seat in the desk next to Maddy and she could feel it again, that same feeling she had felt as she walked him to the booth at the diner. It was like his presence was *radiating* off him. It made it hard to think.

Jacks cleared his throat. "I just wanted to apologize for what happened at the diner last night. And," he said, hesitating, "I wanted to . . . thank you for helping me. I've never really needed anyone's help before. It was a new experience."

Maddy felt the anger and embarrassment of the previous night welling up inside her, mixing and twisting with the shock of the moment.

"Got any more stories for me today?" she almost sneered at him. "Want to tell me about how you need a job? About how you're trying to raise money for college? About how your dad—" A sudden lump in her throat cut off her words. She swallowed it down hard. "About how your dad died too?!"

Jacks's expression registered surprise, as if some expectation had not been met.

"Look, Maddy," he said, and it was a cruel thrill to hear him say her name, "I never meant to hurt you. There was a situation. I didn't think things were going to happen . . . the way they did."

"Well, you thought wrong, didn't you?" Maddy snapped. Jacks's face twisted in frustration.

"Hey, nobody's perfect—"

"Well, you're *supposed* to be!" She glared.

Jacks opened his mouth to speak, then stopped. "I . . . you're impossible!" he finally blurted, getting to his feet.

"Good!" Maddy said, rising out of her desk. "I hope I go down as the one disappointment in your life."

Jacks stopped on his way to the door, as if to consider the words, then turned.

"I just came over here to tell you I'm sorry," he said, fighting to keep his tone composed. Even when she was angry, Maddy looked so pretty to him—and he was startled at himself for even thinking it.

"Well, you should have saved yourself the trouble," Maddy said defiantly. "Please just leave me alone."

She could see the incredulity wash over his face like a black wave.

Just then, Maddy heard the squeak of the turning doorknob.

"Oh my God," she breathed, her head snapping to the door. Mr. Leihew must be coming to check up on her.

"You can't be in here—" she gasped, but it was too late. The knob turned, the door opened.

Gwen's head peered around the door.

"Maddy? You alone?" she whispered.

Maddy looked around the room. Jacks was gone. Her heart was still racing, but she tried her best to make her voice sound calm.

"Y-yeah," she stammered.

"Can I come in?" Maddy nodded unsteadily. Gwen pushed the door open with her foot and came in holding a tray of food.

"Well, I know you're, like, not supposed to have visitors, but this is detention, not prison."

"Thanks," Maddy said unsteadily.

"Were you talking to someone?" she asked. "I could have sworn I heard a voice." Maddy rubbed her sweaty palms against the legs of her jeans.

"Not . . . that I know of," she said.

Gwen talked while Maddy ate with shaking hands. She went on about how she had talked to Jordan Richardson in the lunch line, her new crush and ideal Homecoming date, then said something about how he was going to be at Ethan's party. Maddy tried to listen as Gwen went on and on, but her head was still spinning from Jacks's unannounced—and unwelcome—visit. She could still sense him lingering in the room as she sat there.

Walking home, things felt different. Suddenly she couldn't help feeling the Angel Stars under her feet. She couldn't *not* see the tourist shops and the billboards and the faces of the Angels. As much as she tried, she couldn't erase those piercing pale blue eyes from her mind.

She was so angry.

For once she welcomed her evening shift at the diner; she was looking forward to it, even. Anything to be distracted from her wandering thoughts. She had just rounded the corner to her street when she stopped dead in her tracks. She blinked, not sure if what she was seeing could be real.

There was a line outside of Kevin's Diner. There had never been a line. Even on Sundays, there was no waiting to be seated. This was maybe a hundred people, and not regulars, either. These were hipsters with tattoos and piercings, suburbanites, tourists, and preppy Beverly Hills types. Maddy hustled up the sidewalk and slipped in the back door.

"What did I tell you?" Kevin yelled from behind the fryer as she came in. "It's finally happened. Our luck is changing! I called in extra help." Maddy smiled as convincingly as she could, then disappeared into the bathroom to change.

The diner was alive with talk about Jackson. Maddy couldn't avoid it as she ran between tables, scribbling orders and dropping off armfuls of food. Everyone wanted to know about last night. Girls wanted to know how he looked in person. Even ANN on the Magnavox was drowned out by the frenzy of conversation. If Maddy had been looking for a distraction, this was the opposite.

"Is this where he sat?" a girl asked at one point, pointing to a booth. Her mother hovered in the background.

"No." Maddy sighed. "It was over there."

"Great!" The girl beamed. "Would you mind taking a picture of me in it?" Maddy did as she was asked. Everywhere she looked, people bathed in the afterglow of Jacks's presence.

After a few hours they had cleared the line, but the dining room was still packed. Maddy barely heard the jingle of the front door over the din. She looked up.

Ethan stood there in ripped jeans, a T-shirt, and Rainbow flip-flops. Maddy hadn't seen him since he'd gotten her phone number at school the morning before. He gave a quick scan of the full dining room, not seeing her, then went over and grabbed a seat at the counter. Not knowing exactly why she was doing it, Maddy glanced at her reflection in the window and straightened her ponytail as she approached.

"Hi," she said shyly.

"Hey, Maddy!" he said, looking thrilled to see her.

"You haven't been here in a while. Do you need a menu?"

"Actually," Ethan said, his eyes on hers, "I heard what happened. I have to meet Kyle and Tyler in a bit, but I was driving by and just wanted to make sure you were okay."

Maddy was surprised and a little touched.

"I'm fine. Thanks for asking."

"Great, that's good to hear. I just . . . I don't know. I was worried." He smiled.

"You can't come in here and not order anything," Maddy said, pulling out her notepad. She found she didn't want to see him go. "How about it?"

"I love the food here," Ethan admitted. "But really, I'm not hungry."

"How about a cup of coffee on the house?"

"Sure," he agreed. "That sounds awesome."

She went back and pulled a mug from the rack, then filled it with steaming coffee. Ethan was nice. And, she had to admit, nice-looking, too. They got along. Both quiet, but neither shy. Still, she wasn't ready for him to think that she *liked* him-liked him. She'd have to be careful. She grabbed a bowl of creamers and headed back to where he sat.

"Free cup of joe; I like this place," Ethan said as he took the mug and sipped from it. "Big night, huh?"

"Tell me about it," Maddy said, resting her hip on the counter.

"To be honest," Ethan said, looking around at the excited faces of the dining room, "I just don't know why people care so much."

Maddy looked at him, interested. "I thought I was the only one. Well, aside from people like Tyler, who are against it as like a political thing."

Ethan shrugged. "I mean, I'm not trying to make a statement or anything, I just think we are who we are, and they are who they are. Why worship them?"

A reporter was standing at the hill of the famous Getty Center art museum, Beverly Hills sprawling far below him. He was eagerly reporting on a new save. Spectacular Angelcam footage played on screen: a Guardian ripped open the cockpit door of a plummeting helicopter, its rotors seized up in midair, and pulled out the owner-pilot. They climbed to safety just before the copter smashed into the uninhabited hillside above the Santa Monica Freeway, incinerating into flames. The Guardian flew his Protection to safety at the gleaming white Getty Center at the top the hill, where a fleet of ambulances screamed to meet them. Firefighters rushed to extinguish the roaring fire in the hillside scrub. The Angel was now giving interviews on the open white marble plaza of the museum, his shirt hanging in shreds around him, exposing his perfectly sculpted upper torso, his wings still extended. A plume of smoke rose in the distance. Fans circled all around, screaming and taking pictures. The patrons in the diner all watched, hypnotized by footage of the save. Some were already logging on to SaveTube on their phones to rewatch the clip and find any other footage. Ethan wore a frustrated expression.

"When you see these people saved by Angels, do you sometimes not think about the Angel or the Protection? I mean, do you ever think about the other people? People that maybe got hurt. People that maybe got killed. Do they deserve to be saved any less?"

He looked up from his mug right into Maddy's eyes. She gazed at Ethan, sensing the invitation of the moment, but stood silent, tongue-tied. After another second, Ethan's face broke out into a smile. "Sorry. I guess I've been hanging around Tyler too much."

"It would be easier to ignore them—the Angels, I mean," Maddy said, thinking of Jackson and picking her words carefully, "if everyone didn't *talk* about them all the time."

"Seriously. I'm so glad you feel the same way," Ethan said, still looking at her. Was he blushing? "What I mean is, I knew we had a lot in common."

Now it was Maddy's turn to blush. Sensing her discomfort, Ethan got up.

"Well, I gotta get going. Thanks again for the coffee."

"Anytime," Maddy managed to say, and took the mug from him.

"The other reason I came by was to say I really hope you can make it to my party," he said very softly, leaning forward so she could hear him over the noise of the customers. With that he turned and left.

Maddy watched him until he disappeared from sight.

Maybe she'd be able to forget Jackson Godspeed after all.

When Kevin's finally closed, Maddy had nearly run herself off her feet. Worse, her nerves were raw. Kevin sat in the office, adding up receipts at the till.

"Biggest weekday night . . . ever," he said, typing in figures on his calculator. He looked up at her over the rim of his glasses. "Or any night, for that matter."

"Sleep tight, Kevin," she said as she passed him. Despite everything, she was glad he was happy. She walked out the back of the restaurant and up the adjoining yard to the house. It was an unusually clear night in Angel City, with a light, crisp autumn breeze. She went straight up to her room, peeled out of her uniform, and threw on an old shirt, a lace-trimmed tee from Anthropologie she'd found with tags still on at Goodwill. By now she'd worn it into the ground. Her best pair of jeans were finally dry from the wash and she laid them over the back of her desk chair, along with her gray hoodie. She didn't often have the chance to get new clothes, so she took good care of the things she did get so they lasted longer—even if a lot of the time they came from Target. She ran a washcloth over her face in the bathroom and fell into bed, utterly exhausted. Outside her window the Angel City sign glowed, casting its pale fingers of light into the dark room.

She tried to just go to sleep and not think, but the thoughts came anyway. They gathered like storm clouds in the emotional tumult of her mind. Jackson coming into school and the feel of his presence in the dusty classroom. The evening shift in the diner and the incessant talk of him. That conversation in the back room that her mind kept returning to, and what she had felt.

Then there was Ethan, with his easy way about him and how

comfortable he made her feel. Why couldn't she let him in? He was nothing but nice to her. Why was she so self-destructive when it came to friendships, keeping everyone out except Gwen? Thinking about her conversation with Ethan, she realized something: it was the only time tonight she had forgotten about Jacks. Well, she would never see Jackson Godspeed again. And she was happy about that, she thought. After an hour of staring at the ceiling, she finally felt her mind slipping into unconsciousness.

CHAPTER ELEVEN

Jackson looked in the rearview mirror. His sharp blue eyes met him, filled with uncertainty. He wasn't used to that look—and neither was the world. He was *Jackson Godspeed*, after all. He was confident. He was trained. Nothing could shake him. Or so he had thought.

Jacks tried that uncertainty on for size. It felt strange, like the stiff tuxedo he wore once a year at the gala black tie Angel charity event his mother put on. His iPhone beeped again and he turned it to silent. It'd been going off steadily for a couple hours, but he'd just been ignoring it. Knowing it couldn't be her.

That night Jacks had eaten a quick dinner at home, then left, telling his mom and Mark he was going out to meet Mitch. But instead of meeting up with his friend he'd driven out toward the Santa Monica Pier. Halfway there he had just parked. He'd needed to think. The occasional car crawled past sleepily on the dark residential street. Nobody around seemed to recognize him, and so no one bothered him.

The school—Jacks leaned his head on the steering wheel. He still couldn't believe Maddy's fury. He had gone there to apologize, and she wouldn't even talk to him. Who did that? He was just trying to do the right thing.

After leaving Angel City High, Jacks raced across town to a press junket for the Guardian nominees at the Beverly Wilshire Hotel. Driving there after his jarring encounter with Maddy, Jacks felt like he was in a dream—everything was blurry and distant and muffled. His phone rang. It was Mark. He decided to take the call.

His stepfather was calling to let him know the ACPD had cleared him of any connection with Theodore Godson's disappearance. They'd investigated Jacks's alibi and decided his story checked out. His stepfather told him to get back to preparing for the Commissioning.

"Thanks, Mark," Jacks said. He supposed he should've been more relieved. The last thing he needed was to get tied up in a potential murder investigation. But he wasn't. As strange as it seemed, what had happened at the school with Maddy continued to weigh on him. "I've gotta go now; I'm pulling up to the junket. Think I'm late."

"Sure thing, kiddo. Call me after," his stepfather said.

Darcy was borderline panicked when Jacks arrived. *Where have you been!?*" she whispered harshly under her breath as she whisked him toward the suite where he'd be giving interview after interview after interview. She looked ahead, flashing a thousand-watt smile at the journalists eagerly eyeing Jacks. "Well, our star is here!"

"Sorry, Darcy. I had some, uh, business to take care of," Jacks whispered, thinking back to the Angel City High classroom.

"Jacks, this is your business!" Darcy had responded under her breath. Jackson looked at all the photographers and journalists, hungry for their story. This time he blocked out that disconnected pang before it had a chance to reach his gut.

The interviews all pretty much went the same. *How do you feel about becoming the youngest Guardian ever? Who do you think your first Protections will be? Will you be getting a lottery Protection your first year? What does it mean for you to be a Guardian?* They'd all had to sign documents agreeing not to ask about the incident at the diner the night before, per Mark.

Jacks repetitively answered the questions as each interviewer came one by one into the suite. Occasionally, Jacks sipped from a water bottle. Even the most hardened reporters were starstruck in his presence, fumbling over their words and blushing. Jackson usually pretended not to notice, but this time he actually didn't. After a while it was like he wasn't even really answering the reporters himself, that instead he had drifted away and someone who looked like Jacks was taking questions. *Yes. No. Very excited! Can't wait for the responsibility. Just part of being a Guardian.* The click and whir of the shutters, the lights, the microphone attached to his shirt, recording his every syllable: it all began once again to seem unreal. His mind focused on what *had* seemed real that day: Maddy.

Finally, a reporter's question broke him out of his dazed state, bringing him back to the hotel suite.

"Can you repeat that?" Jacks asked, for the first time actually noticing the man in front of him, an overweight middle-aged reporter sweating in a cheap white cotton shirt and polyester tie. He was poised over a stenographer's pad and a pencil.

"I asked, how do you feel about the growing movement in America that is questioning a lot about the Angels and what's going on here in the Immortal City?"

"Jacks, you don't have to answer that—" Darcy said, getting up. The reporter had broken from the agreed-upon fluff questions.

"No, no, it's okay," Jacks said, waving Darcy back. "What, you mean the HDF? The guy who said he was going to start a 'War on Angels' and picked the Godspeeds out as number-one offenders?" He laughed. "Those guys are completely nuts. If we worried about every—"

The reporter looked at him confidently and finished his sentence. "—'crackpot with a video camera, an Internet connection, and an opinion.' I'm familiar with your statement. No, Jacks, I'm not talking about the HDF, but about mainstream America. As you know, Ted Linden was just elected to the U.S. Senate as an independent, running on a largely anti-Angel platform. He'll be the first senator to go without Protection in twenty years. He wants full transparency between the Angels and the government, and some say he even wants to end protection-for-pay in America."

Blood rushed into Jacks's face. "I—" He was cut off.

"These interviews are over." Darcy stood up again and walked briskly to Jacks, pulling his wireless mic off. "As you all know, Jackson has an extremely busy schedule this week. Thank you all for coming." She glanced daggers at the reporter. He had a faint grin on his face as he slowly put his pen and pad away.

"Jacks, really, you should've just let me deal with that jerk. That's what you pay me for, right?" Darcy said after they'd left the room. She escorted Jacks toward the lobby, where his car was waiting at the valet.

Jackson just nodded silently, already forgetting the man's question, not even seeing the crowd of paparazzi dashing over to get his picture, his mind drawn back to a classroom and a girl's voice.

At home that night, Jacks was almost silent, eating his dinner without even looking at the TV. He'd skipped one of the events set up for the nominees. Mark was apparently working late at the office, so it was just his mom and Chloe around. His little sister talked most of the time, which was just fine with Jacks. He was tired of answering questions.

Restless, but not exactly sure why, Jacks told his mother he was going to meet Mitch and had gone out driving into the Angel City night. Mark still hadn't returned home by the time Jacks left the house.

• • •

Now he found himself sitting in his car maybe thirty minutes later, maybe an hour, maybe two—he didn't even know. He'd come to the pier to clear his mind. But his thoughts kept returning to the girl. Maddy. Why hadn't she accepted his apology? Why was she being so stubborn? He just wanted to make it right and be done with it. Move on.

But if he was honest, he knew there was something more. Something that had gotten under his skin. Something about her eyes and her nonchalant beauty, beauty she clearly didn't even notice, the opposite of Vivian. He thought about what he had felt the night before when they touched. Even though she was human.

He tried to press the thoughts from his mind, but they wouldn't go away. When he thought of her, she seemed to make everything else instantly seem so small.

At last Jacks came to a decision. He turned the key in the ignition and the Ferrari fired to life. He pulled a U-turn, the headlights throwing momentary sheets of light on the slumbering white stucco homes in the otherwise pitch-black night. When he reached Sunset Boulevard, Jacks whipped his car to the right and headed back toward Angel City, his taillights steaming in the quiet night.

CHAPTER TWELVE

Up ahead, Sylvester could see a throng of reporters on the sidewalk and spilling out into the street, lit by the bright lights of their camera crews. On the other side of the street a line of police officers corralled a crowd of tourists who were watching, videotaping, chattering. Overhead, news choppers circled, trying to get the best view of the scene.

The detective pulled up in his unmarked cruiser, looking out at the scene beyond his windshield. He drew a long breath, lifting up his glasses and rubbing his face. He wished he didn't have to deal with the press. He wished he wasn't back on Angel Boulevard for a second straight night. And, most of all, he wished what was waiting for him underneath that white sheet wasn't what he expected.

Blinking red and blue light reflected off the silent palm trees, the closed tourist shops, and the gleaming stars of the Angels. Police floodlights bathed the famous street in a harsh, menacing glow. He got out of the car.

Reporters clamored to him as he fought his way toward the tape.

"Detective, can you confirm this is the second murder on the Walk of Angels in the same week?" one asked.

This sent a murmur through the crowd. "A second murder?"

Another reporter shouted, "Are the two murders related? More gang violence? And when are you going to release the names of the deceased?"

Sylvester raised his hands to the crowd, trying to calm them. Wind whipped against his coat as he cleared his throat.

"I can neither confirm nor deny that any homicide has taken place, and we are not releasing any information at this time. The incident from earlier in the week is still under investigation." He waved off another explosion of questions and ducked under the tape, chewing on his lip.

Sergeant Garcia was waiting for him on the other side.

"Okay, what have we got, Bill?" He had to shout over the buzz of the choppers.

"*What?*" Garcia put his hand to his ear.

"I said, what have we got?" Sylvester shouted.

"Come take a look," Garcia said.

He led Sylvester over to the sidewalk and its gleaming stars. Another white sheet was laid over the concrete. This time Sylvester crouched and lifted the sheet himself.

Another pair of Angel wings. Grisly and severed. Just as before, they were laid neatly one across the other, directly over an Angel Star. Sylvester listened to the drone of the choppers as it mixed with the roar of the crowd beyond the tape. He stared at the wings on the pavement in front of him and knew, without a doubt, the magnitude of what was happening. An Angel being mortalized and likely murdered was rare and extremely serious. But its happening twice, and in one week, was unprecedented. He lowered the sheet, removed his glasses, and polished them.

"Someone is cutting off their wings, sir." Garcia's voice had a hysterical edge. Sylvester nodded, his face grim. "Sir? Someone is cutting off their wings—"

Sylvester placed a firm hand on Garcia's shoulder. "I can see that, Bill. Any body?" Garcia shook his head. Sylvester lifted the sheet again and read the blood-splattered name below the wings. "Ryan Templeton."

"We contacted the Archangels. No one's heard from him in a few days."

"And this is the same spot as before?" Sylvester asked, looking around.

"Sir, look where you're standing."

Sylvester looked below his feet and read the name of the next Angel Star out loud.

"Theodore Godson."

"And now Ryan Templeton," Garcia said. "The very next star."

"They're being mortalized in the order of their stars," Sylvester said slowly. Wearily. He returned his glasses to his face.

The sky roared as another chopper passed close by overhead, its naked spotlight splashing over the scene. Sylvester scowled up at the sky.

"Bill, would you please do me a favor and get those news choppers away from here?"

"I'll see what I can do," Garcia said. He keyed his radio and began shouting orders.

Sylvester stood. His gaze drifted down the sidewalk and down the stars. He looked at the names and stars on the sidewalk, stars that extended as far as he could see. He imagined an endless body count.

Kneeling down, the detective examined the name of the Angel on the next star.

Garcia read his mind. "No contact with anyone since this afternoon. Could have taken a long trip up to Santa Barbara, turned off his cell to get some peace and quiet, or . . ."

Sylvester cursed under his breath. "And this one?" He motioned to the space on the sidewalk where the next star was. It was blank. Workmen had roped it off, preparing to put a name on it.

"Still don't know. One of this year's Commissioning class. We've got calls in to the Angels on this one, but they're not exactly being helpful."

Crossing under the tape and through the crowds, Sylvester walked out into the middle of Angel Boulevard. Away from the scene, it was quiet. Gusts of wind blew a few crumpled papers end-over-end down the street, while a homeless man pushed a shopping cart and hummed to himself. The detective took a look around. It was empty. Yet even at this hour a few straggling tourists still videotaped the sidewalk while shop owners packed up their displays. Angel figurines, plastic wings, bumper stickers that read "I WAS SAVED IN ANGEL CITY."

He heard Garcia shuffling up behind him. Sylvester continued staring down the street.

"What is it, Detective?" the sergeant asked.

"You don't just kill an Angel out here with the whole world watching." Sylvester pulled his keys out of his coat pocket. "Come on, Bill," he said as he walked toward his car. "We're not at the murder scene."

Sylvester's unmarked cruiser turned onto Outpost Road and wound up into the Angel City Hills. The sky over the city was clear and dark, the stars winking in the night. Houses with driveways were quickly superseded by tall hedges obscuring Angel mansions set back from the road. "Always get lost on these roads up here," Sylvester grumbled as he wound deeper into the private retreat of the Angels' perfect lives.

When they arrived at Ryan Templeton's sprawling modernist residence, which hung over the hill, two additional ACPD units were waiting. The officers seemed jittery. Sylvester pulled into the narrow drive.

The house looked like someone had stacked enormous building blocks one on top of the other. Sylvester had never understood the attraction of this so-called style, but now that he was standing right below it, it did have a certain striking appeal. He walked to the front door flanked by two officers. They had their guns drawn. He motioned for quiet. Calm.

He rang the call box. From deep inside the house, he could hear the bell. He looked at the video camera staring down at him from the eave. Silence. Nothing.

"Ryan!" He yelled through the door. He tried again, louder. Empty. He glanced over to the silver Mercedes McLaren in the narrow drive.

"Okay, let's go," Sylvester said.

Drawing a deep breath, the detective touched the doorknob and jumped back as if it had been a snake. The metal handle was scorching.

"Why's it so hot?" he barked, shaking his hand. Carefully, he pushed his toe against the door. It swung open on the hinge, and a wave of stifling air rolled out. Sylvester drew his Beretta 92 FS and signaled wordlessly to the officers. Then he pushed the door open and stepped into the darkened house.

The heat was suffocating. It shimmered in the dark, like a reflection off a hot summer road. Sylvester and the officers moved swiftly and silently into the hallway. Flashlight beams danced in the dark. The walls were lined with framed magazine covers of the home's owner. Ryan Templeton was a sturdy, handsome Angel with sleek hair and serious eyes. The hall opened up into a large, unobstructed living area. The architecture was clean and striking. Paintings. Designer furniture. Marble countertops. The windows looked out onto panoramic views of Angel City, downtown, and beyond. The officers fanned out to clear the rooms.

Sylvester moved passed the kitchen and through an open doorway to the right. He discovered a movie theater. Plush leather chairs. Framed newspaper articles.

A dead end.

He backtracked toward the bedrooms. Rounding a wall, he discovered a pale blue glow filtering through the cracks of a door. Condensation formed on his glasses as he prodded the door with the toe of his shoe. He flipped the Beretta's safety off and slipped inside.

The room was like a sauna, impossibly hot, the air dense with steam.

And something else. The room seemed to be filled with a kind of primal presence. An animal presence. Like fear itself.

At the center of the room, an indoor pool glowed blue-white. The water lapped lazily, sending shimmering reflections across the walls and roof. The windows were fogged. His weapon leading him, Sylvester moved to the edge of the pool.

What remained of Ryan Templeton floated facedown in the water. Where his wings should have been remained only two bloody holes of shredded skin, surrounded by the remnants of his Immortal Marks. Sylvester placed a hand on the fogged window to steady himself. Garcia entered the room. Seeing the body in the pool, he stopped short.

"Oh my God."

The two police officers stood there in silence.

"Rest of the house is clear. I'll get forensics up here immediately," Garcia said after a moment. Sylvester removed his glasses and polished the condensation off the lenses, still not speaking. Garcia couldn't take his eyes off the sight of Templeton's body as it floated in the cloud of bloodred water.

"I mean, an Angel serial killer?" Garcia said. "Is that even possible?"

Sylvester returned his glasses to his face and turned to the sergeant.

"Has to be. Only an Angel can kill an Angel," Sylvester said. "And even that's near impossible to do."

Garcia holstered his weapon.

"But what Angel would *want* to kill another Angel? They've got everything they could want," Garcia said.

"From what I understand, there are some Angels in the upper ranks that aren't too happy with some recent NAS decisions," Sylvester said. "We need deep background investigations on Templeton and Godson. See if we can find a common thread besides their stars."

Garcia's eyes still fixed on the Angel's gruesome remains. After a few moments the sergeant spoke. "What kind of beast does something like that?"

"I don't know," Sylvester said, turning away. "Let's get to work."

The sergeant went out into the hall and began barking orders, his voice echoing through the house. Sylvester stood there motionless, thinking about what Garcia had said. Especially that one particular word. He rolled it around on his tongue.

A *beast.*

The sergeant came back over and stood with him.

"Just came over the radio from the Ventura County police, Detective," Garcia said. "They just arrested three Humanity Defense Front members, heading north from Angel City. They had weapons. Guns. Knives. Hate literature."

"HDF?"

Garcia nodded.

Sylvester's head swam.

"Something serious is going on here. Maybe more serious than any of us could imagine." He stepped away from the window and looked at Angel City through the space his handprint had cleared in the condensation. "Right now anyone on that Walk of Angels is a potential target."

"That's nearly every Angel in the city."

"I need to go talk to an old friend." Sylvester's face tightened. "No Angel in Angel City is safe tonight."

CHAPTER THIRTEEN

Maddy sat up suddenly in the darkness. The dream she'd been having was so vivid, but now it faded from her mind. Something about an accident on Angel Boulevard. The more she tried to hold on to it, the more distant it became. After a few moments she couldn't remember any details at all. The only thing that stayed with her was a feeling—the undeniable feeling of being watched.

She let her eyes adjust to the darkness of the room. Something was different, but what was it? Her gaze moved around the four walls that, since infancy, had been her entire world. The nightstand with her old retainer case. The jewelry box Gwen gave her. The small wooden desk Uncle Kevin bought for her at the flea market, now overcrowded with textbooks and financial aid paperwork. There were even a few tween posters on the wall that she hadn't found the time to take down. It occurred to Maddy that adulthood had been forced abruptly and unwillingly on the little room, and it was doing its best to hang on to the last vestiges of her fading childhood.

A draft caused Maddy to pull the covers tightly around her. That was what had woken her. The window had been closed when she went to sleep.

And now, it was open.

Her eyes darted to the window and, in a breathless, panicked moment, took in the sight of a dark figure crouched on the sill. The letters of the Angel City sign spread out from his shoulders.

"You sleep like an Angel," Jacks said. The shock of his words in the dark room sent Maddy's stomach leaping into her throat. She didn't even realize she had screamed until it came out of her mouth.

"Don't be frightened," Jacks said, sounding worried. "It's just me. I'm sorry, I so didn't mean for that to sound creepy. Let me start over."

"I'm not frightened," Maddy gasped. "I mean, I was, I mean, you scared me to death." Maddy made a conscious effort to slow her breathing and let the knee-jerk fear bleed out of her. Gaining her bearings, she trained a flinty eye on Jacks.

"What are you *doing*?"

"Can I come in?"

"No," Maddy said curtly, "you may not come in." She sat all the way up in bed and drew her knees into her chest. Cool night air rushed under the covers and around her legs like seawater. Wearing only her old shirt and underwear, Maddy began to shiver.

"I wanted to talk to you," Jacks said.

"I don't understand what was unclear about what I said at school," Maddy said coldly, "but I want you to leave me alone. I'm not part of your world, and I really don't care to be." She paused, waiting for Jacks to jump in with something argumentative or clever, or maybe even with another apology. Instead he simply sat there in his suit and V-neck, listening. The silence lengthened. When Maddy spoke again, her voice was softer.

"Look, I'm sure there are plenty of girls who would kill to have you sitting at their window tonight." She paused, thinking of Gwen. "But I'm not one of them. If you're still trying to apologize, then fine, you've apologized. Now you should just go home."

"You're right," Jacks said. "You're not part of my world. You're not one of those girls. And maybe that's why."

"Why what?"

"Why I can't stop thinking about you."

Maddy rolled her eyes. "Guys like you don't say that to girls like me."

"I've never said that to anyone, actually," Jacks corrected. "In fact, I've never done anything like this before." He let out a little laugh. "How am I doing?"

He swallowed hard, trying to push down his nervousness. He was astonished to realize he *was* nervous. Somehow being around Maddy just put him in a different space. Jacks felt so *present*.

Maddy stared at him, letting the anger and frustration surge through her.

"Why are you doing this to me?" she asked finally.

He paused, considering.

"I'm being honest. I know you may not believe me. But I haven't been able to not think about you. When we were in the back at the restaurant, and . . ." Jacks's voice trailed off, his face coloring. "I still feel terrible about what I did. I lied to you and, even though I had good reasons for it, it was wrong of me."

Maddy studied him. Was he telling the truth?

Jacks smiled. "I mean this in the best possible way: I'm not going to leave you alone until you let me make it up to you. I'm serious. I'll be here every night. You might as well get me some pajamas and a toothbrush."

Despite her best efforts not to, Maddy laughed. She looked at Jacks and could see the faintest twinkle of light in his eyes.

"So what you're saying is that I should just give in and let you make it up to me. Otherwise you'll be tormenting me like this for the rest of my life?"

"Pretty much. Yeah."

"Well." She sighed. "What do you have in mind?"

"Come fly with me."

"Fly? I can't fl—I mean, I can't go anywhere with you right now, anyway." Jacks sat utterly still, framed by the letters of ANGEL CITY on the hill. "It's totally out of the question," she protested. "Besides, I have to work the morning shift tomorrow and my uncle would kill me."

The Angel remained silent.

"Plus school," she added, her brow knitted. She could tell by his silhouette that he had folded his arms.

"Maddy, it doesn't matter if you can't stand me. Just do it to *do* something. To make the night yours."

"What?"

"To *live*, Maddy."

"I'm living just fine, thank you very much," she said, haughty.

"Really? By working the morning shift?" He softened. "Maddy, you have the rest of your life to work the morning shift. I'm asking you to come fly with me tonight."

Maddy opened her mouth to say something, then closed it. He was unbelievable. Still, she was surprised to realize her pulse had quickened, and she could feel her heart beginning to pound in her chest.

"I have applications, too," she tried feebly.

"Stop making excuses." Jacks grinned. Maddy eyed her jeans and gray hoodie folded over the desk chair.

"I'm still mad at you," she said.

"Understood."

"And you're not forgiven for what happened at the diner or how you lied to me."

Jacks nodded. "It's a deal. I'll meet you downstairs." Jacks reached into his pocket and pressed something. A car alarm chirped in the driveway, cutting up through the night air.

"I thought we were flying?" Maddy asked, confused.

"Yeah," Jacks said, pulling out his Ferrari keys and jingling them. "Flying."

The Ferrari roared as Jacks expertly shifted, hugging the turns of Mulholland Drive. The car rose quickly and effortlessly into the Hills. Maddy had promised herself that she would not enjoy this. In fact, she had had an idea to pout the whole time. That would show him that he hadn't won. But with the warm leather seat vibrating against her legs and the wind in her hair, Maddy felt the thrill of the moment sifting through her defenses like fine sand.

Jacks navigated a hairpin turn. She shrieked with surprise and held on to the door handle. Jacks looked over and smiled. Ahead, the lights of the Los Angeles Basin beckoned. The most amazing thing, Maddy thought, was that Angel City looked different from inside the Ferrari. It really did. It felt different too. Even smelled different. It wasn't the run-down, dirty city she knew. It was beautiful.

"I like to come up here at night after everyone has gone to sleep," Jacks said. The car rounded another turn. "Up here it feels like you're alone, you know? Away from all the bother. Like the whole city belongs to just you."

"The whole city *does* belong to you," Maddy said, looking at Jacks. "It's a little different for the rest of us."

"Well, you know what I mean," he said.

"And what's the *bother*? All the little people getting in your way all the time?"

Jacks's eyes roamed over her face. "Look, you seem to think I live this charmed existence. And I guess in some ways I do. But the truth is, I have to go through a lot of the same things you do. I have pressure on me. I have expectations. And I'm *not* perfect. I struggle."

"Yeah, right," Maddy groaned, her tone rebellious. "The kid in the hundred-thousand-dollar sports car is telling me about struggle."

"I'm just trying to say we have more in common than you might think."

"You don't know the first thing about me!" Maddy exclaimed. Jacks downshifted hard, the gears grinding in protest. His blue eyes flashed.

"Why won't you give me a chance, Maddy?"

"Because," she nearly yelled, "you think you just get to have anything you want, don't you? You want something, it's yours. That's the way life works for you. Well, that's not how it works for me, so it's not how it's going to work *with* me. I don't fall for the money and the charm and the car. It takes a lot more than that."

Jacks nodded, suddenly thoughtful. He flipped on the car's turn signal.

"Okay, let's ditch the car."

He pulled the Ferrari onto a gravel turnout next to an overlook and killed the engine. "Will you be warm enough?" he asked. Maddy looked out to the bench framed against the twinkling cityscape.

"I think so."

The wooden bench was cracked and worn smooth, yet was surprisingly comfortable as they sat. Just beyond their feet, the earth sloped down gently at first, then dropped off dramatically into a deep canyon. Cut into the hillside like temples, the Angel houses glowed in the night. Jacks took his jacket and draped it around Maddy's slender frame.

"Thanks," she said. No one had ever put a jacket around her before.

Jacks's presence inside the jacket was almost overwhelming. His smell was intoxicating. Maddy took a deep breath, steadying herself. Silence overtook them as they looked at the city together. A cricket chirped nearby, stopped, then started again. Jacks spoke.

"You said I wasn't forgiven for lying to you. Well, it wasn't all a lie." He paused. "I was only two . . . when my father . . ." He trailed off.

Maddy chose her words carefully. "I thought Angels couldn't die."

"True Immortals can't, but there are only twelve of them. Born Immortals can be . . . *made mortal.*" Jacks traced a circle in the dirt with the toe of his shoe. He stared at it, thinking for a split second of the policeman's visit to his house and the mutilated wings that had been found on the boulevard. "I don't even really know what my dad looked like, aside from a few old pictures. He died fighting the rebel terrorists." Jacks looked away, his blue eyes reflecting the lights of the city.

Maddy raised an eyebrow—that's something they definitely hadn't covered in Angel History. But there were a lot of things the Angels kept to themselves.

"Well, I know what he looked like," Maddy said. "He had dark hair. And pale, blue eyes." Jacks laughed a little, shaking his head.

"I have my mother's eyes . . ." he said. "And, I'm told, my father's wings."

"His wings?"

Jacks nodded. "Broad and strong. A Battle Angel's wings."

The question came out of Maddy so fast she didn't have time to stop it.

"Can I see them?"

"My wings?" Jacks asked about his most famous feature in disbelief. "You don't know—" he cut himself off, holding his tongue. Not wanting to come across to this girl as conceited.

"Yeah, your wings," Maddy said, now embarrassed but unable to take it back. "I mean . . . what's the big deal? Can't I see them?"

Jacks got to his feet and pulled Maddy up with him. Maddy watched the muscles move under his shirt. Suddenly, the quiet night filled with the shrill tearing of fabric and Jacks's wings expanded out of his back. Razor sharp, they pierced the night sky, knifing out from behind his shoulders with such force it blew her hair back. The sound of the *whoosh* was deafening. The wings reached out six feet in both directions, then settled, powerful and muscled, awaiting the command to fly. They glowed with their trademark blue luminescence, casting light on Maddy's face. She was breathless.

"What do you think of them?" he asked.

Slightly afraid, but overcome with curiosity, Maddy reached out and ran her finger across the top of the left wing. It was hot to the touch.

"They're . . . great."

Jacks smiled. "Want to try them out?"

Maddy pulled her finger away. "You mean actually fly?"

"Sure. Real deal."

"I don't know," she said, unsure.

Jacks held out his hand to her. "Do you trust me?"

Somehow, strangely, Maddy felt as if the question held within it far more than just this night. She was at a crossroads. She looked at this boy Angel, young and perfect, his hand outstretched before her like the hand of fate itself. It was a simple response—just a single word—but somehow, on some level, Maddy knew that it would change her life in ways she couldn't imagine.

Her lips moved.

"Yes."

Maddy pulled her hood up around her head and cinched the drawstring tight. "Put your arms around my neck," Jacks instructed, kneeling down. "And hold on tight."

When she finally gathered the courage to open her eyes, she and Jacks were rushing through the dark canyon just beyond the outlook. Maddy looked at Jacks's winged body. It wasn't just powerful; it was incredibly graceful too. The wings instinctively and effortlessly adjusted to the air currents as they sailed. Then they curved like airplane flaps, and with a powerful thrust, Maddy and Jacks ascended steeply out of the canyon.

Maddy screamed at first, but then something amazing happened. The scream grew into a shout. And the shout grew into a laugh. A laugh that seemed to start all the way in her toes and radiate throughout her body. Jacks and Maddy soared high over Angel City and into the night, as the stars hovered above.

"I thought you would put your arms out!" Maddy yelled.

"What?!" Jacks struggled to hear her over the wind.

Maddy yelled louder. "I thought you would put your arms out when you flew! Like Superman!"

Jacks laughed. He reached his arms out and let his palms ride on the air current. Maddy gripped his waist with her legs, then traced her fingers over his arms until they found his hands. Fingers laced, they buzzed the palm trees of Santa Monica, the neon pier, and then rushed out over the churning Pacific. Then Jacks climbed, up through the misty marine layer, until they were floating atop a moonlit bed of velvet white.

They flew past spiraling freeway connections swirling with traffic even at this late hour and rocketed over the rooftops of Brentwood, Westwood, and Beverly Hills. Then they dropped low to buzz the lights of Dodger Stadium. Jacks took them out over the scorched deserts of Palmdale and swung so low over an orange grove Maddy could taste the tangy citrus in her mouth. Circling back, they wove through the skyscrapers of downtown. Finally, Jacks pointed them toward a familiar sight. The Angel City sign. He brought them down gently on top of the fifty-foot glowing *C* of the word CITY. When Maddy unlaced her fingers from Jacks's hands, she realized they had gone numb. They sat there together and let their feet dangle over the edge. Everywhere below, humanity twinkled up at them through a fine layer of mist.

"This is my favorite view in the entire city," he said, a little smile playing across his lips.

"It's wonderful," Maddy admitted, her head still spinning from the flight. Jacks's smile widened into a grin.

"It's perfect, right?" But when he turned to Maddy, she was looking away from him. Her gaze had fallen down below and fixed on something. Jacks followed her line of sight until he saw the dormant Kevin's Diner sign.

"So you live with your uncle?" he asked.

"Yeah."

"And you work at the diner for some extra spending money?"

"No," Maddy said, slightly annoyed. "Kevin can't afford to bring on another waitress, so I fill in. It's only temporary, just until the cash flow improves"—she hesitated, embarrassed—"but it's been temporary for four years now. At least I get to keep my tips."

"That doesn't seem fair."

"*Life* isn't fair," Maddy said, irritated. "Well, for me at least. For you it's perfect." She folded her arms. Like in the classroom, Jacks's face fell.

"What's wrong?" he asked, his mind churning with frustration. He looked into Maddy's eyes, trying to figure out anything he could do, what he could say, to break through this wall she had set up against him.

"I mean, don't get me wrong, Jacks, this was . . . amazing," she said. "It's just . . . this isn't me."

"What do you mean?"

"I mean this is *your* life, and it's great. But it's not mine. My life is down there. I'm going to wake up in the morning, and I have to go back to being Maddy Montgomery."

She looked up at him and realized, with surprise, they were face-to-face. Jacks seemed surprised too. It had happened again. It was like a force greater than the two of them was drawing them together. Their lips were now inches apart. The air between them was thick with their body heat. Her lips wanted nothing more than to close the tiny gap between them and kiss. It was more than just how he looked. It was that same feeling she had felt in the back room of the diner. A connection between them. An electricity. As her heart began to pound, it was all she could do to whisper.

"I should go home now."

They drove back listening to the purr of the Ferrari's engine. Maddy watched the view disappear as they descended. Jacks wore the expression of a man trying to work out a difficult puzzle and getting nowhere.

"Here," he said, pulling out his iPhone, "I want you to have my number. Just . . . in case."

Maddy took down his info and added it to her phone's address book simply as Jacks. In silent amusement she stared at the screen. What Gwen wouldn't do for this number. She slipped the phone back into her pocket as they pulled up outside the darkened diner. "I did have a good time," Maddy said at last. "Thank you again."

Jacks nodded and gave her a vague kind of smile. She got out, closing the door quietly behind her so as not to wake Uncle Kevin. She had turned to go when she heard the window rolling down.

"Maddy, wait." She peered back in the car. Jackson hesitated, considering his words. Then he spoke. "I want to take you somewhere.

Out. Tomorrow night." His expression was strangely conflicted, but his tone intent.

"Tomorrow? I—I don't know," she stammered.

"You're not afraid to fly, but you're nervous to go out with me?" Even in the dark car, his eyes pierced her. "Come with me, Maddy. Please."

The word was out of Maddy's mouth before could stop it.

"Sure." What? She hadn't even *thought* the word before saying it.

"Great. I'll pick you up," he said.

"Wait, Jacks," she said, panic rising in her stomach, but he was already rolling the window up. "No, wait. Jacks, I can't!" she yelled, but her protest was lost in the throaty rumble of the Ferrari. In another moment, he was gone. Maddy just stood there letting the dawning anxiety overtake her. What had she just done?

She slid her key as quietly as she could into the lock. Thank goodness Kevin was a heavy sleeper. She went upstairs. Slipping off her jeans and hoodie once again, Maddy sank exhausted into her bed. She turned her head on the pillow and looked at the glowing Angel City sign on the hill.

Absolutely confused and awash with the tingling sensation that she was still flying, Maddy drifted away into sleep.

CHAPTER FOURTEEN

By the next morning Maddy had nearly convinced herself it had all been a dream. Not just the previous night, but the whole thing. Jackson Godspeed entering the diner. Coming into school. Flying. She sat up in bed and looked around the room. The window was shut and locked, as it had been the previous night, and her hoodie and jeans were still lying over the chair back right where she had left them before bed. She got up, grabbed her uniform off the floor, and fished a pair of shorts and a tank top from her dresser for school. Outside her window palm trees swayed in a hot autumn wind. It was going to be a beautiful day.

It wasn't until halfway through the morning shift that Maddy had it proved she hadn't dreamt the whole thing. Kevin switched on the TV, and there it was. A breaking story on ANN that even had Jamie Campbell frazzled. Wearing a pantsuit and the usual caked-on makeup, she announced,

"In an unprecedented development, we're hearing unconfirmed reports

that Jackson Godspeed was spotted flying over Angel City last night and that he wasn't alone."

Maddy froze where she was standing with a plate of pancakes in her hand. The room seemed to shrink as she listened.

"Rumors of a mystery girl have been spreading across the Internet like wildfire all morning, easily becoming the number-one trending topic on Twitter and the most common search on Google. But who is she? Where is she? If you're watching right now, mystery girl, you might as well come forward. The entire world is looking for you."

Maddy didn't even realize the dish had slipped from between her fingers until she heard it smash on the linoleum. She gasped. Someone in one of the booths started clapping. Kevin came around from the counter and eyed her, concerned.

"What happened?"

"I'm sorry, Kevin. I just totally lost my balance." His expression turned to frustration, but he said nothing, and returned to the kitchen. Maddy got down on her knees and began gathering up pieces of the syrupy, broken plate. *Mystery girl?*

The TV continued squawking. *"Stay tuned for more on Jacks's mysterious midnight flight that has tongues wagging worldwide."*

Maddy spent the rest of the shift in a sustained panic. She was so used to being invisible, she even *liked* being invisible most of the time. Could they really have been seen? Of course they could have, she thought. They had gone all over the city last night. Yet she had never planned on anyone finding out—Kevin especially—but really anyone at all. What did this mean for tonight? And how had she ever agreed to go out with Jacks again in the first place? She felt a wave of nausea in her stomach as she realized she had just invited the prying eyes of Angel City—and probably the entire world—into her quiet, uneventful life.

When she got to school, Gwen was nearly hyperventilating.

"OMG. Look!" she commanded as she showed Maddy the Johnny Vuitton blog on her Berry. It read in all caps:

"JACKS FLIES OVER CITY WITH MYSTERY GIRL!!!"

A fuzzy picture taken from a rooftop security camera accompanied the article. It showed an Angel, in flight, holding on to a girl in a hoodie. Maddy's breath caught in her throat.

Gwen was ecstatic. "I know you don't, like, really know or care about this stuff, but this is so huge!"

"Really?" Maddy asked, attempting to disguise her shock as mild curiosity. "What's the big deal?" She squeezed a book into her locker and tried to look as unconcerned as possible.

"Two people, one pair of wings," Gwen said scandalously.

"Meaning . . . ?"

"Meaning she might not even *be* an Angel." Gwen rolled the words around on her tongue as if tasting it.

"Oh, um, interesting . . ." Maddy stammered.

"I know, right? I mean, a human and an Angel? Dating? Sure, there might be rumors every now and then, but never anything *actual*. This is, like, maybe the biggest moment of my entire life! That means I have a shot!"

"But they don't know who the girl is?" Maddy asked, fishing as discreetly as possible. Gwen frowned.

"No. And of course, his publicist is denying everything, but can you believe this week? First Jackson Godspeed comes into your uncle's diner, now he's flying around with some girl . . ." Maddy could almost see Gwen's train of thought connecting the dots and moved quickly to derail it.

"I don't believe it," Maddy said as casually as possible. "I've seen the pictures of him and Vivian Holycross. Like anyone else would even stand a chance."

"Oh, I *know*," Gwen squealed, suddenly distracted by the thought of her idol, "she is *so* gorgeous." Maddy let out a breath and managed a smile. Gwen hadn't caught on. And if Gwen hadn't caught on, no one else had either.

They neared the commons area and saw the group of guys from earlier in the week: Kyle, Tyler, Simon, and Ethan, along with some other students. The boys were sitting around a table, while others stood around them. Tyler was moving his hands around as he talked, apparently in a heated conversation.

"You're just, like, jealous," a blond girl in black leggings and Uggs said to him as Gwen and Maddy approached.

"*Jealous?*" His eyes bulged with incredulity. "We don't even know where these *things* really came from, who they are, what they want from us. Yet the Angels take everybody's money, and all anybody wants to talk about, read about, is *this*"—he pointed to his iPhone, which had a shadowy picture of Jackson flying with the "mystery girl"—"while we have real news, real problems that need to be dealt with. They're just here to help themselves!" Panic shot through Maddy as she saw the picture. Tyler's voice raised high with anger as he continued speaking.

"Ugh," Gwen said under her breath to Maddy. "Tyler's just trying to be cool by being all anti-Angel."

"Hey, Tyler, relax," Kyle said, putting his hand on Tyler's shoulder. Tyler shrugged it off, his face turning red in anger.

"They can't save everyone, you know that, everybody knows that," the girl in leggings said. "But they can save some people, and you wouldn't want them to do that? Just let everyone die? They're doing their best. And you never know, it could be you who gets saved."

"How? The lottery?" he scoffed. "Anyway, I'd *rather* they let me die." Tyler said this last bit dramatically, and a couple students laughed and clapped slowly. His eyes shot out angrily toward them.

Ethan stood up from the table. "Come on, let's go. This is getting too heated."

"No, *I'll* go. Freak," the girl said to Tyler, flipping her hair and walking away with her friends. The crowd of spectators dispersed.

"Dude, that was awesome," Simon said, eyes lighting up from behind his glasses as he pushed his long hair away from his face. "Way to stick it to them, bro!"

Kyle saw Maddy and Gwen. "Hi, Gwen. Hi, Maddy," he said, smiling. Kyle was giving Maddy that look again. *But he couldn't be, Gwen was right there!*

"Hi," Maddy said, looking away from him quickly. She caught Ethan's eye, and she immediately flashed back to their conversation at the diner and how now she was out flying with Angels. Gwen was about to say something to him, but Maddy jerked her arm, pulling her down the hall. "Gotta go," Maddy blurted.

"Ow!" Gwen said as Maddy pulled her along.

"Sorry, I, uh, just don't want to be late."

"That was so weird. It's like, *hello*, you live in Angel City?" Gwen said, looking back at Tyler and the commons. "This is where the Angels are, Tyler. Get used to it. He's just trying to show off."

"Definitely," Maddy said, trying to forget the fact that a picture of her and Jackson Godspeed had been the center of the whole debate. Just a few days earlier she would've probably taken Tyler's side. But now that she had met Jackson, she felt . . . different. There were lots of details people didn't know about the Angels, but maybe they weren't necessarily bad things. Just stuff they wanted to keep private.

The girls made their way down the hall. The conversation turned to Homecoming and who had already been asked from their classes. Gwen reminded her that Ethan "was still single." Maddy relaxed a bit now that the topic had turned away from Angels and, specifically, Jackson. Maybe it really wasn't something to get worked up about. She even started to feel a mischievous sort of pleasure about the whole thing when her phone squawked in her backpack.

"What was that?" Gwen asked, crinkling her nose. Maddy fished out her ancient phone and flipped it open. It was a text message.

From Jacks.

It simply said, *See you at 8*.

Maddy's mouth went dry.

Gwen leaned in to look. "That thing gets texts messages?" Maddy whipped the phone away and held it on the other side of her body.

"It's not a text," she blurted. "I mean it is. But it's nothing."

"OMG, is it a *boy*?" Gwen probed with eager eyes.

"No! Okay, yes. Could you just leave me alone?"

Gwen looked shell-shocked. The very idea of not sharing boy information was a fundamental violation in Gwen's mind.

"I'm, like, your best friend!"

"It's just . . ." Maddy's mind raced. "It was a wrong number." It was a terrible lie. Gwen's eyes flashed with suspicion.

"You're acting strange. What's going on, Maddy?"

"Wrong number, Gwen, honest, I swear. Just seemed like it was from a guy. Not a . . . girl wrong number. Guys are stupid like that, right?"

Gwen flipped her blond hair, annoyed and suspicious. ". . . Right."

The bell rang.

"See you later," Gwen huffed, and disappeared down the hall.

Maddy focused on taking steady, controlled breaths. When Gwen was safely out of sight, she pulled the phone out of her pocket and read the text again. Could she back out? Yes, she thought, she could. Like a complete coward. And worst of all, then she would be proving him right. About her. And all that "living life" nonsense. She wondered where he would be taking her, and what they would be doing, and if she would know how to act. And what was she going to wear? Not her jeans and hoodie, and all that pretty much left was her waitress uniform. She couldn't borrow anything from Gwen without raising even more suspicion, so she didn't even consider it. There was one other option, something she hadn't thought about in a long time.

Maddy sighed. Gwen was right. She *was* acting strange.

She looked at Jacks's text and simply texted back:

Okay.

CHAPTER FIFTEEN

Sylvester drove his unmarked cruiser drove down Wilshire Boulevard, passing the designer stores, luxury car dealerships, and upscale office buildings of Beverly Hills. Though once located at the Temple of Angels itself, the corporate offices of the Archangels had long since been moved to a sleek, ultra-modern building off Beverly Boulevard. Palm trees swayed gently in the breeze overhead as Sylvester drove. The sky was a perfect, cloudless blue.

He turned right at Beverly and pulled into the parking garage entrance under the dark glass monolith of the NAS building. The ramp led him straight to the valet-parking booth. There was no self-park option. He grumbled to himself as he waited for the attendant to make his way over. Having to pay someone just to park your car for you seemed like a crime.

After receiving his ticket, Sylvester called one of the sleek stainless steel elevators and rode it up to the lobby. The architecture of the NAS lobby was striking and minimalist, with dramatic full-length windows and near-futuristic furniture. On the walls, large flat screens played footage of recent saves on a continuous loop. Against the far wall was a glowing reception desk and, to the left of that, a hallway led back to the offices of the Archangels.

Sylvester crossed the lobby to the reception desk and smiled sheepishly at the impeccably groomed girl with perfect skin and blond hair who looked up at him. She eyed his rumpled coat and scuffed shoes incredulously before pasting on a plastic smile.

"Can I help you?" she said in a chirpy voice.

"It's Detective Sylvester to see Archangel Godspeed."

"Is he expecting you?" she asked with a flip of her hair.

"Yes," he said, irritated.

"Have a seat, please, and I'll let him know." She gestured toward the couches while taking a sip of her latte. Sylvester shuffled over and sat awkwardly in a too-fluffy couch. He watched the saves play over and over on the flat screens. After ten minutes, a young assistant appeared.

"Mr. Sylvester?" he asked. "This way, please."

Sylvester was taken past the reception desk and down the hall, passing rows of assistants on headsets busily rolling calls for the Archangels. At the end of the hall the assistant opened glass double doors to the conference room and ushered Sylvester in.

The room was breathtaking. A long, thin conference table with twelve chairs sat in front of a floor-to-ceiling window overlooking Angel City and the entire Los Angeles Basin. In the corner of the room, in a glass display case, stood the armor and sword of an ancient Battle Angel. A reminder of a distant past. Sylvester looked at the armor, then turned and admired the view. After another ten minutes, Mark Godspeed appeared in a crisp, expensive suit.

"I'm sorry, David," Mark said, coming quickly into the room, "I was on a post-save conference call with a Protection. You know how those go. I had my assistant make some coffee; would you care for some?" The Archangel motioned to a coffee service tray that had been set up in the center of the table.

"Yes, thank you," Sylvester said. Mark picked up the carafe and filled a cup with steaming black liquid. He handed it to Sylvester, than began pouring one for himself.

"There's been another incident on the boulevard," Sylvester said. "I wanted you to hear it from me first." Mark paused, then finished pouring his coffee and carefully set the carafe back on the tray. "Another pair of wings was discovered last night. This time we recovered the body in the victim's swimming pool, at his home."

"Who?" Mark asked.

"Ryan Templeton." The detective tipped the cup back, taking a pull of coffee.

The Archangel was quiet for a moment. "Good Angel. I know his family." Sylvester nodded silently.

"The wings were found on his star. Right next to Theodore Godson's star. Although we haven't recovered the body of Godson, it's likely he has also been murdered. We have reason to believe the order of the stars is determining the targets. Lance Crossman's star is next. And sure enough, he's also missing."

After a few moments, the Archangel spoke.

"Angels killed in the order of their stars?" Mark asked. Sylvester nodded. Mark took a seat on one of the sleek chairs. "Does the press know yet?"

"No. But we won't be able to keep it quiet very long. People stand up and pay attention when Angels start disappearing." He paused. "We need to act, Mark."

Mark stared out the window at the city moving silently beyond the glass. "What do you want me to do?"

"Call an emergency session of Archangels, then bring it straight to the Council. Put the Angel community on alert. Afterward, we'll hold a press conference and announce the killings to the media. The whole city needs to be warned."

"Absolutely not," Mark said insistently. "The public cannot know about this. Can you imagine what it would mean? Angels dying? How could the public trust us? We deal with this internally. Period."

"More could end up hurt, Mark," Sylvester said. "This isn't about Angel publicity anymore. Something much more serious is going on here. Don't be a fool."

"There are those who don't live amongst us. Those who have taken, well, how does one say it? A different path?" He turned and studied Sylvester for a moment. Sylvester ignored the implication.

"Sure. Could be. The Archangels have made enemies. But whoever is doing this is ripping off their wings, in some kind of twisted version of the Council's punishment." Mark raised his eyebrow, but Sylvester went on. "We could consider the possibility that someone feels law and order isn't going far enough, a zealot among the Archangels who wants more control. More of their . . . *justice*." He cleared his throat on the last word.

Mark stared directly at the detective. When he spoke, his voice was cold and sharp: "What's past has passed, David. We Archangels didn't make these rules, we simply administer them for the Council. The fact that the ACPD even has you on a case of this nature, due to . . ." Mark trailed off.

"Due to *what*, Mark?" The detective stared at him coldly.

"I think you know what I'm saying."

"I'm not sure I do, Mark." Sylvester pushed his glasses up the ridge of his nose. "Do you mean to say I'm unfit for this case due to the fact that I had my own wings taken by the Archangels?" Sylvester almost seemed to shake as he spit out the words. They hung in the conference room, heavy.

After what seemed like an eternity, Mark Godspeed turned to the window. His voice was calm and even. "Bringing up the past will do no good. That you're implying any one of my colleagues is involved in this bloodshed is outrageous. I hope you're not spreading such filth around the ACPD. That would be unfortunate."

The detective didn't blink.

"The HDF has also been more active than usual recently," Sylvester said. "Three armed operatives were arrested on their way to a safe house yesterday. Do you think a disgruntled Angel could've defected, be working with them?"

Mark shrugged.

"Or it could be something worse," Sylvester continued. He placed his coffee cup on the table in front of him. "The severity of Ryan's wounds . . . and the fact that this is potentially two Angels now in the same week . . . I think we should consider another possibility, too."

"Yes?" Mark said.

"We could be dealing with a Dark Angel, Mark," the detective said. Mark looked at Sylvester incredulously.

"A demon?"

"It's happened before," Sylvester replied.

"Yes, thousands of years ago. You're talking about stuff from the Bible," Mark said. "They were wiped out. The blood of our ancestors, David, don't forget."

"Maybe not all of them. And of the two of us, I'm the one who hasn't forgotten," Sylvester said.

"I just find it hard to believe that some ancient creature that hasn't been seen in millennia comes out of hiding now and starts killing Angels."

"Whatever you believe, do the right thing, Mark," Sylvester said. "Spread the word, and postpone any Commissioning until we know what's going on." He pointed a finger toward the gilded display case in the corner of the room. "I believe that armor stood for something once, represented certain—"

"Don't lecture me, Detective," Mark said sharply, cutting him off. "I know *exactly* what that armor stood for then and still does now. Need I remind you that I'm the one who has stayed and done his duty?" He walked over to the door and held it open. "This conversation is over."

Detective Sylvester sighed as he stepped past Mark, buttoning up his jacket.

"The next star after Lance's has yet to be installed. But it's ready. We made a call." He paused. "It's your own stepson's. It's Jackson's star, Mark. He'd be next."

The Archangel said nothing.

"I'll show myself out," Sylvester said, and disappeared down the hallway toward the lobby.

Mark listened to the murmur of the assistants for a moment, then turned back and looked out the glass wall to the city. The door closed, leaving him alone in the silent conference room.

CHAPTER SIXTEEN

After school Maddy had to tell another lie, after already hiding things from Gwen. She asked Kevin for the night off, saying she and Gwen had decided to work on their senior projects together. It was Kevin's turn to be skeptical.

"You hate working in groups," he said as he plated a Reuben sandwich and fries. "You end up doing all the work yourself. Especially when Gwen Moore is involved."

"I know," Maddy said, her thoughts racing. "I just thought I would help her out. If she doesn't pass all her classes this semester, she won't have enough credits to graduate. She's really worried." Kevin sighed deeply, sending a pang of guilt through Maddy. He picked up the diner's old phone.

"I'll call Suzie and see if she can fill in."

Maddy thanked him, trying not to sound too relieved, and hurried up to the house. The light outside was turning long and golden as the sun set, sending a fresh wave of paralyzing anxiety over her.

She closed the front door behind her and locked it. Upstairs, she walked down the narrow hallway separating her room from Kevin's until she came to a small square hatch in the ceiling. She reached up and tugged at it. After a few smart pulls the hatch swung down with a groan and Maddy unfolded the wooden ladder that was attached to it. With a deep breath, she climbed up into the attic.

The room under the eaves was hot, still, and silent. It smelled of stale wood and rat droppings. Dust particles danced in the air, swirling in the golden shaft of light from the window. As with most old houses, the attic was large and triangle-shaped, and Maddy found she could comfortably stand in it. She took a look around. Against the walls were stacks of cardboard boxes with labels written in black marker. Newer boxes had been added more haphazardly in recent years, mostly without labels, some even left open with their contents spilling out. Kevin was getting soft in his old age, she thought with a smile.

Maddy had only ever been in the attic once before. It was when she was a little girl, and she had still been afraid of every little bump and sound the old house made. Kevin had lifted her up through the hatch one day so she could see for herself there were no monsters living over her bed. When she had looked around, she hadn't seen any monsters, but she had seen something else. Today, she had come back for it.

She pulled the boxes aside one by one as she worked her way back. The newer boxes held together okay, but the old ones were brittle and crumbled in her hands. She had to slide them across the floor, which made a terrific scraping sound, and she cringed as spiders went scurrying for cover. Finally, she saw it. Her heart gave a little leap as she spotted the box tucked far in the back, labeled with a single word.

Regina. Her mother.

Kevin never said much about her parents, and over time he had lost track of nearly all of their belongings. Her parents were gone, he told

Maddy, and so it did no good to hold on to their things. So, it was with quiet amazement on the day she and Kevin went ghost-hunting that Maddy saw the box, and she had never forgotten about it.

She worked it out to the middle of the floor and pulled at the cardboard flaps. The aged packing tape snapped almost effortlessly. She opened the box and peered inside. Jewelry. A watch. Some old books. A comb. She pulled the items out one at a time and set them carefully on the attic floor. It was a lot more emotional than she was expecting. These were her mother's things. Maddy's mother had bought them. Touched them. They had been a part of her—and now they were the only part of her that remained.

After a moment, Maddy found what she was looking for.

It was a stack of clothes, neatly folded. The faintest smell of perfume drifted up to Maddy's nose as she carefully sorted out the dresses. It was sweet and somehow familiar. She picked up and unfolded a cream-colored vintage dress with a lace hem. She sat back and looked at it in the warm light.

Her mother had style, that was for sure.

Maddy dragged an old, cracked vanity mirror around, then slipped out of her shorts and pulled off her tank top. She slid gingerly into the dress, then gently pulled up the zipper. The fabric hugged tight around her curves, wrapping her body as if from memory. It had been a long shot, but Maddy was absolutely right. She and her mother were the same size. She looked at herself in the mirror and felt all the hair on her arms stand up. It was the closest she had ever come to meeting her mother.

She blinked back tears and smoothed the fabric along her body. Then her eyes drifted back to the box and to the small pile of jewelry she had placed on the floor. She picked through the different pieces until she found an unadorned, gold-chain necklace. It was understated and elegant. She fastened it around her neck. Maddy took one last look at herself in the cracked mirror, then put her mother's things back in their box and descended the wooden ladder.

She checked the time. It was 7:52. She went into the bathroom, where she threw on a little eye shadow, mascara, and lip gloss. It wasn't much, but it would have to do. Her hair was going to have to be okay as it was as well. She was just running a brush over her teeth when the sound of the doorbell sent her heart hammering against her rib cage. Through the small bathroom window she could hear the purr of the Ferrari's engine. Running back to her room, she slipped on the only pair of heels she owned and fished out a black clutch that Gwen had forgotten over the summer from under her bed. Then with a deep breath and a tight grip on the rail, she descended the stairs toward the Angel waiting politely for her at the front door.

When Jacks saw Maddy, he took a sharp breath and opened his mouth to speak, but then closed it, as if preferring to keep the thought to himself.

"Hi again," he said at last.

Maddy looked at the nearly impossible sight of Jackson Godspeed standing on her porch. He wore a striking tuxedo jacket over a gray collared shirt, skinny jeans, and crisp, classic Vans. As usual, he looked like he had just stepped off a billboard. His eyes were darker than usual, more of a cobalt, and utterly intoxicating. Maddy collected her scrambled thoughts and tried her best to speak.

"Hey," she managed, and fidgeted in her heels. "Do I look okay?"

Jacks's expression was guarded again. "Maddy," he said softly, "you are beautiful." He stuck out his arm. Maddy took it and he led her down to the car.

They rumbled down the Halo Strip, drawing looks from people in the restaurants and boutiques and waiting in lines outside the clubs.

Maddy felt awkward. She wondered if Jacks could tell how foreign all this was to her. Getting dressed up. Going out. And she wondered what his guarded expression on the porch had meant. Was it possible he had completely changed his mind about her when he woke up this morning? Last night it hadn't mattered who was a famous Angel and who was a waitress from Kevin's diner. But maybe things were different now, after he'd had time to think about it in the daylight. Maybe he regretted the whole thing.

"I'm really glad you decided to come with me tonight," Jacks said finally.

"Yeah," Maddy said, playing with the hem of her dress. "I don't normally do stuff like this."

"You know," Jacks said, grinning over at her, "they got a picture of us last night."

Maddy flushed. "I know, my friend Gwen showed me."

"Well, don't worry about it, my publicist killed it." Jacks smiled. "You'll meet her tonight."

Maddy's heart hammered. "Speaking of, what is . . . tonight?"

"Oh, it's just an event."

An *event*? Maddy felt her palms break out in sweat.

"And what, exactly, is an event?" she asked cautiously.

"Well, it's like a party, but it's also part of my Commissioning."

Party. Even worse. That word carried with it the near inevitability of another word, *dancing*. And Commissioning? Maddy wondered what would happen if she opened the car door and just flung herself into the street. Would Jacks keep driving and let her get away? Unlikely.

Questions pounded inside her head like hammers. Who would be there? Others like her? And why had Jacks invited her in the first place?

"That's okay with you, right?" Jacks asked, snapping Maddy out of her self-induced panic.

"What?"

"Is it okay with you? That we're going to an event?"

Maddy bit her tongue. "Mm-hmm," she lied, and looked out the window. Outside, the first stars of the evening winked in the purple sky. Jacks downshifted and turned, and they cruised down La Cienega Boulevard. Maddy could smell the organic, innovative delicacies of the restaurants and cafés at which she could never afford to eat. Somewhere below them, she could see searchlights knifing through the balmy night air. If she was going to do this, she'd have to do better than her usual Angel-illiterate self. She needed information.

"And . . . this is for your Commissioning?" she asked sheepishly.

"Uh-huh." Jacks nodded. "Me and the other nominees."

Maddy hesitated, trying not to sound like a total idiot. "Is that when you become a . . ." Maddy paused, wishing she had actually listened to Gwen on so many previous occasions.

". . . Guardian Angel," Jacks finished for her. Out of the corner of his eye he gave her an incredulous look. "You really don't follow Angels at all, do you?"

"Not really," Maddy said, a little embarrassed.

"Why not?" Jacks asked, genuinely curious.

"I guess I just don't really get it."

Jacks seemed amused. "Well, I'll fill you in. It's pretty simple. I get Commissioned as a Guardian Angel, and then the Archangels assign me Protections."

Maddy considered the words, then looked over at Jacks. "Why don't you get to choose?"

Jacks's brow knitted together. "What?"

"Why don't you get to choose who you're going to protect?"

Jacks paused. The thought had never really occurred to him before.

"I mean, why don't you say, 'Hey, I think . . .'" She glanced out the window and saw a sign for Carlos's Cleaners. "'*Carlos* . . . is a pretty cool guy. I'm going to watch his back for him.'"

Jacks laughed. "Carlos?"

"Yeah, I mean, whoever. I'm just saying, why don't you get to decide?"

Jacks frowned. "It just doesn't work that way, Maddy. It's not that easy. We can't save everyone."

Maddy opened her mouth to speak but then thought better of it. She leaned back and re-crossed her legs on the vibrating seat. It seemed perfectly simple to her.

"Were Angels always so . . . big?"

Jacks glanced at her seriously, as though really wanting to answer her question. "What do you mean? Like famous?"

"Yes, all the attention and everything." The neon lights of West Angel City spiraled outside the window as Jacks downshifted the Ferrari.

"Well, at first our saves were publicized in the newspaper, you know, like 'Extra! Extra! Angel saves Carnegie this afternoon!' An edition with a Guardian save would sell out almost instantly. Then came silent films. My aunt Clara Godspeed, her saves were famous around the world in the twenties, when she was still a Guardian. They called her the 'Immortal City Pearl.' Now she lives out in Santa Barbara, but she could still kick my ass. Anyway, then radio came, then newsreels. You'd be surprised how many Angels got famous from radio. Once TV came around, they started televising saves, and pretty soon came the twenty-four-hour networks."

Maddy thought about the nonstop ANN coverage on the TV at the diner, how even the non-Angel networks were dedicated to tons and tons of Angel reporting and shows like *American Protection*.

Jackson continued: "Now that we have SaveTube and the Angelcam, anyone anywhere can watch a save instantly. Cool, huh?"

Maddy's eyes lit up in alarm. "Do you have an, uh, Angel . . ."

"Cam?" Jacks laughed gently. "No, not yet, they're still testing them, and I'm not even Commissioned yet, remember?"

They took a right and the searchlights Maddy had seen earlier blazed up ahead of them now, getting closer. A horrible thought suddenly occurred to her. What if *that* was their destination? She realized, with an incredible surge of anxiety, that it probably was.

"Is that . . . ?" she said, sitting up and pointing.

"Oh. Yeah, probably," Jacks said. Adrenaline bolted through Maddy's veins. How had she been so naive? This wasn't just going out. This wasn't just a party. This was a celebration of Jackson Godspeed. It had to truly be an *event*.

Maddy watched the approaching scene with mounting panic. Metal barricades held back throngs of screaming fans all along the sidewalk. Men in suits with earpieces stood in the street directing a traffic jam of black limousines that were jockeying for position along the curb of sbe's SLS Hotel. A red carpet jammed with photographers and journalists came into view. Everywhere, cameras flashed as one glorious Angel after another arrived. Maddy could see them now, beautiful and statuesque. Rows of spotlights lit the scene, so bright they made Maddy squint. Like the glowing gaze of some kind of hungry monster, she thought. A monster hungry for her.

The men with earpieces spotted the Ferrari and waved them in. A pretty woman wearing a headset and holding a clipboard pointed to an open stretch of curb right in front, and Jacks pulled effortlessly into it. The muted sound of screaming girls filled the Ferrari's interior. Fans, photographers, and even other Angels had turned and waited expectantly for the car doors to open. Maddy sat paralyzed in the passenger seat.

She couldn't will her limbs to move.

"What's wrong?" Jacks asked, his face the picture of calm.

"N-nothing," Maddy stammered, "I just . . ." Her voice trailed off as she watched a photographer hold his camera over the hood of the Ferrari and take her picture. *POW! POW! POW!* went the flash.

"Oh, that?" Jacks said, looking at the chaos outside the car as if noticing it for the first time. "Yeah, annoying, I know. I wish the paparazzi would just get a life. Trust me, the only way to handle them is to ignore them. Just be yourself, okay? They're going to love you."

Maddy nodded numbly. What else could she do? For Jacks the moment could not have been more ordinary. For her, it couldn't be more extraordinary. Or horrific. Jacks gave her a final, reassuring smile. Then the attendants opened the car doors, and Maddy Montgomery stepped into the lights.

CHAPTER SEVENTEEN

"*RIGHT HERE!*" "*RIGHT HERE!*" "*RIGHT HERE, DARLING!*" "*WHAT'S YOUR NAME?!*" "*GIVE US A SMILE!*" "*GIVE US A SMILE, BEAUTIFUL!*" "*OVER THE SHOULDER NOW!*" "*OVER THE SHOULDER!*"

The shouts of the paparazzi were so startling, and the explosion of light so astonishing, that Maddy almost fell right back into the car seat. She wobbled in her heels as she steadied herself with the car door, then tried her best to manage a smile. She turned to look for Jacks but was met with only more blinding flashes from the other side of the car. She was surrounded. Trapped in a prison of unwanted attention like some kind of zoo animal. As she tried to take a shaky step forward, the paparazzi shouts gave way to questions screamed at her by camcorder-wielding journalists.

"*IS THAT YOU IN THE PICTURE?!*" "*ARE YOU JACKSON'S MYSTERY GIRL?!*" "*HOW DOES IT FEEL TO BE DATING AN ANGEL?!*" "*WHEN'S THE WEDDING, HONEY?!*"

Maddy stumbled again and reached a hand back for the car door, but the attendant had closed it, and the car was gone. Her eyes darted, searching wildly for an escape. She looked to the sidewalk and saw crowds of hysterical fans crashing against metal barricades like the waves of some violent sea. Their focus had instantly shifted from Steven and Sierra Churchson, brother and sister twins who were both getting Commissioned this year, to Jacks and Maddy. The Churchsons gave an annoyed glance back toward Jacks and began moving down the carpet. The crowds were screaming something at Maddy she couldn't make out and *reaching* for her with a thousand desperate hands. Maddy was suddenly certain that if they could get to her, they would simply swallow her up. Camera shutters whirred on automatic. Flashes exploded like relentless lightning. The screams of fans rang in her ears. All of a sudden she felt the ground begin to move under her feet, rolling like the deck of a ship. Voices echoed now, coming to her as if she were underwater. As if she were drowning. The world spun, and she willed herself to move forward one final time. When she felt the toe of her heel catch on the curb, she was sure, at last, she was going to go down.

A hand reached out and grabbed her firmly by the arm.

It was Jacks.

"You okay?" he yelled over the roar.

Maddy nodded weakly.

"Come on, this way," he encouraged, and led her stumbling up the carpet.

Maddy used Jacks's arm to steady herself as she tried to reassemble the splintered pieces of her consciousness. She kept her head down, but whenever she had to look up, she met pair after pair of disbelieving eyes. They couldn't all be staring at *her*, could they? After a moment, a woman wearing a pantsuit and a scowl marched up to them.

"Where have you been?" she said to Jacks. "They're about to close the carpet and the *Angels Weekly* bitch is breathing down my neck. You have a two-hour commitment, by the way, don't forget that." Then she turned and assessed Maddy coldly. "Who's this?"

"Darcy, this is Maddy," Jacks said, smiling so warmly at Maddy he seemed to glow. "Maddy, this is Darcy, my publicist." Darcy's eyes flickered over Maddy's dress, shoes, and hair. Then she stuck out her hand.

"Hi, Maddy. Nice to meet you."

Maddy attempted a polite smile. "Nice to—" but Darcy had already turned back to Jacks.

"You have to do the A! interview. And please do the gifting suite after, and actually take something this time." She looked at her Berry. "Come on; we need to hurry." She took Jacks by the arm and led him through the crowd. Maddy followed, trying her best to keep up. She could hear the woman hissing something at Jacks, something like, *"You couldn't have told me first so I could have at least done some damage control?"* They approached a large white wall with the *Angels Weekly* logo repeated over and over on it and a firing squad of photographers and TV cameras standing directly opposite. Jacks turned and reached his hand back for Maddy.

"Come on!" he said.

"Jacks, no—" Maddy protested, but with seemingly no effort at all he took her by the arm and pulled her in front of the wall with him.

A blistering explosion of light followed.

Then more shouting: *Together! Individual! Together again!* They wanted to know *who* Maddy was wearing. The question made no sense to her whatsoever, so she didn't try and answer. Instead she focused on staying upright in her heels. After pictures Darcy led them quickly down the carpet and past the press line.

"No press. We're skipping the press," she said, waving off the reporters giving her dirty looks. Maddy wondered if the sudden change of plans had anything to do with her. She had the sinking feeling it did.

"I'll just deal with this tomorrow," Darcy muttered. "We'll tell them—"

"Jacks!" A voice cut through the clamor behind them. Even Maddy recognized it. The three turned.

It was Tara Reeves of A! She was wearing a bedazzled gown cut up the side to expose her tanned leg and Jimmy Choo heels. She pressed her hands together like she was praying and gave Jacks a pleading expression.

"We're not doing press, Jackson," Darcy said sternly.

Yeah, Jacks, Maddy mentally chimed in agreement, *we don't need to.*

"Come on, Tara's really sweet," he said, and pulled Maddy over to the waiting camera crew. Darcy pressed the heel of her hand against her forehead and made a face like a silent scream.

"*The* destination for young Angel City tonight," Tara announced, doing her bubbly lead-in, "this is *Angels Weekly*'s Pre-Commissioning party in honor of this year's class of nominees—and especially Jackson Godspeed!" She turned to Jacks and Maddy. "And here is the star of the evening himself! Hi, Jacks!"

"Hi, Tara, very happy to be here," Jacks said, sounding impossibly relaxed.

"So is tonight the night to cut loose and celebrate?"

"Yes, it is. It's really an honor to see everyone out to support me."

Maddy wondered if she might pass for Darcy's assistant or some other type of attendant who was clearly not intended, or expected, to speak. It would be perfectly fine with her to stand silently next to Jacks like a piece of furniture until the interview was done, thank you very much. But then, without warning, Tara turned toward her.

"And who is your *gorgeous* date for the evening, Jacks?" No one had ever called Maddy gorgeous before. The cameraman pointed the camera at her and focused his lens. Maddy died inside.

"This is Maddy," Jacks said, smiling.

"Well, *Maddy*, how are you?" Tara beamed.

"I'm . . . super," she answered lamely. She barely got the words out, and her voice sounded strange and gravelly.

"And who are you wearing tonight? This vintage dress is *so* cute." Maddy blinked. There was that question again. It was absurd. She was wearing *clothes*, wasn't she? She was certainly not wearing a person.

"W-well," she stammered, "this was my mother's dress."

"Oh," Tara chirped, and raised her penciled eyebrows. "Isn't that sweet?" Darcy made a circling motion with her finger, telling Tara to *wrap it up*. Tara gave a big, bleached-white smile. "Well, there you have it, ladies and gentlemen, Jackson Godspeed, the world's most eligible young Angel, making the *most* of his time before he becomes *Guardian* Jackson Godspeed this weekend!" Tara thanked Jacks, and Maddy felt a hand on her back. Darcy led them quickly off the carpet.

As they walked through the doors of the SLS Hotel, Maddy felt her purse buzz. She discreetly pulled out her ancient flip phone and looked at it.

It was a text from Gwen. It read:

Watching the Pre-Commissioning coverage. Am I insane? Is that YOU?

Maddy felt a curl of nausea in her stomach. If Gwen had seen it, *everybody* had probably seen it. How was she going to explain this to her best friend? Or Kevin? Or anybody else, for that matter?

"Do you need to take that?" Jacks asked, noticing the phone.

"No, it's nothing," Maddy said, and quickly hid the phone back in her purse.

Darcy took a hard right at the lobby and led Maddy and Jacks into a dimly lit room lined with booths. At a folding table they were checked in and given large, empty bags.

"What's this for?" Maddy whispered to Jacks.

"You'll see," Jacks said, grinning, and led her to the first booth. The station was set up in front of a wall of Nike Wings athletic shoes. The girl behind the counter was a pretty Asian in a strapless top and latex knee-high boots. She looked Jacks up and down as they approached, then leaned over and said *hello* with her entire body. Jacks didn't seem to notice.

"Do you have women's sizes?" he asked.

"Of course," the girl said, and turned unhappily to Maddy. "What size are you, love?"

"Oh. I'm a six, but . . ." Maddy trailed off and flushed deep red. "I didn't bring my wallet." She couldn't afford Nike Wings anyway. Gwen had saved up for two months last year to buy a pair. They were $250. The girl behind the counter smiled tightly as she pulled down a box and handed it to Maddy.

"They're free, honey," she said, smirking. Maddy took the box and looked at it. She now owned a brand-new pair of Nike Wings. Her shoes normally came from Payless. It was surreal.

Jacks smiled at the girl, who melted, and then led Maddy toward the next booth.

"Sorry," Maddy said, impossibly embarrassed, "I didn't realize."

Jacks's expression was warm. "It's okay. I should have explained what they mean by *gifting suite*. Just take whatever you want." Maddy stopped and gazed around the room. Cameras, jewelry, watches, phones, perfume, on and on and on. Every major brand name and luxury brands too.

"It's all . . . free?"

"Of course it is."

"B-but," Maddy stammered, "*you* of all people can afford this stuff."

"I know, but look at it from their perspective. If I get photographed with any of these products, do you know how much that's worth to these companies? It can mean hundreds of thousands—even millions—of dollars in additional sales." Jacks was looking at her keenly, as if needing her approval.

"Oh," Maddy said, feeling numb and shell-shocked. She understood the logic, but something about it seemed so wrong. So unfair. Jacks took her around to every booth, filling her bag with the latest gadgets and accessories. It was everything Kevin could never afford to get her. They reached the last booth and Maddy's eyes grew wide. *There* was something she really needed. Jacks saw her expression and smiled.

"She'll take one," he said.

The kid behind the booth set it up instantly, even calling in and activating the service. Then he handed Maddy her own brand-new BlackBerry Miracle. Maddy couldn't believe it. Gwen wouldn't stop talking about this phone, and it wouldn't even be out for another six months. She opened the clutch of her purse and dropped it in, along with her ancient flip phone.

"For nostalgia's sake," she said, clicking the clutch shut. They left the room and found Darcy waiting for them outside. Jacks handed Maddy's bag over to Darcy. He himself had taken nothing.

"Okay," Darcy said, shouldering the heavy swag bag and typing on her Berry, "you guys good? Vivian needs me inside."

"Yeah, we can take it from here," Jacks said, nodding.

"Nice to meet you again, Maddy," Darcy said without looking up, and then sped away, face in her Berry.

Vivian. The name echoed in Maddy's head, and she was surprised to feel a stab of jealousy twist through her.

"Vivian Holycross is here?" she asked.

Jacks shrugged. "Yeah, just a . . . friend. We share the same publicist." Maddy nodded uneasily. But Jacks smiled his hypnotizing smile at her, and Maddy couldn't help but feel good and smile back, Vivian or not.

Jacks stuck his arm out, she took it, and he led her back down the hallway, toward the noise and commotion of the party.

Halfway down the hallway, Sierra Churchson emerged from a bathroom, her twin brother waiting outside for her. Her face instantly turned dark. She was a lithe beauty; her wings were notorious for their resemblance to butterflies'. Jacks pulled Maddy a little closer to his side. Sierra leaned toward Jacks and whispered something in his ear Maddy couldn't fully make out. She thought she caught the word *star*. Confusion crossed his face.

Sierra sauntered away, her hips sliding smoothly under her four-thousand-dollar dress.

"What'd she say?" Maddy asked.

"Something strange . . . Never mind," Jacks said, leading Maddy down the hallway. He tried to put a smile on his face to put her at ease. "Ready?"

For Maddy, stepping into the party was literally like crossing into another world. It was, without a doubt, the strangest place she had ever been. The room was a kind of lounge furnished with mismatched lime-green and orange couches, deer-antler chandeliers, and pink and white chairs of every shape and description. There were life-size plastic pigs for tables and horses for lamps. Nothing matched, and the more Maddy looked, nothing made any sense either. And then, there were the mirrors. They hung everywhere, in every different shape and size, reflecting warped and twisted images of the passing guests. Like they were inside some kind of gigantic fun house.

Jacks's presence seemed to fill the party immediately. Angels offered hearty congratulations and posed with him for pictures. Maddy recognized faces she had seen on billboards during her walks to school and on ANN at the diner. They were all actually *here* now, and so close she could reach out and touch them.

Jacks took Maddy over to where a long serving table had been laid. Even the buffet was bizarre. There was food to drink and drinks to chew. Trays of desserts had been set out that looked more like modern art than anything edible. All around Maddy, the Angels indulged themselves. They munched on foie gras cotton candy and devoured drizzly, melting bonbons. They toasted one another and let the drinks spill over their lips and drip down their chins. A waitress offered Maddy a frozen cocktail that was literally smoking, which she took and then discreetly set down on a pig.

Jacks looked over at Maddy. "Do you like it?"

Maddy saw there were a few humans, Protections. She thought she recognized Sarah, last year's *American Protection* winner, standing around awkwardly, no one talking to her. None of the humans were *with* the Angels like Maddy was. They were hanging out, but there still seemed to be a bright line of separation between them and the Immortals. Just getting invited as a Protection would be enough, though, to get blog coverage that Gwen would've killed for.

"Godspeed, get over here!" a burly voice called out from the bar.

"Come on," Jacks said to Maddy, lighting up. "I want to introduce you to someone."

Over at the bar Jacks embraced an athletic-looking Angel with dark, glassy eyes and a great smile. Maddy found it slightly overwhelming, how good-looking they all were.

"Where have you been, man?" Mitch asked, his tone slightly rebellious. "I've been looking all over for you."

"I want you to meet someone," Jacks said. He turned to Maddy. "Mitch, meet Maddy. Maddy, this is my best friend, Mitch." The Angel looked at Maddy with an expression that bordered at first on sheer bewilderment. His eyes searched hers, as if trying to place her. Finally, he gave a half-smile and reached out his hand.

"Hi, Maddy," he said. "It's nice to meet you." His tone was polite but guarded.

"It's really nice to meet you too," Maddy said. But as she shifted her gaze, she saw Mitch shoot a quick, questioning glance at Jacks. Maddy wondered what *that* meant.

"Mitch and I go all the way back to Basic Flying together," Jacks said. "But seriously, I don't know why I keep this guy around sometimes." Jacks threw his arm around Mitch and punched him hard on the shoulder.

"It's because I keep the world's most famous Angel sane, believe me, Maddy," Mitch said. "Jacks is like a brother to me."

Across the room, Steven and Sierra were talking to a few of the other nominees. In contrast to Sierra, Steven was squat and muscular, looking almost military. The twins noticed Jackson, and brother and sister gave an irritated glance back toward Jacks. They moved away in the room with a few of the other soon-to-be Guardians.

"Sierra just told me, 'can't wait for your star.' What was that supposed to mean? She was serious too, almost crazy, you should've seen her eyes," Jacks said to Mitch.

"Don't worry about them, bro," Mitch said. "They're just mad because rumor is Sierra might get posted to Korea for her first two years before being able to come back to Angel City as a full Guardian. Oh yeah, *and* the fact that the NAS is promoting you every chance they get. Can't win 'em all." Mitch smiled and signaled to the bartender. "Well, now that you're *here*, dude, let's get some shots and celebrate. Maddy, are you joining us?"

Maddy shook her head. "Thanks, but I'm not drinking tonight." She had decided earlier she already had enough to deal with without getting drunk for the first time.

Mitch shrugged, appearing almost relieved, and turned to Jacks.

"Ah, me neither," Jacks said. "I think Maddy and I are just going to . . . walk around a bit. But I'll catch up to you later, man. Cool?"

Surprise flickered across Mitch's face, followed by what seemed like a flash of jealousy and finally concern.

"All right . . . have fun, you two," he said mechanically. They said their goodbyes and turned to leave. Maddy froze.

Walking up to her was the most beautiful girl she had ever seen.

Maddy stared in awe at the approaching Angel in her Chanel sequined black-chain dress and matching Chanel shoes. She didn't even know it was possible to be so . . . perfect. From her flawless skin to her elegant, imposing figure to her shampoo-commercial hair and piercing green eyes, she was so radiant she was almost glowing with supernatural splendor. There was no mistaking her. It was Vivian Holycross. Even with her cheeks stained with tears and mascara, Vivian was the most magnificent creature Maddy had ever seen.

"What do you think you're doing here?" Vivian hissed at Maddy as she stormed up.

"Hey, Viv," Jacks said, startled. His glance flashed to Vivian's swollen, furious eyes. "Let me introduce you to Maddy—"

Vivian ignored him. "Take a look around yourself, *Maddy*," she snarled. "You're not one of us, are you? You don't *belong* here. Why don't you just save yourself the embarrassment and leave?"

Maddy was a statue. Her total awe of this girl had mixed with her panic and the result was utter paralysis.

"Hey, relax, Vivian," Jacks said, his tone angry. "I invited her."

Vivian took a step forward and sneered in Maddy's face. "Do have *any* idea what's going on here? Or how important this all is? Jacks will be saving lives starting Friday. As a *Guardian Angel*. But you wouldn't know anything about that, would you?"

Jacks stepped forward to put a stop to Vivian's attack but stopped when he saw Maddy's face. Maddy had leveled a gaze of such quiet confidence at Vivian that the lady Angel instinctively took a step backward.

"Well, let's see," Maddy said, anger loosening her tongue. The words just came. "I know Jacks brought *me* here tonight and that he didn't bring you. I also know that I met Jacks before I knew he was a famous Angel, and now that I do know, I still don't care. And that's because I like him for *him*, not because he's a celebrity and not because he's going to do wonders for my publicity. But you wouldn't know anything about *that*, would you, *Viv*?"

Jacks looked like he was working to suppress a smile. Vivian's expression twisted with hate. Then she looked at Jacks, and her face softened. "You know what, Jacks? I get *this*, too. A little scandalous fling before all the responsibility, right? Fine. Have fun." She scoffed. "But remember, once you get that Divine Ring, you're mine." Then a smile crept across her lips, and she turned to Maddy. "And Maddy? If you're hoping to become his Protection someday, just trust me," she said, and smirked at Maddy's outfit, "you can't afford him." With that she spun on her heel and was gone.

"That went well," Mitch said. He must have heard the whole thing. "I'll make sure Vivian doesn't kill anyone," he said, and disappeared into the crowd.

"I'm sorry," Jacks said, taking Maddy's elbow and shaking his head. "Vivian gets kind of jealous."

Maddy stared incredulously. "Vivian is jealous of *me*?" She looked at her hands and was surprised to realize they were shaking. The realization of what had happened was still only just sinking in. Vivian might be a fantastic bitch, but Maddy knew she was probably right.

"I shouldn't have come," she said finally.

"What?" Jacks's face darkened in frustration. "Listen to me, Maddy. You belong here because *I* say you belong here, and in case you didn't notice, this is *my* party. Please," he said, more softly, "don't let it ruin your night. In fact, I'm going to make sure it doesn't. Come on."

"Where?" Maddy asked, but Jacks had already taken her by the hand and was pulling her toward a crowd of Angels in another part of the room. A DJ was spinning in one corner, and all of a sudden Maddy's heels were clacking against a wooden floor. She looked down. It was a dance floor.

"Dance with me," Jacks said.

Maddy's heart boomed like a thunderclap. She had never, in truth, danced with a boy before. At her middle school commencement she had let Tom Watson hold her by his fingertips, and they had swayed back and forth to "Total Eclipse of the Heart," but she wasn't going to count that.

"Jacks, I can't," she insisted. "I don't know how."

"It's easy," he assured her. "Just follow me."

The Angel took her in his arms. She felt his hands trace around the curves of her hips and meet at the small of her back. Then he pulled her into his body, and she lost all resistance. It was irresistible. Maddy's breath came is shallow gasps as she breathed him in. She had to reach up on her toes to wrap her arms around his shoulders and then lace her fingers around his neck. Jacks stepped smoothly and began to lead her, and to Maddy's astonishment, she followed. It was nothing like she thought it would be. It was somehow, impossibly, *effortless*.

And they were dancing.

She couldn't feel the floor anymore, but she didn't need to. There was something instinctive, almost inevitable about the way she was moving with him. Even other Angels had stopped and were watching them now. There was no denying it—Maddy and Jacks were a vision. Like they were *supposed* to be holding on to each other. Like they were meant to be.

Jacks pulled back from her, just slightly. "You look so beautiful," he said softly, his eyes dancing in the light. He brought her close again.

Maddy felt that same electricity beginning to move through her, just like the energy she had sensed in the back room of the diner and when the two of them had gone flying. From Jacks's glinting eyes, which he never took away from hers, she could tell he felt it as well.

Yet something was different this time. Somehow, something had changed. As much as she might try, Maddy was surprised to realize she couldn't completely let herself go, lose herself in the moment.

Was it Vivian's words still ringing in her ears? Maybe. But if she was honest with herself, it was more than just that. It was everything about the night—the decadent party, Mitch's distrustful expression, even the discussion in the car on the way over. Something was wrong about the whole situation. Or at least, there was something wrong about *her* in it. Vivian's words reverberated in her head. *You don't belong here.*

As much as she hated herself for it, she couldn't help but agree. She unlaced her fingers from around Jacks's neck.

"What wrong?" Jacks asked, his eyes still drunk with the electricity of their connection.

"Why did you invite me here, Jacks?" Maddy asked. "Tell me the truth."

Jacks looked at her with a questioning expression. "Remember? I told you I would help you get out a little. You know, live life." He gestured around the room, smiling to her. "It's pretty amazing, isn't it?" Maddy bit her lip. He reached for her, but she stepped away from him.

"I'm sorry," she said abruptly, "I just. I can't do this." She turned without meeting his gaze and walked quickly away.

She didn't know where she was going, or even really why. She just had to get out. She saw the twinkling patio through the back door with its shimmering, turquoise pool and headed toward it. She had just gotten outside when Jacks caught up to her.

"What's wrong?" he said, spinning her around. "Is this still about what Vivian said?"

"It's the *truth*, Jacks," Maddy said bitterly. "I don't care what Vivian thinks . . . but she's not exactly wrong, is she? We're different. We don't see things the same way."

Jacks's eyes searched Maddy's face. "What do you mean?"

"Well, first of all, don't you see how *unfair* all this is?" she blurted. "How selfish? Do you think everyone lives this way?"

"No, of course I don't!" he said. He spun his arm to the party. "But it's part of my Commissioning, Maddy. This is how it's always done. I don't have any control over it. And besides"—his expression grew hurt—"you're making it sound like this is all somehow a *bad* thing, when Angels are the greatest force for good in the entire world."

"Yeah, maybe for executives and their kids!" she countered. "Certainly not for anyone I know."

Jacks felt punched in the gut. He had been trying so hard to show her something—how he felt. And she was throwing it in his face yet again.

"Don't you have anything to say?" Maddy said. Jacks remained silent, bowing his head slowly and turning away. Sounds from the party inside filled the silence. After a few moments he spoke.

"Honestly, Maddy, sometimes I really don't get you. I take you out to a party anyone else would kill to go to, and you're unhappy about it." He shook his head. "In fact, you think the whole thing is unfair. There's no pleasing you."

"Would you save *me*, Jacks?"

It came out in a rush.

All of a sudden Maddy realized it was the nagging she had felt deep inside her. It was this single question. It had been gnawing at her ever since he had come to pick her up earlier in the night.

Jacks's eyes darted to hers, intent, then looked away. "If you were my Protection, yes."

"No. As I am now, tonight," Maddy pressed. "If something were to happen, would you save me?" When she spoke again, her voice was gravelly and raw. "Would you come for me, Jackson?"

He just stood there. Maddy watched a procession of emotions move across Jacks's face like rolling thunder. Anger. Annoyance. Doubt. Even sadness?

Finally, he spoke.

"I'm sorry. It doesn't work that way, Maddy," he murmured.

The words cut like a knife.

"It's just not allowed," Jacks said, carefully. "As Angels our duty is to our Protections."

Maddy blinked back the first threat of tears.

"Protections? You mean rich people," she muttered.

"This isn't even up to me. It's just the way things are," Jacks said.

"That's ridiculous!" she shrieked. "It's your choice!"

"It's not! Look, if we just went around saving random people . . ." He paused, his eyes burning. "I mean, my family has to eat too, you know!"

"Your family eats all too well," Maddy snapped.

"Do you think this is a game?" he said, his tone low and intense. The frustration and bitterness welled up quickly. "Tomorrow I'm being Commissioned, and I'm no longer just Jackson Godspeed. Or even just an Angel. I'm a Guardian. I have people's lives in my hands. Do you have any idea of the responsibility that comes with that? Or the pressure?"

"What I know," Maddy said curtly, "is that if I could do what you do, I would use my power to help as many people as I could. I wouldn't use it to get rich." A few traitorous tears spilled over her cheeks, and she wiped them quickly away. "I would save people because it's the right thing to do." Her smile was bittersweet. "I guess that's what makes me human."

"Maddy," Jacks said, his voice like stone, "you don't know what they would do to me."

"I don't care," she said hatefully. She could feel the rage welling up inside her, an uncontrollable anger, and if she didn't get out of there quickly, who knew what might happen. With fury coursing through her veins, she made up her mind and glared at him. "I'm sorry, Jacks, I shouldn't have come tonight. The truth is I don't want anything to do with any of this, and that has to include you. If you were ever my friend at all, you'll stay away from me and just leave me alone."

"You don't—" Jacks began to speak, his eyes in pain as he looked at the girl across from him, but then he stopped himself. He was quiet for a moment, then nodded. His face was bleak and unreadable. "You're right," he said. "I guess it's for the best. To tell *you* the truth, I really don't know why I bothered anyway." His words twisted in her gut. Maddy turned without saying anything else and ran.

She ran through the party and then out to the front of the hotel. The glamorous arrival had long since closed, and workers were now unceremoniously unstapling the red carpet and rolling it up. Maddy spotted a lone taxi sitting along the curb and ran to it.

She waited until they had pulled away from the hotel to let the real tears flow.

CHAPTER EIGHTEEN

Jacks walked through his darkened house, not stopping until he had reached his room and gone inside. He closed the door silently so as to not wake anyone and flipped on the light.

Mark was sitting on the edge of his bed, waiting. He still wore his suit from earlier in the day, but it was unkempt now, his jacket laid next to him on the bed, his shirt collar unbuttoned, the tie drooping in a loose knot around his neck. He had rolled his sleeves up and sat with his hands on his knees.

"Late night?" he said in a subdued tone.

Jacks came in and looked at him evenly.

"Yeah, I guess so," he said as normally as he could manage. "I was going to head to bed."

Mark nodded but didn't move. The silence hung heavy between them. After a moment Jacks went around the bed to the closet and pulled off his jacket.

"I have, of course, seen the pictures from tonight," Mark said. "Chloe showed me, but it would be impossible to miss them, really.

They're all over the Internet, and TV too." He laughed a little. "I'm sure the magazines will be having a field day."

Jacks slipped off his tie. The tie made a *zip* sound as it cleared his collar. Jacks hung it over the rack and turned around to face his stepfather.

"You don't have to worry, Mark," Jacks said. "It was nothing. And besides, it's over now."

Mark nodded again, thoughtfully, and moved over on the bed.

"Sit down, Jackson." He patted the mattress next to him. Jacks came over wordlessly and sat.

Mark regarded his stepson.

"That . . . girl . . . you brought to the party tonight. She's not part of your world, Jacks. She can never *be* a part of your world, and you know that. You know if anything were to happen to her, anything at all, there would be nothing you could do for her."

"I know the laws," Jacks said.

"And there's a good reason for those laws," Mark said. "It's not a"—he paused, choosing the word—"a prejudice, Jackson. It's a safeguard. The laws safeguard the institution of Guardianship."

Mark rose and walked slowly to the window. He looked out at the twinkling city, the palm trees black in the night. Jacks sat on the bed, watching him. *Guardianship. Duty.* The words seemed empty, tied to parties and press junkets and paparazzi, all of it some kind of hollow dream being acted out in the Immortal City when he thought about how he felt standing next to Maddy. But that was over now. He tried to cast these thoughts from his mind. He was just upset, that was all. It would pass.

"As a Guardian, Jacks, your responsibility is to your Protections. If you allow yourself to be distracted worrying about . . . others, then it puts your Protections in danger." He turned and faced Jacks again. "If a

Protection were to get hurt because a Guardian was distracted, do you have any idea the damage that would cause? What would happen to the trust placed in us as Angels? What would happen to people's belief in the system itself?"

He walked toward Jackson, who sat motionless on the bed. Jacks thought about how he would feel if Maddy was in danger, what he would do. If he were totally honest with himself, he knew what Mark was saying was right.

"Don't you understand? Something like what you did tonight could destroy *everything*. Everything the Archangels have worked for, that your mother and I have worked for, even that your father worked for"— he was inches away from him now, standing over him—"fought for, and died for. Do I need to remind you why he fought the rebels? He gave his immortal *life* so that the good work of the Archangels, the good work of Angels on earth could continue."

Jacks nodded wordlessly.

"There's been another incident on the Walk of Angels, Jacks," Mark said, narrowing his eyes at his stepson.

"Who?"

"Ryan Templeton. I wanted you to hear it from me. He was murdered. If this gets out into the media, they'll blow these Angel disappearances out of proportion. There's also a silly rumor going around that these Angels are being murdered in order of their stars. We're sure it's just coincidence. But your star would be next."

"What?" A jolt ran through Jackson's body. He felt something he wasn't too familiar with: fear.

"If this gets out . . . with all eyes on you, it's more important than ever that we keep a solid front. For years, those envious anti-Angel groups have been looking for just this type of opportunity. With Ted Linden being elected, it's only going to get worse. You're—I mean it's—too important to give into fear now. We are putting your star on that sidewalk in defiance of whatever or whoever is out there trying to intimidate Angels."

"But only an Angel can kill an Angel." Jacks's thoughts immediately cast back to what Sierra had said to him at the party that night—*Can't wait for your star*. Was Sierra and Steven's jealousy so great that it would lead them to something like . . . *this*? The look in her eyes had been dark and unblinking. But dark enough for murder?

"Jacks, this is more complicated than you could imagine," Mark said.

The Archangel appraised his stepson. "I know all of this might not seem fair, but it's part of the sacrifice that is asked of us," he said.

Slowly, Mark sat next to Jacks again and let out a long breath.

"This is your Commissioning week, Jackson. I want you to think about your duty as a Guardian. Think about the Protection's life you will be holding in your hands. Think about that. It will be *your* responsibility to make sure they come home to their families each night. So their children can have a parent. So their parents can have a child. So their siblings can have a brother or a sister."

Mark put a firm hand on Jacks's shoulder. "This is not about you anymore, Jackson. It's about the Protections we serve. It's about the duty we are all called to as Angels and as Guardians, and I will not have you mock that. I will not have you mock your duty, Jackson."

Jacks stood up swiftly, irritated.

"You don't have to lecture me about duty, Mark."

In an instant, Mark had risen off the bed in front of Jacks, throwing him back across the room.

"Really? Then can you please tell me why I am seeing pictures of my stepson messing around with trash like that girl? Some *human* girl?"

Jacks steadied himself against the wall.

Mark's tone was ferocious, echoing around the room.

"What were you thinking, Jacks? What were you *thinking*?" Mark spit out. "Do you think all this was coincidence, Jacks, all your media coverage, the success, the fame? Do you think we'll just stand by and let you throw it away, that we'll have groomed you for nothing, that we don't need you to stand as a shining example against our enemies, who are growing every day? *Do you?*" The walls almost shook with his furious tone.

Jackson and his stepfather stood mere inches from each other, eye to eye. Neither blinked. After a few moments the heave of Mark's chest quieted. He began composing himself. Jacks turned away, taking in the weight of Mark's words. He knew it was true.

"Mark, I'm sorry, I wasn't—" Jacks said tiredly. "It's over."

Mark looked at his stepson. The rage was gone from his eyes now; only the disappointment remained.

"I'll talk to Darcy in the morning; we'll take care of it. Try to get it killed by the Commissioning ceremony tomorrow night."

Jacks nodded.

"You embarrassed yourself tonight, Jackson," he said. "Do yourself a favor and never, never do that again. Have I made myself clear?"

"Yes," Jacks said.

Mark walked to the doorway.

"Very soon you're going to be a Guardian Angel. At least try to act like one." Mark paused for a moment on the threshold. Jacks looked at his stepfather, lit from the track lighting above him. There was something off about his blazer, which was normally so crisp and clean, now rumpled and thrown over his arm. It was stained. A red splotch. Like blood.

Before Jacks could even register what he was seeing, Mark closed the door with a slam. Waiting until he heard his stepfather's footsteps fade down the hall, Jacks leapt up from his bed and went to where Mark had stopped. He leaned down and looked at where the Archangel had been standing, but there was no sign of anything. He checked the comforter on the bed, where Mark had been sitting. Nothing there, either. Jacks shook his head. It'd been a late night—he must have been imagining things.

But he hadn't imagined the look in Maddy's eyes when she told him she wanted nothing to do with him.

CHAPTER NINETEEN

"Last call," the man said, wiping dry another pint glass from behind the bar.

A solitary figure sitting at the bar in an overcoat nodded. Dust hung heavy in the dark air. The bartender picked up a broom and began sweeping.

Sylvester slowly twirled the remaining sliver of ice in the glass of whiskey he'd been nursing for the past thirty minutes. The dark bar was almost empty. It had been an Angel City institution for decades, with its dark wood, deep maroon-colored booths, and battered stools. Archangels had sat in those booths in years past, wheeling and dealing, and framed pictures of famous Guardians who used to be regulars in the forties and fifties hung dusty above the mirror of the bar.

The detective hadn't been there in years. But he'd needed to think. The encounter with Mark had left him unsettled. Was the Archangel hiding something? Or someone? Sylvester's mind struggled to put the pieces together. In bringing up Sylvester's punishment, his expulsion from the Angels, Mark had hit a nerve the detective had long since tried to bury. Sometimes he swore he could still feel his wings. Phantom limbs. *Better not to dwell on these things. Think of the case at hand, not time long passed*, he told himself.

It was going to rain. Sylvester felt it in his back. Pressure was in the air.

Why would someone—or maybe some*thing*—be taking justice on these Angels? What had Godson or Templeton done, or was the reason for the murders just the order of their stars? Did the HDF have the know-how to recruit an unhappy Angel to their side? There had to be a part he was missing. Sylvester turned the facts over and over in his mind. Troublingly, his thoughts kept moving to the Archangels themselves. Could the Archangels somehow be cleaning out enemies from within the ranks, and if so, would Mark even be aware of it? *It could go all the way to the Council.* The more he thought about it, the more he began to question Mark's motives. He'd seemed evasive, and not too surprised when he was told his stepson's star was next. The detective's head swirled with possibilities, leads, dead ends. A file ten inches thick was waiting for him on the passenger seat of his cruiser. A peek into the dank underbelly of the Immortal City.

He tipped back the glass and took another sip of his drink. The detective was woozy, but not from the booze. He needed some sleep.

The TV above the bar was tuned to a news channel, but of course they were talking about Angels. A group of talking heads was on a debate-type show. On-screen was the graphic *Angels: Whose Side Are They On?*

"Can you turn that up?" Sylvester asked, motioning to the TV.

The bartender picked up the remote, bumping the volume up a few notches. "You want the check too?" he asked, hopefully. The handful of final other customers was clearing out. Sylvester nodded.

A man with a goatee and glasses was speaking to the two other experts on the show: "So what you have here, what you have is total uncooperation on the part of the Angels, Teri. We have no idea how these guys work. They just show up and do a save for the right price. There's no transparency, no accountability—"

"But the fact is they're saving lives, Will. Pure and simple. Do the math," Teri, a woman in a power suit with short-cropped brown hair, interrupted the goateed man.

"I've done the math, *Teri*, and the fact is that the Angels only save a few, while the vast majority of humanity is left out in the cold," Will responded, his face getting slightly red. "And now with these confirmed Angel deaths happening in what's being called serial killer murders, which we've learned about just minutes ago, and the media hysteria that will certainly come from them, we have absolutely *no* idea what's going on. The Angels are acting as if everything is just business as usual."

Sylvester sat up straight. The murders had gone public. The Angels couldn't keep everyone in the dark forever. The story was too explosive.

None of the handful of other customers in the bar seemed to pay much mind. They went there at that hour to try to escape the Immortal City's woes, not pay attention to them.

The debate continued on the television:

"Okay, okay, let's bring it back to the original—" The moderator attempted to steer the conversation but was interrupted by an irate Teri.

"If we're going back to the original question: they can't save everyone all the time, pure and simple," Teri said. "There's just not enough for humanity. This vocal anti-Angel minority in this country is not useful and will solve nothing. We have to accept the Angels as they are, on their terms. Think of how many lives they've saved! To do otherwise is to give ammunition to hate groups like the Humanity Defense Front, whose stated goal is the extermination of Angels by any means possible!"

The third guest, a man with a buzz cut and a red tie, spoke up. "How do we know they're not capable of saving everyone? And at what cost do we have them save us? And then we have to owe these creatures that just materialized from thin air over a hundred years ago? They know everything about us, but they still won't bring humans into a Guardian training facility except for special staged press events." An on-screen title identified him as former army colonel Davis A. Jessup. "What's really going on over at the NAS? And why has the Council of Twelve all but disappeared from the public eye for the past eighty years? Certainly all of these questions are important from a national security standpoint too." The colonel paused. "I think soon-to-be senator Ted Linden's recent victory at the polls has shown that a large part of this country wants these answers. Now."

Taking a pull from his glass, Sylvester continued peering up at the television. *If the public knew everything* . . . he thought. On-screen they cut to file footage of Ted Linden at his victory speech. He was maybe forty-five years old and handsome, a sleek shock of dark lustrous hair swooped back on his head. He had a winning smile as a he gave a thumbs-up to his supporters.

"What should we think now that Angels are being killed? And scientists also have evidence that the Angels are actually aging faster than we thought," Will stated. "Latest projections have the life spans of these so-called Born Immortals at four hundred to five hundred years. But the NAS maintains total immortality. If the aging is really happening, and these killings are really happening, apparently from within the community, what else are they hiding?"

Teri almost jumped out of her seat. "I've seen that report, Will, and I wouldn't call it 'evidence' as much as total speculation! Anti-Angel elements are just trying for a power play in this country, but it's not going to work. Whipping people into a false frenzy never lasts. It's clear you're just a mouthpiece for Linden and his party."

Sylvester tilted his glass back and took the final gulp of whiskey, laying down the empty glass and a few bills on the bar.

"Thanks," he said to the bartender, pulling on his jacket as he walked to the door. Stepping onto the dormant streets of Angel City, he took in a lungful of night air. The stars high above twinkled dimly in the sky through the light clouds and pollution.

As soon as the door closed, the bartender walked to the window and turned off the neon signs, also flipping the Open sign to Closed. After bolting the door, he walked back to the bar, under the rows of dusty old Angel photos on the wall. He picked up the remote. Will, Teri, and Colonel Jessup were now near screaming at each other on-screen. He pressed the red power button and the TV switched to blackness, leaving the bar in silence as he continued sweeping under the dusty, watchful eyes of glamorous Angels past.

CHAPTER TWENTY

Maddy stumbled down the stairs with her hair still wet, pulling her hoodie over a shirt she had to resurrect from the hamper. In the aftermath of the disaster that was last night, she had forgotten to set her alarm and was late for her morning shift at the diner. Her limbs throbbed with fatigue, and her head ached with the painful memories of the party, but at least, she told herself, that was over now. No more lying. No more sneaking around. She could go back to being just plain Maddy. Beyond that, she tried not to think about it. She tried not to think about Jacks.

She grabbed her backpack from where she had left it on the floor and dropped in her shiny new BlackBerry Miracle. She *would* hang on to that, she decided. She'd needed a new phone anyway, and it made her feel like she at least got *something* out of the whole experience. She grabbed a piece of bread from a bag on the kitchen counter and, holding it in her teeth, hurried across the living room and threw open the door.

Maddy's world went white. A barrage of camera flashes lit up the porch as a dozen voices shouted at her simultaneously.

"MADDY!" "MADDY!" "MADDY!" RIGHT HERE, MADDY!" RIGHT HERE, DARLING!" "OVER HERE, MADDY!"

Maddy had paparazzi.

They crowded together on the lawn in front of the porch steps, shutters clicking automatically, firing away at her. Still more paparazzi were running across the street, pulling their cameras out of their bags and shooting as they ran, men with unkempt beards and unkind, sneering faces. Maddy stood there with her wet hair and the slice of bread hanging limply from her mouth. Jacks's world had followed her home and was now standing on her front lawn.

"Maddy, how does it feel to be dating Jackson Godspeed?!" roared a heavyset pap in the back. Maddy pulled the bread from her mouth and attempted to shield her eyes with it. *"How does it feel to be dating the most eligible Angel in Angel City?!"* he barked again.

"We're not dating!" Maddy shrieked. "I'm not dating anyone!" Maddy saw a few of the neighbors coming out of their homes to watch. A boy of about twelve took a picture with his phone. The humiliation was paralyzing. With her free hand Maddy groped for the doorknob and pulled the front door shut. She dropped the bread, grabbed a textbook out from her bag, and used it to cover her face.

Move, she told herself, and willed her feet forward, quickly down the front steps and walkway. Like a human tidal wave, the paparazzi followed, shuffling backward and trampling the few plants Uncle Kevin kept in the front yard. She broke into a run as she crossed the street, leading them away from the diner. Maddy couldn't risk working the morning shift today. They kept pace with her, backpedaling or dropping their cameras to their sides and running to catch up.

"Did you meet Vivian last night?!" one of them shouted while panting. *"Are you nervous she might try to steal Jacks back?"*

"Just leave me alone!" Maddy yelled, fighting back tears.

"What do you think about the Angel murders? Are you worried about Jacks?"

The last question sliced through the others like a blade. Maddy froze on the sidewalk. The book dropped from her face.

"W-what?" she stammered.

"They're finding severed wings on the Walk of Angels! The story just broke last night!" someone shouted back. She looked around the faces but saw only beady, unwelcoming eyes. She noticed one of them was *recording* the whole thing on a camcorder. He was grinning devilishly as he kept his eye on the device's screen. It was such a violation. Maddy felt utterly naked.

"Angels are being killed in the order of their stars on Angel Boulevard, and they say Jacks could be next! They can't even protect themselves! How does that make you feel, Maddy?"

Jacks could be in danger? Maddy couldn't even let herself process this. She might be mad at him, but the thought of something happening to him made her heart clench. And what was this about a serial killer? All she could do was duck her head and walk even faster. Finally, at the corner, they left her. She hazarded a glance over her shoulder as she gasped to catch her breath. They were inspecting their cameras now, reviewing what they'd got as they hurried to their cars. The pictures would probably be on the Internet within a few minutes.

She pulled her hood tight over her head and walked briskly down Angel Boulevard, not daring to look up. She could just imagine an Angel Tours bus slamming on its brakes and the tour guide announcing, *"You're in luck, folks. If you look to your right, you'll see Jackson Godspeed's girlfriend!"* She ignored the shops now selling T-shirts with Jacks's face on them and the slogan Warning: Protection of Jackson Godspeed. She paid no attention to a guy dressed up like Jackson who wanted to take a picture with her. At the light at Angel and Highland she kept her head down, avoiding the screens that declared, "FULL COMMISSIONING COVERAGE" and the signs that announced, "ROAD CLOSED FOR SPECIAL EVENT."

Then she heard a scream.

It was a girl a few years younger than she was, also standing at the corner and waiting for the light to change. She looked from Maddy, then to her iPhone, and then back to Maddy again. She gawked in amazement.

"It's *you*," she squealed hysterically. Maddy had been recognized. "OMG!" the girl gushed, sounding just like Gwen. "Can I get your autograph?"

Maddy blinked at the girl in horror. This wasn't really happening, was it?

It was.

As she stood there, trying to use her hair to cover her face, a crowd of tourists formed. Disposable cameras flashed. A man wearing a John Deere hat yelled, "Martha, look! It's her!"

The light turned, and Maddy ran the rest of the way toward school.

Entering the hall felt almost exactly like arriving at the party last night. Everybody stared. Except it was worse, because at least last night she was somewhere she didn't belong. Now she was in one of the few places she *did* belong, and people were gazing at her like some strange creature. Like a freak. It was like she didn't belong *anywhere* anymore. As she walked, Maddy became aware of the fact that it was actually growing *quieter*. Conversations died as she passed. People were hushing and pointing. Maddy could hear the sound of her own feet on the linoleum. With her arrival, the usually loud and chaotic hallway of Angel City High had gone dead silent.

She hurried numbly to her locker. Gwen wasn't there, which was unusual. She was avoiding her, Maddy realized. The possibility of just how badly she might have hurt Gwen was beginning to form in her mind. Pulling out her books, she tried to ignore the fact that most people were still staring at her. It felt incredibly lonely. The bell rang, mercifully, and Maddy decided she would try to apologize to Gwen at lunch. If she could find her, that was.

The school day that followed was tense, awkward, and embarrassing. In English, Maddy discovered there was a test she had totally forgotten about. In the middle of struggling through an essay, a phone rang. It was loud and obnoxious, but certainly sounded futuristic and expensive. Then it hit her. It was her Blackberry Miracle.

"Maddy, you know the rules," Mrs. Stinchfield scolded. "Phones need to be off during class." As Maddy fumbled for the Berry, it gave a "new voice mail" chime. Mrs. Stinchfield glared. "You may be a celebrity in the world now, Ms. Montgomery, but in my classroom, you're still just a student."

Maddy silenced the phone as best she knew how. After that, she couldn't focus on the exam. When the lunch bell rang, she had to turn the test in incomplete.

The hall was unusually quiet again, but this time she could hear excited whispers as she passed. People were reading their phones and throwing not-so-subtle glances at her. She didn't even want to think about what the blogs were saying about last night. Or the incident on the porch this morning. And she could only hope Uncle Kevin didn't notice anything on ANN. When she rounded the corner, she saw Gwen at her locker, quickly slamming it and hurrying to escape. She saw Maddy and paused, as if caught. Then she folded her arms over her chest, leaned against the bank of lockers, and tapped her heel in defiance.

"Hey—" Maddy began timidly as she walked up. That was all it took.

"Yes, I worship him," Gwen blurted, "yes, I would probably worship his dirty laundry, but you didn't have to *lie* to me about it."

"I know, I was wrong—"

"What have I ever kept from you, Maddy? Even that time I made out with Brandon Davis while he was going out with Emily, I told you." Maddy withered under her friend's furious stare. "I had to find out from *Samantha*. In a *text*. My own best friend couldn't even tell me the truth! Some friend," she scoffed.

She was right, Maddy thought. Absolutely right. Gwen could be a walking parody of herself sometimes, but she was Maddy's friend. And she had always been a good one—the only one, really. And Maddy had blatantly lied to her.

"I don't know what to say, Gwen," Maddy said, shamefaced. "I'm sorry. I'm so sorry."

Gwen sniffed. "So what, you're Jackson Godspeed's *girlfriend* now?"

"No, that's all over," Maddy said. "I don't know what I was thinking."

Gwen dabbed a finger to her running mascara. "Well, I don't know what you were thinking either, Maddy." And with that, she flipped her hair and was gone.

Maddy felt the eyes of the entire hallway crawling over her skin as she spun the dial of her lock. They had probably heard the whole thing. Was this the way it was going to be now? Was this what she had to look forward to for every remaining day of her senior year? All Maddy could think about was escaping. Her eyes drifted to a nearby stairwell door, and she ran for it.

In the stairwell, she stood gasping for breath. Was her life ruined? Probably not. But what else did she expect to happen when she agreed to go out with Jackson Godspeed? The realization was slow, and bitter. She had been Angelstruck. She slid down and sat on the steps. He had walked into the diner and she had turned into a silly, Angelstruck little girl. And she used to make fun of *Gwen* for being obsessed? She felt like such a fool.

"Spending some time with the Angels, huh?" a voice echoed above her. Maddy looked up.

It was Tyler. He was standing with Ethan, giving Maddy a dirty look. Her face flushed red in embarrassment as she remembered the conversation he'd been having in the commons about Angels. What Tyler—what Ethan!—must think of her right now.

"Go on, I'll catch up," Ethan said to him. Tyler slowly walked into the hall.

Ethan came down and sat next to her on the step. He laughed a little, looking at Maddy with a friendly, comfortable expression. "How's that working out for you—hanging out with the Angels, I mean?"

Maddy shook her head, unable to meet his gaze. With Gwen she had felt like a backstabber. Now with Ethan, remembering their conversation in the diner, she felt like a hypocrite.

"Don't worry, I'm not Tyler. I'm not giving you a hard time, promise. It was a little surprising when I heard about it, though, 'cause you didn't seem like the kind of girl who would get mixed up with those guys."

"I'm not," Maddy said, her eyes flashing. "Nothing happened. And it's over now. He was . . ." She trailed off.

"A jerk?" Ethan offered. Maddy looked at him, surprised. "Conceited? Arrogant? Clueless about how the real world works? Something like that?"

". . . Yeah," Maddy said quietly.

Ethan gave her a reassuring smile. "They're not who you think they are, are they?"

"No." Maddy shook her head. "They're not." She looked down at her shoes again. "I feel like such a joke."

"Well, I don't think you're a joke," he said. "And you know what? Everyone out in that hallway is just insanely jealous. I know the *girls* are for sure."

"Thanks," she said after a moment.

"For what?"

"For . . . *talking* to me," she said with a laugh. "For being there for me."

"Anytime," he said softly. "We should look out for each other."

"We?" Maddy asked, a little surprised.

"We," he said. "You think I don't know you, Maddy, but I do. You're like me. I've felt that way ever since I first ordered a burger from you at the diner. I saw you standing behind the counter watching everyone and I could just tell that you and I, we're so much alike. You feel like an outsider too, don't you? Like we don't fit into this glitziness that everyone is obsessed with. Like you see the world differently than everybody else?"

"I guess so," Maddy said, feeling, for a moment, totally understood. That was exactly it. She had never felt like she fit in. Having it said out loud—and accepted—was liberating.

Ethan gave her a playful punch on the arm. "So we gotta stick together."

"Okay," Maddy replied, brightening, and smiled at him. Gwen might never speak to her again, but at least she had another friend in the world.

"I hope you haven't forgotten my party tonight. We're going to have food, drinks, a great playlist; I promise you'll have a good time. And no Angels. So I'll see you there?"

She had done it again. It was so easy to give him the wrong idea. Or—was it the wrong idea? How *did* she feel about him? Maddy gazed into his sincere, questioning eyes. Then she looked away.

"Ethan, you've been really cool to me. I've just been through so much lately, I don't think it's a good idea for me right now. I think I need to spend some time alone, get caught up on school, just put this disaster of a week behind me." She paused as his expression fell. "You understand, right?"

"Sure," he said, smiling to disguise his disappointment. "Well, if you change your mind, you know where I'll be." He rose and gave her a nod. "The famous Maddy Montgomery. See you around."

Maddy listened to the echo of his departing steps.

After classes ended, she walked alone toward the front entrance of the school—where she spotted more paparazzi waiting impatiently for her outside. They had been joined by television crews, who were attempting to interview some of the students. Maddy couldn't believe it. It was like a nightmare from which she couldn't wake up.

Ducking quickly out the side door of the gym, Maddy cut through the baseball field. She decided as she walked home she would go in through the back door of the house, just in case. Then she could change into her uniform and use the rear entrance of the diner, as usual. With any luck, everyone would forget all about her in a few days time. Reaching the house, she slipped around to the back as planned and let herself in without a hitch.

She tiptoed into the kitchen—and froze.

Kevin was sitting at the table, waiting for her.

"You're not at the diner," Maddy stated, her breath catching in her throat.

"I need to talk to you, Maddy."

Maddy's heart thundered in her chest. She leaned on the kitchen counter for support.

"Okay?"

Kevin let out a long sigh. "I left you a message," he said gruffly. "Where have you been? I've been worried. I was . . ." Kevin trailed off, drawing a deep breath to attempt to calm himself. "The phone company called and they wanted to confirm you added a new phone to your account? And now they're charging me for data? And unlimited calling? And all kinds of other stuff you know we can't afford?"

Maddy stood there, silent. Her mind racing.

"What have I told you, Maddy?" he said. "Homework and emergencies. Is that not clear? And what's this about a new phone?"

She looked at his expectant gray eyes.

"Maddy, do you want to tell me what's going on?"

How could she? How could she begin to explain any of it? Should she just tell him she had been going out with the same Angel who trashed his diner?

"I got the phone from a . . . boy. It was a gift. I'll call the phone company and cancel it right now."

"Is that why you've been acting so strange this week?" he pressed. "Breaking dishes . . . and so tired?"

Maddy let out an embarrassed breath. She didn't know what to say. A realization seemed to wash over his face.

"I'm guessing you weren't studying with Gwen last night, were you?"

"No," Maddy breathed.

"You *lied* to me?" Kevin looked genuinely shocked at this. He looked down at the table. "You were sneaking around behind my back, lying to me." When he looked up, Maddy was surprised to see the genuine hurt in his eyes.

"I didn't raise you this way, Maddy."

It was enough to raise a lump in her throat. Hot tears threatened to overspill her eyes.

"I'm sorry, Kevin," she whispered. "It won't happen again."

Kevin nodded but didn't seem entirely convinced.

"And who was this boy, anyway?" he asked, shifting uncomfortably in his chair. "Some boy from school?"

"Not exactly," she said. "But nothing happened. And it's over now. I promise."

Kevin's expression softened a bit, his shoulders relaxing. "All right."

Maddy looked out the window, out to the Angel City sign looming on the hill. She imagined it was mocking her. Mocking them both.

"You want to take the rest of the night off? I already called someone to fill in for you."

"Sure," Maddy said weakly. "Thanks."

Kevin looked a little embarrassed himself now. Maddy knew these "father-daughter" things weren't easy for him.

"Just do me a favor. I know you're older now, but it's . . . dangerous out there. Especially for . . . you. I mean, young girls like you. Please. Don't walk home by yourself at night for a while, okay?"

"Okay," she said, feeling slightly puzzled. She went over, kissed him on the cheek, and stepped silently upstairs.

Disappointing Kevin was something she rarely did, and she had forgotten how truly terrible it felt. Their modest life wasn't much, but it was everything he had to give her. He had always provided for her, and she wasn't even his daughter. How disrespectful had she been? Very, she decided.

She sat on her bed and pulled out the BlackBerry Miracle. Somehow she had to figure out how to cancel the thing. Then it chimed.

It was a new-blog alert.

Apparently the phones at the party had all been preprogrammed with bookmarked web pages, and, of course, the Angel blogs were among them. Maddy read the screen. It was about Jacks.

"Amid the media firestorm that broke this morning around the Angel killings and last night's *Angels Weekly* Commissioning party, Jackson Godspeed released a press statement today playing down rumors ACPD has him on a list of potential targets. Jacks also emphatically denied there was anything romantic between him and the girl he brought to the party the previous night, describing her as a 'contest winner.'" The blogger continued by declaring, *"Whatever that contest is, we'd love to play!"*

The tears finally came. She had made a fool of herself and betrayed or disappointed everyone she cared about. Gwen first. And now Kevin. And someone else too, a name she was startled to realize was on the list. Ethan. Maddy threw the phone on the floor. From that moment, she decided, she was going to start fresh. A new beginning. A clean slate. She was going to be the fun, social, loyal Maddy she knew she could be. She looked out the window. There was that sign again. Like a ghost. She got up and quickly drew the shade. Then she went digging for her old phone, sat at her desk, and, taking a deep breath, made a call.

Ethan picked up, sounding distracted. "Hello?"

"Ethan, hey. It's Maddy. From school."

His voice immediately brightened. "Hey! Wh-what's going on, Maddy?"

"I just wanted to say I changed my mind. I'd love to come to your party, if that's still okay." The line was quiet. "If not, it's—"

"No! Of course it is!" he interrupted enthusiastically. "That would be great. You have directions?"

Maddy took them down.

"Well, see you tonight, then," Ethan said. "I'm really looking forward to it, Maddy. I'm so glad you changed your mind."

"Me too," Maddy said. She thanked Ethan and hung up. That had actually felt good. Normal. She knew Ethan liked her. Would it be so terrible to not just shut everyone out? And maybe, just maybe, she liked him too.

Then she called Gwen. It rang once and went to voice mail. Still upset, Maddy thought. Well, that was fair. She listened to Gwen's sugary greeting, thinking about what she wanted to say.

"Hey, it's me," she announced after the beep. "I just wanted to tell you I'm really sorry about everything. I was . . . a bad friend. I don't even know what got into me. But I hope you know how much you mean to me, and I'm going to be at Ethan's party tonight, so I hope I see you there. Okay. Later, girl."

Maddy snapped the phone shut and took a deep breath. She even allowed herself to smile. Gwen would be at the party. Maddy would be able to really reconnect with her. She felt terrible about what had happened, that she had broken Gwen's trust. From now on Maddy was going to let her friend in on everything. And no more making excuses: she could find time to hang out with her best friend *and* get all her homework and work at the diner done too. Even if Gwen just wanted to go look at clothes neither of them could afford or obsess over boys they couldn't date, Maddy would find the time. What was the point of all the hard work anyway, if you didn't keep your friends close? She was going to learn to enjoy her normal life starting tonight.

Maddy opened the desk drawer and pulled out her mother's necklace. If there was one thing this whole experience with Jacks had given her, it had, in a strange way, brought her closer to her mother. She put the necklace on and looked at herself. Starting tonight at the party, she would somehow, some way, forget about Jackson Godspeed. She had to stop thinking about the sound of his voice, the heat of his touch, and the radiance of his presence. She had to forget about that connection she had felt between them—like a circuit—that night in the back room.

Then, as she sat there, one final idea came. It was bold and surprising, and she rolled it around on her tongue for a minute as if tasting it. She decided it tasted good. A plan formed in her mind—a final piece of the puzzle for the party—and she resolved right then and there to follow it. It was simple and elegant, and was probably the only guarantee she was ever going to fully blot Jackson Godspeed out of her mind as she became New Maddy.

She was going to go for it. She was going to fall in love with Ethan.

CHAPTER TWENTY-ONE

It was a somewhat long walk to Ethan's, but Maddy didn't mind. The wind had changed directions overnight and was coming off the ocean now, a crisp, refreshing kind of air. Maddy zipped up her hoodie but promised herself she would take it off when she got to the party. That was another thing she had decided—another rule for New Maddy. No more hiding.

Her route took her across the city and up into the lower Angel City Hills. Maddy avoided Angel Boulevard, of course. She didn't need to experience the frenzy that was Jackson Godspeed's Commissioning— she was going to do whatever it took *not* to be reminded, although avoiding Jackson Godspeed in Angel City, she had to admit, was a near impossibility. While she was getting ready, she hadn't been able to stop herself from turning on the TV to find out more about the Angel killings and the speculation that Jackson might be targeted. She tried to remember how angry she was at Jacks, but her heart clenched up as she thought of him in danger. After only a few minutes, she'd had to turn it off. But even now, walking, she could see the news choppers buzzing overhead, circling the boulevard like vultures. In between songs on her iPod she was pretty sure she could make out the distant roar of a hysterical crowd. *That*, she told herself, was why she had come up with her plan. And that, she convinced herself, was why she had to follow through with it. Gwen wouldn't be at the party until after the Commissioning, and that would be a good thing. As much as Maddy wanted to see her best friend, she needed to be alone with Ethan first. Her pulse rose as she thought about it. How *was* she going to do this?

Arriving at the address Ethan had given her, she stood there on the sidewalk for a moment. The house was large and rustic, set into the leafy hillside. The sound of adolescent laughter and thumping bass filtered out into the street. But this was definitely the place. No screaming crowds, red carpets, and photographers like the soiree she had been at last night, thankfully. Just a regular teenage party. The house wasn't lavish, Maddy thought, but its occupants were certainly well off. A silver Audi A5 gleamed in the driveway. Was she really making the right decision by coming here?

As if in answer, another news chopper roared overhead, on its way to join the others and circle over the boulevard. More Jackson Godspeed worship.

Running a nervous hand through her hair and fixing a smile on her face, she marched up the walkway and rang the bell.

No one answered at first, and Maddy had the sudden urge to just turn and leave. Then, with a burst of noise, the door opened. Ethan stood there in the doorway wearing a plaid collared shirt rolled up at the elbows and his usual ripped jeans. He gave her an open, wide grin that made her heart miss a beat.

"Maddy! You found it."

"Yeah!" Maddy chimed back, hoping to match his enthusiasm.

"Well, come in, come in," he said, opening the door wider. She took a step inside, and Ethan moved to hug her. Normally she would have used her shoulders to close off her body and leave the would-be hugger to fumble awkwardly with her arms, but this time she took a step into him and let her body fit closely into his. She felt the hardness of his chest press against hers, then the wrap of his heavy arms. She breathed in his cologne.

"I'm really glad you decided to come," he said as he released her.

"Yeah, I am too."

"Can I take your sweatshirt?"

"Er—yeah. Sure," Maddy said, remembering her promise to herself. She slipped out of her hoodie, revealing an ivory spaghetti-strap top she had actually picked out with some forethought for once. Her mother's necklace rested elegantly on her collarbone. Ethan's eyes flickered over her bare shoulders as he took the hoodie and hung it over a peg by the door. Maddy noticed and blushed. They stood there for a moment like that, neither moving.

"Well," Ethan said finally, and laughed a bit nervously. Maddy laughed too. There seemed to be the sudden pressure to be verbose. "Why don't I get you something to drink?"

"Sure," Maddy replied, and followed him into the house.

The party was already in full swing. People stood around or sat in groups on the couches talking, all holding red plastic cups. The sound of excited chatter mingled with the smell of beer. It was mostly people from school, but no one Maddy was really friends with.

"Gwen told Kyle she was definitely coming, but I haven't seen her," Ethan told her as he led her through the clusters of people. "Simon's here, but I don't know where Tyler is. He's been kind of weird lately; he didn't even answer my text earlier today. And Kyle's on his way."

Maddy thought she spotted Simon across the room. She was also kind of happy that Kyle wasn't here yet. He had been acting strange lately—didn't he know she was Gwen's best friend?

A girl Maddy thought was named Becky danced sloppily next to a coffee table. A couple guys at the TV were playing Xbox. No one seemed interested in watching the Commissioning, which was a relief. She received a few loaded glances as they crossed the living room, but most people were too busy talking or enjoying the contents of their cups. They made their way into the kitchen.

Ethan had somehow managed to secure a keg. It was parked in the middle of the kitchen floor in a large Rubbermaid tub filled with ice. A guy wearing a backwards baseball cap was pouring cups of beer from the tap.

"Keg stands in ten minutes!" he announced loudly.

It was a long way from the sparkling trays of gourmet drinks, Angels in designer outfits, and strange tables made out of fake animals that Maddy had been mingling among just the night before. She pushed that scene from her mind, pigs and all.

"What can I get you?" Ethan asked.

Maddy looked down at the keg. She might be New Maddy, but going to her first real high school party *and* drinking for the first time all in one night seemed like a little much. Besides, she needed to be sharp if she was going to do what she came to do.

"Do you have any soda?" she asked.

"Yeah, totally."

Ethan fished around in the fridge and came up with a Diet Coke. "Hope you don't mind diet," he said as he handed it to her. Maddy took the can from him, and their fingers touched. Instead of pulling away, she let her hand linger on his for a bit longer than necessary. She thought she had seen something like that on TV once.

Ethan looked down at her hand, then moved up to her gaze. His eyes were deep, searching. Nervous but hopeful.

"*Boo!*" a voice yelled right behind Maddy's ear, and she jumped, insanely startled. Ragged laughter followed. "Bet you thought I was the serial killer, didn't you? Don't worry, he's just takin' out Angels," a slurred voice said, with a burp and another laugh.

Maddy turned around. A lean, muscular boy with a buzz cut had stumbled over, bringing the smell of alcohol wafting along with him. It was Jordan Richardson from chemistry. Simon had followed him in.

"Wait, aren't you Maddy Montgomery?" Jordan asked.

"Yeah, man, that's Maddy; I know her, dude!" Simon turned to her. "You're, like, famous or something now, right?" He was talking louder than necessary and knocked over a stack of cups on the counter as he steadied himself. A few people were starting to look over, and Maddy felt the prying eyes of the party begin to shift in her direction.

"How about a tour of the house?" Ethan said loudly, deflecting Simon and the other guy.

"That'd be great," Maddy said gratefully. They walked through the kitchen door and into an adjoining dining room, where a few guys were playing a game with cups of beer and a Ping-Pong ball. Then they crossed through another doorway and into a second living room, this one with white couches and a flickering electric fireplace.

"Thanks," Maddy said when they were finally alone.

"No problem." Ethan smiled. "They're just a little drunk, that's all."

"But you're not drinking?" Maddy said, realizing it as much as asking. Ethan shook his head.

"No. I mean, I want everyone to have a good time, but that's not really my thing."

Maddy looked around the room. The glass coffee table was spotless, and the couches looked like they were sat on very carefully. The house was furnished with nice things, no question, but it lacked the cozy home feel of the shabbier place she shared with Kevin.

"It's a beautiful house," Maddy said as she gazed up at the vaulted wood-beam ceiling.

"Thanks. Still feels kind of new to me. I keep waiting for my mom to decide how she wants to decorate, but . . ." He trailed off and sat on the couch. Maddy took a seat next to him.

"So, your mom's out of town?"

Ethan nodded, looking downcast for a moment. "Yeah, she's out of town a lot for business. Her job keeps her pretty busy."

"What kind of work does she do?"

"Marketing," he replied. Maddy thought of Uncle Kevin. Despite being old-fashioned and set in his ways, he was always there for her. Other people sometimes weren't as lucky.

"So," Ethan said, changing the subject, "college apps driving you crazy yet?"

"Oh, crazy is an understatement," Maddy admitted with a sip of her soda. "I'm *way* behind."

"I know, me too," Ethan said. "Have you gotten that essay prompt yet, *'Please describe what you consider to be the most difficult moment in your life'*?"

"Yes!" Maddy exclaimed. "God, I hate that one."

Ethan shook his head. "I wanted to respond, *'Trying to figure out what to write for this essay.'*" Ethan laughed, and Maddy joined in. She was feeling much more at ease.

"Wow, I had no idea you cared about college, Ethan," Maddy said.

"You assumed I wasn't smart?" Ethan looked mock-insulted.

Maddy blanched and backpedaled. "I've never seen you in the school library is all." Ethan's eyes flashed, mischievous.

"Well, can you keep a secret?"

He pulled out his key chain and jingled it.

"I kind of wanted to study on my own hours, and besides, I prefer being in there by myself without Mr. Rankin to pester me."

Maddy's mouth fell open.

"You have *keys* to the school?"

"Sure. Mrs. Neilson left them lying on her desk one day, so I . . . borrowed them."

"You stole them," Maddy said in disbelief. Ethan shrugged, and Maddy was surprised to find herself smiling.

"I *copied* them. I gave them back, promise. If you ever need to use them, just let me know."

Of course it was wrong to steal the keys . . . but it was also resourceful. And bold. There was something about it she liked. It felt like a New Maddy thing to do.

"Careful what you say," she said at last. "I might actually take you up on that."

Maddy watched Ethan as he laughed. A part of her had always found him attractive, but maybe not as attractive as she was finding him now. Her eyes searched his full lips, his high cheekbones, his hazel eyes. A silent moment passed between them. Almost intuitively, he reached over and took her hand. His felt rough and calloused, but also warm.

As much as she tried to block it, the memory came. The memory of Jacks's touch in the back office of the diner, and the electricity that had passed between them. She pushed the thought desperately away as Ethan turned toward her. They were face-to-face on the couch now. His eyes were doing that thing again. Asking a question. A question she thought she knew the answer to.

"Actually, can I use your bathroom?" Maddy blurted suddenly. "I just need to . . . I'll be back in a second."

"Yeah, of course," Ethan said, looking a little surprised. He pointed. "Go down the hall and make two rights."

Maddy got up, set her soda on the glass table, and nearly ran. After a couple wrong turns she found the bathroom. It smelled pleasantly of coconut. Maddy stood there, breathing hard, looking at her reflection in the mirror. At this point, she nearly despised that face.

"You're such a coward, Maddy," she mumbled as she turned on the faucet and splashed some water on her face. If she was being honest with herself, though, she knew it had nothing to do with courage. Or even with Ethan. She grabbed a hand towel and dried off. Her heart was still pounding, and she rubbed a hand on her chest to calm it. She had made a promise to herself—a promise to start fresh. Her fingers inched up and touched her mother's necklace. The past was the past. She looked at herself again with renewed determination. "You can do this, Maddy," she whispered. She switched off the light and headed out.

The house was large and easy to get turned around in, and soon Maddy was sure she was lost. She went down a long, bare hallway and ended up at the back of the house, facing two doors she thought were probably bedrooms. *Great*, she thought, and was just turning around when something caught her eye. The door on her right stood slightly ajar, and inside, she could just make out something in the middle of the floor.

"Hello?" she asked.

No response. Her curiosity piqued, she went to the door and pushed it open a little farther. It was a bedroom, but clearly not the master. Maybe it was a guest room. A cardboard moving box sat in the center of the floor. The box was open, and she could just make out the glint of light off a stack of picture frames.

So that's where all the pictures are, she thought, a little amused. She stepped inside the room and went to the box.

The photos were crowded together and stacked on top of each other. Maddy picked one up. It was a picture of a man in his early forties, standing with a young boy who looked like Ethan. The man must be Ethan's father, she thought. They were in a backyard, next to a smoking barbecue. The man had a spatula in his hand. Maddy picked up another picture. A slightly older Ethan playing football with his dad at the beach. She fingered through the rest of the photos. They were all of Ethan and his father, until she reached the last frame, which was blank.

"Maddy?" a questioning voice asked from just over her shoulder. Maddy nearly shrieked as she swiveled and saw Ethan standing right behind her. He looked down at the photo in her hand.

"You scared me, I—" Maddy could feel the hot blood rushing into her cheeks. She had been snooping around and got caught. "I got lost coming back from the bathroom and thought you might be in here. Then I saw the pictures . . . I'm really sorry." She had started to put the picture back in the box when she felt a hand on her shoulder.

"Here," Ethan said, reaching forward. He didn't seem angry or upset at all. Maddy turned slowly to face him and handed him the picture. His eyes grew distant as he looked at it. A sad smile passed across his face as though he were witnessing a fleeting memory. Finally, he spoke.

"My dad."

Maddy nodded, understanding.

"He's not—" Ethan broke off when his voice shook. "He's not with us anymore."

"I'm so sorry." Maddy didn't know what else to say.

"It still just gets to me sometimes. Especially when I think about how he died."

Maddy's heart thudded in her chest. She felt terrible. "Ethan, I didn't mean to—"

"It's okay," he said. Maddy watched him as he ran a finger over the picture. She didn't dare speak.

"There was time to save them both, Maddy," he said. "It would have been *easy*. It's effortless for them, you know. But my father, well—" He looked up from the photo and met Maddy's gaze. His eyes were full of unshed tears. "He didn't have coverage."

Maddy's heart was in her throat. She ached with sympathy. No wonder Ethan disliked the Angels. It was a wonder he wasn't as aggressively anti-Angel as Tyler. Ethan set the photo back in the box along with the others.

"That's what they told my mother. That's what they told us both." He gestured around them at the empty house. "No amount of insurance money can buy my dad back. They *could* have saved him, but they didn't."

Maddy thought about their conversation in the stairwell at school, and at the diner before that. She thought about what Ethan must have read about her online. And how he had supported her and been a friend to her anyway.

Almost without being aware of it, Maddy took a step toward him.

"Ethan . . ." Her voice was almost a whisper. "I'm so sorry." She placed a hand on his chest and felt his heart pounding furiously under his shirt. They were face-to-face again, inches apart now.

"I'm glad you told me about him."

Ethan swiped at his eyes with his hand and let out a pent-up breath. He looked down at his feet. "I really know how to set the mood, don't I?" he said, smiling. "Going on about dead people. Real smooth." He laughed, but it was shaky.

Maddy smiled and looked into his eyes. She felt his hand on the small of her back and let him pull her close.

She held his gaze. For the third time, it was as if his eyes were asking a question. This time, she nodded. Letting her mind go blank, she tilted her mouth up toward him and closed her eyes.

She *needed* this. She *wanted* this. She felt his breath on her cheeks and then, ever so gently, the brush of his lips.

It happened in that instant. An image exploding in the blackness of her mind so vivid and clear it could not have come from her thoughts.

It was Jacks's face.

Suddenly, it was as if Jacks was there in the room with her. She could touch him. Smell him. Feel his presence. Maddy pulled herself away from Ethan.

"I'm so sorry, Ethan . . . I can't do this," she gasped, her face twisted and confused. She ran out of the room and rushed down the hallway blindly, fighting tears, Jacks's presence still lingering in her ears, in her nose, and on her tongue. She could hear Ethan's footsteps behind her after a moment, hustling to catch up.

"Maddy, wait!" he called after her.

She found the living room and pushed through the crowd. People glared at her as she shoved past, but she didn't care. She needed to get out of the party before anything else happened, before she embarrassed herself any further. She reached the front door and fumbled with the knob.

"Wait, Maddy, I'm sorry, did I do something?" Ethan panted, finally catching up to her. "You don't have to go!"

"Yes, I do," she said as she threw the door open. "It's not your fault, Ethan, I just need to go." She grabbed her hoodie off the rack and stuck her arms in the sleeves.

Ethan sighed. "Okay, if you say so. I'm really sorry if I rushed things. At least let me drive you home? It's getting dark out."

"No, honestly, it's all right," she said, zipping up her sweatshirt. "Besides, you can't leave your own party."

"Bro, she's right," a drunk voice called. "You can't leave your own *parrrry!*"

It was Simon again. He came over and threw his arm sloppily around Ethan's shoulders. "We'll drive the famous Maddy Montgomery home, right, Jordan?"

The boy with the buzz cut sat up from where he had passed out on the couch.

"What? No!" Maddy said, alarmed. "I'm going to walk."

"*No no no*, we totally got you," Jordan slurred. "There's a killer on the loose; we can't let you just walk around." He laughed, as if he had made a joke.

"I think she's right, man," Ethan said diplomatically. "And besides, should you two really be driving? I'll drive her."

"Dude, I told you we got this!" Simon said. "Just let me get my keys." He stumbled into the kitchen. Jordan tried to follow and tripped over something. Maddy turned back to Ethan.

"Look, I'm going to go before this gets any messier," she said. "Really, I'll be fine walking home. Thanks, Ethan, for having me, and again, I'm—"

"No more apologies," he said, and pulled her into a quick hug, speaking into her hair. "I'll see you soon." Maddy hugged him back, then hurried out the door, passing Tyler coming up the walk. He gave her a dirty look, but she ignored him.

The cool ocean wind had turned blustery and biting now that the sun was down, and Maddy thought it might start raining soon. She pulled her hood up. The streetlights blinked on one by one as the night fell. She had almost made it to the end of the block when she heard the laughing and hollering behind her. It carried down the street in the otherwise quiet evening.

"*Maddy? Maddy? Where'd you go?!*" a voice called out. It sounded like Simon. Maddy paused to listen.

"*I told you I saw her leave,*" another voice said. She heard a question being asked but couldn't make out the words. She thought it was, *Where are you going?*

"*Picking up the Montgomery girl!*" Simon yelled.

Then the other voice— Jordan—answered. "*Not if I find her first! Good luck keeping up!*" Drunken laughter rolled down the street as car doors slammed and two sets of headlights cut into the dark. Maddy started walking again, more quickly this time. Her head throbbed. She wanted nothing more than to put as much distance between her and the party—between her and this night—as possible. If she could get around the corner of the block, they probably wouldn't see her.

Tires squealed behind her and light from the headlights danced down the street. *What are they doing?* Maddy thought. She hazarded a glance over her shoulder and saw the vehicles swerving back and froth, barely missing each other as they rocketed toward her.

They're *racing*, she realized with a spike of nausea in her stomach. She had to get around the corner. Breaking into a run, she headed for the corner and the light post she could safely hide behind. She could hear the snarl of the car engines gaining on her. Kevin's warning echoed in her mind, about how high school parties were dangerous, about how they were *"just dumb kids and alcohol."* What had she been thinking in coming tonight?

Maddy was so preoccupied with the drunken race behind her that she didn't even see the Range Rover approaching from the opposite direction. Apparently, the two boys didn't either. Until it was too late.

The Rover's horn roared as it swerved to avoid the oncoming vehicles, its headlights illuminating Maddy just as she reached the corner. The front tires jumped the curb right in front of where she was standing, stock-still and frozen with panic. For a split second she saw herself in the reflection of the SUV's windshield, her face transformed into a mask of surprise and horror, before she was thrown back by the force of the impact.

Maddy was hit hard.

There was almost no pain as her bones snapped and her internal organs exploded. She didn't even hear herself scream as the Range Rover crushed her fragile body against the light pole.

The vehicle's front crumpled around her as it heaved to one side, then the other, and, finally, came to rest.

It was strangely peaceful afterward, lying with her face resting on the warm hood of the car. Maddy could feel her body surrendering her life, and there was a kind of sublime peace to it. A release. She could feel the breeze playing with the ends of her hair. Somewhere far away, a voice was yelling. It sounded like that boy, Simon, but it was getting farther away now. The world receded. Maddy thought of Uncle Kevin, and Gwen, and Ethan. As her eyesight dimmed, she thought of Jacks. The first few raindrops of an autumn storm pattered on her cheek. Then everything went dark.

CHAPTER TWENTY-TWO

News choppers swarmed overhead, looking down with their telescopic eyes at the thousands of tourists and fans crowding the boulevard below. Traffic in the city had come to a standstill for what was always the event of the year in the Immortal City—the annual Commissioning and the reveal of the Protections. But the mania rose to fever pitch specifically for what was being called the "event of the century"—the Commissioning of Jackson Godspeed.

The preparation had begun before daybreak, with crews bolting together rows of bleachers, laying down hundreds of feet of red carpet, and setting up giant marble sculptures of Divine Rings at the entrance to the Temple of Angels. Teenage girls were camped out along the barricades, where they had slept for days. And, seemingly everywhere, there was security. Crews from A!, ANN, and *Angels Weekly* laid cable, set up cameras, and double-checked their satellite linkups. The feeds would be going live all over the world.

As dawn broke, the city was gripped with excitement, a strange combination of both festivity and fear. The media coverage was nonstop, alternating between Jackson's Commissioning and the Angel murders. The atmosphere inside coffee shops and restaurants was celebratory despite the dark news about the Angel disappearances. Commissioning was always the biggest unofficial holiday of the year, and the scandal around the unprecedented murders only added to the thrill. Many stores around Angel City had shut early, with hastily written signs in doorways reading Closed for Commissioning. By the time the shadows had grown long on the letters of the Angel City sign, the crowds at the Temple of Angels were roaring. They stomped their feet and chanted, waving signs that read PICK ME! and SAVE ME, JACKS! The news choppers had arrived shortly thereafter, eager to capture every possible angle of the story of the decade, or century.

Tara Reeves looked striking in a low-cut silver gown as she covered the lead-up from her exclusive A! stage at the start of the carpet.

"The fans have descended on the Temple of Angels, the red carpet has been rolled out, and the cameras have been turned on as the moment we have all been waiting for has finally arrived. That's right, it's the Commissioning of Jackson Godspeed and his nineteen other fellow nominated Guardian Angels! The guest list is elite. The most famous Angels in history are here tonight, along with the hottest Angel men and their lovely lady Angels. The mayor, the governor, congressmen and senators, luminaries of business and the arts have all been scrambling for tickets, looking for their chance to mix with the flawless Immortals. Stay with us as we bring you the Commissioning, live!"

On the Angel Boulevard sidewalk, a black cover was neatly laid over the section where Jackson's and the other Angels' stars would be unveiled. ANN threw their coverage to a special investigator who was kneeling at the sight of Jacks's star. The network was doing a special story there. The reporter spoke into the camera.

"That's right, Jamie, there is a lone black cloud on this seemingly perfect

day of happiness. The ongoing investigation into what the press has dubbed 'The Angel of Death.' There was some talk that these stars would not be revealed today on account of the investigation into the reported Angel murders. A theory surfaced this morning that the Angels have been disappearing based on the order of their stars—and Jackson Godspeed's would be next. But I'm happy to report that the ACPD feels like it has the investigation well in hand and that all the stars will be unveiled as scheduled. Still, security has never been so extensive. With the city teetering in fear around the potential Angel serial killer, along with repeated threats from the Humanity Defense Front, the Angels are taking absolutely no risks. Security personnel are everywhere, setting up checkpoints and ensuring the safety of all involved. Back to you on the red carpet, Jamie!"

The Angels began emerging on the carpet, taking pictures and giving interviews, each Angel more spectacular than the last. The crowd was whipped into a new frenzy as the most popular Angels began to step out. On the carpet, correspondents maneuvered for the best Angels—of course having agreed not to bring up questions surrounding the Angel murder investigation on this happy occasion of Commissioning.

"Mitch Steeple, ladies and gentlemen!" ANN's Jamie Campbell said as Mitch, looking handsome in a Versace pin-striped fitted suit, waved to the crowd. "A close friend of Jackson, as everyone knows, I'm hearing whispers that you're already a lock for next year's Commissioning. How does that make you feel?"

"You know, it's an honor," Mitch said. "But it's not about me tonight, and it's not even about Jacks or the other nominees." He paused, as if trying to remember something. "A lot of people might not realize it, but being a Guardian, it's not about the fame and fortune, it's about the people we protect. It's about the lives we're going to change."

Jamie nodded, already looking for the next Angel.

"Chloe Godspeed," a reporter for Access Angels announced over shrieks of girls in the bleachers. "Here she is stepping out for her first Commissioning by herself, is that right?"

"Yeah, well, last year I had to come with my dad," Chloe said. "And he kept stepping on my dress. So I didn't want that to happen again."

"And speaking of, this is a *mature* dress. There's been some controversy lately about your fashion choices being, how do we say, somewhat revealing for a young Angel, especially showing your Immortal Marks."

Chloe leaned into the microphone. "I think an Angel's body is a thing of beauty, and we should celebrate it, not hide it. I know everyone fell in love with me when I was young, but I'm growing up now and I just want to express myself," she said, and then smiled sweetly.

The sound was deafening as Vivian stepped onto the carpet. "Vivian Holycross, you look beyond stunning tonight, beyond ravishing," Tara Reeves gushed. "I just, I have no words. Let's get a shot of the dress, guys." The A! camera zoomed out, taking in the red, backless Marchesa gown. "And to think, I ran into you during New York fashion week, and you still hadn't decided what to wear!" Tara exclaimed.

"Thank you, Tara." Vivian smiled gracefully. "You're always so kind. I'm just here to support Jacks the way I always have, and the way I always will. He's a great Angel and he'll be an amazing Guardian. The world is in good hands with him." Vivian waved to her fans, setting off another explosion of screams.

"And speaking of," Tara said, "my producers tell me Jackson is arriving right now with the other nominees!"

The bleachers rocked with the screams of "Jacksaddicts," and the whole world seemed to tremble as Jackson Godspeed emerged onto the scene. Cameras flashed madly, gobbling up the full force of his charm. The other Angel nominees emerged behind him, smiling and waving, fully aware that this Godspeed, the brilliant Angel about to become the youngest Guardian ever, was also the greatest thunder-stealer of all time. Jacks wore a perfectly cut Armani tuxedo, a straight black tie, and a close shave. His blue eyes shone like beams. Darcy appeared instantly beside him, directing the press and photographers like a general at war.

"Jackson Godspeed . . ." Tara shook her head and steadied herself. "Ladies, have you ever seen such a dream come true? Congratulations on the nomination and tell me, Jacks, how does it feel to be here tonight?"

Jacks felt like his polite smile had been glued on his face. "Oh, this is really exciting. It's just a great vote of confidence from the Angel community." Tara hung on every word.

Jacks looked around at the adoring crowds, the hungry reporters, the cascades of flashes from cameras, and he remembered Mark's words the night before. With the story of the murders now out, the whole world was speculating on whether he was a target. He wouldn't allow them to cast him as the victim. He'd show no fear. He was finally going to be a Guardian. He was Jackson Godspeed.

Jacks smiled more widely, drawing a blush from Tara.

"And will you speculate for us on your first Protections? Everyone is on the edge of their seat for your first save!"

"I really have no idea," he protested, laughing.

"And, now I have to ask, the girl you brought to your Pre-Commissioning party, she isn't accompanying you tonight?"

Jacks paused, his expression becoming unreadable. He glanced at Darcy, who stared fiercely back.

"The . . . contest winner?" he said awkwardly.

"Some are calling it a publicity stunt before your Commissioning tonight; what do you have to say to that?"

"I always do my best to give back," Jacks said. He turned and waved to the bleachers, setting off a hysteric roar of adulation.

"Jacks, I hear they unveiled your action figure today," Tara said. Jacks nodded.

"That's right," he said, smiling. "It's a little crazy, but it's great. I'm happy to be buried in the dirt, and stuck up noses, and floating in the bathtub. I'll take that job."

Darcy cut the interview short as the carpet had thinned, the other nominees having finished their interviews and gone in. The start of the ceremony was quickly approaching. Before turning and entering the Temple itself, Jacks gave a final wave to his adoring fans, who screamed and shouted for him in the deepening twilight. He gazed up at the Latin words over the door as he walked beneath them.

Do your duty.

Once inside, Jacks was conducted by temple personnel past nineteen identical doors to his own room, where a stylist waited with his ceremonial dress. It was the official uniform of a Guardian, going back hundreds of years, and for once, Jacks would look like the classic Angel of Renaissance paintings. He put on the white tunic and slipped the long white robes over his head. He felt the silken fabric against his skin as the weight of it came to rest on his shoulders. The stylist made final adjustments, then turned Jacks toward a mirror in the corner of the room. Jacks looked at himself for a long moment. The robes hung straight from his body and seemed to wrap his face in a bright, white glow. He looked celestial. A symbol of perfection and purity and good. It was the uniform he had dreamed of wearing his whole life.

There was a knock at the door. Jacks opened it to see Kris standing there. She looked at her son without speaking, then, wiping a tear away, came into the room and took out a gold sash with the Godspeed crest on it. She draped it around his neck.

"This was your father's crest. He wore it on his Commissioning day, many years ago." She took a step back and looked at him again.

"You look so much like your father, Jacks. He would have been so proud of you." Jacks's heart was swelling unbearably. She wiped her face and smiled bravely. "You've earned this."

"He certainly has."

Jacks turned. Mark was at the door. Jackson eyed him warily, thinking back to what he thought he had seen on his stepfather's jacket the night before. This was *Archangel Mark Godspeed*. Angels were the most important thing in the world to him. How could Jacks even *consider* Mark would be involved with the murders? There obviously had to be another explanation for what Jacks only thought he had seen.

His stepfather had changed clothes as well and wore the ceremonial red robes of an Archangel. He regarded Jacks sternly. "I just wanted to say good luck before we get out there." Then his expression softened; the slightest hint of a smile crept into his eyes. "Jacks," he said, "I know it's been a tough week, it's been a tough week for all of us. But I just want you to know"—he paused, looking at his stepson—"that I am proud of you. So proud." Then he gave Jacks a smile so genuine and pleased that Jacks felt an unexpected warmth radiate through him. Mark turned to go.

"Dad?" Jacks said impulsively.

Mark turned.

"There's no need for luck when there are Angels in the world."

Mark's smile widened. "I'll see you out there," he said, and was gone. After a good luck kiss Kris followed, and Jacks was left alone in the room again. Things were getting back to normal, he thought. The way they should be. The way they were meant to be. He looked at himself in the mirror one last time. His father's crest hung handsomely on him. He found it hard to suppress a smile. Then a man wearing a headset appeared in the doorway and motioned for him to follow.

Jacks was led down a backstage hallway snaked with cables and positioned behind a door at the back of the auditorium, where the other nominated Angels were already waiting. They were being formed into a line. The Churchson siblings were near the front, standing side by side. Jacks looked sidelong at Sierra as he passed, his thoughts moving back to what she had said the night before about his star. Had she known about the killer? How could she have already? It hadn't become public knowledge until this morning. His mind began tracking rapidly, but he was brought back to the present by a hand on his shoulder.

"We have an order. So you're standing here, Jacks," the man in the headset said, putting Jacks at the end of the line. Steven glared back at Jackson, who looked away uncomfortably.

Through the door he could hear the murmurs of the crowd as they waited patiently for the commercial break to end. The ceremony, of course, was being watched live all over the world and so had to work within the confines of the television broadcast. Finally, Jacks heard the disembodied female voice through the door. She announced grandly,

"*Ladies, gentlemen, and Angels, welcome to the 102nd annual National Angel Services Guardian Commissioning. And now, please welcome the nominees for Guardianship.*"

Right on cue the door opened, the music swelled, and the twenty nominated Angels began walking into the Temple, single file. The female voice announced each name as they emerged into the grand auditorium.

"*Jackson Godspeed.*" At this, cheers erupted, almost overpowering the announcer.

Jacks stepped forward, the last of the Angels. He had been in the Temple many times before, but he couldn't help feeling a stir of excitement as he walked down the aisle, surrounded by applause. He looked around the massive main hall with its double row of columns that led toward the altar on a raised stage. This had once been a sanctuary but had long since been converted to a modern theater with state-of-the-art lighting and sound. Two huge screens on either side of the stage magnified his dramatic entrance.

To his right and left, every last seat was packed with the most famous Angels, prestigious politicians, and richest potential Protections. An eager, expectant energy mixed with the applause and cheers that filled the enormous room. Everyone seemed to be waiting for the envelopes to be opened and the names of the Protections to be read. Jacks's gaze flickered to a row of familiar faces in the seats. There they sat, the Angels he had known his entire life. Kris and Chloe. Mitch gave him a subtle thumbs-up. Vivian was there too, and her parents. With the swelling music, the cheers and excitement of the crowd, and the glittering Temple, Jacks found it impossible to ignore the happiness burning inside him. Over the past few days had he forgotten what it meant to be a Guardian? Had he forgotten what he'd worked so hard for? As he felt the exhilaration of the moment, he knew, without a doubt, this was where he belonged.

Jacks followed the other nominees, ascending the steps to the stage. On the platform stood an exquisite altar of red and gold, to the side of which stood four rows of five chairs, one for each nominee. On the walls above the stage, towering stained glass windows told the story of Angels on Earth: from their hidden beginnings, to the Great Awakening, to a Guardian flying grandly over the Angel City sign. Jacks reached the altar and stopped. He gazed down. Sitting on a red satin cloth were the twenty Divine Rings. One of them was *his* Divine Ring. Next to the rings sat a small stack of envelopes. And inside each of the envelopes, Jacks knew, was a list of names. The Protections.

For some reason, Maddy's voice flashed across his mind: *"Why don't you get to choose who you're going to protect?"* He banished the memory and took his seat.

The music ended with a flourish and there was a moment of charged silence. Then the disembodied voice came over the speakers again.

"And now, please welcome the NAS Archangels."

The music swelled again. Applause filled the Temple as a group of Archangels in red robes entered from behind the stage and took their seats in the first two rows of the audience. Jacks looked down at some of the most famous Angels of all time. Mark was, of course, with them. His stepfather's face was drawn and serious, but his eyes glimmered with that same hint of a smile.

Once the music and applause had quieted again, the lights dimmed in the auditorium and the enormous screens flickered to a dramatic title in bold type: THE NEXT GENERATION OF GUARDIANS. Each of the other nominees had a brief clip, showing their faces as they smiled at the camera and then a quick shot of them in action, no more than ten seconds each. Jacks was notably absence from the footage . . . and he began to feel vaguely anxious. He could guess what was coming.

After this series of quick clips, the music swelled and a huge title arose: THE JACKSON GODSPEED PHENOMENON. A few of the other nominees shifted in their seat irritably. Jacks felt his cheeks growing hot, but he kept a composed look on his face. Mark's words from last night rang in his head and now that he knew that his meteoric rise had been the Archangels' plan all along, attention that wouldn't have fazed him a week ago made him feel exquisitely uncomfortable. A lengthy montage played, showing Jacks through his youth, achieving at school, and spending quality time with Mark and Kris. Footage of an eight-year-old Jacks making a funny face into the camera sent a ripple of good-natured laughter through the theater. Then the images changed to the beginnings of the Jackson Godspeed hysteria, from the first few magazine covers, to photo shoots, television interviews, and crowds of screaming girls on the streets. His famous luminescent wings featured prominently in a lot of the shots, leaving no doubt that it was Jacks in action. A shot of Jackson taking Kris as his date on a red carpet elicited *ahhhh*s from every woman in the audience. Finally the montage finished with a dramatic shot of Jackson flying through the sky. Then, almost as an afterthought: THE NOMINEES. Applause filled the auditorium.

The screens went black, and then an image slowly appeared. Twelve figures sat in a semicircle in what looked like a small chapel. It was the Council of Twelve True Immortals, the original Angels to bring the Angel services public, begin Angel families, and found the NAS. They were watching the Commissioning from another location. They rarely, if ever, were seen in public anymore. On-screen, the Council's faces remained hidden in the deep shadows of the gorgeous chapel. One of the True Immortals stood up and stepped to where a light shone down. His face resolved from the darkness. It was Gabriel. He wore a golden robe that seemed to glow all on its own. He was tall and handsome, with a shock of white hair and sharp, piercing features. Gabriel had looked like this for as long as any Angel could remember.

"You, young Angels, have our blessing," he said simply, his voice booming through the loudspeakers and into the Temple.

The crowd began applauding. On-screen Gabriel returned to his seat in the shadows with the rest of the Council. The screens faded to black again. The lights went up and the applause quieted as Mark rose from his seat and ascended the stairs to the stage, approaching the altar and the microphone on a slim stand. Mark adjusted it and stole a look at Jacks before beginning.

"Before us is the next class of Guardians, those who are about to swear their lives and Immortal abilities to serve their Protections under the NAS. Each one of them has fulfilled their training and proved ready to take on this greatest of responsibilities: that of another's life."

Mark began calling each of the other nominees up one by one, swearing them in as Guardians and presenting them with their Divine Rings. Jackson sat in wait, knowing he probably would be last. He was surprised to find his pulse beginning to beat harder as they reached the end: he was nervous. Mark's voice seemed to be in a distant tunnel as he called each of the remaining Angels up, including Steven and Sierra. At last all the other Angels had been announced, received their rings, and sat down again.

Mark turned to Jacks.

"This is the best and the brightest we have to offer. Jackson Godspeed represents the best in us. He is not only one of the most talented and powerful Angels, but is an Angel *dedicated* to the ideals of the Council and the NAS." The Archangels in the front rows nodded in approval. "Step up here, please."

Jacks stood and walked toward his stepfather. Everyone in the Temple seemed to hold their breath in delicious anticipation as he stepped to the altar to be Commissioned at long last. His footfalls echoed in the suddenly silent auditorium.

"Jackson Godspeed," Mark began, "do you offer yourself in the service of mankind?"

Jacks looked into Mark's eyes. He knew the vows by heart.

"I do," he said.

"Do you swear to keep safe, at all times, those under your protection?"

"I do," Jacks said.

"Do you take this burden of your own free will, to do this good work on this Earth?"

"I do."

Mark picked up the ring and slipped it on Jacks's finger. "I commission you Guardian Jackson, of the Godspeed Class."

Jacks could feel the weight of it. He looked down and watched it glimmer on his finger. It was all he had ever wanted. The ring of a Guardian. The ring of a hero. A close-up of the ring on his finger towered, sparkling, on the two screens behind them. In a moment Mark would read the names of the Protections, and Jacks's destiny would finally begin.

"Congratulations, Jackson," Mark said. "Turn and be recognized."

Jacks didn't move.

He stood very still. His mind had suddenly been transported far away from his stepfather before him, from the other new Guardians, from the crowd, from the Commissioning. His face blanched white. His eyes became unseeing and distant.

"Jackson?" Mark said, his face darkening in concern.

The entire Temple sat in charged silence, waiting.

"Jacks?" Kris said, getting up from her chair.

What occurred next happened so quickly it could not be seen. The glass in the windows of the Temple rippled like water—like a wave moving from the front of the hall to the back—and then exploded. Stained glass rained down on the crowd like multicolored diamonds as the doors to the temple were blown open. Wind howled down the aisle, vicious and twisting like jet wash. The crowd outside fell to the ground, some of them covering their ears in pain.

Mark looked up from the floor of the stage, where he had been knocked over.

Jacks had flown out of the Temple and was gone.

CHAPTER TWENTY-THREE

Maddy's eyes snapped open. Her head spun, throbbing with an unknown pain. Stumbling backward, she felt something hard and cold cut into her back. She reached behind her and felt its smooth surface.

The light pole.

In front of her shone the headlights of two approaching cars. Where was she? And what was happening? Fragments of memories swirled in her mind. The party. Talking with Ethan. And *kissing* him? Had that really happened? Then there was some boy named Simon, and . . .

"They're . . . racing," she whispered to herself. It wasn't a statement of fact so much as the recollection of a memory. Like trying to piece together the remnants of a fleeting dream. The headlights grew closer. The cars swerved. She thought she could hear someone laughing.

What the hell is going on?

She forced her mind to function. She had left the party, she had been walking home, and—

A single, terrifying idea rapidly emerged, slicing through all the other muddled thoughts like a shriek.

The Range Rover.

It all came back in a rush. The impact, the sound of her bones breaking, the way the SUV's grill felt as it embedded itself inside her. It was all too real to be imagined, too horrific to be make-believe. There was only one possible explanation.

She'd had another premonition. The grisly vision was the most intense she had ever experienced. Because it was her own.

Watching the headlights bear down on her, Maddy suddenly knew one thing more absolutely and completely than she had known anything in her entire life: she had just foreseen her own death. And unless she did something in the next second to change the outcome of events, she was, without any doubt, going to die.

Light blazed at her, but from the other direction now. She snapped her head around and saw the headlights of the Range Rover. There it was, like the carriage of death itself. Like the reaper's coach. The SUV's horn roared, and she watched helplessly as it swerved in her direction and the tires jumped the curb. With almost detached clarity, Maddy knew it was already too late. It was over for her, and there was nothing left to do but watch it happen. Once again she saw her reflection in the windshield, but this time her face wasn't surprised, or even horror stricken. It was strangely calm. Peaceful even. She closed her eyes and waited for the impact.

She was hit hard.

Pain shot through her body, but not from the direction she was expecting. Whatever struck her didn't feel like the grill of the SUV. What it felt like simply didn't seem possible.

It felt like a hand.

The next thing Maddy knew, she was lying on the pavement looking sideways across the road as the Range Rover plunged into the light pole. The scream of collapsing metal filled the air as the hood exploded, sending deadly pieces of car and windshield tearing through the night. The back end of the Rover jumped off the pavement, fishtailed around, and sailed in her direction.

"No," commanded a voice above her. *A voice?* There was a sound like a hole hammered straight through the night, a flash of all-encompassing white light, and then, silence. When Maddy opened her eyes, what she saw was beyond anything she could have possibly imagined.

The world had frozen.

Everything had just *stopped*. It was as if Maddy had been watching a movie of her death and had simply pressed pause. The Range Rover hovered in front of her with its back end off the ground like some kind of automotive ballerina. Pieces of exploded hood and windshield swam like a sea of destruction all around her. Shards of broken glass hung like twinkling stars. The world held its breath, poised on the knife tip of time, and waited.

Maddy lifted her gaze. In the hard cast of the streetlamp she thought she could make out the silhouette of a figure crouched over her, shielding her with his body, holding onto her hand. Pain was radiating through her now, dimming her already reeling consciousness. She felt her eyes start to close again, but just before they did, she looked at the silhouette and thought she could make out the distinctive outline of *wings*.

She went into shock. Everything went black.

Maddy didn't know if she was alive, dead, or simply dreaming. She had the vague sense she was flying; the wind and the cold on her face were almost unbearable. A jumble of strange, inexplicable images swirled in her head like pieces of a nightmare. Charging headlights and distorted screams, a floating car and a mysterious, shadowy figure. She didn't know if it was real or imagined. About the only thing she was sure of was the pain. A terrible ache throbbed in her lower back, and there was an intense burning in her left shoulder. In the murky neverland of her semiconsciousness, Maddy tried to find something real to hold on to. She forced her eyes to open and focus.

She saw wings. She watched the way the raindrops hit them and beaded instantly off, the lightly glowing wings staying dry. Whatever kind of hallucination she was having, it was undeniably vivid. Then the cold numbed her mind into unconsciousness, and she blacked out again.

The next time Maddy opened her eyes, she found herself sitting with her back against some kind of concrete wall. It was raining, the smell of it everywhere, and she listened to its steady patter on a canvas awning over her head. Not ten feet beyond her shoes the floor ended, and the lights of Angel City glowed in the soggy night. She had to be sitting on the roof of a tall building. She looked up and saw the words *DIVINE RECORDS* glowing on a huge curving sign. Above that, a white spike reached up thirty feet up into the air and pierced the churning sky.

She tried to sit up, and only then did she become aware of the heavy arms wrapped around her. They were so hot they were almost searing. She turned and her eyes traced the contours of a perfect, dripping face. She saw his pale blue eyes.

"How do you feel?" Jackson asked.

It was impossible. He was sitting there with her, drenched, and what remained of a white robe hung in tatters over his body. She must still be hallucinating. Or perhaps she was dreaming. Maybe her mind had escaped her death and taken her here, to some kind of fantasy? She was sure she wasn't experiencing reality, but then again, she could feel the intense heat of his embrace. She could feel the heave of his chest through her wet clothes. Most inescapable of all, she could sense his distinct presence. She was getting to know it now, like the scent of a familiar person. It was undeniably *him*.

Maddy realized the Angel was looking at her intently, waiting for her to say something.

"What?" Maddy croaked.

"I said, how do you feel?"

"I . . . hurt," Maddy said, realizing it as much as saying it.

"I know, I'm sorry," Jacks said gruffly. "I didn't have much time and there wasn't any other way. You hit the ground pretty hard."

"What . . . am I doing here?" she said weakly. "What . . . happened?"

"You were almost in a very bad accident. But you're safe now."

"An . . . accident?" The memories flooded back. For several seconds she was seized by panic as the sequence of events rushed upon her.

"It came out of nowhere. It came right at me!" she said, suddenly panicked. "It all happened so fast . . . I tried to get out of the way—"

"You wouldn't have made it," Jacks said quietly. His tone was absolute. "It would have crushed you."

Maddy felt adrenaline rush into her system. Mortal fear rose in her throat like bile. He was *right*. She *knew* she was going to die. She had foreseen it. She had closed her eyes, waited for the impact, and . . . she remembered waiting for the collision of the SUV's grill with her body and instead being knocked sideways and out of the way. Or *pulled* sideways, she realized. She felt pain in her shoulder flare angrily. It must have been *him* standing over her, protecting her. The reason she was alive.

"What did you do?" she in a desperate whisper.

Jacks looked away from her, out to the boiling storm.

"I broke the law."

"You *what*?" she choked. "*Why?*" Somewhere in the distance, a ribbon of lightning flashed.

"For you," Jacks growled.

Maddy reeled. Had Jackson Godspeed rescued her from certain death? And after everything he had said to her at the party? And how badly he had hurt her? And humiliated her? And insulted her? Sudden, uncontrollable anger welled up, but now it was much worse than it had been at the party, because if he had really saved her life, she now *owed* him. After everything he had done and said, now she was going to have to be *grateful* to him?

"I told you to stay away from me," she said cuttingly. "What part of *leave me alone* was unclear to you?"

Jacks released her from his grip, and she immediately slid away. The cold bit through her wet clothes almost instantly.

"I should have guessed you'd be this way," he said in exasperation.

She struggled to her feet and had to lean against the concrete wall to keep from falling over. She was still dizzy. "You had no *right* to do that."

A snarl escaped Jacks's lips, startling her. In an instant he was on his feet, walking out into the pouring rain, his shoulders heaving. Then he turned and glared at her. Maddy winced at his hostile expression.

"You stubborn, impossible girl!" he yelled through the raindrops. "Why are you always like this? I save your life, and you're *angry* with me?" His blue eyes were blazing, his tone ferocious. Maddy felt her own anger evaporate in his burning gaze.

"I just, I told you to leave me alone," she said again, desperately. "Please."

"Why?" he demanded. "Why do you push me away? Am I not good enough for you?" He was stalking toward her now.

"You don't understand, Jacks," she said, the emotions twisting inside her. She walked out from under the awning and felt the rain soak into her skin.

"What don't I understand?!" he demanded.

"I *have* to stay away from you," she burst.

He stopped. "What?"

"Self-preservation!" Maddy screamed. The words rushed out of her as if some internal dam had finally broken. "Don't you get it? I have to keep myself away from you so I don't get sucked into the illusion that you might actually *like* me," she said, water dripping off her lips. "I can't let myself believe you actually have feelings for me, Jacks. If I do that, I'll wake up one day and realize that you're a famous Angel and I'm . . . I'm nobody." She felt a lump rising in her throat and swallowed it down hard. She wasn't going to let him see her cry. "My life hasn't been easy like yours, Jacks. Things like this don't happen for me. So, I've just learned it's easier to push them away."

Jacks stared, astonished, through the downpour. "You have to keep away from *me*? I have to fight to keep away from *you*. Do you have any *idea* how hard this has been for me? I meet you one night, and just like that, I can't get you out of my head. When our hands touched, and I saw this . . . streak of *beauty* in your eyes . . . I'd never felt anything like that before, nothing even *close*." He began to pace furiously, the rain flicking off him as he went. "All of a sudden, every fiber of my being is drawn to you, to be with you, and I don't know why." He stopped and pointed an accusing finger at her. "I didn't ask for this. But I felt something in that back room with you, and it's stayed with me ever since. I want to be with you. I need to be with you." His tone was both angry and helpless.

"And that's why you took me to your party, to show me how important you were, how everyone loved you, how I'd just be one more speck in a sea of girls who wanted you and your fame and your car. You did that because you wanted to 'be with me.'" All Maddy could do was scoff.

Jacks's face rippled with disbelief. "Maddy, I took you there because I wanted to show you the night of your life. I wanted you to have everything, to show everyone else you were special! If I thought you'd see it that way, I *never* would've taken you to the party. Those things aren't important to me. I just wanted to spend time with you, to make you feel as special, as alive, as you made *me* feel when we met."

"Why are you being so cruel?" Maddy said, her voice cracking. "Please, just leave me alone." She turned and walked away from him farther into the rain, her emotions twisting inside her. She didn't feel the hand on her arm until he had spun her around. Then she felt the fingers of his other hand lace into her hair, and in an instant, his wet mouth was against hers.

The kiss was raw. Hungry. She opened her mouth and his immortal breath rushed into her. He pulled her against him and kissed her again. The storm raged around them.

When their lips finally came apart, his breathing was hard and ragged. She felt the steam of his breath against her hair. Her feet touched the tops of his, and standing on him like that, she let him hold her. The downpour was steady all around them. Maddy concentrated on slowing her racing heart. She could still taste him in her mouth. She could still hear his words echoing in her head. Could she really believe him? Could he really have feelings for her?

She stepped back off his toes and looked at him. He was watching her through wet stabs of hair, scrutinizing her. Waiting. Another ribbon of lightning glowed in the sky and she saw a flash of his eyes. She felt desire welling up inside her. She wanted to kiss him again. But she didn't want to be a silly, Angelstruck girl. She took another step away and looked out into the storm, embarrassed. Jacks's face fell in frustration.

They stood there quietly, neither speaking.

"I was scared, Jacks," Maddy finally whispered. "I mean, not about what happened to me. But scared for you. The reporters . . . they said you were next. With the murders on the Walk of Angels."

Jacks nodded, gently wiping water away from her cheek with his thumb. "Well, now I have something much worse to worry about."

"What happens now?" Maddy said.

"Now they'll come for me." She looked back at him. His face had hardened.

"What?"

"The Angels." He paused. "The Council's Disciplinary Agents."

"Because you saved me?" she asked in disbelief. The idea of Angel Police flickered in her mind. What would that even look like?

"Because I saved someone who wasn't supposed to be saved. There are consequences in my world, Maddy."

"What consequences?" The lightning flashed again and this time she saw *fear* in his eyes.

"They'll take my wings," he said quietly.

"They can make you . . . they can take them?" A stab of panic hit her stomach.

"Yes," he said, his mouth a grim line. "The Archangels would never admit it officially, although somebody out there sure seems to know about it. They'll remove my wings, which will draw the immortality out of me. They'll do it slowly and make sure they do it right."

"They can't do that. You're Jackson Godspeed."

"They can. And they will. There is a system to uphold. Disciplinary Agents are hunting me as we speak." Jacks's face was miserable but resolute. "Nothing is impossible when you break the rules."

Maddy shook her head, as if the movement could somehow shake the reality away. She simply couldn't believe it. That by saving her he had actually, knowingly put himself in line for a consequence this severe. So much was kept hidden about the Angels, about how they handled their internal affairs—brutally, it turned out. All the while they put on a smooth, clean exterior for the public and the media.

"What can I do?" she said finally.

Jacks looked at her through the deluge.

"Come with me."

There he stood in the pouring rain, the image of shirtless soaked perfection. He stood before her offering her a choice just like he had the night they went flying. She was at another crossroads. She knew she could just leave. Knew she probably should. But they were going to take his wings, and it was all her fault. Her fault for going to the party, her fault for trying to follow through with her plan, her fault for leaving and insisting on walking home. Could she really leave him now? Before she had even decided, her mouth opened.

"Yes," she said. Just like when he had invited her to the party. It simply came out, as though her true desires could no longer be repressed.

Jacks smiled a dripping, radiant smile. A flash of lightning lit the roof, followed closely by a bark of thunder.

"There are Angels I know who will help us. I can't fly or the ADC will take me immediately. We need to get off this roof and lie low, travel on foot."

Maddy nodded. Her decision made, questions began pounding her mind. She pulled out her BlackBerry Miracle and tried to power it up. The screen was black and lifeless.

"Dead from the rain," Jacks said. "Mine too. They can track them anyway. Come on, let's get going."

Jacks began walking toward a door on the far end of the rooftop. Maddy lingered for a moment, thoughtful.

"How did you know?" Maddy asked.

"What?" He strained to hear her over the roar of the downpour.

"How did you know I was in trouble?" she said again. She might not follow the modern Angels, but one thing she did know from her required Angel History reading was that they never disclosed how they made their saves. They simply performed them, leaving the public to guess about their trade secrets.

Jacks's eyes searched hers. How many rules could he break in one night? "You know I'm not allowed to tell you this."

Maddy stood where she was. Something in her *needed* to know. "Do you trust me?" she asked quietly. The rain continued pounding down across the Immortal City.

After a moment, Jacks let out a long breath and spoke. "I saw it," he said simply.

She looked at him through the cascading liquid.

"What do you mean?"

"Well, I *felt* it first and then saw it. After I focused on your frequency," Jacks said. "Every person has a frequency. In Guardian training we learn how to tune to them so we can then do it for each of our Protections. We learn people's frequencies. That way we can instantly feel when something bad is about to occur and then tune in through the static of all the other human beings. It sounds more complicated than it really is."

"But with me?"

Jacks paused. "I felt your frequency that first night in the diner. How could I not?" He looked out into the night. "It's the big secret of how we always know when our Protections are in danger. Tuning to the frequencies. Otherwise it would just be random images, feelings. Like jumbled static."

Maddy's heart stopped in her chest. The world around her halted. Everything faded into the background as Jacks's words rang in her head. The Angel looked at her stunned expression.

"I know it sounds amazing, but to us it's really no big deal, like flying or anything else we train for that the NAS keeps secret. It's just one of those things. Like being double-jointed or something." He laughed.

Even soaking wet, Maddy felt every hair on her body standing on end. Jacks walked over to the roof access door and tried the handle. It was unlocked. He turned to her. Despite the rain, he could see she had gone white as a ghost.

"What is it?"

"We need to go back to my house," Maddy said. "I have to talk to my uncle." Lightning flashed right overhead, followed by a vicious crack.

"I'm sorry, Maddy, it's just too dangerous. They'll be looking for us there."

"I have to, Jacks." Her voice was growing hysterical. "I have to talk to my uncle. It's important."

"Maddy, we can't. It's out of the question," Jacks said.

"You don't understand. I'm going to my uncle's house," Maddy yelled through the storm, "and I'm going whether you come with me or not."

Then the night seemed to literally explode.

It was like a terrible firework lighting up the sky as a finger of lightning reached down and struck a power line on the hill not far away. The crack of the contact deafened Maddy's ears, leaving them ringing. A plume of blinding sparks erupted from the transmission tower, momentarily illuminating the ghostly Angel City sign, and then, like strands of Christmas lights being unplugged, the streets and neighborhoods of Angel City went dark. They blinked off one by one until Maddy and Jacks were consumed in blackness. The rain continued to splash down, washing the Immortal City's streets clean under the cover of darkness, churning filth into the overflowing gutters.

A square of light formed in the abyss as Jacks opened the roof access door, bathing them both in the dim light cast from the building's emergency power.

"Is there any way I can get you to change your mind?" he asked.

"No," Maddy said stubbornly.

"Okay." Jacks sighed. "Then let's go." He gestured to the door.

Her heart still racing, Maddy followed him out of the rain and into the cold—but dry—stairwell. She couldn't feel her feet on the metal steps as they descended. Maddy's scattered mind had focused into a single laser of a thought. It was time to find out what really happened to her mother and father. Time to find out who her parents really were.

CHAPTER TWENTY-FOUR

Sylvester sat in his darkened cubicle in the Homicide Division, bathed in the blue glow of his computer screen and the yellow cast of the emergency lighting. The storm had knocked out the power, but the backup generator at the station had kicked on almost immediately. The reduced output was running the computers and the televisions and the few dim emergency lights. The amber glow made the normally bright and sterile police station look strange and eerie. Rivulets of rain traced down the windows as the downpour continued outside.

Sylvester's cubicle was a temporary one that had been set up for him in the open-air bull pen the detectives all shared. He himself was usually downstairs in a windowless room, double-checking paperwork for other investigators or handling the occasional small property crime. It had been years since he had been invited upstairs. He hadn't had time to unpack yet. All around him were unorganized stacks of folders and still-unopened file boxes. On top of one of the boxes sat a tub of Red Vines. An indulgence.

The detective had been up at 5 a.m. that morning, investigating another pair of gruesome severed wings. Another star, another Angel—Lance Crossman, who had already been missing. Now probably dead, though they hadn't found the body yet, only his wings, which had been broken in many places, twisted and cracked. This time the killer hadn't left them on Lance's star—with the police barricades and the media coverage, there was no way he or she would have been able to do so unnoticed. Instead, they'd been securely wrapped and delivered anonymously to ACPD headquarters. The desk sergeant who'd had the misfortune of opening the package had been taken to the hospital in severe shock.

After that, Sylvester had gone down to Long Beach. Local police had fished a mutilated, bloated body out of the bay just hours before—Theodore Godson. At least the press hadn't been able to get any pictures.

Other detectives in ACPD had no leads on this case, and the Angels weren't being helpful. They'd just wanted it swept under the rug until after the Commissioning, although someone had already leaked to the press the night before that Angels were being killed. A surge of calls with supposed tips flooded the ACPD offices. Sylvester had been out interviewing potential witnesses all day and all night, trying to unearth solid intel. Or the body of this third victim. Instead all he'd been able to collect was gossip, like the fact that Ryan Templeton had had a secret cocaine problem. Not very heavenly of him.

On Sylvester's computer screen were gruesome images of the crime scenes. Disembodied wings. Glistening blood splattered over the famous stars of the Walk of Angels. He studied the images, scrutinizing them for details that he had missed. As he did, the glitz and glamour of the boulevard seemed to mix and blur with the blood and carnage in a very unsettling way.

He flipped to a prison photo of a man with an unkempt beard

and an otherworldly look in his eyes. William Beaubourg. Sylvester had interviewed the three arrested HDF members at the Tombs jail downtown, trying to figure out what they knew about the murders and Beaubourg's current whereabouts. After being released from San Quentin prison earlier this year, Beaubourg had immediately disappeared, releasing videos on the Internet that talked about the coming "War on Angels." The jailed operatives seemed to hint to Sylvester that the HDF was behind the Angel murders. But were they just trying to gain notoriety for their cause? Sylvester was unable to piece together what Angel would be helping the HDF. But he couldn't rule them out.

And then there was Mark. Sylvester was still hunting for hard evidence—all the dots weren't connecting to point to Mark Godspeed as the culprit. But Sylvester's gut told him that the Archangel was somehow involved. The detective had already cleared Jackson. His alibi had entirely held up, and he had been seen in public during the time at which forensics figured Templeton was murdered. Plus Sylvester's long-honed intuition told him the Godspeed kid was clean. Unlike most of the Immortal City.

But Mark: the way he had almost totally discounted Sylvester's findings, even basically threatening to discredit the detective. How he merely wanted to cover up the murders, not help with the investigation. Was he going for a strange power play among the Archangels? Was managing this panic somehow going to allow him to consolidate control? Sylvester thought back to Mark's actions almost twenty years before. With those actions in mind, Sylvester would put nothing beyond him. There was no way he could be trusted.

Sylvester flipped through more files, rubbing his burning eyes. He leafed through a stack of reports Garcia had gathered from locals living near the crime scenes. Anybody who thought they had seen something strange had been interviewed. Most were nothing of interest, just fancies of worried people, but he took the time to scan through them anyway. One of the reports he stopped on was from a homeless man who had been sleeping in a doorway next to Theodore Godson's star on the night of the first incident. The report was several pages long and appeared to be nothing more than the rant of a drunk or a drug addict. Sylvester groaned, pulling the report out of the stack and setting it aside.

Then he stopped. Something on the page had caught his eye. He looked at Garcia's neat handwriting. There was that word again.

Beast.

He began reading. The man described seeing a *black, shimmering beast* on the boulevard that night *that had seven heads* and *horrible, twisted horns.* But then again the man went on to say the beast looked nothing like the alien spaceship he had seen the previous week. Sylvester sat back in his chair and thought. The witness was clearly unreliable, but the *description* was familiar to him. And specific. The man had counted *seven heads.*

He felt a sudden surge of adrenaline as his mind made the connection. He slid the tub of Red Vines off the file box and dug around until he found what he was looking for. His King James Bible. He flipped the book open, paged through to Revelation, and started to read.

It took him only a minute to find it. Revelation 13:1. He read it twice to himself to be sure:

And I stood upon the sand of the sea, and saw a beast rise up out of the sea, having seven heads and ten horns, and upon his horns ten crowns, and upon his heads the name of blasphemy.

A *beast,* he thought. He sifted through the reports again, reading them with new eyes. He picked out key phrases from the interviews, *felt a strange presence at night,* and *sinking feeling of terror in the dark.* They weren't just worried. They were feeling something. Sensing that something was wrong. He was convinced. Something as old as time itself, something terrible and forgotten—a myth—was in fact real. And it was loose in the city. His intuition had been right the whole time. He couldn't prove it, but he knew it as surely as he knew anything. He reached back into the file box and rifled around again until he pulled out a small, ornamental box made of brass. The outside had a series of engravings between small jewels inset in the metal. He looked at it and took a deep breath.

Suddenly a voice from behind startled him.

"Sir?"

He turned to see Garcia.

"What is it?"

"You better come see this," the sergeant said.

"Jackson Godspeed flying out of his Commissioning? I heard. But I've ruled him out already."

"You'll want to see this anyway." Garcia's expression was grave. Sylvester set the box carefully on the desk in front of him and rose out of his chair.

They walked down the hall together, their bodies throwing long shadows in the amber glow of the emergency lights. Garcia led him to the TV in the waiting room, where several people had already gathered to watch the ANN special report. A serious-looking anchor was announcing the breaking news.

"Angel City police officials won't comment at this time," he said, *"but in what may turn out to be the story of the year, Jackson Godspeed has been linked to the series of gruesome Angel attacks on the boulevard this week. And amid the outcry in Angel City, Senator-elect Ted Linden has called for special hearings on Capitol Hill around what he calls the 'Angel Question.'"*

Sylvester turned to Garcia.

"Jackson? Who did this?"

"Wasn't me," the sergeant said. "And it wasn't anyone on our team, either. I checked."

Sylvester turned and walked quickly back down the hall. Passing his station in the bull pen, he walked back toward the offices and burst into Captain Keele's office without knocking. The captain, who was signing some paperwork, barely raised an eye as Sylvester came in.

"Oh good, David, we were just about to have you join us." He motioned with his pen behind Sylvester. "These gentlemen are here from the NAS. From the Council's Disciplinary Department, I'm sure you're . . . familiar with it?"

Sylvester looked behind Keele. He could just make out the outline of two large figures in the darkened office. They seemed imposing, ominous. He couldn't see their faces. He turned back to the captain.

"Sir, Jackson Godspeed has nothing to do with this. That is a totally unrelated situation."

"You yourself had him questioned—"

"And quickly ruled him out."

The captain regarded Sylvester patiently.

"They seem to think otherwise, Detective. They say they have good reason to suspect him, and I'm inclined to believe them. I think they have more experience in these matters, wouldn't you agree?"

Sylvester looked at the captain in disbelief.

"Then show me the evidence," he countered. "They can sit down with me at my desk and show me what they've found. If I think it's relevant to the case, I'll share what we know from the crime scenes."

Captain Keele leaned forward in his chair, the leather chirping.

"David, how long have we known each other?"

"A long time, sir."

"Good. Then you can trust me when I tell you to just leave this one be," he said. "Let this go."

Sylvester was furious.

"This is my investigation—"

"Actually, it's not," the captain said, his voice turning impatient. "The chief and I are handing the investigation over to the NAS. They're simply more experienced and better prepared to handle this sort of thing than we are. The department will, of course, still be involved, but in an auxiliary capacity. You'll be providing them with any assistance they need, and they will be making the decisions. Understood?"

Sylvester glanced at the two shadowy figures again. They had not moved since he entered.

"These orders didn't happen to come directly from Mark Godspeed, did they?" Sylvester asked.

The captain looked down at his desk.

"Sir, whatever's doing this is extremely powerful, and extremely dangerous," Sylvester said. "Something terrible is out there, something from another world, and I'm getting closer to finding it. This investigation is too important to be used as a public relations stunt for the NAS. In fact, there is reason to believe high-standing members of the Archangels might be involved in this violence."

The captain's gaze flickered briefly to the agents standing in the back. His expression was almost embarrassed.

"David, I think I made a mistake when I pulled you off your light duties. I can see now that you're not emotionally equipped to handle something like this at present. Starting Monday, you'll resume your work downstairs. Now I want you to go home and get some sleep. You look like you need it. That's all."

Sylvester turned without saying anything and left the office.

He walked slowly back down the hall to his temporary cubicle and sat. His computer monitor had clicked over to a colorful screen saver. He removed his glasses and polished them.

After a moment Garcia appeared from the hall again.

"I heard," he said.

"Go home, Bill," Sylvester said. "Your wife and daughter haven't seen you for days." Garcia looked regretful, but nodded in assent.

"For what it's worth, sir, you did a hell of a good job on this one."

Sylvester looked up.

"You proved a lot of people wrong, sir, including me." Garcia hesitated a moment longer, then turned and shuffled away down the hall.

Just as he was getting closer to the truth, the NAS was pulling him off the case. *Mark Godspeed* was pulling him off the case.

Sylvester sat back in his chair and stared at the small box he had set on his desk. A minute passed. Then two. Suddenly he sat forward and began scooping up files and papers and stuffing them into his satchel. He threw in his Bible, along with a handful of Red Vines from the tub. Then he picked up the small box again, opened the lid, and looked inside. Appearing satisfied at what he saw, the detective snapped it closed and put it in his pocket. Standing, he pulled on his overcoat from the wobbly rack in the corner and prepared to face the weather outside.

It was going to be a long night, and he had work to do.

CHAPTER TWENTY-FIVE

Jacks kept a watchful eye on the sky as they worked their way across the city, using side streets to avoid Angel Boulevard, then cutting up north toward Maddy's house. The power outage, if anything, had worked to their advantage. Inky blackness covered all of Angel City. It was much easier to go unnoticed in the dark. Twice Jacks had pulled them into alleys to wait as helicopters passed overhead.

By the time they arrived at the house, rainwater had soaked through Maddy's shoes and socks. She was shivering. They stayed out of sight and worked their way around to the kitchen window. Maddy peered in. There was Kevin, face drawn with concern, lighting candles and placing them around the house. The beginnings of a fire crackled in the fireplace. Maddy felt a lump rise in her throat.

"Is he alone?" Jacks whispered.

"I think so."

Jacks touched her shoulder, and she turned to him.

"Maddy, are you sure we have to do this?" His tone was uneasy. "It's dangerous."

"Yes," she said simply.

Jacks nodded reluctantly. "Okay, let's give it a try, then."

They slipped around to the front porch and Maddy knocked quietly at the door. Kevin came at once. He was wearing his plaid robe over an undershirt and slippers. Maddy did her best to still her shaking body. The raindrops clung to her hair.

"Hi, Kevin," she said.

"Maddy," he breathed. "Thank God. Come in out of the rain."

He pushed the door open and saw the world's most famous Angel standing on his doorstep. Anger flickered in his eyes, but not surprise. There was something else, too. A kind of deep tension Maddy had never seen in her uncle before.

Kevin looked from the Immortal to his soaked niece and back again.

"You too, young man," he said finally.

Once they were inside, Kevin pulled Maddy quickly into an embrace. She couldn't remember the last time they had hugged like that. Jacks waited quietly, seeming to sense the rarity of the moment.

"I was so worried," Kevin began to growl, anger edging the relief in his voice. "Are you okay? They said that—"

"I'm fine, Kevin," Maddy said. "I want you to meet—"

"I know who this is," Kevin said. His tone wasn't unkind. But it wasn't warm either. He didn't offer his hand. With everything that had happened, Maddy hadn't had much time to think about how her uncle would react. She watched nervously as Jacks smiled and said hello.

"You'll want to get out of those wet clothes and get dry," Kevin said. Then he turned to Jacks. "I think I have something that will fit you too. Why don't you come with me?"

Maddy went upstairs to her room, peeled out of her sodden clothes, and showered. There was still hot water in the lines and it burned painfully—and wonderfully—against her cold skin. She thought about Jacks's words on the rooftop again. And the kiss. Could he actually be telling the truth? Was it possible he had *feelings* for her? She had never allowed herself the thought, and now she tested it delicately. It felt . . . wonderful. That's what she was afraid of. It felt too good to be true.

When she got out, she lit a candle and took stock of her injuries in the mirror. She had a deep bruise forming on the shoulder where Jacks had shoved her, and she also had a raised discoloration under her shoulder blades that was tender to the touch. She must have hit the light pole harder than she thought. She dried off, put on clean jeans and a dry hoodie, and went downstairs.

Maddy sat in the living room toweling her hair dry while she waited for Jacks to emerge from the downstairs bathroom. Kevin had found something for him to put on in a box at the back of his closet and sent him to change. She looked anxiously around the room, from the embarrassing school photos on the wall, to the secondhand furniture, to the old, boxy TV. Compared to Jacks, they were staggeringly poor. She quickly got up and scooped up a pile of Kevin's laundry that was sitting on top of the couch. She tried to arrange the magazines on the coffee table like she had seen in fancy offices, until she noticed the magazines were *Family Circle* and *Reader's Digest*. She sighed. It was hopeless.

Jacks came out of the bathroom wearing Kevin's old jeans and a tattered shirt, which, on him, looked like an advertisement for worn-out vintage chic. He crossed the living room and, to her relief, passed the wall of photos without inspecting them. If she got out of tonight alive, she thought, she vowed to stash them forever.

"I like your place," Jacks said, looking around. "It's homey."

"Thanks," Maddy said sheepishly, and grabbed a stray pair of Kevin's underwear from the couch. "Let's go into the kitchen."

Maddy and Jacks sat down at the table while Kevin took down three mugs from the cupboard. The gas for the stove was still flowing, and he prepared fresh cups of tea for all of them. Outside, the rain fell constantly against the roof, filing the kitchen with its soft murmur.

"Thank you, Mr. Montgomery," Jacks said as he accepted his cup.

"It's just Kevin," Maddy's uncle said. He handed Maddy a cup, then busied himself around the kitchen again. The hot liquid scalded her tongue as she drank, and the warmth spread down through her chest.

"They've been calling, you know," Kevin said.

"Who?" Maddy asked.

"Everyone. ANN, *Angels Weekly*, MSNBC, and some blogger. Vuitton . . . something. I thought about unplugging the phone, but I was afraid you might try and get in touch. I was worried."

"I told you, I'm fine," Maddy said, and looked at Jacks. "He saved my life."

"That's not exactly what they've been saying," Kevin said evenly. "But I've heard a lot of things tonight."

Maddy watched Kevin as he took out more candles from under the sink and set them around. She drew in a long, deep breath. At last her lips parted.

"My parents, Kevin," Maddy said, her voice small but firm. "I want to know the truth." Kevin froze where he was standing with his back to her, then struck a match and lit one of the candles.

"What do you want to know that you don't know already?" he said, without turning.

"Jacks told me he could save me because he saw I was in danger, like a premonition. Well . . ." She took a deep breath. "*I've* had premonitions all my life, and always when something bad is about to happen." Kevin still didn't move, but stood listening. "I've always just explained it away to myself or tried to ignore it. I figured I was just, I don't know, different. A freak." She swallowed down the beginnings of another lump that was threatening in her throat. "Now I think maybe there's more to it, and maybe you've been keeping something from me."

"Maddy, don't you think you might be imagining—"

"I'm not," Maddy said sharply. "I'm done pretending it doesn't happen, because it *does*. It happened today when I was almost crushed by that car. I saw it all happen in my head first, and that's impossible." From the corner of her eye she could see Jacks's astonished expression. He had set down his cup and was scrutinizing her intently. "So. Who were they, really?" she asked quietly.

Kevin turned and met her gaze. Jacks's eyes darted between them. Kevin brought one of the candles over and set it in the center of the table. Then he sat looking at the flame, his glasses reflecting the flickering light. Maddy realized she was holding her breath.

"I wondered if this day would come," he said at last. "I thought it might, but not this soon, and certainly not under these circumstances. I told your father it wasn't fair that I'd be the one to have to tell you, but he said he was glad it would be me. That I had always been good with you. Now, I'm not so sure."

Maddy looked at her uncle in the dancing candlelight. There sat the man who had cared for her, and provided for her, her entire life. Suddenly she felt like she didn't know him. Or at least didn't know a part of him. He looked abruptly older to her. Worn somehow. His face was drawn in grim lines.

"Please," she whispered. "I have to know."

"Are you sure you want to hear this story?" he asked, his expression darkening. "If I tell you, I'm going to tell it to you straight. I'm not going to edit. And I can warn you now, it's not always pretty." Kevin's glasses caught the candlelight again and gave him burning embers for eyes. Maddy considered his words and then nodded. Jacks sat still with suspense.

"Okay, then," Kevin said. "Where do I begin? With the Angels, I guess." Kevin rose and walked over to the cupboard as he talked.

"You should know from your history class at school about the Awakening, when Angels revealed themselves to us? And you know about the establishment of protection-for-pay and the NAS Archangels?"

"Yes, of course," Maddy said, remembering Mr. Rankin's tedious lecture.

Kevin had begun taking the remaining mugs out of the cupboard and setting them on the counter. Maddy wondered vaguely what he was doing. A draft blew through the house, causing the candles to flicker. As Maddy watched, Kevin removed the back of the cupboard and pulled out what looked like an old scrapbook. Maddy's heart began to hammer relentlessly in her chest. She had never seen the book before. What was it doing hidden in the cupboard?

Kevin brought the book back to the table, sat, and set it in front of him.

"A little less than twenty years ago, a young Guardian, what they call a Born Immortal, had a radical idea. He believed the Angels had become corrupt, and the system had become corrupt along with them. He argued that Angels should return to performing miracles anonymously, and for free."

Kevin opened the book. The binding cracked as the cover came up. He started leafing through the brittle pages. There were pictures of people Maddy had never seen before. Young, beautiful faces peering out at her from the pages. Jacks craned his head to see as well. Kevin stopped on a faded photo of a young Angel. Maddy didn't recognize him, but she was immediately struck by him. He had kind eyes and a striking, statuesque figure.

"This is him?" Maddy asked, tapping the photo.

"Yes, this is him," Kevin said. "This is Jacob Godright." Kevin pointed to a handsome man in his twenties standing next to him. "And this is a young human activist named Teddy Linden."

"The senator?" Jacks asked in disbelief. "He hates Angels."

"Or hates what they have become. That was another place and another time. You see, Jacob Godright and his followers were convinced that Angels and humans could live together as equals, work together, and even have families together. To prove his point, he secretly married a beautiful, brilliant human girl he had fallen in love with." Kevin's voice wavered under the weight of the words. "That girl was my sister, Maddy. She was your mother. Montgomery is your mother's maiden name. Your real name is Madison Godright."

He paused.

"Your father was an Angel."

It was a full ten seconds before Maddy could speak. Or move. Or even breathe. Her galloping heart threatened to tear through her chest. She heard her uncle's words ringing in her head.

"That's . . . impossible." She hadn't meant to say it aloud, but the word broke through her paralyzing shock. She became aware of Jacks sitting like a sculpture next to her, his face a stony mask of disbelief.

"I'm so sorry I haven't been able to tell you until now," Kevin said. "I can't tell you how much I wish things were different. How much I miss my sister."

"But I'm not an Angel," Maddy managed to get out.

"No," Kevin said, "you're not. You are human, but you have Angel blood flowing in your veins. You are one of a kind, Maddy, unique in all the world." He smiled and gave her a quick squeeze on the shoulder. Then his face darkened. "Your birth, which was thought to be impossible, became the catalyst for everything. Your parents said you were a miracle, and a sign, but the NAS called you a bastard, a half blood, and"— he paused on the word—"an abomination." Kevin's eyes were apologetic, but his tone was cuttingly honest. "And so, a power struggle began within the Angels."

"The Troubles," Jacks said.

"That's right," Kevin said. "The Angel Civil War."

"My father . . ." Jacks said. Maddy watched his knuckles go white as he gripped the armrests of his chair.

"Yes, your father, Isaiah Godspeed, was a rebel along with Jacob."

"What?" Jacks glared at Kevin, his eyes narrowing into distrustful slits. "My father fought the rebellion. He was killed putting it down."

"No, Jacks," Kevin said calmly. "That's what your stepfather, Mark, wants you to think. The truth is, your father wanted to reform the Angels too. He supported Jacob and his child."

"Why wouldn't Mark want me to know that?" Jacks asked.

"Because when Maddy was only a few weeks old, Jacob and Isaiah approached him for help. They were all classmates, and Mark—Isaiah's cousin—was already a rising star, an ambitious political prodigy. The Jackson Godspeed of his day," Kevin said, nodding toward Jacks. He turned the final page of the scrapbook. It was blank. Maddy looked at the yellowed, brittle page. Like a future cut unnecessarily short.

"Mark refused to support them and turned them away. With the ranks closed against them, Maddy was brought to me under cover of darkness. The next day, both Jacob and Isaiah were captured by the Council's Disciplinary Agents, mortalized, and killed in cold blood. Regina, my sister, was also murdered. Kris Godspeed and her child, Jackson, were spared. In exchange for not helping the rebels, Mark was given his position as Archangel and quickly rose in the NAS.

"Jacks," Kevin said, his tone suddenly gentler, "your mother didn't know. And still doesn't. She is innocent. In her grief, she gave in to Mark's advances and they married."

Kevin closed the scrapbook and put his hands on the dusty cover.

Jacks had turned and stared unseeingly out the kitchen window. Kevin looked at Maddy.

"The Angels promised never again to interfere with your life so long as you lived it out normally, without any knowledge of your past or what you actually are. I agreed, and you've been with me ever since."

The lump in her throat was back and throbbing as it rose. She had come to speak to Kevin in hopes of finally clearing up the foggy dream world of her past. Now she realized that dream was a nightmare, a nightmare he had been protecting her from. She wasn't just an average, unremarkable girl. She was a perversion of man and Angel. A monster. No wonder she had always felt like a freak.

She literally was one.

Maddy could feel her eyes swelling, and she didn't know if she would be able to stop the tears. Unsteadily, she got up from the table and walked through the living room to the window. The rain had finally stopped, replaced by fog that hung low over the wet street. Maddy watched a man out walking his dog in the mist.

Jacks sat unmoving in his chair. Now it was his turn to decide what to believe.

"And now they're hunting me for saving her," he said softly.

"They're probably hunting you both," Kevin said. "Now that you've saved Maddy, Jacks, both of you are a threat to the Archangels' power, a reminder of other . . . ideas about how the Angels should be. Descendants of the rebels, acting rebelliously. Dangerous. They will never allow the two of you to be together. No matter what it takes. If they can, Council Disciplinary Agents will kill you both."

Maddy heard the scrape of chairs on the linoleum as Jacks and Kevin got up.

"You'll have to excuse me when I say I don't like Angels," Kevin said, and then he offered his hand. "But thank you for saving my niece's life." Jacks looked at Kevin's hand for a moment and then took it. The two shook.

Maddy continued staring out the window in silence. She watched as Jacks's reflection appeared behind her in the glass. She wondered if he would have some lame condolence. The Immortal Angel telling the freak of nature *I feel your pain* or something pathetic like that. At least she could stop wondering if he actually cared about her or not. Now, for sure, she knew he would want nothing to do with her.

Jacks stood beside her. Instead of saying anything, she felt his fingers trace up her palm and then lace into hers. He had taken her hand before, quickly and for functional reasons—usually to drag her off to someplace she didn't want to go—but he had never *held* her hand. Not the way couples did in parks or lovers did in old movies. Maddy stood there and felt the heat of his grip. It made her think of that first night in the diner, when they had talked about pretend memories and she had felt so connected to him. But now they were further apart than ever, she had to remind herself. One an Angel and the other an *abomination*.

"We should get going," he said finally. Maddy couldn't believe he hadn't said *I* should get going, but she was too numb to care. Or think.

"Who is that?" Jacks said. He was looking at the man with his dog.

"I don't know," Maddy said. "A neighbor, I guess."

"How long has he been there?" His tone at once severe.

Suddenly the lights inside the house sprang to life. The refrigerator whirred back on, and the TV in the living room blinked to life.

"*—Manhunt under way for Angel Jackson Godspeed . . .*" a reporter was announcing under a scrolling breaking news banner.

Outside, the neighborhoods of Angel City lit up one by one along the grid as power was restored. The man with the dog suddenly looked directly at Maddy standing in the open window and vanished. He disappeared in a literal blur and was gone, leaving the dog to look around inquisitively and sniff at its lifeless leash.

Maddy turned toward Jacks, breathless.

His face was twisted in sudden despair.

"How much time do we have?" she asked.

He grabbed her by the back of her hoodie and pulled her away from the window.

"It's already too late."

CHAPTER TWENTY-SIX

From Maddy's point of view, three things seemed to happen simultaneously. First, the house itself seemed to simply explode. The windows, which a moment before had been cold and still and covered in raindrops, suddenly disintegrated into a thousand glittering pieces. The front door disappeared, blown into razor-sharp splinters that knifed their way through the living room. In the kitchen, utensils, teacups, and plates were tossed into the air like lethal confetti.

Second, something collided violently with Jacks. Maddy saw it only out of the corner of her eye. It came through the window, moving so fast it was nothing more than a blur in her peripheral vision. A blur with *wings*. Jacks was propelled backward through the furniture and into the old TV, which gave a buzzing death cry as it shattered.

Third, as she turned to look back at Jacks, Maddy felt the fingers of an iron grip wrap around her throat. Another winged blur had come through the living room window, and this one had come for her.

She flew backward like a pinball, hitting the wall of school photos and sending most of the frames shattering to the floor. The impact was so violent she was momentarily disoriented. *Angel blood . . . perversion of nature . . . Council will kill you if they can.* The words mixed with a strange image of a dark figure with *glowing* eyes. She must be dreaming. She had to be imagining the phantom before her.

The need for oxygen brought Maddy suddenly, painfully back to the present. She was staring into an expressionless black mask with gleaming, computerized eyes. The Angel stood larger than Jacks by nearly a foot, was muscularly built, and wore some kind of futuristic black armor that covered his entire body. His wings were armored too and black, like bat wings. Whatever Maddy had imagined Angel Police would look like, it wasn't this. The mask made the Angel look like a ghoulish robot.

Her mouth opened to scream, but the vise-like hand that was around her throat simply tightened and choked off the sound. She flailed. She clawed at the enormous arms and willed her feet to move, but the Angel's grip constricted like a snake. Her knees buckling under her, Maddy felt her body surrender. The Angel lifted her by her neck and threw her against the far wall.

She heard the crack as her head smacked against the stone fireplace. A high-pitched ringing began in her left ear. She tried to roll over and scramble away, but the Angel was over her at once, pinning her to the ground. His speed and strength were spectacular. Overwhelming and absolute. She saw a heavy glass paperweight sitting on a stack of bills on the corner table, grabbed it, and swung it at the Angel's head. He caught her arm midswing. She heard the crackle of a radio from somewhere within the mask. The voice was cold and indifferent.

"I have the girl. Prepare for extraction."

It was already over.

Behind her, in the direction of the kitchen, Maddy heard a male scream. She recognized it at once. Kevin. She had never heard him scream before. The sound made her blood run cold. This was all her fault. She had led them to a trap.

Maddy looked into the masked Angel's glowing, electronic eyes. His mouth was hidden, but Maddy had the strangest feeling that he was grinning at her.

In an instant, the glowing eyes looked up, as if in surprise.

Jacks's hand whistled through the air, catching the Angel's arm and bending it in an impossible angle. Jacks's other fist blurred, his Divine Ring a flick of light in the dark room, landing a crushing blow into the black mask.

The look on Jackson's face was something she had never seen before. His eyes flared, ferocious. They burned with a kind of fire. Maddy could only think of one word to describe it: *wrath*. His mouth opened to release an inhuman roar. Wings burst from behind him, broad and menacing. Maddy's mind flickered back to what Jacks had told her at the outlook: *a Battle Angel's wings*.

The black Angel came at Jacks again. He thrust his hand forward as she had seen Jacks do in the diner and at the street corner, but Jacks was faster. For a moment the Immortals shimmered in time, flickering like television static. Maddy saw Jacks blur a hand around the Angel's leg, and with a howl of rage on his lips, he threw the winged creature into the wall.

Jackson's murderous eyes shot back to Maddy.

"Are you okay?" he thundered.

"I think so."

The sound of Kevin's screams came back to her. She struggled to her feet and stumbled into the kitchen.

Maddy found Kevin sitting against the cabinets below the sink. A jagged cut on his forehead had begun to ooze blood. The candles that he had so carefully set up were now cracked and broken on the floor around him. The scrapbook sat mangled in the corner, its pages wrenched out, pictures scattered everywhere. One of the photos had caught on an overturned candle and was starting to burn.

"Kevin!" Maddy screamed.

"I'll be fine!" Kevin yelled. Another explosion shook the walls as more winged silhouettes crashed into the house. Steps thundered on the stairs as they swooped down from above. The siege's noose was tightening around them.

"You have to go *now*," Kevin said, and looked at Jacks. "Fly!"

They would only have a moment to escape or never.

Jacks's wild eyes were on Maddy, but he didn't move. He waited for her decision. Maddy looked in Kevin's eyes. Something in them didn't want her to go, but begged her to all the same.

"Okay," Maddy said, turning to Jacks. "Let's go."

She felt his heavy arm scoop her up and had only a moment to dig her nails into his skin before they were torn skyward. They shot through the jagged opening of the window, Jacks's wings thrashing the air, and climbed into the foggy night.

The wet rushing air burned against Maddy's face. Compared to now, the first time they had gone flying had been a leisurely stroll. Now they rocketed through the night, ferociously, painfully. Angel City receded below them until it was nothing more than an indistinct glow. The night fog enveloped them.

The muscles of Jacks's back rose and fell with the exertion of his wings. Maddy looked back through the lashing air. She saw nothing at first, just the fog and inky black night. Then the unmistakable outline of Angel wings emerged. Three dark shapes were coming toward them in the dark, their yellow eyes glowing like banshees'.

"There are three of them!" she yelled over the rush of the wind. Slowly, surely, the pursuing Angels seemed to be nearing. Maddy watched helplessly as they began to close the gap.

Then, through a break in the fog, she spotted it. The Los Angeles skyline. In the foggy night the twinkling buildings hovered like ocean liners on a sea of mist. When Jacks spoke again, his voice was little more than a whisper in the wind.

"Listen. This will probably be the worst pain you have ever experienced in your life. Everything in your body will tell you to let go, but you have to hold on. You have to hold on, Maddy, no matter what. No matter how badly it hurts. You can never, never let go. Can you do that for me?"

Maddy nodded. She crossed her arms around his neck and gripped her elbows with as much strength as her hands would bring to bear. Jacks wrapped his arms around her arms, pulling them so tightly around his body she winced. Banking steeply, they soared toward the towers of glass.

The Angels behind them had gained. Maddy didn't need to look back. She could hear the hiss of the wind over their wings. Jacks rushed forward with disorienting speed. She watched as a towering building emerged from the fog like a ghost. It quickly eclipsed her vision, a wall of glass rushing eagerly to greet them. Jacks didn't change course. He didn't slow down. Maddy felt a primal panic well up inside her. She watched the wall approach until she could see her reflection in it. The raw terror overpowered her rational thinking, and she screamed. In that exact instant, Jacks buckled at the waist, pumped his wings, and wrenched Maddy straight down.

They dove. Viciously. The thrust nearly tore her off Jacks's back. It was like the first big drop of a roller coaster—except excruciating instead of fun. Every cell of her body screamed at her to let go. Pleaded. The tearing sensation in her arms and fingers was overwhelming. Blood drained from her head.

They flew directly down the tower's surface, so close she could touch it, so fast it appeared as a single, unbroken sheet of glass. A strange popping noise filled her ears, and she realized the windows were exploding as they passed. A wave of shattering glass pursued them as they rushed toward the fast-approaching ground.

Maddy's eyes opened in agonized slits and she saw the street. It was like death itself rushing up at her. Then, with impossible precision, Jacks leveled and shot straight forward over the ground. Streetlights, signs, cars: all flew by at deadly speeds, missing them by inches.

The acceleration bled away and Maddy found she could breathe again. She looked back. Sure enough, the first Angel had been pulled into Jacks' trap. He was not as nimble—or as strong—as Jacks, and as he leveled, his wing caught on a streetlamp, sending him tumbling over the pavement and taking several parked cars with him.

One down, she thought.

"Are you okay?" Jacks's voice was strained with exertion.

"Yes," Maddy gasped. She hazarded another look behind her.

"There's two now!" she shrieked.

"Hang on."

Zigzagging through the jungle of downtown, Jacks banked hard and low. Maddy looked up at a gaping concrete mouth. They were going into a tunnel. She heard the snap of air as one of the Angel agents swooped in right behind them.

The tunnel was bathed in an eerie blue-green. Headlights reflected off the tunnel's glossy ceiling, giving it a cold, futuristic feel. Up ahead Maddy could see a row of orange lights coming right at them. She heard the blare of the semitruck's horn. The sound seemed to come from everywhere all at once. Jacks put on more speed. The big rig bore down on them, filling the claustrophobic tunnel, its trailer only a few feet from the tunnel's ceiling. Maddy realized with sickening certainty they were going up over the top. They would have to squeeze through the tiny gap between the top of the truck's trailer and the ceiling of the tunnel.

"Do you trust me?" Jacks yelled. Maddy pressed her lips against his ear.

"Yes!"

In an instant, Jacks rolled so they were flying flat against the ceiling. Maddy pressed her body against Jacks's chest, knowing that if she moved, she would be killed. They slipped over the top of the truck, instant death mere inches away. Maddy felt, more than heard, the impact behind them as the agent collided with the semi. The shock of the Angel's body against the windshield clapped her ears like a bomb.

Jacks rolled level as they soared over the tops of the cars behind the semi. They approached the end of the tunnel, the damp night air getting closer.

Two down.

Maddy looked back. Nothing.

"I don't see anyone!"

"What?!" Jacks yelled.

Maddy squinted to be sure.

Before Maddy could respond, she felt the crushing impact from above.

He must have gone around the tunnel.

A gloved hand wrapped around Maddy's wrist. The crackling voice was older and surprisingly genteel through the black mask.

"Hello, Madison."

Jacks thrashed his wings and rammed hard against the Angel, then dove. The agent's grip on Maddy's arm ripped loose painfully, and he fell back behind them. As he flew in evasive maneuvers, Jacks's eyes scanned the sky, his head darting back and forth, until he trained on a hazy, blinking light above them. A chance.

"Maddy," he yelled, banking sharply and preparing to climb. "I need you to hang on for me one more time. Will you do it for me?"

"I'll try," she said weakly.

Jacks wrapped her arms in his vise-like grip and, using his last ounce of strength, climbed straight up like a rocket into the night sky. The weight of the acceleration was crushing against Maddy's small frame. Faster. Higher. Her eyes became long tunnels as the blood rushed out of her head.

"Just hang on, Maddy! Hang on!"

Jacks's voice echoed somewhere far away.

She simply didn't have any more strength in her fingers as they began slipping. The world began to recede. Her eyes closed as the blackout swept over her. She barely heard the sound of the jet engines growing closer or felt the sizzling heat as they passed through the jet wash. The next thing Maddy knew, she could feel metal below her feet.

Groggy, she opened her eyes. She saw riveted metal and glowing, round windows. They were on the wing of an airliner. Jacks maintained balance on the wing as the 747 banked to land at LAX. He pulled Maddy close against the side and they waited there, unmoving. The metal of the roaring aircraft was frigid against Maddy's skin. She watched a woman inside the plane as she glanced out her window. The passenger's eyes grew wide, and her mouth hung open as she took in the image of the two of them on the wing.

They left the airliner moments before the 747 touched down. Jacks flew them low over the palm trees until black, silent canals came into view. The pungent smell of stagnant water filled Maddy's nostrils as they landed and Jacks pulled her under a white footbridge. They sat there next to the water, listening for anything. The lap of the canal was the only sound. Otherwise it was silent. Nothing.

For the moment, they were safe.

"Are you okay?" Jacks asked, panting, exhausted.

"I think so. What about you?" Maddy asked.

"I will be."

"Was that . . . ?"

"Yes," he said. "Those were Council Disciplinary Agents."

"This is all my fault," Maddy said quietly.

"No, it's not. You had no idea."

"I forced you to go to see my uncle when you knew the danger, and now"— her breath caught—"I've put him in danger too."

"He'll be okay, Maddy."

They sat there listening to the lap of the water.

"What do we do now?" Maddy said.

"Hide. Find someplace safe and dry where I can recover my strength. I can't trust any Angels. Not even my stepfather. We need someplace they won't be looking."

Maddy thought of the one place she had known as safe her whole life. The image of Uncle Kevin crouching in the kitchen as the ADC tore into her house made her shudder. There was Gwen's. But that was just down the block from her home, and her friend's entire family would be there. And for all Maddy knew, the Angels would be watching her best friend too.

After a moment, Maddy thought of it. It was far from ideal. But under the circumstances, it was the only place they could go.

"I know somewhere. We'll be safe there, I think."

"Where?"

"A . . . friend. He might not be all that excited to see you, but I think he'll help me."

Jacks looked at her. "Who?"

CHAPTER TWENTY-SEVEN

They worked their way up the streets, taking care to stay out of the cones of streetlight. Maddy's injuries were throbbing—her shoulder and back bruise from the almost-accident and now her neck where the Angel's hand had tried to strangle her. She noticed Jacks had begun to step unevenly. He wasn't hurt exactly—she didn't even know if Angels *could* get hurt—but his strength had left him for the moment. They both needed somewhere dry and safe to rest.

By the time they reached the residential street, the fog had lifted. The air was clear and cold. Puddles of rainwater stood eerily still as they reflected the streetlamps overhead. They stopped in the shadow of a parked car and looked at the large, rustic home.

The house was now dark and quiet. A few red cups littered the lawn as the only evidence of the party earlier that night. To Maddy, it already seemed like a distant past. Like a memory from another life.

"Who is this person again?" Jacks said, scrutinizing the house.

"Um . . . a friend," Maddy repeated, keeping her tone neutral.

He turned to her and searched her gaze. In the cast of the streetlight he looked like an old-time superhero. Once again she hated herself for finding him so attractive, even when he was exhausted, beat up, and on the run.

"Can we trust him?" Jacks said.

Maddy considered. "I know he would never do anything to hurt me," she said finally. The answer didn't quite seem to satisfy Jacks, but he nodded. They made their way around to the side of the house, slipping on the leafy hillside, until they came to a dimly lit window. Maddy peered in.

Ethan sat against the wall in the soft glow of a desk lamp. The box of photos sat next to him. He was looking at the pictures.

Maddy recognized the room, of course. It was where they had nearly kissed. She found herself thinking about how his lips had felt as they brushed against hers. Then she thought about their last conversation, when he told her how his father had died. *Maybe this wasn't such a good idea after all*, she thought, but it was too late to turn back now. She reached a hand up and tapped on the glass.

Ethan jumped, then looked over at the window.

"Ethan!" Maddy hissed in a loud whisper. "Over here."

He stared out at the darkness for a moment, then cautiously rose and came over to the glass.

"Ethan, it's me," Maddy whispered.

"Maddy?" He slid the window open and looked at her with wide eyes.

"Can I—we—come in?"

"We?" He looked into the shadows behind her and saw Jacks. His expression hardened.

"Please," Maddy said, searching his hazel eyes. "I didn't know who else to turn to."

Ethan hesitated as he considered. "Go around to the back," he said. "I'll meet you there."

Ethan let them in through a sliding glass door at the back of the house. He was still wearing his ripped jeans and sandals from the party, but he had thrown on a white thermal under his plaid shirt and corralled his hair under a backwards baseball cap.

"Thank you," Maddy said as she came in the door.

"I'm so glad you're okay," Ethan said, genuine relief in his voice. "You left the party and I heard those two *idiots* racing down the street. I should have never let you leave like that."

"No, you shouldn't have," Jacks said. His eyes were flinty. Ethan flinched at the Angel's words.

"Ethan, this is—"

"Yeah, I know," Ethan said. He studied the Angel before him.

"Maddy tells me you two are . . . friends?" Jacks said.

Ethan nodded. "And you two are . . . ?"

"Friends," Maddy said quickly. She could only imagine what was happening under Ethan's controlled exterior. She wondered what she must be putting him through by inviting an Angel into his house.

"Come in," Ethan said at last.

Ethan led them down the hallway toward the kitchen. He had cleaned up everything since the party.

"I wish I had something to offer," Ethan said as they walked. "But there isn't really anything left. There's some old Chinese food in the fridge, I think."

"It's okay," Maddy said. They came into the kitchen and Ethan leaned against the counter.

"So," he said. "How can I help?"

"Ethan, we need . . . a place to hide." Maddy paused. "I was hoping we could stay with you."

Ethan looked between Maddy and Jacks. "Look, Maddy," he said honestly, "I'd let you stay here, but you can't. And it's not because I don't want you to."

Maddy bent her head.

"They've already been here," Ethan said. Maddy's heart hammered against her chest.

"Who?" Jacks asked, alarmed.

"The Angels. They left, but I'm sure they'll be back. They were looking for you and for . . . *him*." Ethan motioned to Jackson.

"Ethan, please," Maddy said. "Jacks saved my life."

"He *saved* your life?" Ethan said, incredulous. "That's not what I heard."

"What do you mean?" Maddy said, her eyebrows pulling together. "What have you heard?"

"That he kidnapped you, of course."

"That's ridiculous," Maddy said in a low voice. "Who's saying that?"

Ethan raised an eyebrow. "You really don't know?" He walked over to the TV in the living room. He grabbed a remote off the couch, and clicked on the flat screen. Tara Reeves's exhausted face filled the screen as she continued to report on the breaking news story.

"We're bringing you the latest updates on the Jackson Godspeed situation in this continuing ANN Special Report. At this time, the hunt continues for Godspeed, who allegedly kidnapped seventeen-year-old Maddy Montgomery of Angel City earlier tonight and is now believed to be connected to as many as three Angel disappearances over the last week."

Maddy sat paralyzed with shock. What was going on?

"It's already started," Jacks murmured, as if in answer.

"What has?"

"The cover-up," Jacks said.

"It's worse online," Ethan said. He nodded over to his laptop, which was sitting open on the kitchen counter. Maddy went to the computer. She tapped the space bar to wake up the machine, and there it was:

Ethan's browser was open to all the most popular Angel blogs, with bold headlines like "COMMISSIONING GONE WRONG," "ONE DISTURBED ANGEL," and "SCANDAL IN THE IMMORTAL CITY!" She clicked through the various sites. They all had their own spin on the same basic story—how Jacks had disappeared from his own Commissioning, and allegedly kidnapped her, and was behind the Angel murders. There were even some rumors that he was working with the extremists HDF to bring down the Angels.

"But none of this is true," she said, her eyes darting across the screen. "This isn't fair; Jacks didn't kill anyone. And I wasn't *kidnapped*."

"Well, that's not what you're telling everyone."

"*What?*" Maddy gasped. "How?"

"You've been updating your Facebook page."

Maddy's eyes narrowed.

"*Facebook?* I don't *have* a Facebook page."

Ethan went over to her and, reaching his arms around her, navigated to Facebook and typed in Maddy's name. There she was. Her profile picture was her hideous junior-year school photo, and the pictures in her album were paparazzi shots from the diner, the party with Jacks, and the walk to school the day after. Her status was listed as *It's complicated*, and her wall was filled with sympathetic comments from "friends," of which she saw she currently had 560. Under *What's on your mind?* she had written. *Getting kidnapped by Jackson Godspeed.*

Maddy couldn't help but lean her back against Ethan's chest as she absorbed the shock. Jacks came up behind them, noticing and unhappy.

"Oh, you're on Twitter too," Ethan said. He navigated to the Twitter home page, typed in her name, and there she was again. Her most recent tweet was only fifteen minutes old:

Everything okay, will get back to everyone soon. Thanks for all the love and support!

"They're even selling T-shirts," Ethan said. He quickly typed in *celebritytee.com*. Maddy's mouth dropped open. There was a shirt for sale with her face on it. "'Team Maddy' or 'Team Jacks,'" he said, reading off the site. "So I guess you get to pick what side you're on. There's also 'Team Macks' if you can't decide or are rooting for you both, I guess."

"All this happened . . . *tonight*?" Maddy asked in disbelief.

"It's the world we live in now," Ethan said. He stepped back and leaned against the counter again. "Congratulations, Maddy, you're a celebrity now."

"And now they're hunting me," Jacks said, almost to himself. "Whoever, whatever is really out there killing Angels is just getting a pass so the Archangels can cover up their dirt." He turned to Maddy. "He's right. We can't stay here. If they've been here looking for us once, they'll return."

Maddy thought about the Angels coming through the windows of her house. It was an image she never wanted to see again. Ethan turned to her.

"Maybe it's none of my business, Maddy, but is staying with Jackson really such a good idea right now?" Ethan murmured.

"That *is* none of your business," Jacks said, his jaw set.

"As her friend, Maddy's *safety* is my business," Ethan countered icily. Jacks turned away from him.

"Let me check the street outside, then we'll go." The Angel walked quickly down the hallway. Maddy wondered if he didn't want to leave her with Ethan. Was he actually . . . *jealous*?

Ethan and Maddy stood in the silence that followed.

"I know what you must be thinking," Maddy said finally. "But if it wasn't for Jacks, I'd be dead right now. He saved my life, Ethan, more than once tonight. Things are just *different* from what I thought."

Ethan's eyes flashed to her. They were vulnerable, almost hurt.

"I know, things *are* different," Ethan said. "Like I said before, you just don't seem like the kind of girl who gets mixed up with these guys." He looked sad and tired. "But I guess I was wrong."

She bit her lip. She didn't know what hurt more, her injuries or her friend's disappointment in her. Jacks came back into the room.

"Okay, we should go."

"Where?"

"Anywhere but here. They'll be back, I guarantee it."

Jacks started toward the front door. Ethan watched them. Then he sighed and pulled a ring of keys from a drawer.

"I told you to borrow this whenever you wanted, so you might as well borrow it now. It might not be the most comfortable place in the world," he said, peeling off one of the keys. "But it's dry, and I don't think anyone will think to check it. I mean, besides you, Tyler's the only person who even knows I have these, and he's sleeping it off in my bedroom." He walked over to Maddy. "This opens the maintenance door on the east side; do you know it?"

". . . Yes," Maddy said, realizing what he was talking about.

Ethan looked down at the key, then up at Jacks, regarding him coldly.

"I'm sorry, Maddy, I don't trust him. But if this is your decision, I'll do everything I can to help." He turned to her. "Are you sure you're okay?" As he spoke, he stepped in to her. Close. Jacks's eyes flashed with that same anger.

"Yes," she said, blushing. "And thank you."

"Anything for you, Maddy," Ethan replied quietly.

"Let's go," Jacks said gruffly.

They made their way carefully down the sleepy street. Maddy looked back over her shoulder. The windows of the house were dark, but she could see Ethan's silhouette standing there, still, as he watched them go. His idea *was* a good one. No one would ever think to look for them there. He was actually helping them, as much as it probably killed him inside. Ethan. Steadily there for her. She found herself wondering again what she thought about him. What would he think if she ever told him the truth about her parents? Would he be enraged? And become as cold to her as he was to Jacks? Or would he accept her for who she was, no matter what blood was flowing in her veins? She had a feeling he would support her, no matter what. She wondered if Jacks would do the same.

Jacks turned to her at that moment with a smile that made her heart melt.

"Okay, Maddy, so where are we going?"

CHAPTER TWENTY-EIGHT

Crickets chirped steadily in the grass. Palm trees stood motionless, watching.

"Here?" Jacks asked, looking at the slumbering Angel City High.

"Yes, here." Maddy laughed. "I can't imagine anyone would think to look for you at a public school." Their feet squished in the wet grass as Maddy led Jacks around the classrooms to the side of the school. They came to the unmarked maintenance door, and Maddy slid Ethan's key in the lock. Holding her breath, she turned it. She heard the click as the dead bolt retreated.

The hallway was dark and quiet. Homecoming posters hung sleepily from the walls. The only light came from a vending machine down the corridor, a soft red and blue fluorescent glow. She looked around and got her bearings.

"It's this way," she said.

Maddy ran her hand along the banks of lockers as they walked. She had strolled down this hallway a thousand times before, but now it was different, and it wasn't just the dark. Everything had changed. She came to her locker and paused. She thought about herself at that locker just days ago. That simple, comfortable life she'd known for so long. *One day you return to your normal surroundings and everything just feels different*, she thought. *Except the surroundings aren't different. You are.*

"What is it?" Jacks asked.

"It's nothing," Maddy said. In truth, it was everything, because she had just realized nothing would ever be the same again. The lockers and the scuffed linoleum and Gwen gossiping about the Angels, it all seemed irretrievably gone now. Even if things did somehow go back to normal, there'd be no forgetting the truth of her parents' identities or their horrible deaths. There was no escaping it. Whether she was ready for it or not, her childhood was, officially, over.

"It's not much farther," Maddy said, and started to walk again.

Then she froze.

She could hear a *voice*. It was coming from down the hall, from inside one of the rooms. Her eyes darted to Jacks. He was already listening intently.

"We should go," Jacks said, his voice low.

"Wait," Maddy said, and listened again. She *recognized* the voice. It was a girl, a girl she knew. The voice gave her a strange, sinking feeling she couldn't place. Who could possibly be there with them? And at this time of night? She gave Jacks a look, then crept forward, staying close to the wall. Up ahead a faint light filtered out through the frosted window of the teachers' lounge. With her heart galloping in her chest, she noiselessly turned the handle and cracked open the door.

The room was empty. There were a few half-drunk mugs of coffee still sitting on the table. And a glowing TV left on in the corner. Someone must have forgotten to turn it off. Maddy registered the face on the screen.

It was Vivian Holycross. She was radiant in a silver sheer Alexander McQueen dress as she sat on a couch across from the irrepressible Tara Reeves. It was an ANN exclusive interview. Even though a tear streamed down her cheek, it was a perfect tear. Hair and makeup had done a great job making her look sufficiently distraught.

"It's a big misunderstanding," Vivian said, taking a tissue she was offered from Tara and wiping her eye. The scrawl on the bottom of the screen stated "*ANGELHUNT on for suspected serial murderer Jackson Godspeed.*"

"Would you like to say something to Jacks, if he happens to be watching?" Tara asked. Vivian sniffed.

"Come home, Jacks, and we'll get this all worked out."

Even crying, she looked amazing. Maddy watched the screen, and jealousy twisted through her. She had almost gotten used to the tempting idea of Jacks's affection. Vivian's perfect image was an icy reality check. How could she ever compete? She, an abomination. How could she have ever let herself think Jacks would truly have feelings for her when he had Vivian to come home to?

Jacks gazed at Maddy, seeming to guess what she was thinking.

"Come on," he said, walking to the television and punching a button. It turned off with a slight buzz. "I'm sure Vivian made a great appearance fee to do that."

Maddy looked at him uncertainly.

"Before I collapse right here in the hall, why don't you show me where we're going?" Jacks said, leading her out of the room.

The faded mural painted on the side of the gymnasium depicted a muscled, red-and-white cartoon Angel dribbling a basketball under its wing. The banner read This Is WINGS Territory!

Maddy tugged on the handle. The door opened with a metallic clang. The gym was dark and cool and smelled of hardwood and cleaning solvent. Their footsteps echoed in the dark as they entered. Jacks walked forward and sat heavily on the floor. Maddy groped along the wall until she found a metal control panel and a row of switches. She threw the switches on one at a time, and slowly the gym lights started to glow. Jacks sat there in the half-light, his arms resting on his knees and his head bowed. Even for an Immortal he looked utterly exhausted. Maddy knew well enough the school was only a temporary solution, that on Monday teachers and students would be streaming into the halls again. But for now it would do—it simply had to. Jacks needed to rest. Even Maddy herself was too exhausted to think straight anymore. They could plan their next steps in the morning.

She found a stack of gymnastics mats in the corner and pulled the top one down. Awkwardly unfolding it, she dragged it to half-court.

"Come lie down," she said.

He walked over and fell hard on the mat.

"Are you really going to be okay?" she asked.

"I will be, I just need some time," he said wearily.

Maddy sat beside him and pulled her knees up to her chest. She listened to Jacks's deep breathing. Vivian's crying face still played in her mind.

"Can I ask you a question," Maddy said finally, "if I promise not to be stubborn about it?"

"Sure," he said.

"What you said on the rooftop," she said, her voice small. "About being . . . meant to be together. Was that really the truth? I mean, do you really believe that?"

Jacks looked at her. Maddy was very still, her eyes at her feet. "I just don't understand. Why would you go through all this trouble when you have someone like her?" She huffed in defeat. "I'm not blind, Jacks. She's . . . incredible."

"Vivian?" Jacks asked. Maddy nodded.

Jacks studied her for a moment in that way he did, scrutinizing her, then lay down slowly on the mat and looked up at the lights.

"When I got home that night after you and I met, things were chaotic in my house. The police were there, my mom was crying, Mark was yelling, but my mind, Maddy, my mind kept returning to you. I couldn't understand why. I went and sat on the deck outside my room and searched the city lights until I found your uncle's diner. I watched the sign until it went off."

Maddy's expression had turned incredulous.

"You don't believe me?"

"I don't believe your *room* has its own deck." She groaned.

Jacks laughed a little.

"I was thinking about our conversation. I didn't even understand why. My mind just kept returning to that flash in your eyes, and what I had felt when we touched. I'd never felt anything like it before in my life. I had to see you again. So . . ." He paused, suddenly embarrassed. "The next day I did a little research and found out where you went to school."

"I was wondering how you found me." Maddy laughed.

"Angels have their ways," he said, grinning. "I went, expecting you to be thrilled to see me, but you pushed me away. No one had ever done that to me before. It made me crazy—and only more determined. I went to your window that night, not knowing what I was doing there, almost unconscious. I just had to. Then you woke up, and we started talking. I told myself I was there because I just wanted to *win*, you know, I just wanted you to say you forgave me. Then it would be over. But then after I took you flying, you pushed me away *again*." He shook his head. "And every time you pushed me away, Maddy, it only made me more . . . fascinated by you. More interested."

"That's hard to believe," Maddy said. "Even *I* have to admit I was being impossible. I tried hinting so many times that I wanted to be left alone, but you didn't even seem to notice. Or care."

"You were dropping *hints*?"

"Sure. Girls do that. I guess you don't have much experience in the rejection department, but every girl knows how to get rid of unwanted boys. I think it's part of our DNA."

"Ouch," Jacks said in a mock grimace.

"You know what I mean," Maddy said, and felt her cheeks flushing.

"You have to understand how predictable people are to me. Every day, everyone does whatever I say. They smile and say yes to everything I want. They're either scared of me, or Angelstruck by me, or *paid* by me. So once I got over being furious about it, and I *was* furious—you get used to getting what you want from people all the time—I realized something. You were acting that way because you weren't treating me like a celebrity. You were just treating me like anybody else." He paused. "No one had ever seen me for me, Maddy, not Vivian, not anyone."

Maddy shrugged. "I didn't do it consciously. I've just never understood what the big deal was about Angels."

"I know," Jacks said, and laughed. "You've already made *that* point very clear to me." He rolled on the mat, trying to get comfortable, and winced.

"Are you scared?"

Jacks's open eyes looked up into the darkness of the gym's roof. "I don't know. I don't think so."

Maddy sat up slightly. "Maybe we can just somehow find out who the real killer is and prove you're innocent. And I'll explain I wasn't kidnapped. They'd have to believe me. I'd make them. This could all go away." Hope edged her voice.

"It wouldn't work. There's still the unsanctioned save. They won't stop. The NAS would come up with something else. They always do."

"But it could be . . . less bad somehow, if they knew part of the truth at least. You're not a killer, Jacks."

He silently nodded.

"Who could it be?" Maddy asked.

Jacks's thoughts immediately cast back to the strange thing that Sierra Churchson had said to him at the party he had taken Maddy to—"can't wait for your star." And the way the twins had looked at him at the Commissioning, malice in their eyes. Was it more than just jealousy? The twins had always been a little intense. And then there was what Jacks had learned tonight about Mark's past and the stained blazer that his mind wouldn't let him forget. How could he trust Mark about *anything*? Something much bigger was going on, and Jacks's brain tried to get hold of something, anything that would make things clear. But it eluded him.

"I don't know, but does it really matter?" Jacks said, sighing. "For now the world thinks it's me."

"Vivian's right, though," Maddy said, unsure again. "None of this is your fault. It's mine."

Jacks shook his head.

"No, it's not. I went along with the decision to go see your uncle."

"I mean everything," Maddy said. "I shouldn't have gone to Ethan's party, I shouldn't have said yes to that date with you, and I *definitely* shouldn't have taken you into the back room with me at the diner." She played with the drawstrings of her hoodie. "Every decision I've made has been wrong, and now look what's happened."

"Why *did* you go to Ethan's party?" Jacks asked, his tone curious.

Maddy shrugged. "I only went because I was upset at you. I was trying to . . . forget you."

"Really?"

"Really. Girls do that too."

"Well. He seems nice. Even if it kills me to admit that."

Jacks rolled again, trying to get comfortable.

"Here," Maddy said. She sat closer to him and leaned back on her elbows. "Rest your head on me." She delicately placed a hand on the back of his neck and pulled his head against her shoulder.

Jacks's head moved heavily from her shoulder to her chest. She could feel the weight of it as she inhaled. Maddy leaned back all the way and wrapped her arms around him, holding him against her. He lay there quietly, as if listening to her heartbeat. Neither spoke. Neither wanted to. After a few minutes, the heave of his chest quieted.

Maddy looked at his face against her chest, at the divine, flawless features that still took her breath away. She reached out and, with the tip of her finger, touched his forehead. Then, as if it were a healing instrument, she traced the finger along his skin, across his temple, and down the line of his jaw, feeling the stubble of his beard. Finally, she traced up his chin and brushed his lips.

Jacks's eyes opened. He sat up and faced her, his wings expanding behind him, bathing the two of them in faint blue light. She watched him carefully and waited for him to stop her. He didn't. She touched him again, this time on his arm. She traced her finger along his forearm, up past his bicep, to his shoulder. Then, after hesitating only a moment, she moved her finger delicately onto the ridge of his wing. Jacks let out a heavy sigh, and suddenly, faster than Maddy could see, his powerful hands were on her arms. The grip was almost painful.

He kissed her fully and deeply. She pressed herself into him. The electricity began to thud like a hammer between them, back and forth, growing. Their bodies entwined in the dusty light of the gym, at half-court, the empty bleachers their only witnesses. Maddy drew a gasp of pleasure as Jacks lifted her onto his lap. He wrapped his wings around her body and she wrapped her legs around his.

Then suddenly, he stopped.

"We can't," he said, pulling himself away from her.

"What's wrong?" she said through gasps.

"It wouldn't be right. Not here. Not like this," he said.

Maddy's heart was racing in her chest, her breathing quick and erratic. She had to concentrate on taking slow, controlled breaths before she could speak again.

"You don't want to?" she said at last.

His eyes flashed.

"Of course I do. It's just more complicated . . . for us, Maddy. There's a lot more to it." Then softly, almost to himself, he murmured, "Or so I've been told."

Maddy nodded, feeling the excitement begin to bleed out of her. She sat back on the mat, feeling suddenly cold and alone without his touch.

"I've never done anything like that," she said with an embarrassed smile.

"Me neither," Jacks said. He was thoughtful again. He looked down at his Divine Ring and ran his fingers over the sacred inscription. Then his eyes flickered back to Maddy.

"I want to give you something." He slid the ring off his finger. "Up until this week, I've never wanted anything more in my life than to wear this ring. Not as a piece of jewelry, but because I thought I could find meaning in saving others, in being a hero. But the meaning I've finally found in my life is from meeting *you*." He set the ring on the palm of his hand and held it out. "I want you to have it."

Maddy looked at the ring. The light created a million tiny reflections that danced around his palm.

"I can't take it," she said, and closed his fingers back around it.

"I'm not asking," he said.

He took Maddy's hand and slid the ring onto her finger. It was stunning, but far too heavy for her to wear. She reached up to her neck and unclasped the simple chain necklace that hung there.

"This was my mother's," she said, taking the chain and threading the ring through it. "It's one of the only things I have to remember her by." She pulled the chain back around her neck and clasped it. The ring rested heavily in the basin of her chest, just below her collarbone. She looked into Jacks's eyes.

"Will you explain it to me sometime?" Maddy asked in a quiet voice. "What else there is to it. For . . . you."

Jacks smiled. "I promise. Later." He contracted his wings, wincing as he did.

"They're sore," he said.

"Come here," Maddy said. She sat cross-legged and held out her arms. He laid his head on her lap.

She sat there holding his head, playing lightly with his hair with her fingers. In response he lifted a hand and ran it along her back.

"Doesn't it feel strange?" he asked.

"Doesn't what?"

"Not having wings."

Maddy considered.

"I guess if you've never had them, you don't miss them."

Jacks smiled at her. "I guess."

His breaths became slow and measured. After a minute, Maddy realized he was asleep. *Even Angels have to sleep*, she thought. Then, before she was even aware of it, her head had dipped, her eyelids closed, and she slept too.

CHAPTER TWENTY-NINE

The neon sign for Kevin's Diner had long since been extinguished, but the parking lot was populated with ACPD police cars, as well as a number of strangely uniform, black Escalade SUVs. A single light filtered out from the nearly empty dining room.

Kevin sat in one of the booths, the lamp over his head making his eyes look sunken and hollow. He gazed out the window at the dark, foggy city. A patch of gauze was taped over his forehead where the shattering window had cut him, but otherwise, he was okay.

He turned his attention back and looked at the Council Disciplinary Agent sitting across from him. The Angel was imposing, with a build at least a foot taller than Kevin, a perfectly symmetrical face, and a sharp, square jaw. Other agents stood around them or milled about the darkened diner.

Kevin sighed and eyed the Angel, who hadn't moved.

"Even if I knew where they were going, I wouldn't tell you. I've already told the police everything I know. You don't even have the right to question me."

"We're working with the police now," the agent said in a smooth, articulate voice. "Jackson is suspected of kidnapping, as well as three homicides."

"Is that what the police think or the NAS?"

The front door opened with its usual chime. A shadowy figure walked between the dark tables toward them, obscured in the darkness until the cast of the lamplight fell on his face. It was Mark Godspeed.

"I can take it from here," Mark said to the agent.

The agent nodded and slid out of the booth. Mark sat down in his place.

"How are you, Kevin?"

"What do you want?" Kevin asked icily. Mark regarded him.

"I'm sorry about what happened to the house. The agents, they saw an opportunity, and they took it." He reached into his jacket. "I think this should probably cover it." He took out an envelope from his jacket pocket and slid it across the counter. Kevin hesitated, then picked it up and peered inside. It was a check for five hundred thousand dollars. "I put in a little extra for the damages Jacks did to your diner, too," Mark said, looking around. "I kind of thought this place could use some renovation anyway."

Kevin looked at the check for a moment, then set the envelope back down on the counter and slid it across to Mark. Mark looked surprised.

"If it's not enough, I'm sure we can do a little better."

"I don't want your money," Kevin said. "I told you and your boy to stay away from my niece. That was the agreement."

The silence hung heavy between them.

"I didn't come here to fight, Kevin," Mark said. "What's done is done. Let's talk about what we can agree on."

"And what's that?"

"I think we can agree that we both didn't want this to happen. Any of it. And we both don't want it to go any further. Am I right?"

After a moment Kevin nodded reluctantly.

"So please, Kevin, just tell me where they were going. Any clue you may have where they could be, where Maddy could have led them, would be vital. Anything that could help us."

"Why? So you can hunt them both down? Finish what you started twenty years ago?"

Mark leaned back in the booth, exasperated. He took a long breath, eyes intense. "I just want things to go back to the way they were before, Kevin. Before Angel wings started turning up on the boulevard, before police were chasing my stepson and he was taking waitresses to Commissioning parties." Kevin seemed to bristle at the word *waitress*, but he stayed silent. "Please," Mark went on, almost imploring, "don't you want her back in here? Working the morning shift? Going to school, getting ready for college, living the life she was meant to live?"

Kevin held up his hands in defeat.

"Yes, Mark. Of course. But the truth is I don't know where they went or what they were planning. We hadn't gotten that far when your agents came smashing in. That's the truth."

Mark nodded, accepting this.

"Does she know now?" he asked.

"Yes. She knows everything now," Kevin said, pausing. "And so does Jackson."

Mark's body stiffened almost imperceptibly.

"What are you going to do when you finally catch him?" Kevin asked.

Mark's expression hardened, and he looked out the window and into the darkness. Another silence settled over the booth as Kevin watched the Archangel. Kevin's eyes followed Mark's out to the parking lot, where there was some movement—more Council Disciplinary Agents arriving. What looked like maybe a girl, together with a broad-shouldered guy, neither in uniform but both clearly Angels, were lit for a moment by the light above the lot. But they disappeared back into the shadows. Kevin rubbed his eyes. He was exhausted.

"You haven't changed at all, have you, Mark?" Kevin said. "Your own stepson. Your wife's child. How could you?"

"Jacks was Commissioned a Guardian Angel and, as such, is subject to the same laws that govern all Guardians. Including me."

"Get out of here," Kevin said. "Take your bribe with you."

Mark regarded him coolly, then tucked the envelope back in his jacket.

"It's not as simple as that, Kevin," Mark said as he slid out of the booth and rose. "The situation has changed. I can't discuss it, but all I can say is I hope we find them. I hope we find them before something else does."

Kevin's face darkened in confusion and concern.

"Some*thing* else?"

But Mark turned without replying and disappeared into the darkness.

CHAPTER THIRTY

Maddy woke in utter darkness. A few moments passed before she remembered where she was. The gym. Angel City High. She was hiding with Jacks, and they both must have fallen asleep. Something was different from when they went to sleep. Then she realized it: all the lights were off. Reaching for Jacks, she discovered, with sudden panic, he wasn't there. The air around her suddenly felt harder to breathe. Her hands groped in the darkness. She opened her mouth to speak, but before she could, she felt a finger press delicately, but firmly, to her mouth.

It was Jacks. Silencing her.

She could just barely see him now in the dim light that crept in from the cracks under the gym doors. He was sitting up and utterly still. Something was wrong. In that same moment Maddy realized it hadn't just been her panic—the air around her *really was* harder to breathe. It scorched her lungs as she sucked it in. The entire gym had grown blisteringly hot while they slept. It was stifling. What was going on? A bead of sweat rolled down Maddy's forehead and splattered against the mat. Her hair was damp and sticky. She turned to Jacks.

"What is it?" she whispered.

"I'm not sure," Jacks whispered back. "Something's in here with us. I turned the lights off, but it knows we're in here."

"What is it?"

"I don't know. I've never felt anything like it. It's like pure evil. It's not friendly," Jacks said.

Maddy began to tremble. Taking her hands, Jacks wrapped them around the ring on her neck.

"We're going to go into the hall together, and then I want you to run. Don't look back. No matter what you hear, just keep running."

"What? What are you going to do?"

Jacks was silent.

"You're saying goodbye, aren't you? You're going to try and fight it."

"Whatever it is, it knows we're in here. It will never let us just walk down the hallway and out of here. It's our only chance."

"What if there's another way out?"

"A way we can go without using the halls?"

Maddy willed her terrified mind to think logically. Rationally. Then she saw it.

"Yes. Some of the classrooms connect. If we go out through the locker room, we could cut through the classrooms to get to the other side of the school. Once we're there, let's just hope the gate is open."

She could barely see the silhouette of his face in the darkness.

"Which way is it?"

Maddy led them silently toward the girls' locker room door. When they had passed through it, she made sure the latch reengaged without making any noise.

In the dark, the silent rows of lockers seemed alive and menacing, like some kind of horrific, hallucinatory maze. Fog covered all the mirrors. Condensation dripped down the glass, reminding Maddy of rivulets of blood. Could something be hiding in this labyrinth, waiting for them? She looked at the lockers hanging open, the few towels left on the ground. Everything was utterly still. Maddy took Jacks by the hand and led him down one of the rows. They passed the coach's office.

A voice called out to them from the darkness.

Maddy felt Jacks's hand crush down on hers. He turned to shield her from whatever might leap out at them from the darkness.

"Baby, when I think of you-ou-ou, I get so blue-ue-ue."

It was the gym coach's radio, no doubt left on by a custodian after cleaning up the locker room. Jacks relaxed his grip on her hand.

"Ain't gonna just stand around while you run off with somebody new-ew-ew."

Then, from the opposite side of the gym, they heard the click of the door latch. This was no radio, no TV. Something was trying to get into the locker room.

Maddy pulled Jacks through the dry showers.

She could see, for the first time, a glint of fear in his eyes.

The door to the gymnasium began to open. Whatever was out there, in another second, it would be in the room with them. They rounded the shower stalls and Maddy spotted the door at the end of the short corridor. It had a small, square window in it, which let in light from the hallway outside. They were close. And that's when Maddy heard it.

Footsteps in the locker room behind them. Panic surged up her throat. Whatever it was, it had feet. There was a thump, followed by two clicking sounds, like knife blades against the linoleum tile.

Step, *click click*. Step, *click click*.

Jacks squeezed her hand and mouthed a single word.

"Go."

They glided over the floor in silence. Maddy reached the door and applied just enough pressure on the handle to check the lock. The handle depressed and the door moved effortlessly out of the jamb. It was unlocked. She swung the door open and they slipped through, leaving whatever it was—the *thing*—behind them in the locker room. They emerged into the hallway next to the vending machines. The whir of the refrigerators made it impossible to hear behind them. Maddy scanned down the stifling hall. The heat and humidity had fogged the windows to the classrooms. There was no way of seeing inside them.

"Come on," she whispered, moving to the nearest door. "I have class in this room. I think it connects to the bio lab. The lab goes to a hall that can take us to the other side of the school."

"Go, go," Jacks whispered urgently. They went.

Maddy put a hand on the door handle and steadied her trembling heart. Cracking it open, she peered inside. Silent. Nothing. She swung the classroom door open. The empty desks cast long shadows in the light from the hallway. It was her AP History class. On the board the assignment for the weekend was still written there:

Read New History of Angels, pages 220–256

They moved into the classroom and Jacks shut the door silently behind them. Maddy could almost hear the chatter of her classmates as she moved through the desks and the drone of Mr. Rankin at the board. They were the sounds of safety, the sounds of wonderfully commonplace well-being. If she ever got out of this alive, she promised never to take those mundane sounds for granted again.

They passed Mr. Rankin's desk and suddenly Jacks grabbed Maddy by the hoodie and yanked her down to the floor. His eyes darted to the window, where a black silhouette moved across the light. It was large, taller than the windows. *Big.* Maddy held her breath as it passed the classroom. Her heart was pounding. Then it stopped and came back, shadowing the windows again. It was *smelling*, Maddy thought. Hunting. The latch on the door began to turn.

"Don't look back," Jacks whispered as they moved toward the door at the far end of the classroom. Jacks pulled the door shut behind them just as the entrance to the hallway swung open.

It knew where they were now, Maddy thought. It was closing in.

Jacks pulled Maddy down behind a long counter. She listened to the sound of her shallow, quick breaths, trying to control them. The lab was divided by four counters running the length of the room, bordered by narrow alleys on either side. Test tubes, beakers, and other glassware sat atop the tables awaiting next week's use. Maddy peered at the far door, across the room. She could see the hallway through the door's square window. The hallway, she knew, led directly out the school's side entrance to the street.

"Let's go," Maddy said. "We can make it if we run." Jacks held her arm with an iron grip.

"No. We can't," he said quietly.

"Why not?" she whispered, almost pleading.

"Because it's in here with us."

Maddy heard the door to the classroom click shut. The darkness felt suddenly alive all around her. Then she heard it. The faintest sound of air.

She could hear the thing breathing.

A suffocating heat permeated the darkness like growing fire that gave off no light. The pungent smell of earth, decay, and something worse wafted out of the darkness toward her. It smelled like death, Maddy thought. Stinking death itself.

A scream rose up her throat and she slapped her hand over her mouth. It took all her strength to stop it.

Maddy listened as the thing began to move through the room.

Step, *click click*. Step, *click click*.

Jacks held up one finger. Maddy stared at the silent signal, willing her terrified mind to understand. Then she got it. *One*. It was behind the first counter. Jacks crouched with his feet under him and beckoned her. Maddy shook her head. She was frozen with fear.

Jacks pointed toward the door. Through a red fog of terror Maddy realized what he was indicating. They had lured the thing into the maze of the lab, and they were going to slip out while it searched for them. They crawled on their hands and knees, listening to the steps of the creature.

Step, *click click*. Step, *click click*.

Then the footsteps stopped.

Silence descended over the room. Jacks put a hand on Maddy's forearm, an indication to be absolutely still. She held her breath. At last, Jacks pointed up.

It was right above them, on the counter.

Maddy felt the scream rising up inside her again, and this time she didn't know if she could stop it. She pressed her trembling lips together, but they were numb. She felt herself losing control of her body. Her mouth opened to scream.

Jacks's hand closed around her mouth like a vise. His other hand wrapped around her waist and pulled her toward him. He held her in the darkness as the scream died silently in her mouth.

The second passed like hours. After what seemed like an unbearable length of time, Maddy heard two footfalls as the thing stepped off the counter.

Step, *click click*. Step, *click click*.

It was back on the ground, continuing its methodical investigation of the lab. Jacks released Maddy from his grip and mouthed a single word.

"Move."

On their hands and knees again, they circled around the second counter and headed for the third. Maddy saw they were close to the door now. A tiny spark of hope leapt inside her. They could do this, she thought. They could make it. She scooted quickly around the corner and her shoulder collided silently with the counter, jarring it.

Perrrring.

It sounded like the ring of a delicate bell. The sound seemed to roll and then disappear. In the rush of adrenaline, Maddy recognized the sound instantly. A test tube had just rolled off the counter in front of her, and it was heading toward the floor. She thrust her hands out blindly in front of her. She was terrible at any sport that involved catching anything—or really, any sport at all. Miraculously, she felt the slap of the delicate glass cylinder against her palm. It leapt up again, and for a single breathless moment it danced across her reaching fingertips. Then it was gone.

The sound of the tube shattering was like a gunshot in her ears. It was followed by the most awful, inhuman sound she had ever heard. It sounded like tearing metal, like the growl of some rabid animal, hungry and guttural. It was so loud it was painful. Instantly Maddy felt something grab her by her hood. She heard fabric tearing.

It was a claw.

Maddy shrieked and threw her arms backward, wriggling out of the hoodie as the claw cut it cleanly in half. She felt Jacks's strong hands around her waist, pulling her away from the beast.

"Run, Maddy!" he yelled.

Maddy tore into the black hall. She was alone now, terrified and blind, running through the darkness. Arms that were not Jacks's wrapped around Maddy. She screamed.

CHAPTER THIRTY-ONE

"It's okay, it's okay," a voice whispered. "You're okay now." Maddy looked up at the man who was holding her. He was older and wore glasses. His face was creased and worn.

"It's got Jacks!" Maddy protested, her voice muffled against the man's jacket. "We have to help him." Maddy twisted away from his grasp and ran back down the hall. The man followed quickly. They found Jacks crouched like an animal waiting to attack. His wings trembled in the air, ready. In a blur, he had thrown the man against the lockers. The Angel's eyes burned in fear, almost unrecognizable.

"Jacks, wait!" Maddy said.

"It's . . . gone . . ." the man choked. "Please, it's gone." It was several seconds before Jacks released his grip on the man's throat. The man slumped, coughing, against the lockers. Jacks's chest was heaving. His eyes darted to Maddy and then back to the man.

"Wait a minute, I *know* you," Jacks said furiously.

"My name is Sylvester. I'm a detective with the ACPD. We met when

I interviewed you at your house earlier this week." Jacks's face tensed. Sylvester held up a hand in surrender. "I'm alone. If my intention was to arrest you, this place would be swarming with police right now."

"What are you doing here?" Jacks asked. Sylvester rubbed his throat.

"Up until tonight I was leading the investigation into the Angel attacks on the boulevard. I started tracking the demon two days ago. I tracked him here."

Demon, Maddy thought. She had heard the word before but never thought they were real.

"It just left," Jacks said, his eyes bewildered. "It was right there, facing me, and then it just disappeared."

Sylvester nodded. "I was hoping this would work if I ever made contact, and it did, but it likely won't again." He opened his fist. A small amulet with an ancient inscription sat on the palm of his hand. He retrieved the brass ornamental box from the pocket of his jacket and carefully placed the object on the crushed purple velvet inside. He closed the box securely.

Jacks studied the tall, tired man before him. His eyes narrowed.

"You're an Angel," Jacks said in disbelief.

Sylvester nodded again. "Yes, I am."

"How is that possible?"

"Not every Angel is still a Guardian, Jackson," Sylvester said, "and not all Angels are loyal to the Council."

Jacks stepped back. Sylvester straightened up and smoothed his coat.

"You have a theory?" Jacks said. "About this . . . this *thing*?"

Sylvester shrugged. "It's just a hunch."

Jacks considered his words. "We need to talk," he said after a moment.

Sylvester's brow furrowed. "Technically I should be bringing you in."

"But you're not going to do that," Jacks said carefully. "Are you?"

Sylvester sighed.

"No, I'm not," the detective said. He removed his glasses and rubbed his face. He looked between Jacks and Maddy.

"My car is parked out front. I'll pull it around."

They rode in the back of Sylvester's unmarked cruiser through the sleeping streets of the Immortal City. The car tracked past the pockets of nocturnal homeless and criminals, fluorescent-lit twenty-four-hour donut shops, the occasional fogged window with lights creeping out from behind drawn curtains. Unsavory business getting transacted. The Angel City underworld. In another hour or so, it would start to get light, street sweepers would scour the roads and alleys, and the Immortal City would be camera ready again.

Maddy settled into the seat quietly next to Jacks and let the relief course through her veins. She had never experienced fear like that she had felt in that biology lab. She wasn't sure she trusted the rumpled detective who was driving them to who knew where, but at least they were headed away from the school. At least for now they were safe.

Maddy looked down at the small gap of vinyl between her and Jacks on the seat. When they had gotten into the backseat, she had instinctively left that space between them, like she always did. A minimum of protection from Jacks's intoxicating presence.

In the terror of the moment she had almost forgotten the new deal she had made with herself. To believe he actually had feelings for her. To let him in. Carefully, she leaned toward him and closed the gap between them. Her heart thudded irregularly as her shoulder touched his, and the wave of his warmth washed over. It was so lovely to be close to him. Jacks reached over and rested his hand on her leg. The casual touch was thrilling. Like he was familiar with her. She sat there feeling the warmth of his hand through her jeans, listening to the sound of her pounding heart, and trying to control her suddenly erratic breathing as Sylvester pulled up a narrow driveway and parked.

The apartment was in a Spanish-style building from the 1930s. Old Angel City, Maddy thought, a reminder of a forgotten past. They followed him upstairs and into his corner unit. The apartment was simple and unadorned. There was a living room with a fireplace at its center instead of a television and chairs for sitting instead of a couch. Through the glass door of the tiny balcony she could see an old Catholic church. She had never noticed it before; it was beautiful.

Newspaper clippings and articles haphazardly covered the walls. The apartment must double as an office, Maddy thought. She went to the wall and read some of the clippings. Bizarre sightings, unexplained tragedies, natural disasters. Descriptions of a strange, burning creature with wings. Maddy began to feel uneasy. When Sylvester spoke, it made her jump.

"I know it's not much," Sylvester said, a little self-conscious, "but please make yourselves at home." Maddy turned and glanced at Jacks. He gave her a nod as if to say he thought things were okay. They sat in the old chairs.

"It's not every day I have a Godspeed and a Godright over," Sylvester said as he settled into his chair.

"You know?" Jacks said, surprised.

"Of course," Sylvester said, looking at them both. "I'm one of the very few who does."

Jacks nodded. He was silent for a moment as he considered this.

"That thing," Jacks said finally. "At the school. I've never felt anything like it. I've never seen anything like it."

"Most of us haven't," Sylvester said grimly. "It's been years since anyone has encountered a Dark Angel."

"A what?" Maddy asked.

"A demon," Jacks said.

The word hung ominously in the tiny room.

"But there's no such thing," Maddy said, as if saying the words would make it so. Sylvester looked at her evenly.

"If you can accept there are Angels in the world, then you must also realize that there are demons." His face was deadly serious. "Just as there is a world above us, there is a world below us too, Maddy."

"But they were destroyed. Thousands of years ago," Jacks said.

"The world is a darker place than you think, Jackson."

Maddy thought about the *thing*. She felt the claw trace down her back again. A demon. It sent a chill slithering down her spine.

"Demons can be found in the darkest corners of our world. They're in the shadows, causing catastrophic earthquakes, tsunamis, even hurricanes. I think if someone went looking for a Dark Angel and looked hard enough, they could find one."

"Even if what you're saying is true," Maddy said, "and even if they do still exist, what was one doing in my high school?"

Sylvester's face faltered. "I don't know. Ancient writings, even the Bible, describe demons attacking cities and laying waste to villages. Causing chaos. What's going on in Angel City is entirely different. This demon is attacking specific Angels. It's choosing its targets. It tracked Jackson there. It feels like premeditation to me, like there's a motive behind it. It feels like a good, old-fashioned, regular crime."

Jacks studied Sylvester intently. "Meaning what?"

Sylvester removed his glasses and began polishing the lenses against his shirt.

"Meaning I think someone could be controlling it. That's my theory at least. We talk about demons in our lives, and we talk about *controlling* them. Where do these metaphors come from? I think a long time ago it was possible to hire a demon, much like Angels are hired today. Not with money, of course, but with something much more valuable. Something the demon wants. It may still be possible today. Someone might have brought a demon to the city and be using it to carry out these attacks." He finished his polishing and returned his glasses to his face. "I know it sounds incredible, but I think someone is playing a very dangerous game with a force they can't possibly comprehend."

Maddy's heart was racing. "But who would do that? Who would be using it to kill Angels? And sending it after *us*?"

"The Archangels," Jacks said miserably, thinking about the stain on Mark's jacket. "It has to be the Archangels. They must be using it to eliminate their enemies, and now that includes us."

"I wouldn't jump to conclusions," Sylvester said. "It's one possibility. Although . . . hmm." He got up and started pacing. "I haven't been able to put my finger on why the NAS would want to eliminate Godson, Templeton, and Crossman. They weren't with the anti-Angel movement. I found no evidence of ties between them and Senator Linden, say, or the HDF. But Godson was known to be a womanizer and a drunk, and Templeton had a secret drug addiction. It could be that the Archangels are pruning the tree, cutting off embarrassing branches. I'll have Garcia look into Crossman's background."

"It's the only possibility," Jacks said through his teeth. "Kevin said the Archangels would do whatever it took to keep us apart. We'll, that's exactly what they're doing. They're going to kill us just like they killed Jacob and Regina. Just like they killed my father."

The detective looked unblinking at the young Angel in front of him.

Jackson stared back, narrowing his eyes. "What happened to you? Did they take . . . ?"

"Yes, the NAS took my wings. Punishment," Sylvester said. Maddy's eyes grew wide. "Not for missing a save, like most police at ACPD would think."

"What was it?" Maddy asked.

"It was for saving someone who wasn't a Protection."

"The Archangels let you live?" Jacks said, astonished.

"It wasn't public. They didn't consider me a threat. Found it more of a punishment to mortalize me, discredit me, send me as a 'failure' into the human world." Sylvester studied him gravely. "You can be sure they won't have the same leniency with you. You're too involved with Maddy, everyone was watching your Commissioning. You're just too big, Jackson."

Maddy held her breath. The detective was silent. Jacks sat very still. She could see him thinking intensely.

"What should we do?" Maddy said finally.

"We're getting out of here," Jacks said. It surprised them both. "I want to get as far away from Angel City and from the NAS as I can."

He turned to Sylvester.

"We need to figure out a way to get out of the city. Will you help us?"

Sylvester looked back and forth between them with searching eyes, then nodded.

"Yes, of course."

"Thank you," Jacks said, giving him an appreciative nod. Maddy watched as despair washed in waves over his face. She wondered if he was replaying the detective's words in his head, or Kevin's words, or maybe even Mark's. Was he remembering the chase through the skyline or the demon? Maddy wished she could know what he was thinking. That she could help. Jacks got up and left the living room. He went out to the tiny balcony and slumped down in a chair. After a moment, Maddy followed.

The balcony faced the street, with a view of Sunset and of East Angel City. Jacks sat in one of the rusted metal chairs. A few dead plants sat in pots on a wire table. Maddy sat in the chair next to him. They watched the first light of the gray dawn spread along the streets.

"Everything I've believed in is a lie, Maddy," Jacks muttered. "Everything I've worked for since I was ten. Angels aren't the heroes. We're the villains."

Maddy shook her head firmly. "You are not a villain," she said.

He looked at her with searching, intense eyes. "Will you come with me? Leave the city. I mean, haven't you ever just wanted to get out of here?"

It was all she had ever wanted. She had always imagined it would be with her bags packed for college, and not escaping as a fugitive. But it was still leaving, all the same.

"Yes," she said. It was the only answer. Not just because it was what she had always wanted, but because, she suddenly realized, she was going wherever Jacks was going. It was just like when he had invited her to the party and asked her to come with him on the rainy rooftop. There was only ever one answer.

"Good. We'll leave this morning and never come back to Angel City again."

He smiled at her, but the smile was edged with sadness. Reaching over, she placed her hand over his on the table. Just as he had done for her at her house, she supported him by saying the most important thing she could say. Nothing at all.

She felt the contours of his hand around hers and realized it was becoming familiar to her. Like much of him. Sitting next to him in silence, Maddy was surprised to realize she was totally happy in this moment. It was incredible. She wasn't used to being happy. She didn't want it to end.

"It's going to be dangerous," Jacks said, interrupting the silence.

"I know," Maddy said. She thought about what would be involved in trying to escape Angel City while not being recognized. Her stomach filled with a heavy feeling. There was something she was missing, even if she couldn't put her finger on it.

"I'm willing to risk it if you are," he said.

"Yeah," Maddy said. "Me too."

"We'll be okay so long as we're together," he said, leaning over and putting his lips in her hair.

Maddy reached up and put her hand on his face. "We will, together."

They were silent a moment longer before Maddy heard Sylvester shuffling around inside.

"We should get going," Jacks said, drawing away.

They got up and went back into the apartment, leaving the balcony and the dawn, silent behind them.

CHAPTER THIRTY-TWO

Kevin sat motionless in the sea of empty tables in Kevin's Diner. He wouldn't be opening today. The sound of silence in the usually bustling dining room was so loud it was nearly overwhelming.

After the Angels left, he had just wandered about the abandoned tables and booths. He thought about going home, but he didn't know if he could face the house without Maddy, if he could look at the gaping, jagged windows that had swallowed her into the night. So he had decided to stay in the restaurant, but it wasn't much better. He still hadn't slept.

When dawn finally came, he rose from his seat and shuffled back into the kitchen. There was no great hurry. The cold kitchen smelled of stale grease and cleaning solvent. He picked up the coffeepot to rinse it out, but it was already clean. He checked the burners again to make sure they were off. They were. He picked up the broom from the corner and ran it over the floor. The bristles against the linoleum made the only sound in the restaurant. He stopped after a moment and put the broom back. Silent again. Absolute stillness. His gaze drifted to the counter, where he was surprised to see Maddy's notepad. He must not have noticed it in the dark last night. It was sitting haphazardly where she had thrown it after her last shift. When had that even been? He couldn't remember. It seemed like ages ago. Another life.

He went to the notepad and picked it up. He flipped through the pages. He looked at her scrawl, which he always criticized her for. Even now he could barely read it. Did that say with onions? Or no onions? *It's unreadable*, he used to scold her. *I can't cook the food if I can't read your writing.* He would be okay with it now, he thought. He would be fine with however she wrote the orders, if only she were here to write them. He set the notepad back down and leaned against the fryer, fighting the first tears he had felt in years.

The steel lock of the front door banged as someone tried to open it, followed by a knock on the glass.

"We're closed!" Kevin yelled from the kitchen. The knock came again. Kevin looked up. He could see a silhouette on the other side of the door framed by the colorless glow of the morning.

"I said we're closed!" he yelled again, anger edging his voice.

More raps on the glass. Insistent.

With an annoyed sigh, Kevin rounded the corner of the kitchen and walked to the front door. He unlocked the door with a jingle and looked out.

Standing there was an intensely beautiful woman he had never seen before. She seemed to be middle-aged but was slender and impossibly striking. There was something about her that was strangely familiar.

"I'm sorry, but we're closed," Kevin said in a suddenly softer tone, almost startled by her beauty. The woman just stood there, a dark Hermès scarf wrapped around her hair.

"Mr. Montgomery?" she asked.

"If you're a reporter, I don't have a comment," he said.

"I'm not a reporter. I need to talk to you about your niece, Maddy. And my son. It's important."

"Your son?" Kevin asked.

She nodded.

"Jackson."

Kevin blinked at her. It was Kris Godspeed. He had only ever heard about her, and maybe seen a few pictures over the years. He had never met her. Now he knew why she had seemed familiar to him. The likeness between her and Jacks was almost uncanny.

"Come in," he said reluctantly. She quickly stepped in and Kevin locked the door again behind her.

Kris looked around the diner. She appeared somewhat on edge, unsure of herself. She was clearly out of place. Kevin motioned for her to take a seat at a nearby booth.

"Please," he said.

They both sat.

"Would you like some coffee?" he offered.

"No. Thank you," Kris said politely. "How is your head?"

"My head? Oh." He touched the gauze on his forehead. He had completely forgotten. "I'll live."

He regarded her. Beneath the layer of hastily applied makeup he could see the lines of fear and worry framing her face. He wondered if she had slept.

"What is it you want?" he asked.

She looked like she was considering her words, maybe even reconsidering her decision to come and see him. For a moment he thought she might even get up, apologize, and ask to leave. Then finally, she spoke.

"No one knows I'm here," she said, "But I had to come see you."

"I don't know where they are," Kevin said preemptively.

"I'm not asking. I know the Council Disciplinary Agents have already been here, as has my husband."

Kevin nodded.

"I also know your general opinion about Angels, Mr. Montgomery." She paused, her eyes intent on him. "I came here hoping you might listen to me not as an Angel, but as a mother. Can we talk one parent to another?"

"Go on," Kevin said after a moment.

"I don't care about the law. I just don't want them to hurt my son. I don't want Maddy to get hurt either. I want to end this thing before it goes any further, before something terrible happens. To either of them."

"When I talked to Mark last night, he seemed determined to follow the law to the letter, no matter what," Kevin said. "And no matter who."

Kris nodded. "As an Archangel, that is his duty. But as a father, he has a duty too, and he's managed to do something extraordinary. He has spoken to the Council."

Kevin's face showed surprise, but still remained skeptical.

"There is a chance now, a chance for Jacks to walk away from all this and be forgiven. A chance for Maddy to come home, and for all of this to go away."

"I don't understand what you need me for then," Kevin said. Kris regarded him. He wondered suddenly if she understood something about what happened that he did not.

"I know the way my son feels about your niece." She shook her head and looked at her hands on the table. "It's something Mark could never understand, and so that is why I have come to you. I need you to get a message to her."

When she looked up at him again, her eyes were wet.

"Only you can make this happen. Only you can save my boy. So I'm coming to you, and"—she swallowed hard—"I'm begging you. Please help me. For my son. For my only son. Please help me save his life and bring him home."

Her face dropped again and her shoulders shuddered as she stifled her crying. Kevin considered her—considered not the Angel, but the mother before him. He took a deep breath and spoke.

"What's the message?"

CHAPTER THIRTY-THREE

Palm trees stood dead still in the windless morning. The marine layer had settled in and hung low over the city as they drove. Maddy and Jacks sat in the back of Sylvester's unmarked cruiser. Jacks wore a long trench coat, dark glasses, and a fedora he had borrowed from the detective to hide his identity. Maddy had taken a thick scarf and another pair of dark shades. They looked a little oddly dressed, but hopefully not so much so that they would attract attention. Sylvester had the slightest of a grin, looking at the two of them in the rearview mirror as he drove.

"It's going to work," he said.

Jacks watched out the window as they passed under the huge Angel billboards. The largest advertisement of all was of him, of course, plastered on the entire side of a building. There he was, twenty stories high, wearing the latest pair of Nike Wings.

"Feels different now?" Maddy asked, gazing at it too.

"Yeah," Jacks said thoughtfully. "It does."

After a few minutes they pulled into Union Station.

"Be safe," Sylvester said as they got out. "Call if you need me, but remember, no cell phones." He wrote his number down and passed it over. They said a quick goodbye and walked into the terminal.

The train station was busy and loud. Maddy had, in fact, been there before, when Kevin used to take her on day trips to San Diego as a little girl. The station had a single, sprawling lobby under a vaulted wood-beam ceiling, with a marble floor and arched windows that looked out to courtyards. It had always reminded her of a scene from an old movie. Directly ahead stood an advertising kiosk that Maddy couldn't help but notice with dull annoyance. On it was a picture of Vivian running her hand seductively through her hair to show off a twinkling diamond Cartier watch on her wrist. Could she ever get away from that Angel? Beyond the kiosk, an ornate, arched hallway extended under a tunnel that read TO ALL TRAINS.

Maddy looked on the crowded station with equal emotions of fear and excitement. The terror of being recognized in such a public place fought in her heart with the thrill of finally getting out of Angel City. With Jacks at her side. Maddy wondered how many times she had dreamed of this, of seeing Angel City disappear in the distance forever. It was everything she had ever wanted, and yet, she was surprised when Sylvester agreed to drive them to the station that she didn't feel more, well, excited. As much as she tried to deny it, something was nagging her. Again. She told herself it was just the fear of going out during the day and the risk of being recognized, but in truth, she knew it was something else. It was another voice in the back of her head, like the night at Jacks's party, speaking words of warning she couldn't quite make out.

"Come on," Jacks said, taking her hand. "Just act normal."

They headed toward the large electronic departure board and the ticket windows at the far side of the lobby. A few people looked askance at their overdressed appearance, but no one cared enough to say anything or really take a second look. Jacks let Maddy lead the way for once. She knew the terminal already, and besides, Jacks had only ever traveled in private jets; she wasn't sure how familiar he was with the concept of public transportation.

She gathered fragments of conversations as they passed crowded waiting areas. Most people were talking about them, it seemed, chatting excitedly about the scandal and the ongoing manhunt. They intently watched flat screen TVs distributed around the room as ANN reported on the latest developments. Maddy tried to raise her gaze discreetly and catch a piece of the broadcast but looked quickly away when she noticed a little girl peering at her curiously. The girl had on a Team Maddy shirt. Her sister was wearing Team Jacks. Maddy couldn't help but stare for a moment. It was unreal. The girl looked at Maddy and opened her mouth to say something but then was quickly pulled away by her parents.

With a horrible jolt, Maddy thought of the demon they had encountered just hours before. In her mind, every person who passed was looking at them. Who could they trust? What if this was a trap?

"Jacks," she said under her breath. "What if the detective is leading us into something? Wasn't it convenient that he arrived just as the Dark Angel was there? How did he *know*?" Maddy's mind flashed to the maps, the articles on Sylvester's apartment wall. She hadn't actually inspected them too closely—could it have been that those were for *planning* the attacks? That *he* was the one controlling it?

A shadow crossed Jackson's face as she watched him consider it. Her pulse quickened. The detective knew so much. But wouldn't he have taken the opportunity to kill them right there, in the school?

"No. Maybe. It's too late anyway, Maddy. We have to go ahead; it's our only hope of getting out of Angel City."

Maddy scanned the spacious hall. Streams of travelers moved past, not taking notice of them. She took a deep breath and calmed a bit. Jackson was right. But she still had that nagging feeling that there was something she was forgetting.

"Okay."

Maddy led him to the ticket kiosks. Sylvester had given them a prepaid debit card to use at the machines; they couldn't buy tickets from the staffed windows or they would have to show ID. They stopped in front of the electronic boards displaying departure and arrival information.

"I'm going to find a pay phone and call my uncle," Maddy said. Jacks gave her a hard look. "I need to make sure he's okay after last night. And . . . I want to say goodbye."

Jacks hesitated for another moment, then his face cleared in understanding.

"Okay. Let me handle tickets, then," he said, squeezing her hand. "It'll be a surprise."

"Let's meet on the train platform," Maddy suggested. "Better not spend any more time out here in the open than we need to." Jacks agreed.

She walked over to a row of pay phones. Each phone was housed in its own glass booth, another relic of the old station. She stepped inside the nearest one and closed the door behind her, cutting the terminal noise to a muted murmur. She picked up the phone and listened to the dial tone. What was she going to say? What could she say? *After seventeen years of your taking care of me, I'm just leaving forever? Nice knowin' ya?*

Through the glass, Maddy looked back to where Jacks was standing in front of the departure and arrival board. She watched him scratch his head as he considered destinations. San Diego. San Luis Obispo. Bakersfield. Maddy sighed. It was too late to second-guess anything now. They had formed their plan; now they had to follow through with it. She fed in two quarters and dialed.

Kevin picked up after the first ring.

"Kevin, it's me," she said.

"Maddy?" His voice was ragged, as if he hadn't slept at all. "Are you okay?"

"Yes, I'm with Jacks. Are you . . . okay?"

"I'm fine. Just a scratch on the forehead. Maddy, where are you?"

She looked out the window at the station but bit her lip. "I can't tell you."

"I need to talk to you, Maddy," he said, his tone urgent. "Jacks's mother came into the diner this morning."

Maddy froze. She had been expecting him to try to convince her to come home or maybe go to the authorities. She was completely unprepared for this. *Jacks's mother*? Her eyes darted back in the direction of the departure board, but Jacks had vanished. Buying tickets, most likely, or already down at the train platform.

"W-what?" she managed to stammer at last.

"She wanted my help in getting a message to you."

"What's the message?" Maddy's heart suddenly raced.

"Jacks's stepfather has managed to negotiate a deal with the Council and the rest of the Archangels. It's a chance for Jacks to get out of this situation Immortal and alive. They're willing to forgive everything so long as the two of you never see each other again. Jacks goes home this morning, alone, and becomes a Guardian Angel; you come home to me and go back to being Maddy Montgomery, senior at Angel City High. You both live out your lives separately, as it was meant to be." Kevin paused. "They just want this all to go away, Maddy."

The phone booth suddenly felt claustrophobic and suffocating.

"We're leaving, Kevin," Maddy said, trying to sound resolute. "That's why I'm calling."

"They will never stop hunting him," Kevin said, his tone abruptly hard. "They *will* track him down. You've seen how powerful they are. We both have. Does he really think he can run from the Angels forever? This is Jacks's one chance, and it's in your hands."

"It's his decision," Maddy said quickly. "Why is it in *my* hands?"

"Because you're the one who has to leave him. He thinks he's protecting you, so he'll never leave your side. But if you stay with him, you'll kill him."

Maddy listened in silence to the buzz and crackle of the line.

"I don't understand. What is it you expect me to do?"

"Leave him." Kevin's words were like daggers. "Tell him you've changed your mind. Get out of there, and get him to go home."

"How could I hurt him like that?"

"Hurt him to save him," Kevin snapped. "If you don't, they will find him, and when they do, they *will* mortalize him. If you care about him, you'll do this for him." His tone took on a kind of naked appeal Maddy had never heard before. "Maddy, listen to me, what do you think you're doing? You can never be a part of his world, and he can never be a part of yours. He's a Guardian Angel and you're my niece and I love you, but you're just . . ."

"Nobody?"

Kevin sighed.

"Normal, Maddy. You're just normal. You're not meant for what he's meant for. He's going to be the Guardian Jackson Godspeed and this is where he needs to be, in the city of Angels." He paused. "The truth is I don't care what happens to Jacks, but I care what happens to you. I tried to tell my sister what I'm telling you now, and she wouldn't listen to me. Look what happened to her, Maddy. Look what happened to them both. Please, don't make the same mistake she did. I don't want to lose you. And if you care about Jackson, do this for him too."

Kevin's words echoed in the tiny booth. Suddenly she realized the thought that had been nagging at her since Jacks had come up with the plan at Sylvester's apartment. It was the same inevitable truth her uncle was talking about: they could never run from the Angels. It hadn't been twelve hours since Jacks saved her life, and they had barely made it this far. Were they just deluding themselves by believing they could get away?

"This is what's best for both of you," Kevin said. "But of course it's up to you. It's your decision."

She watched the bustle of the travelers outside. When she spoke again, her voice was barely more than a whisper.

"If . . . I did, do I have your word, and Mark's word, that nothing bad will happen to Jacks?"

"Yes," Kevin said.

Maddy let the ice water of reality wash over her. This was the only way to save Jacks. The word was out before she could stop it.

"Okay," she said.

"Good girl," Kevin said. "Now where are you?"

"Union Station," Maddy said.

"I'll call Kris right now and they'll send someone to pick him up. I can be there in ten minutes for you. It's what's best, Maddy. Now go tell him you're leaving. Do it now. I'll see you soon."

The line went dead.

Maddy stood there with the phone still pressed to her ear. The dial tone droned. She pressed a hand to her temple and leaned her throbbing forehead against the glass. Nausea came with the pain, rolling and lapping against the walls of her stomach. She began to tremble.

Suddenly there was a rap on the glass. Maddy turned to see a security guard glaring at her. Her heart leapt into her throat. Maybe this was it, and she had been caught, and she would be saved from what she knew she had to do. She opened the door.

"No loitering in the booths, miss," he said in an annoyed tone.

Maddy nodded, moving numbly past him.

She entered the tunnel at the end of the lobby under the TO ALL TRAINS sign. Slowly her thoughts began to break through the brick wall of shock and to plan. She was going to hurt him. She had to. Then she was going to go back home and be Maddy Montgomery again, and forget she had ever met Jackson Godspeed.

Anxiety welled up in her as she emerged onto the platform and found herself alone. She looked around. Maybe he had left without her. She almost hoped it. Then she saw him, standing at the far edge of the gray platform, waiting for her.

Standing there for a moment, Maddy just watched him. She took a picture in her mind that she would keep forever after this was over and she had gone back to being just another girl. She knew she would see him on TV and in magazines and on billboards—she had already prepared herself for that—but this image of him would be different because this moment was hers and hers alone. Jackson Godspeed, waiting on a foggy train platform next to a hissing locomotive, waiting to whisk her away to an impossible future they would never share.

He turned and saw her. His face brightened at her approach. She allowed herself to bask in his magnetic presence one last time.

"The train should be here any minute," Jacks said. "I tried for California, but there were only short trips to Anaheim and Solana Beach. Anyway, I've never been to"—he checked the ticket—"Kansas City."

Maddy stood quiet.

"What's wrong?" he asked, seeing the look on her face.

She had pushed him away so many times before, but now she didn't know if she could. Her head was throbbing in protest. She met his gaze.

"Jacks, I can't do this."

He stepped toward her, confused.

"What are you worried about? We're almost there." He glanced down the track. "I think this is it approaching now. We can get on right here; no one will see us."

"No." Maddy's tone was cold. "This isn't right for me."

Jacks paused. An announcement for Kansas City echoed on the platform.

"What do you mean?"

"What I mean is I want you to leave me alone, Jacks," she said tonelessly. Almost robotic. "I'm going home and I want you to stay away from me."

It was as though the words had physically struck him.

"Both our lives are in danger, Maddy," he said in a low, urgent voice, color draining from his face.

"My life is in danger because I'm with *you*, Jacks," she snapped. "It's like Sylvester said. They will never allow us to be together. If I go back to being a normal girl—"

"But you're *not* a normal girl," Jacks said.

"I *am*, Jacks. When are you going to realize that?" Her voice was almost hysterical now. "We come from two different worlds, Jackson, and I'll never be allowed to be a part of yours. You belong here, in Angel City, saving people's lives. I belong in my uncle's diner. It's just the way things are." She was trembling now. The nausea rose in her stomach and her head screamed.

Jacks shook too.

"It was *you* who told me I have control over my own actions. It's simple, remember? So I've made my choice. I want to be with you. I'll keep you safe. We'll get away."

He held out his hand with the ticket in it.

"Do you trust me?"

Maddy thought about the night he had held out his hand before they went flying for the first time and then last night, when he had held it out to her in the pouring rain. She wanted nothing more than to take it now, but doing so, she knew, would seal his fate.

"Jacks, I don't want this anymore. I *want* to go back to the way things were." She said the words clearly and carefully. His hand dropped to his side.

"Will you listen to me just this once?" he nearly yelled. "I . . . I *like* you, Maddy. I mean, more than just as a friend. Are you so stubborn you can't see that? Maybe last night meant nothing to you, but it meant something to me." His eyes were vulnerable, almost tortured. "Did you ever even consider that I might love you, you stubborn, impossible girl?"

The words hit her. Another announcement blared over the platform speakers. It was the final boarding call for the Kansas City train. The words poured out of Jacks.

"You know, there's something when you just know you fit together. And I fit with you. I don't care what you are, human or anything else. It's like a need, Maddy. So please." He stopped and looked at her desperately. Nakedly. "Give me a chance, Maddy."

She turned away. Tears threatened to spill from her eyes; she couldn't let Jacks see her face. She pushed the pain violently away. She *had* to keep her emotions under control. When her words came, they were unapologetic and hard.

"You're a superstar, Jacks. The only person you know how to care about is yourself. You don't love me. You're just . . . in love with the idea of loving me. It's all about you, Jacks, don't you see?"

He didn't move or make a sound. Then he spoke.

"All about me? I saved your life."

"You did," she said. "And now I'm saving yours."

She didn't need to say more. There wasn't even time. At that moment something huge and powerful landed on the platform, pushing a wall of wind past them. It almost knocked Maddy off her feet. Panic shot through her system. She put her hands up in defense, waiting for a repeat of the attack at her house, for the Angel to grab her by the throat again. But nothing happened.

A moment passed before she could open her eyes and see the Angel who had just landed.

It was Mitch. Shrieks of surprise and fear gave way to screams of excitement on the platform as all eyes turned toward them.

"*Oh my God!*" someone on the next platform yelled, and pointed. "*It's Mitch Steeple!*"

Mitch looked at his best friend.

"Come on, man," Mitch said. "There's a car waiting for us out front."

Jacks's eyes darted to Maddy. She watched the full realization of her betrayal hit him.

"*Jackson Godspeed!*" a young girl shrieked. "*OMG, it's Jackson Godspeed!*"

The chaos was abrupt and all encompassing. People began shrieking "*WE LOVE YOU, JACKS!*" and "*FREE JACKS!*" Maddy saw travelers drop their bags and push toward them like a gathering tidal wave.

"*Maddy! There's Maddy!*" someone else screamed. A sudden mob rushed at her, pulling her away from Jacks.

"Wait!" Maddy called frantically. "Jacks!"

But it was impossible to be heard over the bedlam. The crowd closed around her, and Jacks disappeared from her sight. Phones were held high and cameras snapped as the travelers pressed in desperately to get a picture with her. Maddy shoved her way through the mob, trying to get back to Jacks, but the more she struggled, the farther away he became. It was like they were being carried apart on a violent sea.

When she caught a glimpse of him again, Mitch was pulling him away toward their waiting car. Jacks's face was still shell-shocked. Expressionless. Blank.

Maddy yelled his name over and over, but Jacks was gone. All that was left was an ocean of strangers screaming and reaching for her. Her head snapped back as a hand behind her yanked at her hair.

"I want a picture!" a little girl demanded.

Maddy turned and ran.

She pounded out the tunnel and into the now-empty lobby. Behind her she could hear dozens of feet and glanced over her shoulder to see a literal crowd of people running behind her.

"Wait! We're your fans!" a middle-aged woman yelled. *"Will you sign my T-shirt?!"*

Maddy didn't dare look back again. She pelted out the front entrance and saw Kevin already there, idling at the curb in their station wagon. Maddy said nothing as she tumbled into the passenger seat and closed the door on the horde of people. Kevin quickly put the car in gear and drove away from the station, wordless.

CHAPTER THIRTY-FOUR

Maddy had thought she would never see her room again, and now here she sat on her bed, back as if nothing had happened at all. Her eyes stared unseeingly at the wall. She listened to the tick of her old alarm clock on the nightstand. If not for the throbbing in her back and the lingering headache, Maddy might have convinced herself she was dreaming and any moment she would wake, back at the train station. With Jacks.

The drive back had been silent, Kevin looking straight ahead at the traffic while she sat numb and bewildered in the passenger seat. At home she had gone straight upstairs. On her way through the living room she realized the house was much less damaged than she had imagined. It appeared only the windows and the front door had been destroyed beyond repair, along with some picture frames and dishes, and, of course, the old TV, which Maddy was kind of glad had finally been put out of its misery. Otherwise, the house was fine. Kevin must have cleaned up most of the mess in the morning, and some company had already been by to cover the window frames in plastic sheeting in preparation for new glass. In a day or two, the house would be back to the way it had always been. Normal.

Maddy wondered vaguely if that's what would happen to her too. Kevin and Gwen and maybe even Ethan would clean up the emotional mess, and then the irreparable wounds, the memory of breaking Jacks's heart at the station, would simply be covered in plastic until the damaged parts could be replaced. Time would do its job eroding the memories, dulling the sharp edges and fading the once-vibrant colors. And pretty soon she would be back to the way she had always been. Habitual, average, routine. It was a terrifying idea, she thought. Some wounds were meant to be remembered. Some scars should never disappear.

After an hour of sitting motionless on the bed, Maddy startled at a knock on the door. It was Kevin, in his plaid robe. He sat on the edge of the bed.

"I ordered a pizza. It's downstairs if you want some."

"I'm okay," Maddy said.

"You did the right thing," Kevin said after a moment. "I just want you to know that."

"I do know that."

He sighed and started to explain something about healing, but Maddy couldn't focus on the words, and eventually she tuned him out. Her eyes drifted to her book bag on the floor. It was Saturday. Monday would she be expected to go to school like she had almost every morning of her life? She wondered if she really could just get up, work the morning shift, and then go to class like nothing had happened. Was she capable of that?

Suddenly something Kevin said caught her attention, breaking through the thickness of her thoughts.

"What?" Maddy said.

"I'm just saying, I know you think you're in love with him, but—"

"I'm *not* in love with him," Maddy said, quickly defensive. She saw him flinch at her tone and immediately wished she could take it back. He looked at her with helpless eyes, then shrugged.

"Well, like I said, pizza downstairs." His parenting now done the best he knew how, Kevin got up and shuffled out the door.

His words hung meaningfully in the once-again silent room. *In. Love. With. Him.*

She knew it was true, despite her knee-jerk rejection to hearing the words out loud. She was in love with him. Could it be possible that she had just made the biggest mistake of her life?

Her gaze drifted around the room, looking for any distraction, any escape, and came to rest on her bedroom window. There to greet her, as always, was the sign. She thought about what Kevin had told her on that first morning of school. That their luck was going to change. He had been right, she reflected bitterly, he just didn't realize it was going to change for the worse. That's the funny thing, she thought. You always want things to get better, but you never know how good you already have it. Maddy certainly hadn't. She hadn't realized that she was happy, with an uncle who loved her, a loyal best friend, and a chance at a good life. It was more than a lot of people could say.

Before, she hadn't ever hurt anyone, and she hadn't known what it was like to care for someone and then have them taken away just as quickly. And she didn't know anything of her own traumatic past. Would she truly be able to live with the knowledge of who her parents were and what really happened to them? If nothing else, there was some small, bittersweet satisfaction in knowing the truth now. Her hand reached up and felt for her mother's necklace. When she touched it, she discovered something heavy hanging against her chest, near her heart. She pulled the necklace out from under her shirt.

There, dangling from her neck, was Jacks's Divine Ring.

For a moment she just stared at it in numb disbelief. In everything that happened, she had completely forgotten about it. She held the ring in her hand and inspected its exquisite beauty. She watched the way the light reflected onto her palm and how when she turned the ring, those reflections danced. It was the only thing he had ever wanted, and he had given it to her. Seconds ticked by while she fought to keep her fracturing emotions together. Was she feeling sadness? Yes. But was it also regret? And despair?

Maddy made a decision. He deserved to know. Although she could never be with him, and even though she would never see him again, he deserved to know the truth about how she felt. After what she had done at the station, she owed him that much. Getting up, she rummaged through her dirty jeans on the floor until she found her old flip phone. She turned it on, navigated to the recent call log, and dialed Gwen's number.

The phone rang three times, then picked up.

"Maddy?" Gwen asked skeptically. Her familiar voice caused Maddy's throat to tighten.

"Hey," Maddy got out.

"OMG! Where are you?"

"I'm back home. Gwen, I have a favor to ask."

There was a brief pause on the other end of the line.

"Yeah, anything. What do you need?"

Maddy looked at the Divine Ring in her hand.

"I need to drop off something. Do you think you could borrow your mom's car and drive me?"

"I can't," Gwen said.

"Oh," Maddy said, her heart sinking, "okay, then—"

"But I can drive you and then return it before my mom finds out, how about that?"

Maddy smiled in relief.

"That sounds perfect. Can you wait down the street?" She didn't know if Kevin would let her go, so she wasn't going to take any chances.

"No prob," Gwen said. "I'll come right now."

Maddy flipped the phone shut. She dropped the necklace and the Divine Ring back under her shirt and felt the ring thump lightly against her chest.

Rifling around in her drawers, she found some old stationery and a pen. She thought only for a moment, then wrote:

Jacks, I'm sorry for being stubborn and impossible, and I'm so sorry for what happened. I know now that I am drawn toward you just as much as you are drawn toward me, and without you, I will always feel incomplete. I lied in the station, but I did it for a good reason. The truth is . . . I care about you very much. Please know that—and please never try to find me or contact me again.

—M

Fishing out a blank envelope from the desk, Maddy stuffed everything in her pocket. Then she stopped.

She didn't know where he lived.

He had never taken her there, and she didn't even know where to begin looking—beyond the assumption it was somewhere in the Angel City Hills. She paced back and forth for almost a minute before something occurred to her. She got down on her knees and looked under her bed. It was too dark to see, so she stuck her hand out and swept it back and forth across the carpet. Hair ties, old homework, her iPod box. Then her fingers curled around a folded crinkled pamphlet, and she pulled it out. Bingo. She threw her hoodie back on, stuffed the pamphlet in her pocket along with everything else, and slipped as quietly as she could out her bedroom window.

CHAPTER THIRTY-FIVE

"We're going *where*?" Gwen's tone was incredulous as she drove. She had just picked up Maddy in her mom's blue Volvo, greeting Maddy with a crushing BFF hug. She was wearing a Team Maddy shirt that she had perfectly distressed to match her denim skirt and high-heel sandals.

"Relax," Maddy said, "I know how to get there."

"Oh, really? And how's that?"

Maddy produced the crinkled, dusty Angel map from her back pocket, the one Gwen had bought last summer that had almost gotten them both grounded.

"This thing really works, right?" They took the turn onto Outpost Road from Franklin and wound their way up into the Angel City Hills.

"And how did you even *know* about those shirts anyway?" Maddy asked, looking again at Gwen's outfit.

"Duh!" Gwen chirped. "You tweeted about it."

"That's *not* me, Gwen." Maddy groaned. "It's someone pretending to be me."

"Really? OMG, you have, like, impersonators? That is so cool!"

As Gwen navigated with the map, Maddy took out the envelope and placed the note in it. She unclasped her mom's necklace from around her neck and slid the heavy ring off it.

"Is that a *Divine Ring*?" Gwen gasped in disbelief.

"I'm returning it," Maddy said, dropping the ring in the envelope. "I'm just going to leave it at the front gate." Gwen looked like she might hyperventilate, but seeing Maddy's expression, she did her best to stifle her excitement and nodded solemnly. Maddy turned the envelope over and wrote *JACKS* on it.

They had nearly reached the top of the hill when a tall, ivy-covered fence came into view. Beyond it, Maddy could just see the spires of a breathtaking mansion. The fence ran almost a full block before a gated drive appeared. Gwen looked at the map, then squinted out the windshield.

"I think we're here."

They parked, and Gwen cut the engine. Being so close to Jacks again, Maddy was surprised she didn't feel the painful emotions she was expecting. She still sensed the despair and the regret, the pain of what had happened, but these were crowded out by an altogether different, new emotion. She was uneasy. She had expected to find the street full of people by now, swarms of paparazzi and live television reports, a grand homecoming for the prodigal son. Instead, the street was empty, almost eerily so. Had Darcy forgotten to tip off the media that Jacks was coming home? It was possible, but still, it bothered Maddy.

"Do you want me to come with you?" Gwen asked. Maddy shook off her anxiety.

"That would be great, thanks."

Getting out of the car, they walked toward the looming gate. It was quiet. Maddy reached the mailbox and discovered it was locked. She should have figured that. What now? She looked at the gate, not really expecting to find any solution there, and paused. She stared. The gate had been left *open*. Maddy's intuition flickered again. Why would the gate be open? Someone could have forgotten to close it, but that was silly. She was sure Jacks's family had a staff that monitored the grounds.

Maddy walked toward the gap between the ironwork doors and peered through it. It must have been *left* open on purpose, she thought. But why would you leave a security gate open? The answer came quickly: so someone could get in.

"Just leave it inside the gate, Maddy, and let's go."

Maddy looked at the envelope in her hands.

"I'm sorry, Jacks," she whispered. "Goodbye."

That's when she heard the scream.

It echoed down the long drive and seemed to die just inside the gate. Had she not been standing so close, she was sure she wouldn't have heard it at all. It was a woman's scream, one of sorrow, not of pain. A wretched sound that sent a shiver down Maddy's spine.

"Did you hear that?" Gwen asked, startled.

Maddy hesitated only a moment before squeezing through the gate and motioning to Gwen.

"Come on," she whispered. "Follow me, and stay quiet."

They stayed low against the wall of the driveway and crept noiselessly up the curving drive.

"Wait," Maddy whispered, and pulled Jacks's Divine Ring out of the envelope and threaded it back around her neck for safekeeping. They moved forward, and the spectacular estate came into view, nestled in immaculately manicured gardens.

"OMG, his house is amazing, right?" Gwen whispered behind her.

"Shhh!" Maddy hissed. She stopped where the wall was just high enough to conceal them and looked at the house. Jacks's Ferrari was in the driveway, but there were also three black Escalades with tinted windows parked in front of the house. They stood, ominous. The front door to the house had been left open. She could hear an argument coming from somewhere inside.

"I need to get closer," Maddy whispered. Scrambling forward, she ducked down behind a circular fountain next to the SUVs that sat directly in front of the house. Maddy could make out the words of the argument now. She flinched at their hostility, their agony.

"It was the only way to bring him in quietly," a deep, authoritative voice barked.

"He's your son! You promised! Do something!" It was the woman again, her voice jagged like broken glass.

"I'm just doing my duty, Kris," the deep voice retorted.

Maddy felt her heart twist. Kris. Jacks's mother. Then someone was coming out of the house, or being led out of the house. Maddy froze.

It was Jacks. Four broad-shouldered men in black suits led him. They had chiseled, flawless faces. Not men. These were Angels. One of them had his hand on Jacks's shoulder. Another turned to say something over his shoulder, and Maddy saw a split tailored into the back of his jacket. For wings. *Angel Police*, Maddy thought. Her heart sank.

It had all been a lie. Kevin couldn't have known, or Jacks's mom, but they all three had been fooled by it. The "deal" must have been nothing more than a trick to get Jacks to turn himself in so he could be quietly dealt with. No big Angel battle with the whole world watching. No black mark against the Immortals. No scandal. Sylvester had been right, Maddy thought. The Archangels were willing to do whatever it took to protect themselves.

And she had helped them. She had delivered Jacks.

They were walking in her direction now, headed toward the waiting SUVs. Jacks's face was expressionless. His eyes had turned colorless and gray. His arms hung limply at his side.

"Fight," Maddy whispered furiously. "Dammit, Jacks, fight."

But he didn't. He let them take him. His face was the same blank mask she had seen at the station. Maddy fought back a paralyzing despair. She had taken the fight out of him. Once again, everything was her fault.

Maddy focused all her energy on overcoming the paralysis. She had to think. Because she had to do something. She watched carefully as they loaded Jacks into the middle vehicle, and made a note of which seat, which side. All three Escalades started up and began to move. Already leaving.

A new commotion erupted from the house. Maddy's eyes darted over. A middle-aged woman was struggling against her husband and another Angel in a suit. She was trying to leave the house. If she hadn't been screaming with her hair tangled in her face, she would be strikingly beautiful. Regal, even. It had to be Kris Godspeed. Behind her, in the hall, Chloe stood helpless and crying, her face wrought with grief.

Suddenly, as Maddy watched, Kris's wild eyes darted in her direction.

Maddy froze. She watched recognition dawn on Kris's face. She knew Maddy was there, crouching behind the fountain, and she knew who she was. Maddy fought the urge to turn and run. Would Kris give her away? Sic the Angels on *her*? Instead, something flickered in Kris's eyes. An unspoken message. Some understanding had just passed between them, but in the adrenaline-fueled rush of the moment, Maddy wasn't sure just what.

Kris pulled hard against the two Angels holding her and, with a small cry, sent all three of them slamming into the wall just inside the foyer. Maddy heard the unmistakable sound of keys dropping to the floor as the three Angels collapsed to the ground in a chaotic tumble. Kris's eyes narrowed in concentration. Her free leg kicked. The keys, which she had knocked off the wall next to her, jingled across the tile and came to rest in the open doorway.

Maddy didn't think. She didn't have time. She leapt to her feet and ran toward the front of the house. She heard Gwen yell behind her, but the rushing wind and pounding of her heart drowned out the words. She hit the doorway at a full sprint, more running into it than stopping, and flattened her body against the outside wall. Kris had done enough flailing to keep her captors occupied. Maddy slid down onto her knees, reached her arm out into the doorway, and grabbed the keys. The ignition key with a prancing horse on the yellow shield looked right at her.

Kris's eyes shot over and fixed Maddy with a meaningful gaze.

Go.

In an instant Maddy was on her feet again and sprinting toward the Ferrari. She fumbled with the smart key while she ran, finding the unlock button. The Ferrari chirped to life. She hazarded a quick look down the driveway. The SUVs were already turning out the gate. In another moment, they would be gone. She saw Gwen running out from behind the wall. She must have seen Maddy's frantic dash for the keys. Gwen reached the car first, jumping into the driver's seat just as Maddy arrived.

"What do you think you're doing?" Maddy gasped.

"What does it look like I'm doing?" Gwen said.

Maddy opened the door. "No way. I don't want you getting involved."

"You need all the help you can get," Gwen hissed. "Seriously, get in." Then she put both hands on the wheel. "God, this car is so sexy."

"Move over, then," Maddy said as she got in, pushing Gwen into the passenger seat. "I'm driving." She might not have a car of her own, but she'd never gotten less than an A in any class she'd ever taken, and that included driver's ed.

She fed the key into the ignition and adjusted the rearview mirror. In the reflection, she could see Kris's husband looking in her direction. She might only have seconds. She punched the start button on the Ferrari and six hundred horses roared to life. The machine crouched like a wild animal, ready. Maddy depressed the clutch and moved the manual transmission into first. The Ferrari purred with anticipation. Gwen lifted an instructorly finger.

"Always adjust your side mirrors before putting the car in drive—"

Maddy released the clutch and shoved her foot down on the gas. The Ferrari lurched forward much faster than Maddy thought possible, throwing both girls violently into their seats. Maddy heard a voice behind her but didn't dare look back.

"Put your seat belt on," Maddy commanded. Gwen immediately obeyed. Maddy pushed the clutch in again, shifted to second, and smashed the accelerator. The Ferrari shot down the driveway like a whip and cleared the gate like a red marble out of a slingshot. She threw the wheel over, pivoting the screaming race car on its front right tire, and stomped on the gas again. In an instant they were rocketing down the street in pursuit of the caravan.

CHAPTER THIRTY-SIX

Maddy didn't look back to see if she was being chased. It didn't matter now. This was her only chance.

"Okay, but his house was, like, so amazing, right?" Gwen said again as she looked in the rearview.

"Need to concentrate," Maddy said curtly.

Maddy downshifted and the Ferrari's engine snarled. Needles jumped on the gauges as they roared down Outpost, glimpsing the caravan of black Escalades and then losing them again on the winding road. Sparkling Angel mansions flew by in a blur.

"So would now be an okay time to ask *what is going on*?" Gwen asked, holding on desperately to the door handle.

"They're taking him," Maddy said miserably.

"Who's taking him?"

"The Angels. The deal must have been a lie and now they're taking him."

"Deal?"

"Jacks saved my life, which is against their law. Mark supposedly made a deal with the Council and the Archangels for Jacks's life. But the deal was a trap and now they've caught him and they're going to kill him and it's all my fault."

"What?" Gwen choked in bewilderment on all the information. "But they can't kill him. He's an Angel!"

"They're going to make him mortal," Maddy said. "*Then* they're going to kill him."

Maddy caught a glimpse of the caravan again. They had reached the bottom of the road and were turning left onto Franklin.

"Angels can be mortal?" Gwen gasped. "And there's a law? And wait, who's Mark again?"

"Honestly, Gwen," Maddy quoted as she braked for the turn, "how can you live in this city and not know these things?"

She threw the wheel over and they roared off the winding road onto the trafficked street.

"OMG, are these seat warmers?" Gwen asked as she fiddled with the buttons on the dash.

"If you could just not touch anything . . . !"

Gwen frowned and folded her arms across her chest. Maddy squinted into the glare of the late-afternoon sun, panicking. She had lost sight of them. Maddy ground the gears into fourth and pushed the gas pedal to the floor. The engine screamed a high-pitched whine as they streaked forward like a crimson bullet.

"Hold on to something!" Maddy commanded.

The light had turned red. They flew into the intersection. Tires squealed as cars swerved, missing them by inches as they careened through the light.

"Where are they?" Maddy's eyes scanned the street ahead as they tore past the other cars, horns blaring. "I've lost them!" she shrieked. "I've lost Jacks!"

"Just keep going straight!" Gwen said, her neck craning. "Maybe they're going to the freeway." Maddy swung into the bus lane and blew past the tourist traffic.

"Right there! Right there!" Gwen shrieked as she pointed to where the Escalades were turning up the on-ramp onto the Angel City Freeway. "They're getting on the freeway! Going south!"

Maddy threw the wheel over. Horns roared in protest as she swerved in front of oncoming traffic, across the lanes of traffic toward the rushing on-ramp.

"We're going to make it, hold on!" Maddy said. Their heads snapped back as they clipped the curb at the corner of the on-ramp, but Maddy straightened the wheel and they sailed up toward the elevated freeway. Gwen had gone white in the passenger seat.

"You are *so* losing your license after this!" she said.

Downtown lay ahead in the red haze of the dusk as they merged into freeway traffic. The sky itself seemed to be burning.

The caravan moved into the fast lane. Maddy followed. She could count five cars between them. She began to weave through traffic using the left two lanes, methodically closing the distance.

"How did you learn to drive like that?" Gwen yelled over the howl of six hundred horses.

"Watching Jacks." She gunned the engine and slipped around another car.

"What?"

"You know, watching his shifting."

Gwen gasped. "You've been looking at his *shifter*?"

"Would you just shut up!" She swerved around another car.

They were only three cars back. She looked at the back of the Escalade with its tinted black windows. The license plate had no numbers on it. It sent a chill down her spine. She wondered where they were taking him. Out of the city, maybe. It didn't matter. The beginnings of a plan were forming in her mind. It was simple, but effective. She would offer them something. Something, she was sure, they would be interested in.

Maddy changed lanes and jumped another car length ahead. The Escalades were only two cars ahead, although traffic was teeming.

"We're almost there," she said, feeling a sudden surge of hope.

Then it happened.

What Maddy saw, her brain could not process at first. Her mind registered it only as a *shape*, a dark shape landing on the roof of the last Escalade. She heard the crunch of collapsing metal, followed by a rain of broken safety glass that pelted against the Ferrari's windshield.

Slowly, slowly, her brain began to accept the images her eyes were sending, and the shape became clearer. It had a shimmering black body and vast, bat-like wings.

It had *more than one head*, she realized, like black snakes bursting forth from its body, horns that erupted out of its back like twisted tree limbs. A long, black tail whipped against the palm trees. Framed by the famous skyline, looming over the busy freeway traffic, the burning thing turned to look at her with strange, iridescent pairs of eyes. A sudden, overwhelming feeling hit her. It was the same feeling she had felt in the bio lab that previous night. A kind of mortal, suffocating dread.

Maddy now knew what she was looking at. She knew what had just landed on top of the Escalade. She froze in the driver's seat, paralyzed by terror.

"What is *that?*" Gwen cried, the sound of her voice like tearing metal.

"Dark Angel," Maddy whispered.

"What?" Gwen shrieked.

Maddy watched as the demon leapt off the moving Escalade and onto the next. The Escalade buckled and spun wildly against the concrete median before rolling back into traffic, right at them.

"Maddy!" Gwen yelled.

The destroyed SUV tumbled toward them like a bowling ball of death. Maddy snapped the wheel to the right and the Ferrari swerved. The car growled like a wild animal as they swung around the rolling vehicle.

Gwen started screaming something, but Maddy couldn't hear her. She was hypnotized, riveted with fear. She watched the demon tear open the roof of the SUV with its various mouths and begin pulling Angels out of the vehicle and tossing them onto the freeway. Guardians were torn to pieces, their wings ripped from their bodies. Immortal parts rained down on the road. The demon reached in and pulled a struggling Angel out like he was a doll. Maddy's heart hammered in her chest.

"Jacks!" she screamed.

She could see him now. He was in the arms of that burning thing, his eyes wild. *It's taking Jackson.* It was the first rational thought Maddy had since the demon appeared. *It's got him now and it's going to take him.*

The demon lifted off the SUV and rose. Ascending over Angel City in the twilight, it was gone.

Maddy could barely focus through the fog of shock and terror as the second Escalade clipped the first and both vehicles rolled over and tumbled across the freeway, knocking cars into one another.

There was no time to think anymore, only to react.

"Crashing car!" Gwen yelled as a Civic ricocheted toward them.

"I see it!" Maddy yelled, and yanked at the wheel.

"Another crashing car!" Gwen yelped, and pointed at a truck that was hurtling toward them. Maddy veered around it; the twisted metal missed them by inches.

"Tell me where it is, Gwen," Maddy said, keeping her eye on the chaos in front of her, trying to snatch glimpses up at the sky.

"Where what is?!" Gwen panted, her fingernails digging into the leather seat.

"The demon. Tell me where it is."

"It's a *demon*?" Gwen gasped in horror, "Like in the olden days?"

"Yes! Now tell me where it is!" Maddy shouted. Gwen squinted up through the sunroof.

"I don't see anything, Maddy," she said breathlessly, peering out the window to where the demon had disappeared with Jacks. "It's gone."

Maddy's heart bottomed. Despair radiated through her as the Ferrari continued snarling down the freeway. Despite everything, she had failed. Even the Angels couldn't protect Jacks from the horror that had come for him.

"Wait, I see it!" Gwen suddenly shrieked. "It's ahead of us!"

Gwen pointed out the windshield. A dark image was crossing the still light sky.

"Which way is it going?"

"Toward downtown. It's moving so *fast*."

Maddy's mouth became a grim line of determination. She mashed the gas pedal to the floor and the Ferrari sang as the speedometer climbed past 100. Cars swerved all around them, drivers no doubt transfixed by the image of a demon flying over Angel City.

"I . . . I think it's going to the top of that really tall building ahead of us," Gwen announced.

"Which building?"

"The . . . the tallest one. Maybe it landed, 'cause I can't see it anymore."

Maddy squinted up at the looming, semicircular skyscraper towering above the rest of the buildings on the skyline. At its top was a design of windows like a crown. Maddy couldn't see if anyone was up there, but she thought of Sylvester's words again. They would hire someone, or something, to do their dirty work for them. Whatever trick of the Archangels this was, Maddy was about to see the endgame.

With a flick of the wheel the Ferrari tore down the exit ramp for downtown. Maddy whipped through the streets, ignoring stop signs, lights, and oncoming traffic. All around them, sirens began to ricochet off the buildings. She could see the lights in the rearview. The police were after them now.

The tower's entrance came into view. Maddy downshifted and hurtled toward it, braking hard to a halt right in front of the building. Her heart was galloping uncontrollably in her chest. She looked out at wide marble stairs leading up to the lobby.

"Come on," Maddy yelled as she threw her door open. Gwen jumped out with her, leaving the Ferrari still rumbling behind them.

They ran up the stairs toward a row of glass doors. Maddy didn't need to turn around to know police cars were pulling up behind them. She heard the footsteps and shouts of the officers as they emerged from their vehicles. Reaching the glass doors, she furiously tugged at the handles until she found one door all the way to the left that was still unlocked.

She ripped it open as the footsteps pounded up the stairs.

Gwen turned to her, out of breath.

"Go. I'll slow them down," she panted.

"What? No!" Maddy cried.

Gwen's eyes were suddenly, inexplicably calm.

"Maddy, I'm your best friend, and there's nothing I wouldn't do for you. There *is* something you can do to help him. I've always been amazed by you, Maddy, you can do anything you put your mind to. I know you'll think of something. Now go to him. He needs you."

Maddy met Gwen's eyes. The unexpected words had tightened her throat.

"Gwen—" she started.

"Don't say anything, just hurry," Gwen said, and shoved Maddy inside the lobby. Closing the door, Gwen wrapped her arms through the handles, using herself as a human shield. Maddy could see police streaming up the steps. They slowed, advancing on Gwen.

Maddy turned and ran toward the gleaming bank of elevators.

CHAPTER THIRTY-SEVEN

Sylvester tore down Wilshire Boulevard in his unmarked cruiser, weaving around the teeming Beverly Hills traffic. Overhead, palm trees swayed anxiously in the wind, leaves glinting orange in the fiery dusk. Careening across oncoming traffic on Beverly, not bothering with the red light, he pulled into the NAS building, scraping the belly of the car on the garage ramp. He screeched into the valet parking and left the car without waiting for a ticket. He took the stairs up to the lobby.

The chirpy receptionist seemed startled to see him again as he strode across the sleek lobby.

"Can I help you, sir?" she said in her pseudo-polite tone.

"Save it, honey," Sylvester grumbled as he passed her. She rose out of her chair, sending her latte spilling all over the desk.

"Wait! You can't go in there!" she shrieked. He ignored her.

Turning the corner, Sylvester blew past the rows of assistants on their headsets. They gave him curious, uncomprehending stares as he passed. He could hear the receptionist's clacking stilettos on the tile behind him, most likely trying to raise an alert, but he didn't bother to look back. He reached the end of the hall, turned, and threw open the glass doors of the conference room.

The Archangels were sitting around the conference table in intense discussion. Their jackets were thrown over chair backs, their ties loosened. An assistant had apparently brought in coffee and trays of sushi that were set in the middle of the table, along with glasses of imported sparkling water. On the flat screen, news chopper footage of the attack on the freeway was playing.

At Sylvester's entrance the Archangels fell silent, looking up at him with surprised expressions. Sylvester glared back. He looked at the faces of the Archangels, backbone of the NAS. His eyes found Mark, who still wore his suit jacket and appeared stunned.

Finally, Mark spoke.

"What can we do for you, David?" he said calmly.

Sylvester came into the room, letting the door close with a clang behind him. Outside, assistants watched through the glass, horrified. One of the Archangels held up a hand to them, as if to indicate everything was all right.

Sylvester felt suddenly unsure of himself. His hands instinctively went to his glasses to polish them, but he caught himself, and instead he let them drop back to his sides. He took a shaky breath and spoke.

"You know how I feel about you and the NAS."

He paused. They were silent.

"You know I believe all of this is wrong," he said, motioning around at the lavish surroundings of the conference room. "I believe it was never supposed to be this way, saving mortal lives for mortal money, for mortal vices. I believe you have led us astray. I believe your greed and corruption is directly responsible for the threat this city faces."

Mark was silent, scrutinizing Sylvester intensely.

Sylvester felt his passion loosening his tongue.

"Now I want you to prove me wrong. I want you to prove to me that you still remember the old ways. That you still remember who you are. I want you to prove to me that you can defend those who can't defend themselves, the victims, the sufferers, and the mortally endangered. Prove to me you can do your duty." He looked around at their flawless faces. "This city needs you. Now rise up and protect it."

A blond, chisel-faced Archangel rose.

"David. We're working on it. These things have to be discussed first. Plans have to be approved with the city, as well as, of course, a price."

Sylvester's face darkened.

"You have to understand we can't just ask Guardians to risk their lives—"

But Sylvester had stopped listening. Reaching down to his waist, he drew his service revolver.

The blond Archangel's eyes grew wide.

Sylvester pointed the pistol at the large glass display case in the corner, the case holding the ancient armor and sword of a Battle Angel, and fired. The glass fell instantly in a cascade of ringing pieces. The bullet ricocheted off the armor and buried itself in the ceiling tiles. The room went deafeningly silent.

The armor and weapon stood in the shattered case. Ready.

Sylvester reached in and closed his grip around the hilt of the ancient sword. The weight of it was heavy in his hand as he brought it out. He turned to the Archangels and threw the sword onto the conference table, sending sushi rolls scattering, water glasses shattering under its tremendous weight.

Sylvester looked around at the startled faces of the Archangels. They had all gone silent.

"Now," he said, his tone resolute, "where are the others?"

CHAPTER THIRTY-EIGHT

The cold against his face. That was the first sensation he felt, the first coherent thought Jacks had since riding in the back of the SUV. His fingers became aware of the ground, cold and absolute beneath him. The wind whistled in his ears. As he lay there, fragments of a nightmare began to return to him. Terrible images swirled in his consciousness. Archangels ripped out of their seats next to him. Cars colliding violently with one another. Black-orange fireballs of death. And some kind of terrible *thing*. A monster. But the worst image of all was simpler than all the others. It played over and over like a horrible movie, refusing to stop.

A train station and a goodbye.

He opened his eyes and looked out at a sideways world. The lights of the Immortal City twinkled all around. The moon, pale and bloated, had begun to rise. He must be on a rooftop. Then he realized he was not alone. The presence of the demon surrounded him. He could feel the heat of its horrific body and make out its shimmering presence.

It was only then that he noticed the other figure standing silhouetted against the moon, framed by the enormous rising disk. The figure stepped forward into the light and smiled.

"You . . ." Jacks murmured in disbelief.

"Yes," the figure said. "Me."

Maddy paced back and forth in the claustrophobic elevator car, listening to her pounding heart and the mechanical whir of her seventy-three-story ascent. The mirrored walls created endless reflections of her. She looked around at all the Maddys staring back. Their hair matted, their faces lined with fear and determination, pain and guilt. Jacks's Divine Ring dangled near her heart. She hit the palm of her hand against the gleaming steel of the compartment's wall.

"Come on, come on!"

Trapped in the elevator, there was nothing to do but face her racing thoughts. No matter who, or what, was up there, they wanted Jacks mortal and dead. She made her decision. It really wasn't a hard choice at all. She would offer herself. Her life in exchange for his. Instead of making Jackson mortal, she would offer them a mortal life. On some strange level, it seemed to make sense . . . She had never imagined the end coming this way, and this soon, but she was surprised to find she was okay with it. Really, what else was there for her?

She was kidding herself if she thought she could go back to her old life of high school and Kevin's Diner. Not with the knowledge of what really happened to her parents, who she really was. Yet there was no going forward, either. To the Angels she was a perversion of nature, a revolting half breed, and to everyone else she was a now-infamous tabloid joke. It was a bitter truth to face: she could never be accepted by anyone. Maybe she really was an abomination. If the world was better off without her, at least she could cause some good with her death.

Without warning the whir of the elevator quieted. Maddy's stomach leapt into her throat as the car slowed and came to a stop. The floor numbers paused at 60 and the doors slid open. Maddy punched the button for 73 again and again, but the car didn't move, and the button would no longer light up. The elevator chimed and the doors began to close. *The top floors must be restricted*, she thought in a panic. *It's going to take me back down to the lobby.* With a gasp Maddy leapt forward and slid between the doors just as they clamped shut.

The hallway she found herself in was dark, cool, and quiet. Motion-sensor security lights blinked on with her presence. Her eyes searched wildly for a stairwell door as precious seconds ticked by. Nothing but drab, unmarked office doors. She bounded down the hall and around the corner. More office doors, but at the end of the corridor she saw the green glow of an exit sign. She sprinted toward it and threw her shoulder into the door, nearly falling into the dark stairwell. Then she steadied herself with the handrail and began to climb.

The burning pain was everywhere, indescribable. The demon was engulfing him, smothering him in flaming arms. Jacks screamed as he felt his wings emerge from his back and catch fire. The licking black flames left no burns. The fire wasn't consuming his body. It was consuming his immortality. It was literally *eating* the Angel inside him. The pain was like glass coursing through his veins.

The beast threw him back down on the roof. He crumpled against the concrete, helpless. He could suddenly *feel* his mortal body. It felt feeble. Breakable. Even the ground underneath him was all of a sudden hard and uncomfortable. He watched as the figure approached, eyes dark and pitiless.

"What's the matter, *Jacks*, aren't you going to resist? Aren't you going to fight back?" Jacks said nothing.

"You surprise me, Jackson. I thought you had more in you, but, I guess, well . . ."

The fist smashed into Jacks's face, sending his head violently against the ground. Something wet dripped from his nose. Then he felt the kick of a boot up under his rib, snapping it. He cried out. He couldn't help it. He had never felt his body break.

"The great Jackson Godspeed." The figure laughed. "Look at him now."

Jacks's eyes grew distant as he was beaten. His mind left this place, left this rooftop, and went to the only place he wanted to be. With her. He imagined they really had gotten out on that train. He imagined they had escaped. He thought about sitting next to her, watching Angel City slip away outside the window. He would have joked about getting used to life without his Ferrari, and she would have rolled her eyes and given him a hard time. In the end she would just look into his eyes like she always did. She would look into his eyes and only see him. Not the famous celebrity, just him.

White-hot agony finally broke through the fantasy. His head was being pushed into the concrete again and again. Blood streamed from his mangled lips. He let the pain flow freely though him now. Welcomed it. Yearned for it. It wouldn't be much longer now. The end would come soon.

He was pulled onto his knees, and the figure stood over him, a brutal grin on his face.

"Don't worry," the voice said. "Despite your really pathetic performance tonight, I'll still make sure your wings get to your star." Jackson looked up through blurred eyes and saw a vicious-looking knife. The ten-inch blade glinted in the moonlight.

Maddy sprinted up the stairs as fast as her feet could move, her sneakers skipping up the concrete steps. Adrenaline rushed into her veins as she saw a pale shaft of moonlight filtering down from up ahead. She was close. Finally, she saw a door at the top of the stairwell with a sign that warned ROOF ACCESS. CAUTION: HELIPAD. No time to think now. No time to imagine what might be waiting for her on the other side of the door. She reached for the door handle and exploded out onto the rooftop.

She saw the moon, pale and huge as it rose behind the tower. Then her eyes adjusted, and she saw Jacks. He was on his knees, as if praying or kneeling before an altar. What was left of his clothes hung in tatters around his shattered body, and his wings were draped limply across his back. Their beautiful blue luminescence had almost totally faded to nothing.

"Jackson!" she screamed.

He didn't move. He didn't even seem to hear her. The Jacks she knew had gone out of him. Then she saw the shadowy figure standing over him. As she watched, the figure turned and looked at her.

Maddy was so shocked it took her several seconds to speak.

"Ethan?" she finally gasped uncomprehendingly.

Ethan straightened, and the cast of the moonlight fell fully on his face. He was wearing his usual ripped jeans, and his sandy hair whipped in the wind. Maddy's mind reeled. The puzzle pieces refused to fall into place. She couldn't make sense of what she was seeing.

"Maddy?" he said, surprised. His expression turned almost thoughtful, apologetic. "I . . . I didn't want you to see this."

"What are you doing?" she said through the numb shock. Conflict played in his eyes. The Ethan she knew fighting with some other part of him she did not. Then he looked down at Jacks, and his expression hardened.

"I'm doing my duty."

Raising the knife over Jacks's back, he brought it swiftly down.

There was a sound like a pop as the blade sank into the Angel's flesh at the base of the wing, then a wet snap as the knife severed the wing from the body. It went lifeless and fell to the concrete with a thud.

"No!" Maddy screamed. She reacted on instinct and ran toward Jacks. At once a black shimmer crossed her vision. A low, inhuman growl made her blood run cold. The last time she had heard it, she had been in the high school.

The demon emerged from the night in front of her. It was large, at least ten feet tall, but it had no definite features. Its shape kept shifting and changing. Maddy froze, her limbs refusing to move.

"I see you've already met *my* Guardian Angel," Ethan said, smiling. Maddy realized the thing was hard to see because its skin really *was* shimmering. It was more than just shimmering. It was on fire. The creature was literally burning; the licking flames were black instead of orange. The fiery monster circled around Ethan and then crouched next to him, ready to strike.

"You don't know what you're doing, Ethan." Maddy shook with fear and fury. "Do you think you can control that thing?"

"If people can hire Angels, why can't I hire a demon?" Ethan said. "The price may be different, but . . ."

He began to raise the knife again.

"Leave him alone!" Maddy screamed through numb lips. Ethan's eyes flashed with anger.

"Why should I!?" he demanded. "What about our discussions at the diner and at school? Angels are all the same, Maddy, shallow, vapid, overly privileged creatures who do more harm than good." His tone had a note of hysteria now. His mask of calm was beginning to crack. "Don't you understand? They aren't the heroes, they're the *villains*. I'm giving them what they deserve."

"Why Jacks?" Her voice was barely more than a whisper now. "He never did anything to you. Or to your dad." She could see Ethan wince at the mention of his father, but he quickly recovered, his mouth turning into a cruel grin.

"I have you to thank for that, Maddy. At first I just wanted to kill Angels, any of them. Make them suffer. They're all guilty. Then I saw you with Jacks." He sneered, standing over Jackson's trembling form. "*I* wanted you, Maddy. We were supposed to be together, but you didn't see it—yet. Was I not good enough for you? Not enough of an *Angel*?" Ethan spat the word out like venom. "You wouldn't have me, so I just wanted to make sure you wouldn't have him, either."

The words stabbed like knives.

Maddy struggled for breath as the truth sank in and the world began to spin around the rooftop.

"It's been you all along. Not the NAS. You've been murdering Angels on the boulevard." Her entire body shook as the final pieces fell into place. "We came to you for help, and you sent the demon after us at the school."

Ethan's eyes narrowed.

"Don't blame me, Maddy. Blame yourself. It was *you* who did this. The truth is, he's far too powerful. If you hadn't abandoned him at the train station, none of this would've been possible."

Maddy blanched. He was right. It was all her fault. Ethan seemed to smile at this.

"I know all about it. I know how you left him standing at the platform like he was nothing to you, left him to be delivered into the hands of the Archangels." He shrugged. "I thought about just letting the NAS mortalize him, but I don't know. I guess after I saw him with you again, I took it a little personally." He raised the knife over Jacks's maimed and bleeding back. "So anyway, since you obviously don't care about him, let's get on with it, shall we?"

"I love him!" she screamed. The words just came out. She had never spoken them before. She looked from Ethan to the trembling Angel below him. "Do you hear me, Jacks? I came back to tell you that I love you." She saw a glimmer of recognition in Jacks's eyes. The gray had turned the palest shade of blue again.

Ethan smiled like the devil himself.

"So much for true love."

He brought the knife swiftly down again. Maddy heard the whistle of the blade through the air.

Then the slap as Jacks caught Ethan's arm midswing.

Ethan grunted. A surprised, painful sound. Jacks's hollow eyes had filled with color. The blueness blazed. The Angel's fist collided with Ethan's jaw on the left side and shattered it. The knife dropped from Ethan's hand and skittered harmlessly to the floor.

The black shimmer crossed Maddy's vision almost instantly as the demon lunged at Jacks.

"Jacks, look out!" Maddy yelled.

Then it happened.

As the demon sprang forward, it was hit rapidly by something that came out of the sky, something moving so fast it was no more than a blur in the night. The demon tumbled back across the roof, growling and snarling. Ethan crumpled like a rag doll to the rooftop and Jacks was on top of him at once, his fists raining down.

The demon rose up but was hit again by a blur, this time from the other direction. The blur stopped on the roof only for a moment, and Maddy saw the Angel. He was dressed in matte black ADC battle armor. He unsheathed a primeval-looking sword. *A sword?* Maddy looked up.

They came streaming down through the night, seemingly from nowhere, a legion of Battle Angels in close formation. All wore the futuristic, black battle armor of the ADC. The Angels rolled one by one like fighter jets and dove toward the hell that awaited them on the rooftop. Turning, the demon launched itself away, disappearing into the black night without a trace. The legion rocketed over the rooftops of downtown in pursuit.

Maddy looked back to the Angel and the boy fighting in front of the full moon. Jacks roared with fury as his iron fists found their mark again and again. Maddy turned away as Ethan's nose exploded.

In a movement so fast it was almost invisible, Jacks picked Ethan up and pushed him to the edge of the roof. Ethan let out a surprised cry as his heels balanced on the edge of the abyss. Then his expression hardened, and he smiled.

"Do it, Jacks," Ethan's bloody mouth mumbled. "Do it and prove me right. Prove that you're no hero."

For a terrifying moment Maddy fought her own urge to run forward and push Ethan off the edge.

"No, Jacks," Maddy at last shrieked from where she stood. "No!"

Jacks looked at her. She could see the conflict in the Angel's burning, murderous eyes. Then slowly, slowly, they softened. Relief rushed into her as Maddy looked at the old Jacks she knew. He pulled Ethan away from the edge and let go of him.

Ethan's broken body crumpled to the ground. He coughed, then sucked in deep, rasping breaths wet with blood.

Jacks turned toward Maddy. His one remaining wing drooped behind him. "Maddy?" Jacks said, still in disbelief. "You came for me?"

"Of course," she breathed. She took a step toward him, then found herself running toward him. She wanted to collapse into his arms. Like a silly Angelstruck girl, she thought. Like Gwen. She didn't care. Maddy watched him smile as he took a step toward her. Then she saw a strange gleam move through the air behind him.

Jacks stopped. And stiffened. His eyes looked to her desperately.

"Jacks?" Maddy said.

Then she saw it. The knife tip protruding from his chest. Ethan stood up shakily behind Jacks, holding the hilt of the blade with both hands. He shoved the knife in again and then let go. Jacks began to fall.

Maddy dashed forward and made it to Jacks just in time to catch him.

She fell back as the weight of Jacks's body hit her, collapsing on the concrete. She was barely aware of the roof access door flying open and the police streaming out, the two officers shoving Ethan to the ground. She struggled to sit up and took Jacks's face in her hands.

"Jacks?" she panted, hysterical.

His eyes were already draining of their color again, turning that same unseeing gray. She could see him try to smile.

"You love me?" he asked, his voice raspy. "I thought you . . . never understood what the big deal was about Angels." He coughed, and blood began dripping out the side of his mouth, faster and faster.

"You're going to be fine, just hang on," she said desperately. But as she watched, the light in his eyes dimmed and then finally went out, extinguished. His body became impossibly heavy, and still.

Maddy shouted his name again and again. He couldn't be gone. He couldn't. She shook him violently, but he only bobbed lifelessly like a doll. Somewhere nearby, a girl was sobbing uncontrollably. Maddy looked at the perfect, divine features that had become so familiar to her. They were still so beautiful, but cold and vacant now, like an abandoned house. She tried to hold on to the feeling of his presence, but it was fading too and, in another moment, would be gone forever.

Maddy listened to the sobbing girl again before choking and realizing it was *her*.

She had been too late after all. She closed her eyes and let the agony overwhelm her.

In the darkness, she heard a voice.

"Maddy?"

It was Jacks. She must be hallucinating. Her mind had taken her away with him as he died. She savored the sound of his voice.

Then he spoke again. *"You came for me?"*

Maddy's eyes flew open.

Her vision focused.

There was Jacks at the edge of the roof again. Ethan lay coughing blood where Jacks had just thrown him to the ground. Maddy stood where she had before.

"Y-yeah," Maddy stammered. "Of course."

Jacks was walking toward her again. Maddy's mind crystallized around a single thought.

It was a final premonition. A premonition of Jacks's mortal death.

The moment became impossibly clear to her. Maddy had the sensation of near-perfect clairvoyance. She felt her body and soul unite. With perfect clarity, she could make out every speck of dust on the rooftop. Her hearing registered every breath, every rustle of clothes, every gasp of wind.

She could still save Jacks.

Maddy ran. She willed her feet faster and faster. It was the fastest she'd ever run in her life. The rest of the world blurred on all sides of her as she focused on this one thing.

Jacks's face grew confused. Maddy flew right by him. She ran at Ethan, colliding full-force as he lunged at Jacks with the knife. Maddy fell on him, and the two tumbled toward the edge of the roof.

Ethan was on top of her, gasping in surprise. Maddy felt something tugging at her side, like her clothes had snagged on something. Then a warm sensation, not altogether unpleasant. She looked down. Both her and Ethan's hands were wrapped around the knife handle. The blade was deep in her side.

She looked at Ethan. His eyes were blind with rage. If he could pull the knife out, she thought, he would go after Jacks again. She was sure of it. She had one instant to make a decision. She closed her hands tightly around his and pushed the knife as far inside of her as it would go. Then she let out a ragged, agonized breath. The blood began to flow.

The pain was startling at first, then unbearable, and finally it engulfed her, sucking her consciousness away and closing her eyes. She heard a metallic clang as the door smashed open. Willing her eyes open for a moment, she saw Detective Sylvester burst onto the rooftop with his gun drawn, followed by a fleet of cops. Her eyes fluttered closed again. Many voices, and the pounding footsteps over the rooftop. She heard Ethan shout something as the detective drove him to the ground and handcuffed him. Then everything went black.

In the darkness of her mind, she drifted. To that first night when Jacks came into the diner. Back to the night they went flying together, and how the city had looked reflected in his eyes. To the gym, and the way his lips had felt against hers. Looking down, she realized she was floating over the rooftop now. It was quiet up here. Peaceful.

She could see her body and the dark pool growing underneath her. The police were everywhere now. She watched with detached curiosity as they pulled Ethan up and took him away. Angels began landing on the roof. She saw Mitch, wearing the black armor of the ADC, an ancient broadsword flashing in his hands. Maddy also recognized a couple other Angels as they landed, sheathing their swords. The demon must have fled.

Then she saw Jacks. He was yelling something as he knelt over her body. On his back was a bleeding, bloody stump. She saw him take her in his arms and hold her. He was calling her name over and over. *I'm up here*, she tried to say, but he didn't seem to hear her. He shook her body again and again. The drone of a helicopter filled her ears, and suddenly, she felt herself being pulled back. Steadily, painfully, pulled back down toward the roof.

Her eyes opened. Jacks was holding her. A spotlight shone down on them from a chopper hovering above. Maddy squinted up at Jacks in the glare of the spotlight.

"Just hang on, they're coming for you right now," he said. She watched his eyes dart helplessly over her body. "They're going to fix you, Maddy!"

She moved her lips. "I'm sorry for what I said . . . at the station. I'm sorry for being so impossible all the time. Can you . . . forgive me?"

"You have nothing to apologize for," Jacks said urgently. "This is all my fault. If I had never convinced you to leave with me. If I had never kept bothering you. If I had never gone into your uncle's diner." He trailed off, his throat closing. Maddy shook her head. The pain drilled through her.

"I'm glad you did."

The darkness took her again. She was dancing with him at the party now. Maddy couldn't even feel her feet moving over the floor. She didn't know how long she danced with him. It could have been minutes or only a few seconds. When she opened her eyes and found Jacks again, he was looking at her with terror-stricken eyes.

"Don't do that," he said. "Stay with me."

"I'll try," she said. Her response was barely more than a whisper.

"Tell me how to help you, Maddy," he said desperately. "What can I do?"

"Hold my hand."

She felt his fingers lace into hers. Her hand was sticky against his. His hand was trembling. He leaned on one elbow. His strength was leaving him. Maddy felt the darkness coming for her again, and this time, she was sure, she would not be back. It was almost impossible to move her lips. When the words came out, they were slurred.

"Promise me something," she said.

"Anything."

"Be the best Guardian you can be. Save lots of people. And every time you save someone, think of me."

"No, don't you dare say that. We're together now; everything is going to be okay." He looked across the roof with agonized eyes. "I can see them coming. They're coming for you right now, Maddy."

Maddy realized there was no pain anymore. It was becoming peaceful again. "Jacks," she said, "I think I have to go now."

"Please. Don't leave me, Maddy." He was begging.

"It's okay," she said. "It really is. Do you remember my pretend memory?"

"The park," Jacks said.

"I can see it. I'm looking at it now. I can see my parents; they're beautiful, Jacks. I think I'm going there now. And if I'm lucky, they'll let me stay with them. Forever." Tears spilled over Jacks's eyes. "I'll wait for you, Jacks," Maddy whispered. "I'll be waiting for you there."

Her eyes closed. She felt Jacks's hands reach down and unclasp something from around her neck. Then she felt the cold, hard weight of a ring on her finger.

"You are *my* Guardian Angel, Maddy," a voice said, but it was far away from her.

Everything was far away now. She tried to smile, but her body was no longer obeying her commands. It was all happening so fast. Then the darkness came and took her.

Jacks collapsed next to Maddy. They lay there, side by side on the cold rooftop. The paramedics descended on them. Maddy was no longer breathing, but Jacks thought she could still see him. A medic unclasped their hands.

He watched as they shocked her again and again. If he could've talked, he would have begged them to stop. But he couldn't. The strength had gone out of him. He watched Maddy's eyes empty of life, but she still lay there looking at him, somehow seeing him. She seemed happy to be with her Angel, finally at peace.

"Call it," he heard one of the paramedics say. Then they stopped shocking her and, finally, let her be.

CHAPTER THIRTY-NINE

Beep. Beep. The sound at first was distant, then came closer. It grew clearer. *Beep.*

Jacks faintly moaned. The sound of his own voice seemed strange. He tried to swallow, but his tongue felt numb and paralyzed. Struggling to open his eyes, he made out a gauzy shape to his left. He was lying on his side. Then his eyes closed shut, the effort too much. He groaned slightly again. Consciousness began slipping away.

"Jacks? Can you hear me?" a voice said. *Beep. Beep.* Jacks made another effort to open his eyes and was more successful this time. He saw a white curtain and gray, blinking machines. The blur took shape as he focused. It was his mother, Kris. She moved in and out of focus. He felt her take hold of his hand.

"Hi, darling," she said.

As if from an electric shock, Jacks jolted up, reaching for his back in an attempt to push away Ethan's plunging knife. His mind swirled in panic. It took Kris and three nurses to restrain him, ultimately getting him to lie down on his side again. Jacks reached back and touched the place where the knife had severed the wing. Instead of an Immortal Mark, he now felt only a mass of destroyed flesh and bandages. He lay there trembling as the awful memories returned to him. The demon. That boy Ethan. And Maddy's glassy, lifeless eyes.

"Maddy," Jacks whispered.

"Rest, Jacks," Kris said and squeezed his hand. Moving his head as best he could, he realized he was in a hospital bed. The room was clean and impossibly white.

"You were . . . hurt," Kris said. "The doctors were worried. But everything's going to be okay. You're going to be fine. They've performed emergency surgery on your wing."

Jacks looked at his body. He was covered in bandages. He forced air in and out of his nostrils, trying to keep consciousness, trying to keep the one thing at the top of his mind from overwhelming him. The girl who had died in his arms.

"That boy," Kris said.

"I know," Jacks rasped.

"He was troubled. It seems his father died in an accident in which a Protection was saved. He used the father's life insurance money to travel the world in search of . . . revenge."

"The Dark Angel," Jacks said.

Kris nodded.

"It appears his mother didn't even live with him. She had been institutionalized ever since her son's return. When she saw what he became."

Jacks heard the hallway door open, and a familiar voice spoke.

"The demon should have known it would take more than that to mortalize a Godspeed."

Jacks turned his head stiffly.

It was Mark.

Jacks tried to sit up again, the cords of the monitors tangling around him.

"Get out," Jacks croaked. "I know what you did. *All* of it. Get out."

His stepfather didn't move, although something unreadable flickered in his eyes.

"I will. Just as soon as I tell you something."

He took a step into the room.

"The NAS and the Council have dropped their case against you. I made a personal plea that, based on special circumstances, you had done nothing wrong."

"Nothing wrong?" Jacks said incredulously, rage edging his weakened voice. "She's dead."

Kris put a hand on Jacks to calm him.

"Maddy is dead because of me," Jacks said again, his voice cracked with misery.

Mark just smiled. For an instant Jacks hated him.

"Only an Angel can kill another Angel, Jackson."

Tears welled in Kris's eyes as she looked at her son. Mark stepped forward and pulled the curtains aside.

Maddy lay in the next bed. Her breaths were long and deliberate, her vitals steady. Kevin sat asleep in the chair next to her. A magazine was open on his lap, facedown. The sound of the curtain woke him. His eyes were red and bleary from keeping watch over his niece, but he smiled when he saw Jacks awake.

"It's good to see you up," Kevin said. He gently rubbed Maddy's arm.

Maddy's eyes fluttered open. She lay there blinking at her uncle for a moment, then turned her head and saw Jacks.

"Hey," she breathed.

Jacks attempted to get up, cables and tubes tangling up as he went. His foot touched the ground and he almost crumpled. He was much weaker than he had thought. Kris helped him back into bed.

"I thought I had lost you," Jacks said, his voice saturated with relief.

Maddy just looked at him, tired but radiant, her eyes never leaving Jacks's. He felt like he could live in those eyes forever.

"I've taken care of all Maddy's recovery costs," Mark said. "The doctors assure me she's going to be just fine. Apparently there's more Angel in her than we first thought . . . More than anyone thought. Because she's half human, though, her Angel traits have only begun to develop in the past few years. So that's what I argued to the other Archangels. Technically it wasn't an illegal save, Angel saving Angel. There's a lot to talk about, but it can all wait for later."

Jacks took his gaze off Maddy long enough to see Kevin eye Mark coolly.

There was a light knock at the door. It opened, and Mitch stuck his head in.

"Are we interrupting?"

Jacks smiled.

"Come in, Mitch."

"You're awake, man!" Mitch beamed. He stepped into the room. Just behind him followed Gwen. They both carried cups of coffee from the hospital cafeteria.

"This is Maddy's friend Gwen," Mitch said.

Gwen came in, utterly Angelstruck. For a moment Jacks was worried she might actually faint.

"Hey, I'm Jacks," Jacks said.

"I know," Gwen said, blushing impossibly red. "I'm . . . Gwen."

"Nice to meet you, Gwen."

"I've heard so much about you," Gwen said, then caught herself. "Er . . . from Maddy, I mean. I like your car, by the way."

Mitch laughed and Gwen punched him playfully.

Then the door flew open again. This visitor, apparently, didn't see the need to knock.

"Once I get done spinning this, they're going to give you the Medal of Honor, Jackson," Darcy said as she came in. As usual she had her head buried in her BlackBerry and was furiously typing something on the keypad. In her other hand she held a heavy-looking black garment bag. She glanced over at Maddy's bed.

"Oh, good, you're up too. I've got *Teen Vogue* and *Angels Weekly* in a bidding war over your fall fashion spread. We're going with *Teen Vogue*, of course, but let's let them sweat it out. And ANN wants your first televised interview, but we're holding out for the *Today Show*, which, trust me, we're going to get."

She threw the garment bag over a chair in the corner. "And Free People was hoping you'd wear this when you leave the hospital. They didn't know your style or sizes, so there are four options in the bag. Keep them all if you want."

"What?" Maddy said weakly.

Darcy paused and for the first time looked up from her Berry. "Maddy, I'm the fiercest bitch in PR, I *always* get my clients what they want, and you'll never look better in the public eye, or make more money, than with me. What do you say?" She stuck out her hand.

Dazed, Maddy just blinked.

Then Darcy's Berry went off again.

"Hang on, babe," she said, and picked up. Her brow drew together as she listened. "What? Forget it. If you think Maddy Montgomery is showing up for *that* appearance fee, then you're wasting both our time." She held up an apologetic finger to the room and stormed out the door.

Jacks smiled. He looked over at Maddy's bewildered expression.

"Trust me, she won't take no for an answer."

Maddy swallowed and spoke in a surprisingly strong voice. "Please tell her thank you, but I don't intend on doing interviews. Or talk shows."

Jacks turned to Mark. "What happened to the demon?"

"The Dark Angel is gone."

"How is that possible?" Jacks asked. Mark's expression turned heavy.

"It has the soul it came for."

"Ethan?" Maddy asked.

Mark was silent.

"Dark Angels—demons—have been kept at bay for thousands of years. Now that Ethan has done this . . ." He trailed off. Mark's eyes were distant. "We can only hope this is the last time."

"Mark?" Jacks asked. His stepfather's gaze focused.

"Yes, son?"

"That night I took Maddy to the party—when you were in my room. What was on your jacket? It looked like . . . well, like blood."

Mark was silent for a second, looking genuinely saddened. "I'm sorry to realize that you were suspicious of me," he said at last, "but I suppose my conduct has been such that I deserve it. The truth is that the demon left Lance Crossman's body in the NAS lobby for us to find that night. I'm ashamed to say that I hid it rather than informing Detective Sylvester. I thought we could handle finding the killer ourselves. Obviously, that wasn't the case. David and I have spoken at length about it."

Then the Archangel's face lightened. "But don't worry about any of that now. What's important is that you two get better. I'll leave you to it."

Kris looked away from Mark as he stepped out into the hallway.

Jacks wondered how long it would take for her, for both of them, to fully trust his stepfather again, despite whatever strings he had pulled at the NAS.

After a few more minutes of small talk Mitch and Gwen left to get more coffee, and Kris stepped out to make a call and check up on Chloe. Kevin, feeling awkward about being the only one in the room, excused himself to use the bathroom.

Maddy and Jacks lay on their sides, facing each other, and let the silence overtake them. Maddy gazed into Jacks's pale blue eyes. Jacks looked right back.

"Thank you," Jacks said finally.

"For what?" Maddy said.

"For saving my life."

Maddy blushed slightly.

"You . . . do you remember what you did up there. You saved me?" Jacks said.

Maddy nodded.

"I know. That's what we perversions of nature do, I guess."

"Maddy, please."

She rolled over onto her back, wincing a little, her eyes growing tired again.

"Well, I don't care," Jacks said.

"But everyone else does. I'll always be a freak. Even if they say I'm 'a bit more Angel' than they thought."

"Can you not be impossible just for one day?" Jacks asked.

Maddy laughed a little. "I'm too tired to argue anyway."

Her eyes fluttered shut. Another silence drew out and Jacks watched her, still in happy disbelief that she was here, alive. Then he spoke.

"Was it true?" he said quietly.

"Was what true?" Maddy said, her eyes still closed.

"What you said on the rooftop. When Ethan was going to kill me."

Jacks waited for her to respond. He waited until he heard her slow, steady breaths. He sighed.

She had fallen asleep again.

CHAPTER FORTY

The ACPD credentials and authorizations got Detective Sylvester through every checkpoint he needed. A guard at the jail rode with the detective in the elevator, down to the maximum security level. The Tombs. The lift whirred. Sylvester merely stared forward, the ride passing in silence. The entire time the guard attempted to hold his hands still, but they wouldn't stop shaking.

Eventually the guard drew his pistol.

"That won't be necessary, Officer," Sylvester said as calmly as he could.

He'd been expecting this. But that didn't mean he was ready for it.

With a ding the elevator reached its destination. The door slid open, revealing chaos in the bowels of the jail. Prisoners screamed to be let out, banging anything they could against the inside of their cells. Begging. Two guards with drawn rifles stood on each side of the elevator, waiting for Sylvester. Droplets of sweat had formed on their foreheads.

"Right this way, sir," one officer said shakily, leading him to the corridor on the right.

"Get me out of here!" a prisoner screamed as Sylvester passed. "For God's sake let me out! You're murderers to leave us in here!"

"They must have seen something," the guard said, indicating the prisoners.

"I'm sure they did," Sylvester said. He walked steadily, despite the stench of fear that hung in the air.

The solitary cells had small, thick windows looking out to the corridor.

"This is it," the guard said. Sylvester stepped close to the steel door, drawing a deep and wary breath. His shoe stuck to the floor, leaving an imprint. Blood had seeped under the door.

The guard peered in the window quickly.

"Are you ready?" he asked.

The detective nodded.

The door opened with a squeak and a clang. The guards stood with their rifles at the ready. Sylvester stepped into the cell, followed by two of the guards.

His face remained calm, inscrutable, as he took in the sight.

Ethan's body, or what was left of it, lay in the corner. The only recognizable feature was his face. Where his eyes had once been were two black, decomposed pits, larger than his eye sockets. The veins running away from his eyes had all turned black and gray. It was like looking into an abyss. The rest of his body looked like it had been turned inside out. As if he had been torn apart from inside. Gore covered the walls of the cell. Deep scratch marks had penetrated the concrete.

The demon had taken his payment.

"I've never seen anything like that before," one of the guards said, collecting himself. He ran his sleeve across his mouth.

"I hoped I would never have to," Sylvester said. He looked at Ethan's gruesome remains for a few moments longer. "Thank you, Officers, that is all." Turning on his heels, Sylvester exited the cell.

The guard took one last look before leaving Ethan's cell. The door closed, reverberating throughout the jail.

CHAPTER FORTY-ONE

Kevin's Diner was unusually busy that afternoon. The booths were overflowing, the dining room filled with the chatter and laughter of customers. In the corner the dusty TV crackled, tuned, as usual, to ANN. A snowy-bearded anchor announced the day's top story.

"Breaking news: the identity of the teen responsible for three Angel murders has been released. Ethan McKinley of Angel City was being held without bail in a Los Angeles jail but died in a mysterious incident authorities are currently investigating. In a related story, rumors are swirling that Jackson Godspeed was injured in last week's incident following his Commissioning. Mark Godspeed as well as Jacks's publicist will neither confirm nor deny. And in Washington, Senator Linden has pushed forward for a special congressional committee to handle Angel affairs in America."

Maddy barely glanced at the TV as she moved between the tables, dropping off steaming plates of food and cups of coffee. She could still feel a pinch where the knife had penetrated her, but all things considered, she had healed surprisingly well. She seemed to have no ill effects from the incident downtown. Well, no physical ill effects, at least. She picked up a table of dirty dishes and headed back into the kitchen.

Kevin stood behind the fryer, as usual, pulling cook duties and plating orders.

"Hey, Kevin, can I take a break?" Maddy asked.

"Okay," Kevin said as he whipped up another hamburger special. "But it'll have to be quick. It's getting pretty busy out there."

Maddy went into the back room and sat heavily into the old chair. Her feet were aching. She felt like she hadn't even had a chance to breathe since that first group of tourists arrived on the Angel Tours bus at the start of her shift. She reached into her book bag on the desk and pulled out her BlackBerry Miracle. She unlocked the screen and checked it. No new messages. Still. She tried her best to ignore her disappointment.

"Hey, you've got a new customer," Kevin called from the kitchen. Maddy sighed. She powered off the Berry and threw it back in her bag. It was going to be a long night.

She walked back through the kitchen and out into the bustling dining room.

And stopped.

There Jacks stood, bathed in the golden afternoon sunlight shafting through the windows. Even in a simple T-shirt and jeans, he was gorgeous. He saw Maddy and gave her a delighted, unassuming smile.

"Looks like he could use a table," Kevin said. Maddy looked at her uncle. His gray eyes crinkled around the edges. Then he squeezed her on the shoulder and disappeared into the kitchen.

Maddy tucked a stray hair behind her ear and smoothed her uniform. Then she approached him.

"Can I help you?" she said.

The slightest grin played across Jacks's lips.

"Yeah," he said. "A table for one, please?" His eyes danced.

"Of course," she said, lowering her eyes. "Right this way."

She pulled a menu from behind the counter and led Jacks to the booth she had just cleared. As they walked together, she let his presence wash over her like a wave. She couldn't help herself. Every time she felt it the blood still raced in her veins.

"Here you are," she said. Jacks took a seat and Maddy handed him the menu. He made a show of opening it with ceremony and inspecting it. A little laugh escaped Maddy's lips. Then he set it down.

"Actually, I think I'd like to apply for a job," he said.

She gave him an incredulous look.

"Well, I'm sorry to say I'm not so sure about your qualifications," Maddy said.

His forehead creased. "Oh, I've got a lot of experience," he said.

"Such as?"

"Lots of stuff." Jacks shrugged. "And I know the cutest waitress in Angel City; that's got to count for something, doesn't it?"

Maddy felt her cheeks burning as she blushed.

"I think you just want to get me alone in the back."

"Okay, maybe," he confessed.

They both laughed.

"Actually, I'm concerned," Jacks said, looking sly.

"Concerned? Why's that?"

"Yeah, I mean, you're going to have to hire someone quick, or else the restaurant is going to be short-staffed on Monday."

Maddy smiled at him but was confused. That hadn't been part of their exchange so far as she could remember. She looked into his eyes.

"And why would we be short-staffed on Monday?" she wondered.

A bell rang in the kitchen. An order was up.

"Because I've spoken to the Archangels," Jacks said softly. "And they've asked me to tell you that your training starts on Monday."

He wasn't joking anymore. His gaze searched hers intently.

"Training?" Maddy said. "Training for what?" ·

Jacks smiled at her.

"Training to become a Guardian Angel."

EPILOGUE

Maddy reached the top of the stairs, went into the bathroom, and shut the door. She had been waiting for this all day. After Jacks's visit and his unexpected news, she hadn't even had time to process what he was telling her because the diner was so busy. By the time they closed, she had been on her feet for almost eight hours and smelled like sweat, food, and who knows what. She had been looking forward to a shower all day—and to thinking about what Jacks had told her.

Maddy peeled unceremoniously out of her uniform and threw it on the bathroom floor. She turned on the hot water first and waited until it scalded her hand to add the cold. When the temperature was just right, she pulled the plunger on the faucet and the shower coughed to life.

The hot water burned wonderfully against her skin. Maddy let out a sigh as she washed away the shift at the diner. She inspected her bumps and bruises. There were still some remnants of the rooftop incident to be sure, and she was still tender in places, but she felt almost well. Maddy let herself stay a full ten minutes, a luxury she rarely afforded herself. She still wasn't fully ready to confront the decision that lay before her.

When she was finished, she stepped out onto the old bath mat and wrapped a towel around herself.

Steam had fogged the mirror around its edges, but a circular porthole of reflection in the middle had remained somewhat clear. Maddy toweled off her body, then her hair. She turned around and looked over her shoulder at the mirror to check how bad one of the bruises on her back was.

Water droplets patted noisily against the bath mat as she stood there, frozen in place.

Under her shoulder blades, the angry bruise that had formed as a result of smashing into the light pole had faded—or simply evolved—into the beginning of what could only be described as *marks*. They looked like graceful tattoos that ran parallel to her spine and came to rest in two elegant flourishes at the small of her back. They were simpler than others Maddy had seen, but all the same, they were unmistakable. She watched them shimmer in the fluorescent light of the bathroom.

They were Immortal Marks.

Acknowledgments

This book would not have been possible without the enthusiasm and belief of a select group of people. My mother and father, first of all, thank you for teaching me to believe in myself and to believe in the power of imagination. Mom, thank you for teaching me to believe in magic. I cannot imagine two people more brilliant and capable of being great parents, and in that way, I am absurdly lucky. My sister, Julia, whom I love very much and who has always been patient with me. Simon, my agent, who has championed and believed in me from the beginning. Thank you, brother, for reading a fifty-page draft full of typos and seeing something special. Claudia, my book agent, who decided to take on a music-video director with no writing experience and muscle through countless drafts and revisions. Brian, you know how instrumental you have been, and without you, none of this would have been possible. Alicia, another key cheerleader who decided to stand up and back the project. Without your enthusiasm, the book would still be unfinished. Ashley, for your love, faith, and support, for early morning coffees, and for all those fashion ideas. No project is accomplished without the support of great friends, friends like Lucas, Steve, Michael, and Brandon—thank you all for reading drafts and giving your feedback and notes. Finally, my editor, Laura, whose unrelenting passion for the book has seen it through its final transformation. Laura, you made the decision to invest yourself in a dream I had about celebrity Angels two years ago, and for that, I am forever grateful.